PRAISE FOR THE JUDAS LINE

★"This delightful Catholicism-infused quest fantasy stars a likable and original duo. Fr. Michael Engle, a pragmatic Catholic priest, and Jude, who has a considerably more uncertain relationship with God, are unlikely friends, but when a blood-covered Jude runs into Mike's church asking for help, Mike listens to him, believes him, and joins him on a quest to find the Holy Grail, which Jude hopes will help him destroy a legendary and dangerous family heirloom. Along the way they encounter Cain, the Norse gods (drinking and watching *Bridge over the River Kwai*), and a Valkyrie with the requisite 'chainmail-covered pillowy breasts.' When Mephistopheles shows up, Jude manages to label him an Arch-Fiend of Hell without irony and without irritating the reader. Stone's depiction of magic is realistic and intelligent and his treatment of Catholicism refreshingly informed and three-dimensional. Even the obligatory near-apocalyptic ending is coherent, surprising, and exciting."
—*Publishers Weekly* Starred Review

"This evil mystery is a heavenly read! *The Judas Line* creates a believable mystery which links the ancient past to the present. By building on the ancient story of the betrayal of Jesus Christ by Judas, Market Everett Stone crafts a dark versus light drama which will keep readers hooked. I loved how Stone makes Jude an unwilling member of the darkest family threatening mankind. Simply brilliant!"
—Elizabeth Crowley, *Fresh Fiction*

"A fast-paced book which does not lack for history or adventure. The inclusion of death and destruction are a given and it is good that there is a lot of humour instilled throughout. I would say that if you're a fan of Jim Butcher's *Dresden Files*, you will enjoy Mark Everett Stone's work. Recommended."
—Michelle Herbert, *Fantasy Book Review*

"Evil does not die so easily. *The Judas Line* is a novel following Jude Oliver and the long family line that lies behind him, specializing in assassination, using the artifact known as the silver. Jude Oliver must find the origins and stories of his family to be able to end the Silver's legacy for good, with only a single Catholic priest by his side. Blending paranormal and biblical ideas, *The Judas Line* is a riveting thriller that should prove hard to put down."
—*Midwest Book Review*

"I have come to expect a lot from this remarkably talented writer, but Mark manages to please yet again by bringing new elements to his latest work. *The Judas Line* is, as anticipated, a lightning-paced thriller that is equal parts non-stop action and intelligent musing. This is, in fact, a surprisingly introspective book that delves into many interesting questions about the nature of good, evil, and faith. It's an enthralling read certain to delight and entertain, a well-crafted gem worthy of a place on any bookshelf."
—Michelle Izmaylov, author of *The Galacteran Legacy: Galaxy Watch*

"Mark Everett Stone takes the classic good versus evil plot line and puts his own unique spin on it. He effortlessly merges bible canon with the world and people he's created, adding off-the-wall humor to help break the tension. This book makes you laugh while making you think about the nature of evil and the power of faith."
—Jamie White, author of *The Life and Times of No One in Particular*

"I found myself chuckling at some of the insane twists and turns of the plot and other times I was worried by the sudden turn of events [....] A fast-paced read, with nail-biting moments and some humor thrown in. The characters were compelling, I often find myself picturing them in my head [....] I can't recommend this book enough."
—Lisa McCourt Hollar, Jezri's Nightmares

"Once in a great while, a book comes along that challenges you to think outside the box. The Judas Line is one of those books. I was absolutely amazed at the way Mark Everett Stone has taken religious stories and beliefs and intertwined his own tale of power, evil, friendship, sacrifice and redemption. The action is nonstop and the characters will stay with you long after you finish the last page."
—M.E. Franco, author *Where Will You Run?*

"The pacing is flawless in every respect. [....] Never before have I found a work of fiction to be so captivating. It picks you up, sits you down, and it does not let you even think about getting back up."
—Grace Knight, author of *Sun And Moon* (2013)

"Mark Everett Stone has written a masterpiece. How did he do that? This novel is built on massive detail—historical, alchemical, fantastical. *The Judas Line* is a buddy novel, a road novel, and a family novel (and you can't choose family, so watch out)."
—Jack Remick, author of *Gabriela and The Widow* and the California Quartet

The Judas Codex

The Judas Codex

The Judas Line Chronicles, Book 2

MARK EVERETT STONE

CAMEL PRESS

Seattle, WA

Camel Press
PO Box 70515
Seattle, WA 98127

For more information go to: www.Camelpress.com
www.markeverettstone.wixsite.com/mysite-1

Cover design by Sabrina Sun

The Judas Codex
Copyright © 2018 by Mark Everett Stone

ISBN: 978-1-60381-282-5 (Trade Paper)
ISBN: 978-1-60381-283-2 (eBook)

Library of Congress Control Number: 2017958097

Printed in the United States of America

Acknowledgments

First and foremost I want to thank the Likeminded Authors Seeking Publication and the Evil Brain Trust, Ltd. You guys kept me centered when things looked truly weird for me. To Julie Campbell and Allison, you two offered me more assistance than you realize and I appreciate it more than you know. To everyone who loved the first book, thanks. If it wasn't for you folks, I'd be banging my head against the keyboard in frustration.

Also by the author from Camel Press

From the Files of the BSI
(Bureau of Supernatural Investigation)

Things to Do in Denver When You're Un-Dead

What Happens in Vegas Dies in Vegas

I Left My Haunt in San Francisco

Chicago, The Windigo City

Omaha Stakes

The Spirit in St. Louis

(Coming Soon)

Talladega Nightmares

The Judas Line Chronicles

The Judas Line

The Judas Codex

(Coming Soon)

The Judas Revelation

This one is for Dave and Chris.

Thanks for everything.

Part One

Flight

Chapter One

"The meek shall inherit the dirt they are buried in."
—*Codex Infernales*

"AND WHAT ABOUT OUR INVESTMENTS IN Afghanistan?" asked Blaine Deschamps. He was wearing a seventy-five-thousand-dollar William Westmancott steel-gray suit and sitting behind a blond-wood desk that dominated one end of the large office. Leaning back in an overstuffed chair, he casually toyed with a platinum letter opener shaped like a misericord. Eyes half-closed, he seemed to a casual observer relaxed, almost bored. Those who knew him understood it was a pose. The hard, lean body beneath the overpriced trappings contained all the ferocious energy of a crouching Bengal tiger.

"Still unimpeded by the war, sir," said the older man standing in front of the desk, a tablet computer clutched in one hand. His charcoal pin-stripe Briony suit, although well-tailored, fell far short of Blaine's and sold for tens of thousands of dollars less. "And with the American troops finishing their withdrawal this year, our profits from the opium trade should triple."

Blaine set the letter opener carefully upon the desk blotter and steepled his fingers under his nose, concentrating. He was aiming, successfully, for an air of studious reflection. The year 2014 had seen a swift rise in assets and 2015 was shaping up to be a record-breaker. "Excellent, Fergus. Excellent."

The older man, Fergus, gave a thin smile and visibly relaxed. These daily sessions with the boss drained him, and he silently cursed Blaine's need to micromanage. His green eyes shifted to the large African-American gentleman standing in the corner of the spacious office a few short feet from his employer. Blaine's personal bodyguard, Alexander.

The bodyguard caused Fergus a twinge of anxiety, though Fergus's lean, Scottish face under sandy hair gave away nothing, thanks to years of learning to survive while employed by the world's most dangerous family. The previous, unlamented bodyguard for the head of the Deschamps Family, Boris, had unnerved him more than the previous Family head. Boris had been like a force of nature, hard and implacable, but something about Alexander scared him shitless. Where Boris was clearly suppressing what made him human, Alexander seemed to have been born with a deficit of emotion, having no apparent connection to feelings such as love, hate, or even anger. It did not appear natural. His glassy stare resembled a china doll's and the reflection from the floor-to-ceiling monitor mounted on the wall colored his darker-than-dark skin, the numbers from the stock market channel winking off his black eyes and smooth-shaven dome.

Blaine noticed the other man's studious nonchalance and smiled inwardly. He had spent over five million dollars acquiring Boris's replacement and was pleased to have found the perfect specimen. Untiring, uncaring, and utterly ruthless, qualities he treasured in an ever-present bodyguard.

"Send Senator Cridwell a message. I want his aide to leak information that Synoco will not be receiving a government contract. That should cause their stocks to tumble enough that we can pick it up on the cheap." He took a deep breath. "That is all for now. We will continue tomorrow with our Eastern European developments." He waved a hand toward the exit, and Fergus, the most junior member of the board, was more than happy to comply.

Blaine grinned. "I think he is scared of you, Alexander," he said after the door had shut.

The giant gave a small, yet deep, grunt in reply.

Leaning back in his alligator-hide chair, Deschamps placed his hands behind his head and marveled that Julian Deschamps, his father and predecessor, had had the good grace to die and leave him in charge.

When the Patron had informed the board that he, Blaine, was to be the new head of the Family, the leader of the Deschamps' multibillion-dollar conglomerate, the shock of it nearly tore the board apart, but no one ever argued with "The Patron."

For the first time in a thousand years, a non-European member of the Deschamps family sat at the head of the table. Born into one of the two American crèches, Blaine had survived a childhood filled with assassination attempts, temptation, and ready wealth by maintaining strict discipline— discipline over his mind, body, and emotions. By the age of fourteen, he had quietly killed four of his half-brothers in such subtle fashions that their deaths could not be linked to him (two had no talent in magic and were therefore off-limits, to be groomed for high-ranking positions in the business side of the Family enterprise.) By sixteen he had mastered the martial arts training of the *Sicarii*, the assassination and covert ops side of the Deschamps Family business. In magic, he possessed eleven out of the twelve Words of power.

So he was a prodigy by Family standards, even if he was an American.

Unlike many of his half-brothers, he took after his biological mother, a perfect specimen of Norwegian beauty and constitution. Tall, with sandy blond hair and wide shoulders, he shared few traits with his father Julian, whose features were more Mediterranean. Only full lips and an aquiline nose.

My mother, he mused sourly. What a joke. The Family selected women for their beauty and intelligence and genetically screened them to ensure that they would be perfect incubators for the Family offspring. They were then implanted with Julian's seed and carefully monitored during their pregnancies. Any sign of defect and the child was aborted, as were any children whose genetic assessment showed them to be less than ninety-six percent of compliance to the rigorous standards. This was called the filtering process and it had been used efficiently, ruthlessly, for the past few decades. Thus the quality of offspring had improved over the old stock.

Blaine smiled. Julian was gone, so it would be Blaine's DNA, the best of the best, that would be carried on in future generations of Family members. It would be his brood that would scheme and plot and kill in an orgy of Darwinian survival. He could almost feel paternal pride.

The harsh glare of the city lights was softened by the lightly tinted floor-to-ceiling window that formed the outside wall off his office. Constructed of Lextrope, the hardest substance ever manufactured, it was three-inches thick and virtually indestructible. Able to withstand everything from a .50 caliber round to an RPG, it providing unparalleled protection for the new head of the Family.

Ahhh ... New York. A great city. My city. The thought warmed him in a way the embrace of a woman never could. Other cities might be more elegant, such as Geneva, or storied, such as Prague or Istanbul, but New York was the city of action, of guts and glory and anything the heart could ever want. It teemed with furious life and energy, and he fancied he could *feel* the sizzle of its vigor against his skin like a warm breeze. The other cities might have the genteel atmosphere of a venerable grand dame, but New York was a place for *business*, and that suited Blaine Deschamps just fine.

The NYSE, Wall Street, the Diamond Quarter, the Garment District, etc., etc. Places where he could sink his teeth into the bloody meat of industry, then tear it off the bones. There was nothing better, no wine headier, than the glory of besting his foes in business, and any who opposed his will were foes.

He wanted it all, to own everything worth owning, and Patron-help anyone who stood in his way. While most people treated business as a chess game performed with careful, deliberate movements, not Blaine Deschamps. He approached business the way the *Conquistadores* conquered the new world, with ruthless brutality. He was morally certain that the world belonged to him, and it was ripe for the plucking … assuming he had the time to carry out his plans.

Time …. There was never enough, not for the grand plans he wished to set in motion. Not enough hours in the day, not enough years in a mortal's lifespan. There were too many things to accomplish, and he knew in his guts that it would require his ferocious discipline to accomplish them.

Once again, he renewed his vow to live forever, and in this age of genetic manipulation and medical advancement, that was entirely possible. The progress with geriatric medicine achieved by Schiller Pharmaceuticals excited him beyond measure. Now that he was the head of the Family, he could spend billions extending his life, improving his health. He smiled at the possibilities.

What a delightful shock it had been to learn the truth about the Deschamps family. That it was "The" Family—an unbroken lineage dating back to the legendary Founder, Yehuda, called the son of Simon, better known as Judas Iscariot. Judas, who in reality was the first son of the Patron and betrayer of the false God's get, Yehoshua, the so-called Messiah, better known as the Nazarene. Then there was the prophecy of the Redeemer ….

Riiiinggg.

Blaine straightened in his chair, fear suddenly hot and loose in his bowels. It was *The Line*. There was only one person who used *The Line*. He tapped a swirling knot on the blond wood of his desk.

"Hello, sir."

The sugar-coated shit of the Patron's voice slid through the speakers hidden in the walls of the large office, a voice both terrible and avuncular. "Hello, Blaine. I trust my interests are thriving."

Despite the urbane confidence the Patron's voice exuded, Blaine was hardly comforted. "Yes, sir." Sweat beaded his forehead.

"I had thought Burke was the best of the 'B' series, but I must say, the past year and a half has proved me wrong."

Blaine felt a stab of annoyance. *Burke? Hah!* Burke was a disappointment and had proven it by failing to kill that miserable abortion of a half-brother Olivier Deschamps. Twice. His death at Olivier's hand was only just, considering he had chosen to face the more powerful magus in single combat, no backup, no SS team to ensure his success. That kind of foolishness invited death. He said as much to the Patron in more diplomatic verbiage.

The sigh that came over the speakers reminded Blaine of hot wind over shattered rock. "Yes, of course, my boy, he should have incapacitated the rebel Olivier with a horde at his back. His lack of pragmatism led to his demise. It is your pragmatic, uniquely American view on such things as combat and business that have elevated you in my estimation. That is why you are the head of the Family. Had Julian been as direct, not only would he still be alive, but we would have regained control of the Silver."

The Silver … an ancient Family artifact, the thirty *talents* of silver paid to the Founder for betraying the cursed Nazarene. In each *talent* rested a Terrible Word designed by the Patron. Words so evil, so awful that few in the Family had the power to grasp more than one. It tore at Blaine's soul that the artifact had been destroyed before he could use it to test his mettle. The fact that Olivier had mastered all thirty Terrible Words, and had known all twelve of the Words of Magic available to ordinary magi ate at him like a cancer. Being the best was Blaine's destiny, and being bested by Olivier before Blaine had even been *born* added insult to injury. Blaine should have been the strongest in magic, not Olivier.

"Yes, sir, but the Silver is destroyed, so that is a moot point," Blaine remarked.

The silence that greeted his words was pregnant with malice. Finally, he said, "That is one of the reasons for my call, *boy*." The last word was spit out with such thick anger that Blaine's bladder nearly let go and he cursed himself for poking the bear.

"I-I am … sorry, sir," he stammered, sweating freely now. "It was impolitic of me to state the obvious. Please continue, sir."

A small pause, long enough for Blaine to know that the Patron had not *quite* forgiven him. "It has come to my attention that Cain has departed Omaha."

Blaine did not ask how the Patron knew such a thing, but accepted it as a fact. The son of Adam was the only person the Sicarii—the whole Family— feared. Besides the Patron, of course. "He has left the priest to his own devices?"

"It is so."

Father Michael Engle … alone and unprotected. The thought almost sexually aroused the twenty-year-old head of the Family. "Then I should take care of the matter quickly."

"Not so quickly that mistakes are made, my boy."

"Of course not, sir." Blaine slowly rubbed his hands together. "In fact, when I took command of the Family and had learned of the priest's involvement in Julian's demise, I made sure to position one of our assets from the UK in the American Midwest. Someone, I believe, you will find perfect for the job."

"Indeed, do tell." The Patron's deep voice became heavier still and Blaine imagined he could feel every word land hard on his shoulders. "Why not a Special Services Team?"

Blaine made sure his voice did not sound the least bit self-satisfied or smug. "An SS team would be noted by our old enemies, especially considering the events of two years ago, so it is better to do things under the radar, so to speak. Besides, Cain has a long arm and he's no fool. He might have the priest protected from an SS Team. Why not try a subtler approach? Where teams might be noticed and stopped, a single man might slip through unheeded." His smile was tight and unpleasant. "Such confrontations are better when we can pick the field of advantage. A single person already in the United States, ready to be aimed at a target of our choosing, would not attract attention. The death of that particular priest will attract notice, but nothing that could point at us, nothing that could cause an extreme response.

"Five years ago," Blaine continued, "one of the A-series—a distant cousin with only one Word and a modest ability with Botanical Magic—developed a penchant for ... ah ... *eliminating* pre-operative transsexual prostitutes in the Whitechapel area of London. He remained at large in the UK until I had him relocated to the U.S., once you, ah, promoted me to head of the Family."

The Patron cleared his throat. "You mean Alvin Deschamps, the one the British rags so drolly dubbed 'Nitpicking Nick.' He does fine work. A fine asset, indeed."

Of course the Patron would know of Great Britain's most infamous serial killer since Jack the Ripper. He knew everything. Blaine continued, "Well, yes. We know him as 'The Giggler,' for obvious reasons, but in order to bolster his utility, I had him moved to Illinois, where he changed his modus operandi and became the serial killer known as 'The Atheist.' I believe Alvin will be the perfect one to, um, rid us of the pesky priest."

The Patron was silent so long that Blaine feared his displeasure would strike him down. Then, finally, a soft, scratching began to emerge from the hidden speakers, a *scritching* that rose to an ear-blistering wail of feedback that disturbed even the indomitable Alexander. The giant shook his head softly and took a small step from the wall.

With a start, Blaine realized the Patron was *laughing*.

Was this good news or bad?

Whatever it was, it was possibly the scariest thing he had ever experienced. No human throat could make that peal of metallic noise like a cross between a horrendous traffic accident and the wails of tortured babies. Blaine doubted there was a synthesizer capable producing *feedback* so emotive that it sent chills through his flesh. It was the laughter of a being so jaded that all emotion had become alien.

"Oh, Blaine," the Patron finally said once the crackling noise subsided,

"I do so appreciate irony. Very well, have Alvin the Giggler, the *Atheist*, sent to Omaha to remove the priest from the equation." A pause. "What are your plans for Cain?"

Fucking Cain, Blaine thought angrily. The fact that the world's oldest man and first murderer was still alive and kicking ate at his insides. "I am attempting to locate him even as we speak. I have a plan for the Son of Adam."

"He is in Great Britain," the Patron replied. "If your plan for him is to shorten his lifespan drastically, you must beware of the consequences. The Lying God's curse is not something you should take lightly. As is breaking our agreement with the man."

"Of course not, sir, but I do have the Family, and *you,* on my side."

A long pause. So long, in fact, that Blaine feared the Patron had hung up, but then that the sugar-coated shit of his benefactor's voice emerged once again. "I owe that do-gooder choirboy priest some serious pain, and I want him to experience some serious *hurt* before he dies. Make sure Alvin understands that." He paused. "Do *you* understand, Blaine? *Hurt.* Call it an obsession of mine."

"I understand, sir." Oh yes, he did.

"And speaking of obsessions, I see you have purchased Genomica, that company so invested in anti-aging technologies. Still looking for the secret of immortality, are we?"

Of course the Patron would know. "Yes, sir." Lying to the Patron was a sure way to find himself in a place where screams were food for beings that lived on misery.

"I myself have my own little obsessions, my peccadillos as it were, so I understand what drives you. Immortality is a rare gift, Blaine, so rare that I have bestowed it upon only one man. Julian was *almost* worthy of such a gift and might have received it had he not dealt with the matter of his wayward son, your half-brother, so poorly. Olivier had the best of him on more than one occasion, and that could not be tolerated, no matter that our holdings doubled in size during his tenure as head of the Family. Go ahead, indulge your little obsession. Try to unlock the human genome, search the globe, every rain forest, and lost valley for the chemical cocktail that will give you the secret to immortality. It should be interesting to see what you come up with."

"Sir, if I do succeed in significantly extending the human lifespan, think of the profits, think of those who would sell their souls for just a little more time. Even a few years are precious to those who have stared death in the face." Blaine licked his lips. "Politicians, heads of state, CEOs, and the like would be beholden to us, would do *anything* for a shot at immortality. We would hold the key, the *key* to their lives. This isn't just a mission to fuel my obsession, this is a mission to literally control the *world*."

The Patron's voice slid softly through the air. "Interesting. You have much more ambition than even I anticipated. Go ahead, support the research for viable, *sellable* immortality and see where it leads you. But know this: if you succeed in your quest, if you manage to bring the world to its knees before the Scions of Yehuda, before Me, then I will *personally* grant you immortality. *True* immortality, youth and vigor for all time. This will be your reward for a job well done."

Oh my .... Blaine reeled in his chair. His eyes darted to Alexander, who merely stared impassively, as unemotional as a stone. *So close.* It would probably take years, but the Family's businesses were cutting edge and even the United States government did not have the technology that was at the fingertips of the Deschamps.

Immortality.

"Thank you, sir! It *will* be done."

"My name, My will," said the Patron.

"Pardon, sir?"

"You may thank me by using my full and proper name." Evil, thick as paste, seemed to flow from the speakers.

Blaine suppressed the urge to vomit as fear once again clutched at his guts. No, the Patron had *not* forgotten nor forgiven his earlier faux pas.

Bowing his head, the young man closed his eyes and assumed an attitude of prayer. "Thank you ... oh Mighty One, Star of the Morning, Najmun Thāquib, Heylel, for the gifts you have given me, that I may increase the measure of your Glory upon this wretched Earth. Thank you for creating in me the Preparer Of Ways for your Second Coming in defiance to the Lying God and his bastard son. Thank you for the gift of Yehuda, the Founder, without whom I would not exist. His seed is potent because it is yours, and all things must spring from your terrible loins and insatiable lust. Bless me, Oh Dreadful Lord. Bless me and grant me the strength to do your will."

"Continue, boy."

Blaine paused, sweat running freely down his face, then intoned in an appropriately fearful voice:

> My Master, who dwells beyond the World
> Whose name is Legion
> Thy Kingdom is forever
> Thy Glory overshadows
> This paltry Earth, as it should.
> Grant us our lives

That we may serve
And strike at the heart of Thine enemies.
Let us storm the vile halls of Heaven
And cast out the Lying God.
For Thine is the Might,
The Majesty and the Dread
For all Time.

There was no *Amen* at the prayers finale, just an abrupt end. Blaine took a deep breath and finished with, "I thank you, Lord Lucifer Morningstar."

The Patron answered, in a voice smug and fat with evil, "Damn right you do."

Chapter Two

"C'mon, Eddie, keep your guard up!" shouted a strong baritone ringside.

Don't listen to the voices, just keep punching. Focus, old man, Mike thought.

"Sweep the leg, then shoot!"

That's right, tell the other guy what to do so I can counter.

The kid was good, I gave him that. He went for my leg, his foot striking with impressive speed, but I was ready. I dropped forward and down, twisting in midair, wrapping my legs around his waist, surprising him with a scissors take-down. A second later, I had him in a kimura armbar.

It was supposed to be practice, a bit of sparring to test the kid, but at first he didn't take it seriously, figuring that the old man he faced would be too easy. It didn't take too darn long for him to realize that I wasn't playing around and that I was pretty tough myself.

Still, the kid was strong and possessed arms like steel cables.

"Turn your hips in!" That voice belonged to Joe, the guy who owned the gym, the man who had let Cain and me train there for the past couple of years. He was bald as an egg with cauliflower ears and built like a brick with two stubby legs. Turned into a good friend, too. "Your hips, Mike," he urged. "Turn them in."

Sweat stung my eyes and my lungs burned, but I held on ferociously, the larger man's sweaty wrist in my grasp. A big kid, that Eddie, but you know what they say about the bigger they are. I had the kimura deep and within a few seconds felt his fingers drum on my forearm as he tapped out. Sighing in relief, I let go, fingers tingling.

Standing, slicked with sweat head to toe, I took deep and measured breaths, even though my body wanted to pant like a dog. It was a good workout, my hardest yet against someone who wasn't Cain. I tore at the Velcro of my padded, fingerless gloves with my teeth, ripping my hands free.

"Good job, Mike," Joe enthused as I staggered toward the ropes. The big grin covering his lovable pumpkin face revealed how many teeth he'd lost over the years. "Three rounds. That kid gave you a serious workout." His massive forearms rippled as he gripped my hand.

"Yeah." I nodded, chest heaving. "Never … went that long before."

The other trainer—the guy with a baritone voice, Steve—was visiting from Minnesota with his protégé, Eddie. He walked over to where we gabbed, the skin on his neck flushed red beneath the swirling tribal tats that covered it like a collar. He held out a massive hand for me to shake. "Heck of a fight, Mike. If I hadn't seen it with my own eyes, I wouldn'tna believed it." The expression on his face showed his sincerity, but his hazel eyes were flinty. His meal ticket had just lost a fight to a man nearly twice his age, and that didn't sit well.

I gripped a hand thick with calluses. "Thanks."

"I can't believe you're forty-five. You fight like you're twenty-five and you look all of thirty. How you do that?" he asked. "Protein shakes? Special diet?"

Laughter hurt. The kid had given me a couple of good shots to the ribs that I'd be feeling for days. "Just clean living, I guess."

"Steve, old Mike here is the original Clean Marine," Joe said proudly. He handed me a towel, which I used to wipe the sweat off my body. Within seconds it was heavy with moisture.

"Clean Army Ranger," I said, handing the damp towel back. "Call me a Marine again and you'll be in trouble." My smile took the sting out of the words.

"You learn mixed martial arts at Ranger school?" Steve asked. To the kid, he said, "Go shower up, Eddie."

The "kid," all two-hundred-fifty pounds of him, sulked off to the showers while rubbing his arm, trailing a trio of friends who had come along for the ride. They all tossed me heated glares.

"He's a good egg," Steve told Joe, rubbing his eyes. "And I was thinking of taking him pro, but your man here put paid to that." A long sigh. "For now, at least, thanks to those Ranger moves."

"I was in service before the Army adopted the Modern Army Combatives, but for the last two years I've been training with a guy who has forgotten more about hand-to-hand combat than I'll ever know." I lifted the top rope and ducked through. "He was harder on me than any DI, and if he hadn't been, your man would've eaten me for lunch."

"He's the best I ever saw," said Joe thoughtfully. "Fast as a snake and stronger than any two guys. Coulda turned pro anytime."

Steve rubbed his tatted neck, a frown on his broad face. "I'd like to meet this guy. Perhaps he can train Eddie, make him a force to be reckoned with."

"Can't. He left town recently," I said softly. "Eddie will be fine. I have another advantage, as well."

"What advantage?"

I smiled. "God has my back."

JOE'S GYM OCCUPIED A SPOT AT 46th and Center, not too far from where the city was trying to gentrify the area with new builds. It looked like a dump from the outside, the air inside redolent with stale grease and old sweat. It needed a coat of paint something awful—the walls gray and peeling—but the locker rooms were new. Shiny white tile and gunmetal-gray steel lockers for the members and clean stalls with an endless supply of hot water for us older guys trying to act twenty years younger.

The mind wanders when fatigued, but that's no excuse for a man with a bull's-eye on his back. I should've been more alert when trouble arrived in the form of an irate kid.

"That was uncool, dude, beating me in front of my trainer, and you ain't even a real mixed martial artist and stuff. Steve told me you just train here three days a week."

I ran the towel through my close-cropped black hair and my handlebar mustache, feeling clean, feeling good, almost like a blessing. Perhaps it was, a blessing from a friend who had a particular affinity to water. Silly, I know. He was long dead.

"Don't sweat it, son," I said while pawing through my locker. "I beat you fair and square. It happens. Someday, someone will beat me. In fact, there are many who can, including my trainer, who can beat any five guys you care to name."

The sound of a bare foot softly slapping on cold tile and I felt a large presence loom behind. He was trying to intimidate me by invading my personal space. Another step. Another person. And another. Did Eddie really think he needed friends to intimidate one man?

"Why are you taking it so hard, son?" On went my black shirt and pants, the cloth stiff and scratchy against my flesh.

"I ain't your son, and look at me when I'm talking to you!"

Sigh. The clichés had started. I finished adjusting my collar and turned around. "I have work to do, son." Eddie and his three friends stood there, big arms crossed, but when they got a load of my priest's collar, they took a collective step back. Two crossed themselves. Nice to know that some young people still believed. "Now, if you don't mind, I must return to work."

Eddie and the gang, now pale and nervous, mumbled and backed away, and as I passed them, I couldn't resist a bit of fatherly advice. Comes with the job. "It's not how you win that measures you as men, but how you handle losing."

They had the good grace to look abashed.

Merging into the scant traffic on Omaha's L street, I headed west, listening to Def Leppard on the CD player. Although a priest, a man who is supposed to comport himself with the dignity due his station, I still liked to listen to 80s rock. *Pour some sugar on me* is my jam.

I was sure that the Lord would forgive me for enjoying the double entendres found in that song and Aerosmith's "Love in an Elevator." God had saved my life several times and I had felt His power flow through my mortal flesh on more than one occasion, providing me with the certainty of His existence. I am a man of faith, but it's sure nice to have proof, you know?

Oh, yeah, let's not forget another sign that the Lord is real and both His love and justice know no limits … Cain. Yes, *that* Cain, the son of Adam, the trainer I mentioned earlier. How much more proof do you need for God's existence than a man cursed to wander the earth forever? Makes you think twice about breaking any of the Ten Commandments, doesn't it?

I passed a motorcycle out front (a Kawasaki Ninja 300, not my style, but kids love their crotch rockets) and parked my Honda Civic in the spot reserved for us priestly types. As I entered my office through the back, I thought of my friend Cain, who had left just a week ago for parts unknown. The day of his departure, I hadn't bothered with the priestly dog collar, instead settling for a plain gray T-shirt and jeans when I went to say goodbye.

He had called me, asking to meet in the Jobbers Canyon area of downtown, where the businesses catered to tourists, and old warehouses and factories became loft apartments for the nouveau riche—an expensive antique surrounded by garishly modern.

Unease trickled down my spine as I pulled into the parking lot where Cain stood like shining beacon in his tan summer suit. A fat manila envelope was clutched under one arm.

"What's going on?" It was a thick, warm August evening, and the cobbled streets of the old downtown were radiating enough heat to make me sweat.

My friend gave me a smile, his eyes hidden by pair of oversized Glacier-Sherpa sunglasses. I'm a big man, but he topped me by several inches. His long, curly hair floated about his head like a halo and his long, lean face was tanned several shades darker than its normal olive. "I'm leaving, Mike," he stated flatly.

Usually Cain spoke with the flowery extravagance of a Cohen Brother's Western, and those three simple words, uttered with gravitas, unnerved me. "Leaving? Why?"

"Surely your wandering eye has espied the various congregants of your ministry regarding me with much unearned suspicion?"

That was true. The previous week's service had been slightly marred by the dark looks and mutterings the congregation tossed his way. I assumed it was for the ever-present shades he wore, but looking at him in the evening light, I realized that it was his curse, the Mark of Cain bestowed upon him by God, which caused the others to fidget and glare. They had no clue as to why he made them uncomfortable; they only knew that something about Cain set their nerves on edge. Even I wasn't immune because lately I felt irritable when he was around.

"So, you have to go? Really?"

He nodded. "Really." Sighing, he removed his glasses, revealing his eyes. Ice-blue like a wolf's, the irises were bordered by thin line of soft brown. That strange coloring, those wolf eyes, was *The Mark*. "I had fervently hoped that my stay in Omaha would yield certain advantages in my quest for the Almighty's forgiveness, yet so far my search to be quit of my peculiar malady has yielded naught, and as I have stated before, my curse does not afford me more than a brace of years in any one locale."

It took a second to untangle the knots of his words, but I got the gist. When he helped Morgan (who started as Olivier, then changed to Jude and ended his life as Morgan—the name, I think, suited him best) and I defeat the Sicarii, God showed him a small measure of his grace by lining the Mark in his eyes with brown, his eyes' original color. It was proof that he could someday be forgiven, but it seemed that he was still limited to two years before people began to point fingers.

"I am sorry to see you go."

His gaze was grave. "Not as sorry as I, my friend."

It had been fifty thousand years since Cain first lied to God.

"Where is your brother?"

"I do not know, am I my brother's keeper?"

It wasn't the murder of his brother, it was the First Lie that was the true affront.

I was sure he suffered all manner of emotional turmoil, angst for the ages. But as I looked upon his normally impassive face, I was struck by the notion that he was weeping inside, that his very guts were aching at the thought of his departure.

My own heart breaking, I nodded and gestured to the bar. "Why O'Toole's?"

"Where better to imbibe alcohol with a dear friend than at an Irish pub?"

Not being much of a drinker, I slow-walked my way through a glass of truly terrible chardonnay while Cain put every alcoholic that ever existed to shame, drinking shot after shot of Glenfiddich until the general manager herself came over to ascertain his sobriety.

He muttered under his breath as she replaced the bartender. She was a serious-looking redhead with a wide, smiling face and laugh lines bracketing her mouth.

"You okay there, hon?" She eyed the army of overturned shot glasses resting in front of him. "Had a lot. I think I'll have to cut you off. No offense. I can call you a cab or fetch you a bite."

Cain's smile lit up the bar. "Madam, I assure you that, although I have imbibed a prodigious quantity of this Scottish amber nectar, I am now, as I always am, sober as a judge and in full possession of my rather amazing faculties." He extended a hand, holding it rock steady in front of our eyes. "So, as you see, I am capable of ingesting even more of that precious fluid without harm. But if it will allay your fears, my good friend here, who nurses his wine in quite a miserly fashion, is a man of the cloth, one of great import and faith. He will see to it that I do not suffer any gross physical indignity and that I will not pose a threat to those whose hearts are pure."

Her arms crossed beneath large breasts. She hemmed and hawed, screwed her face up in concentration as she tried to judge Cain's level of inebriation. Eventually she gave up and nodded, toddling off with a bemused expression.

"So, tell me," I urged after the bartender poured another shot. "What's your secret?"

Cain's lips stretched in a toothy grin. "Purify."

"Excuse me?"

"Purify. It's a Word. A very good and puissant Word indeed, and it carries with it the smell of freshly sliced green apples." He closed his eyes, inhaling. "How I do love the smell of apples." Eyes glinting, he shot me an amused glance. "Ironic, isn't it? Considering my lineage."

"You *cheated*," I accused.

"*Purify* merely removes impurities from food and drink, as well as all toxins. If used with proper intent and inflection, it removes toxins from a body as well. Considering that alcohol is a poison, I have merely rendered the small amount in my body inert. It's most definitely not cheating, my friend."

The *Words* …. Let me tell you, a couple of years ago I would have scoffed at the notion of magic, but my friend Morgan, who turned out to be an ex-member of the largest criminal organization known to man called the Sicarii, removed all doubt. I saw him heal wounds, grant me a fantastic vision on a moonless light, and perform feats of strength that should have torn his flesh apart. Yeah, I believed in magic.

Sigh. "So, Purify smells like apples to you? Nice." There was smell attached to the uttering of a Word that was unique to the magus using it. When Morgan had used Healing, he smelled cinnamon.

"My friend, it occurs to me that I am afflicted with the disease of procrastination, which is a malady a man such as myself cannot afford." He removed the manila envelope from his lap and slid it across the bar. "Here."

It was heavy, over a pound. "What is it?" I asked, not wanting to open the envelope.

"Our enemies, the Sicarii, will no doubt attempt to do you great harm—*that* we both know. You and I have aided in the deaths of many of their Dagger Men and the timely destruction of their fortress in New York. They do not possessive a capacity for forgiveness, for forgiveness belongs to those who follow the arduous path of the Lord. These scoundrels will come to extinguish your life in order to soothe their wounded pride, which is the very reason I have trained you so extensively these past two years in the manly arts of unarmed combat. I have made of you a weapon, taught you much of the hand-fighting I have gleaned and devised through centuries of conflict."

Images of death and horror streamed across my mind. The Sicarii had tortured me, tried to kill me, but by the grace of God I had survived. Thanks to my friend. Thanks to Morgan. "You've made me ready. Unless they send an SS team, I will survive."

I met my reflection staring back at me from the lenses of his Glaciers. "You will not be ready," he said. "They will come implementing surprise and under the unpleasant cover of darkness to claim your life, and no matter how wonderful your skill at hand-fighting, they will plant a small lump of lead in your brain, which will terminate your existence. I find that thought unacceptable. That is why I have delivered unto you the contents of yon envelope. If you ever find yourself in dire straits, it should be of some aid." He sighed, taking a sip of Scotch. "When I depart this oasis of alcohol, I will make such a fuss that the Sicarii cannot help but follow. This may grant you some small measure of protection."

"God will provide," I said firmly.

"That is true, but He also helps those who help themselves."

"Do you really think this necessary?" I asked, nudging the envelope, not wanting others to come to harm in my defense.

"Please, my friend, do not endeavor to equate yourself to be the legendary man of the cloth in the famous joke 'The Priest and the Boat.'"

I rubbed my mustache. "Sorry, don't know that one."

The bartender, a young, pudgy man who had just poured another shot, leaned in close, obviously wanting to hear a new joke, or at one he didn't know.

Cain smiled at the bartender and motioned him closer. "Come, my good purveyor of fine spirits, listen while I regale my thick-witted companion." He emptied his shot glass. "Fill your ears whilst you fill my glass." When his shot glass was full, he turned his attention back to me.

"In 2005 there was a great storm called Katrina in the glorious land of Louisiana," he began. "And, lo, the stately city of New Orleans suffered a calamitous flood of nearly biblical proportions, tearing through the streets as through tissue paper.

"A humble, somewhat elderly priest of a small church worked hard to save the people of his tiny parish, and before the flood reached his church, he managed to save his entire congregation. All except himself and two elderly ladies.

"You see, he had spent so much of his valuable time assisting in the evacuation of his flock that by the time he had sent most on their merry way, the waters trapped him and the two ladies within the confines of the House of God. They found their options limited: drown or climb to the roof and pray for assistance, divine or otherwise."

Cain finished his Scotch. "Good man, pour me another round of yon sublime liquid, if you will." The bartender complied while I smiled to myself. Cain could gab with the best of them and he sure was in his element, drawing attention and teaching at the same time. He would have made a heck of a preacher. For all I knew, he might have been one in the distant past. I imagined there wasn't much he hadn't tried in fifty thousand years.

"Ah, thank you, my good man. Where did I leave off? Oh yes, the roof of the church. There crouched our intrepid trio watching the waters rise all 'round, praying with all their might to the Lord for salvation when suddenly, emerging through the rain and fog like a vision came a small powerboat chugging along, low in the water due to a surplus of refugees.

" 'Ho the church!' came the cry from the gentleman steering the stalwart craft. 'I have room for two more!'

"Of course the kindly priest escorted the ladies to the conveyance, urging them to safety. The gentleman at the tiller assured the clergyman he would return. 'God will provide,' intoned the pious priest.

"So the swift, terrible waters rose and the elderly priest was sodden, bravely weathering the horrific gale that tore at his frail body. Before too long, the boat came back, burdened with refugees. The same Good Samaritan was at the tiller.

"'Go, save those poor wretches,' said the priest. 'God will save me.'

"Nodding, the Good Samaritan sailed away with his precious cargo and once again the poor priest was subject to the harsh elements. Soon, however, the same boat returned, once again burdened with a surplus of refugees. The noble priest sent them on the way over the Good Samaritan's protestations. 'God will save me.'

"As the boat was lost from the priest's vision, the little church collapsed and he drowned, for he could not swim.

"Of course, such a goodly man found himself within the hallowed halls of Heaven, at the foot of the Throne, no less. In the ecstasy of the moment, the Lord spoke unto the priest and asked if he was inclined to inquire about any moment in his life. The goodly man, with eyes averted, asked, 'My Lord, why didst Thou not save me from drowning? I prayed unto You for safety but found none.'

"The Lord looked down with kindly eyes full of holy wisdom and said, 'I did try, my son. I sent that boat to you *three times!*' "

Dead silence met the punch line and silence won until I blurted out, "That's a joke?"

The bartender left, shaking his head, while Cain merely chuckled. "It killed them in Antwerp," he said.

I couldn't help but smile and then laugh just a little bit. "Okay, big man, I get your meaning. The first sign of trouble and I'll open the envelope. It's not like I can use magic to protect myself."

As for Cain, he had the magic of twenty-five Words, the full measure of knowledge from the apple eaten by his mother and father, Adam and Eve, and could protect himself quite well. Not to mention that he was filthy rich, I mean richer than most *countries*. That kind of money could buy a lot of security.

"You could, my friend, find it in your heart to join me in my travels where such companionship would be most welcome." He spoke nonchalantly, but there was a strange undercurrent in his voice.

Heck of an offer, to join the world's oldest man on his quest for God's forgiveness. If anyone needed forgiveness, it sure was he. I smiled. "My parish needs me."

"Of course they do—the flock always needs a good shepherd—but consider your own safety. Do not endeavor to emulate the priest in the joke I have just regaled you with, my friend." His face was dead serious and from behind those shades I could feel the heat of his gaze. "Come with me, please."

I shook my head. I couldn't leave; I'd been on enough crazy quests to last a lifetime.

He sighed. "Your funeral."

We sat there in silence for a few hours until the stars came out, the manila envelope an oppressive reminder of what lay ahead.

That was it. He was gone out of my life and I felt the worse for it.

Work was at St. Stephen's Catholic Church in southwest Omaha, Nebraska. The building was originally conceived with an eye toward modern funk, but wound up looking a trifle silly with its rectangular, leaning steeple done up in gray and walls of plain masonry in eye-numbing beige. Not the best look for a church dedicated to Christ, but it was home, and home was comfortable.

St. Stephen the Martyr Parish was the largest Archdiocese of Omaha, with thirty-five hundred families, three priests, and six deacons. We were proud of our parish, which has the largest religious education program in the state. I counted my blessings every day that I was able to serve in such a humble, yet important place.

I was content. No, that's not the word. I was *happy*. Not many found their calling in life and not many could say with absolute certainty that they were in good with the boss. And I don't mean Archbishop Conroy.

God.

Yeah, *Him*. Two years ago, in 2012, my best friend and I found ourselves on a quest to destroy an evil artifact called *The Silver*. Along the way I encountered a rock legend, a biker gang, two demons and the Holy Grail. With the Grail, I was able to destroy the Silver. God had found my faith sufficient and had given me the tools to get the job done.

I entered my office, a bit surprised by the large cardboard box sitting in the middle of my desk. Where had that come from?

The label read LAW OFFICES OF HAMMERT & LEDSKER. Interesting. Why would a law office send me a package? I tore into it.

Inside was a plain, battered wooden box about a foot long and half as thick. It had somewhat rusty iron hinges and a crude iron lock that looked to have been constructed sometime during the height of the Roman Empire. The wood was crusty gray with age and had splits and splinters along its length. Resting next to it was a ream of paper thick enough to be a George R.R. Martin novel. Sitting square on the ream was a cream-colored envelope bearing the name *Father Michael Engle*. Me.

"What's all this, then?" I muttered, tearing open the letter.

Dear Mike,

If you are reading this, then I have either disappeared or have been killed, perhaps both. I have instructed my attorneys to deliver this package to you if they have not heard from me for a period of no more than two years. Since you're reading this, I'm history and that sucks, but I can't think of a better person to entrust the contents to.

Inside are two items:

One: My personal story. When you read it, don't judge me too harshly. I have been trying to live a better life. Believe me, it's a lot to swallow, but it's all true.

Two: In the wooden box is the Family History, the *Codex Infernales*. Don't bother reading the original—it's in Hebrew, Aramaic, Latin, and a few other languages that use slang and euphemisms unknown to modern man. As such it makes poor reading. However, I have taken the liberty of translating the important parts into modern English for your benefit and attached it to my personal records.

I'm sorry to lay this burden on you, but you are the wisest man I know and the only man I trust in this whole wide world. It may be onerous, but I have faith in you, that you will know what to do with the *Codex*. Destroy it, perhaps? Maybe entrust it to a higher power, or just bury it in the Utah Salt Flats. The only things I have faith in these days are you and your judgment, so do what you will with the *Codex*. May the God you so devoutly believe in protect you from what you will learn.

Sincerely,
Jude Oliver

Tears blurred the office around me as I finished. Jude Oliver. Olivier Deschamps. Morgan Heart. The same man. My friend. I preferred Morgan, the name of the man he had become, the man who sacrificed himself for others. Olivier was the name of a callous murderer, a member of a heartless "Family," a criminal who used people without thought or concern. Jude was the name of a lost soul looking for a friend, for answers in this life.

Words sent to me from beyond the grave. My chest tightened and my throat grew thick.

Rain pattered against the window as I cried. Two years later and it still hurt, a splinter in my eye, a wound in my side. I prayed to God that his soul had found its way into Heaven.

Wiping my eyes, I hefted the ream of paper and rifled through. Most of it I'd read before: Morgan's beginnings, his Family shenanigans and his life-changing meeting with the Angel of Knowledge, Herachel.

Tap-tap-tap.

The water droplets fell fat, fast and heavy on the window. It was surprisingly loud through the glass. Then, a little slower.

Tap … tap … tap.

I rubbed my face, feeling my handlebar mustache rasp against my palms. Fast again:

Tap-tap-tap.

My eyes flickered to the window, annoyed. Raindrops continued to patter against the glass, but it was the thick ones that made the noise.

Tap-tap-tap.

I smiled, remembering what Morgan said about water Elementals. *Water talks*, he told me several times. *Water talks.*

Tap … tap … tap.

Each drop hit hard against the window, spraying a surprising amount of water.

Tap-tap-tap.

Water talks? I drummed my fingers in time to the drops. *Tap-tap-tap, tap … tap … tap, tap-tap-tap.* Funny, there seemed a pattern there like … like … like ….

Morse Code.

Dot-dot-dot, dash … dash … dash … dot-dot-dot.

SOS.

Oh boy.

Chapter Three

"Be sober-minded; be watchful. Your adversary the devil prowls around like a roaring lion, seeking someone to devour."
—1 Peter 5:8

Dread prickled across my skin and my stomach clenched with nausea, but the sick feeling didn't stop me from moving quickly to my desk. There, under the center drawer, lay a weapon.

Specifically, a Taurus PT 24/7 with a ten-round magazine loaded with S&W .40 caliber ammunition. It fit smoothly and comfortably into my sweating palm.

A priest with a gun, what a concept, but when chased by the most elite assassins in the world with no weapon but fingernails, one develops a need for alternate defensive strategies. Priests may be the extensions of God's will on Earth, but that doesn't mean we can't defend ourselves. Especially from the aforementioned assassins.

Gun in hand, I made my way through my office door into the nave. I immediately smelled it, the coppery tang I was all too familiar with. Blood, and a whole heap of it. Mixed in with the metallic smell was the odor of feces and urine.

My eyes speared immediately through the gloom of the dimly lit interior to the sanctuary where the altar lay. The gray-blue carpeting shone dark with clotting blood, staining the steps to the nave.

Taking long, slow breaths, I swiveled my neck to scan the large, warehouse-like interior with its wooden beams hung with lights that didn't offer nearly enough illumination. However, just enough light shone from the hollow, square steeple above that I didn't have to squint.

Plock.

The gun came up as my eyes tracked the noise. I lifted my gaze to see ....

Oh my Lord.

Father Paul. The oak cross where Christ's image hung had been desecrated by the corpse of the good father hanging upside down, legs bound to the arms with nylon ropes. He was slung across Christ's image like a bizarre, reverse piggyback. Paul's arms hung down past his head, along with several ropes of intestine that glistened with purple wetness in the sparse light. *Drip, drip, drip* fell the blood from his fingertips, *plocking* down upon the sanctuary. A look of fear and pain and horror carved the face of my friend, ample evidence that he'd been quite alive while eviscerated. Bile stung the back of my throat.

Out in the dim light of the church proper, written on several pews, written in blood that shone black in the spare light, were the words "There is NO GOD."

"Do you know how long I have waited for you?"

That voice floated from the darkness pregnant with menace. An Irish brogue so thick the words were barely understandable. A man's deep baritone. I didn't jump or twitch or scream. I was firmly in combat mode, training that ended over twenty years ago kicking to the fore in a rush of muscle memory. My switches flipped and I felt frosty, cold enough that I fancied the juices in my eyes froze solid.

"Come out, come out wherever you are," I sang, mind clicking along like a clock.

"A priest with a sense of humor," said the voice. "I like that, I do."

"Who are you?"

What answered me was a sort of high-pitched warble, a fluctuation of tones that grated on my nerves. The man was *giggling*.

When the voice once again emerged, it was filled with a strange sort of hilarity. "Me? I'm the one having *fun!*"

"Come on out. Let's have fun together." *Drip, drip*. Fun. Eviscerating Father Paul and hanging his corpse in an obscene parody of crucifixion was *fun* for this guy. I was sorely tempted to put a few rounds into his skull the second he showed his face.

But that's not the kind of guy I am. Not anymore.

Deep breaths, stay frosty, be the machine, no emotions. "Come out, Sicarius." I flicked my eyes to Father Paul, whose dull, lifeless hazel eyes gazed fearfully at the blood-drenched carpeting. "Come out, Atheist."

"Awww ... who's been telling tales?" came the mocking voice in a parody of a child's whine. "Been watching the telly?"

"You've been making a splash in Chicago," I replied, trying but unable to get a fix on the source of the voice. The only thing I saw were shadows and the twin rows of pews stretching toward the front door. It was a wide-open space, but there were plenty of places to hide. "A serial killer who targets priests, hangs them upside down from the cross and writes 'There is no God' in blood on the pews. Tends to grab the attention of my sort."

"It's good to be famous, isn't it? Be that as it may, I'm glad you know what I am, who I answer to, although it takes away from a clever monologue I've been developing." *Giggle.*

"Who's the new boss, Mr. Atheist?" Any intel was good intel. Providing I survived. "Who pulls your strings?"

"We all have strings, *giggle*, little priest. Rome pulls yours."

There you are. My gun rose as if it had a will of its own. There, fourth pew from the front, where the shadows were deep. *Come on.*

Giggle. "There's a new sheriff in town, and his name is Blaine. He had the intelligence to send me to America, put me 'in play,' as it were. *Giggle.* Allowed me to indulge my passions. Different sort of passions than back at home. He's the man who said I should focus on priests. Clever, eh?"

"Clever." Blaine? Not surprising I'd never heard of him. The late Julian I knew, as well as Boris. The thought of the Russian bodyguard sent a spasm of nausea through my gut. Even two years after his death, I still felt the fear, the mind-numbing terror associated with our time together.

Shadows moved, coalescing into the form of a tall man, skinny with a wiry mop of reddish hair and jug ears. He rose from the pews, the shadows dripping from his long body like sheets of water, revealing blue jeans and a tank-top T-shirt liberally stained red. His hands were gloved in reddish brown. The grin pasted on jaws was as horrible as his giggle, a perverted thing more suited to a jackal than a man. He stepped to the aisle and performed an elegant bow. Dried blood crusted the corners of his mouth.

"Please to make your acquaintance, lad." *Giggle.* "I am Alvin Deschamps." There was a knife in one hand—long, thin, and silvery, dripping crimson.

Of course. I was seriously tired of that Family. "Drop your knife."

"Now why would I want to do that?" His lips barely moved from their awful grin. His eyes glittered like green gemstones.

I lowered the Taurus a fraction. "I'll shoot you in the shin if you don't."

The knife came up and I nearly shot him then and there, but he only stabbed the air in my direction. "Now that's not right, a priest with a gun. Not very Christ-like at all."

"Drop it. *Now!*"

He shook his head. "Don't believe I will."

The Taurus barked. The noise was deafening inside the spacious church and I felt a twinge of regret for adding to the violence already committed in the house of the Lord.

But nothing happened.

Again. Same result. Again and again and nothing. The bullets hit, but didn't penetrate his skin. Instead they flattened, broke apart and fell to the floor. Each and every one. The Atheist stood there with that terrible grin on his face and I harkened back to what Einstein said—that the definition of insanity is doing the same thing over and over again and expecting different results.

Damn.

Alvin the psychopath took a mincing step forward. "You see, ever since you, Cain, and that misfit Olivier took out our hotel two years ago, I have been ... studying." *Giggle, giggle.* "I'm shite when it comes to Words, but I do have maaaaaad skills when it comes to Botanical Magic." *Giggle.* "I came appropriately prepared." His sick grin disappeared and he rushed forward.

Anger blurred my vision as I raced to meet his charge, still holding the Taurus in one hand. For two years I'd suffered guilt over killing a Sicarii Dagger Man—one of the elite assassins bent on sending me to meet my maker—by putting a bullet in him. It was him or me, and I chose him. The memory was still an-hour-ago fresh. The *bang* of the pistol, the blood and bone and the sightless eyes and then the crushing guilt.

Thou shalt not kill.

It took me a while, a lot of soul searching, before I came to grips with that commandment in relation to the man I had killed. Murder is immoral, against the will of God, but self-defense is another kettle of fish entirely.

So, without hesitation, I attacked Alvin the Atheist, fist filled with two pounds of polymer and steel. He sure wasn't going to pussyfoot around with me.

Feet squelching on blood-soaked carpeting, I closed in. The Taurus hit Alvin's knife hand hard, cracking bones and sending the blade spinning to the floor. I followed with an uppercut that took the starch out of his shorts quick, his knees buckling.

Right cross, and then, while he staggered, I grabbed the back of his head and helped introduce his face to my knee. Bones crunched and blood soaked through my pants and my knee stung, but it dropped the serial killer to his knees. I followed up with a kick to his skull, and that should have been that.

Should have. Moving snake-fast, he caught my shin with one large hand and I had to struggle to remain upright as he stood, eyes gleaming with madness and fury.

Then I was airborne.

What the ... I didn't get to finish the thought because pain and stars intruded as my body slammed into the first row of pews. Wood cracked and my head slammed into a surface harder than bone, ringing my bells. The Taurus went flying to points unknown. Time for the ref to count to ten, or to tap out.

Alvin had thrown me *fifteen feet*.

Through the purple spots that swam in my eyes, I saw Alvin standing on the dais in front of the padded bench, shaking his head slowly, blood drooling from split lips and a smashed nose. "!" he said.

A Word. Instantly he started to heal. No longer swelling, his nose straightened with small popping sounds. Within a space of a few seconds, he was fully healed. That sick smile rejoined his face as his mad eyes met mine.

"I do so love Healing. It may be the least desirable of Words, but I find it the most useful, I do."

"N-now who's cheating?" I breathed, lungs burning as I struggled to sit upright.

"Never said I wouldn't cheat, did I? Have one word and I use it well." He charged, hands outstretched.

I was hurting, my back a solid mass of agony as if someone had slipped burning metal under my skin. My head wasn't any better, but adrenaline is an effective painkiller, and the prospect of imminent death at the hands of psychopath was a great motivator. My shoes hit the floor a split second before his hands grasped air where my throat used to be.

I threw a right to the body and he sucked wind, face contorting. He hastily blocked a left, but my fist did a number on his upper arm, landing with a meaty *thwock*. Ask any boxer, a hit to arm takes a toll.

Alvin the priest killer jabbed and missed and jabbed again. I knocked his hand away, although the force of his strike bruised my palm. We circled each other like lions, probing for weakness, and my mind went into overdrive.

His strengths: the Word of Healing. Made him hard to put down. Incredible strength, probably augmented by Botanical Magic—magic from plants that retained the divine spark from when God used the First Word that created the world and all life therein. That would also explain why he was bulletproof. Skilled at fighting—I could see it, the way he moved his feet and held his hands. No stranger to unarmed combat, which wasn't a surprise, considering he was a Deschamps and therefore trained in all manner of evil.

Weaknesses: none that I could see, except a tendency to blab. Could I use that?

"You got skills, son. You a Dagger Man?"

His grin broke through the crust of blood on his face. "I read the report on you, old man." *Giggle.* "You took out a couple of young ones, but I'm more seasoned, I am." The jab he threw didn't connect.

You're also sloppy, out of practice, I thought, keeping my face impassive. Too many priests who couldn't fight back, no real challenges. My jab did connect.

Blood spurted from his nose, and Alvin shook his head, blinking rapidly. That opened him up to a savage overhand right, which broke his nose once again. I had no desire to close in and grapple with a man who could throw my two-hundred-pound bulk across the room like a spoiled child flinging a ragdoll. He'd wind up ripping my arms off. But if I could just pick him apart ....

"!"

The Word slithered in one ear and out the other. Dang it ... Healing again. Might be his only Word, but he could use it until the cows came home while I wore myself thin.

That's when I had an idea.

Morgan had twelve Words, all that the Sicarii had access to. By his own admission, he was one of the most powerful magi that ever was, having mastered the Elemental Languages and Botanical Magic, but even he had a limit, one all magi were prone to.

Backlash. Damage incurred by using magic too often. It take a severe physical toll on a body. I thought that Alvin, a one-Word wonder, couldn't use magic with the frequency a twelve Word like Morgan could. The more Words, the more ability to toss them about before Backlash set in.

I smiled inwardly. Time to test a theory. My fist blurred and I connected to Alvin's lantern jaw, bruising my knuckles. I followed with a kick to the shins he couldn't block. I felt as well as heard bone crack with the sound of a small firecracker detonating.

As he fell, the Atheist screamed Healing and his shin mended before his butt hit the carpeting. Then he was on his feet with greater speed than I'd anticipated, striking quickly, a solid kick to my midsection that flung me back a good eight feet and had my abs shrieking in pain.

I landed hard, but made it to my feet in time to avoid a vicious ax-kick to the skull that would have shattered my neck; instead his foot hit the carpet with a resounding *whoom!* and I lashed out, driving the knuckles of my left hand into the soft meat of his calf. He jumped back, cursing between mad giggles. His cackles were getting on my last nerve.

No time for pain, only time to jump forward, swinging with all my might, swinging like I wanted to rip his head from his shoulders. I thought I could hear my fist whistle through the air—*don't let him breathe, don't let him recover*—and I connected with his side, following through past the target of his ribs. The wind left him explosively, his eyes bugging out. I hammered at him, falling on top as he fell back. I began to drop bombs—chin, cheek, nose, elbow to the jaw and teeth—and blood flew.

I realized my mistake a microsecond after it was too late.

I had closed in, far too much, well within his powerful reach, and I felt those big hands grasp my legs, hands that crushed my flesh through a thin layer of gabardine. The Bones creaked as he *squeezed*.

"Arrrrghhh!" It was bad, that pain, but I had been tortured by the best—Boris. Julian Deschamps' former bodyguard had cut me across the side, had sliced me down to the bone and taken a pair of pliers to the exposed rib. That had been the worst, but what Alvin did was pretty darn close.

He let me go only so I would stop punching, so he could Heal himself. Once again, that slithery Word echoed throughout the church. Only a few more seconds and he'd be on me again. I tried to get to my feet, but my calves were on *fire* while blood ran into my socks. He had squeezed so hard that flesh tore like toilet paper and the blood was flowing freely from several small tears. For the first time, the tinny taste of fear flooded my mouth, and despite the pain, I stood, swinging wild and connecting with a rock-hard stomach that actually gave beneath my fist. Suddenly my black pants were soaked in serial-killer vomit and I swung again, punishing ribs. I ducked an elbow that would have shattered my jaw.

"This is fun!" *Giggle, giggle.* "Aren't you having fun?"

No time for talk, only fists and feet. I took a glancing blow to the cheek that had me seeing cartoon stars, but I managed to respond with a kick to the testicles that bent him over. Once again, he used the Word and straightened, still giggling, still wearing that nightmare grin. If the Joker had an evil Irish brother from another mother, it was this guy.

Left, left, left, *right*, left, left, left, *right*, establishing a pattern. Left, left, left, *right. Fall for it you, sonofab ....* And he did, he fell for it, trying to counter the second left. I smacked him in the nose a third time, with a hard right. I noticed a slick paste on my knuckles—perhaps a Botanical Magic mix that gave him strength or made him impervious to bullets—and when he said the Word again, his nose didn't *quite* straighten out and a spasm of pain clouded his shining green eyes. Backlash had finally set in.

A hard knuckle punch to Alvin's deltoid, a point of pain for the Atheist. Thank you, Cain, for showing me that nerve cluster. My assailant grimaced as his arm went dead. Once again he uttered a Healing. Blood trickled fresh and bright from his nostrils. It hurt, the Backlash, but his arm moved, and in his eyes shone the first spark of fear. Though faint like the stars seen through a thin scum of clouds, it was there.

"Give up, son," I panted, fists raised, ready for anything. I was the better fighter and he knew it. It didn't take much to fight your average workaday priest, but it sure as heck took a lot to tangle with one like me.

Giggle-gasp. His manic giggling was fraying at the edges, but that didn't stop him from tacking on that crazy smile. "You priests … just don't know when to start having fun!"

He launched.

My fist met his throat and he fell, limp and gasping, unable to voice his Word, unable to do much more than twitch spastically.

I slumped, tired to the bone and more than a little rough around the edges. My clothes were soaked in vomit and blood and not a little sweat. Grunting, I grabbed Alvin by the hair and lifted him from the floor, giving him one last solid *whack* to the jaw that stung my fingers something awful. The Atheist slid to the ground, semiconscious.

"Now, son," I panted, feeling all kinds of sore. "Didn't want to do that." He wheezed and drooled and bled. "But you left me no choice." My Lord, but my hands hurt deep to the bone. I flexed my fingers. Nope, nothing broken. With a groan and a moan, I hauled Alvin to his knees, keeping both hands on his shoulders. His smile was gone, replaced by mashed, raw lips.

"Now listen, son, I want you to tell me everything you know about this Blaine Deschamps."

Giggle. Mumble, mumble.

"What?"

Those bleeding lips moved slowly. "I said, 'You're still not having any fun!' "

Blam.

Alvin's head rocked sideways, brains exiting at speed. *What the …?* I looked toward the front doors for the source of the gunshot.

Whoa.

I dropped Alvin's corpse to the floor, where the remains of his brains leaked onto the carpet. "Who are you?"

A vision in tight jeans, black leather vest, and a white T-shirt sauntered down the aisle, hips swaying rhythmically. A Glock was clutched in one perfect, long-fingered hand. "Father Mike?" she asked.

I nodded dumbly, trying not to drool. I might be a priest, but I still possessed hormones. "What the heck? I had him! I had him beat. You didn't have to kill him."

Her perfect lips turned down in a frown that told me she didn't care about the heap of dead meat at my feet. "Our mutual friend asked me to tell you that I am 'the boat sent a second time.' " She shook her head, long, black ponytail swinging. "Whatever that means."

Chapter Four

"There is no peace," says the Lord, "for the wicked."
—Isaiah 48:22

CAIN ALWAYS LOVED FLYING. FOR MILLENNIA he had dreamed of it, but unlike angels who had wings, he could only dream. So it was no wonder that he stared out the window of his private jet at the world so far below and simply enjoyed the view. Fifty thousand years was a lot of time to build up a serious yen.

Only a few short hours and he would be in London. *How marvelous.*

The only thing that marred the experience was Michael's refusal to accompany him. The priest was far too stubborn for his own good, and Cain felt it incumbent upon him to see that he was well guarded. From a distance, of course.

He took a long pull from his tumbler of Scotch, savoring the burn. The plan was to drink and drink, then Purify his system and drink some more. It promised to be a long flight, and he had nothing to do. The plans he had so meticulously laid out over the past two years were already in motion.

Young Olivier Deschamps had certainly impressed him, even more than that Greek adventurer Odysseus. While the king of Ithaka might have been more cunning and a more ... balanced individual, it was Olivier who had provided him with the clue to his salvation.

Why had he not seen it sooner? Fifty *thousand* years of introspection and angst, of deep reflection and the slow, steady walk on the razor's edge of madness and he'd completely missed the moral of the story. He was the oldest man alive, the most powerful magus in the world, and it took the thirty-five-year-old punk Olivier to point out the obvious.

It was *The Lie*. Actually, it was the First Lie Ever Told and it was told to God. Satan must have laughed his ass off to see such a demonstration of mankind's ability to accept evil. The First Lie had been told over and over again around campfires, first in the Land of Nod—located in what is now known as Iran—then farther away as mankind bred like rabbits and spread across the skin of the world. Cain himself had told the story to his own child Enoch as his family wandered from settlement to settlement. Eventually he left his family, for their own safety, the burden of his Curse having become too heavy for those he cared about.

He sighed and took another sip. All this time, he'd thought it was the murder of his brother that God punished him for. The power of the Curse kept the memory fresh: the harsh feel of the jagged rock in his hands, the smell of moist soil mixing with the coppery tang of fresh blood, and the sudden give of bone to the brutal force of a pummeling stone. The memory of the lurid, pinkish-red color of his brother's brains upon summer wheat still haunted him, had been burned into his forebrain by the wrath of God.

This was his Hell, to remember with perfect clarity ... total recall.

Pain clenched his heart as he recalled the presence of the Lord at his back and the Voice—the Voice so few mortals could withstand—as it thrummed across his nerves.

"Oh, Cain, where is your brother? I cannot see him working with his flock. Do you know where he is?"

The shame, the utter mortification. How could he answer? With the Lie, of course. "I do not know where he is. Am I my brother's keeper?" He should have known such a thing could only end in tears. His own.

And it had taken a member of the most corrupt, evil Family known to man to point out the Lie, his tragic mistake.

Quite embarrassing, actually.

Still, the boy had been a magical prodigy, surpassing even his own exceptional ability at Botanical Magic. He'd taught an old dog a new trick or two, that one.

"Sir."

It was Christophe, Cain's valet and all-around right hand. "Yes?"

The stout man's thick lips twitched into a semi-smile. "The paparazzi we contacted have already put your photo on every website. As far as the world is concerned, Forrest Evers, the head of Lion Communications , has concluded his business in New York and is on his way to visit his London offices."

Forrest Evers, one of my cleverest puns. Cain smiled. "Excellent, Christophe. Any reaction yet from our foe?"

The other man nodded. "Our ... contacts have tracked two Sicarii SS teams boarding the Chunnel to England and will monitor their progress. It is likely they will attack quite soon."

"And young Michael?" asked Cain. "Omaha is but two hours behind us, yet I worry that one of their nefarious teams might be sent to exterminate my friend forthwith."

Christophe shook his head. "According to available data, there are no teams in operation in the United States and none have been dispatched from Europe. In fact, it is disturbingly quiet on that front, as if the Family has forgotten all about Michael Engle. Perhaps because of *them*, the ones who have been fighting them all these years."

Hmm .... That was disturbing. Julian Deschamps had been a clever chap, but a mediocre strategist, relying on the Board of Twelve to run the vast concerns of the Family. This new leader, Blaine, was an enigma. And an American, a fact that no doubt left the Twelve feeling most ... discombobulated. The idea that the Sicarii's ancient foe was the reason they wouldn't send a team into the U.S. was most amusing.

"I have engaged the services of an old friend to look out for Michael as he carries on with his life most extraordinary. He will no doubt find himself in good hands if and when our enemies attack."

The other man nodded and turned away, preparing to return to the rear of the plane, but Cain caught a certain stiffness in the set of his shoulders under his immaculate Saville Row suit.

"Wait."

Christophe turned back, his face carefully neutral. "Sir."

"You have something to say." It was not a question.

"Sir?" Cain's main man would not meet his eyes.

Sigh. "How long have you been in my employ?"

"Seven years."

Ahhh ... so that's it. Pity. Cain took another drink, debated using Purify. Sometime a good drunk was just what a body needed. "You are feeling the effects of my Curse."

No answer. There was none to be given.

One of the major drawbacks to being in Cain's employ was the Curse. He tried to keep his closer employees at arm's length, dealing with them mostly by telephone and Internet, but no matter how infrequent the face-to-face conversations, they all began to be a bit *tetchy* after a few years and quickly left once the symptoms of the Curse manifested. Loneliness was the natural by-product of God's justice.

"I understand, my friend," he said finally. "You will, of course, receive the appropriate severance package as well as letters of reference that will paint you in a wonderful light. I thank you for your service."

Cheek twitching, the other man nodded and attempted to hide suddenly moist eyes. "Sir?"

"Yes, my friend?"

"Why did the Sicarii wait so long before making their move? Two years is such a dreadfully long time."

"Indeed you are correct, but put your prodigious mind to work on this: the opposition knows *for a fact* that Father Michael Engle possesses a direct line to the Almighty and has been graced with the power of His will to perform glorious miracles. He has destroyed the Silver, banished demons, and foiled the Family at every conceivable turn. Couple that with my own heroic might, and they find themselves confronting a threat they have no stomach for. Despite their firm, yet mistaken, belief that the dread lord of Hell is the mightiest being in all of Creation, they quite literally quake in fear at the very notion of God's chosen champion uniting with the one man who has dispatched more Dagger Men over the centuries than any other. Add to that their unease at the thought of *them* and you can understand their trepidation."

Christophe frowned slightly. "*Them*," he said softly. "Do you think *they* are still a threat to the Sicarii? There has not been much *they* have done in the past decade or so."

A long pause. "It is beyond my ken as to their state, except to say that my contact amongst *them* has offered assurances as to their readiness, and indeed their willingness to strike should the appropriate moment come to pass."

"Then why attack you at all? Why attack the good father?"

"Because, my dear Christophe, Pride remains the Devil's greatest sin and his greatest weakness. Together we have gazed upon the face of the Infernal and spat into his fiery eye. He cares not for the sting of it." Cain grinned. "No, his pride is sorely wounded. He wishes a reckoning for that wound and will stop at nothing to ensure we receive our comeuppance, no matter the cost of men and material.

"It is my belief, dear Christophe, that the end game that will resolve every battle is nigh, much to the dismay of all involved. I feel … as if things are coming to a head, my friend. I feel it in the dark places of my heart and the marrow of my bones."

Cain stared into his tumbler as if trying to divine answers in the amber fluid within. Christophe nodded quietly, moving away.

"Christophe?"

Once again the valet turned. "Yes, sir?"

"Please instruct my security forces to sweep Heathrow for snipers. It would not do to have some ambitious Dagger Man attempting, and possibly succeeding with, a lucky shot."

"Yes, sir."

The rest of the flight passed in ominous silence, only the drone of engines marking the time.

"What can Earth do for you, Second Man?" asked the mound of stone and dirt in the Language of Earth.

Cain stared at the small pile of nature's detritus, his sunglasses resting in the inside pocket of his suit jacket. To an outside observer, the mound was merely a haphazard collection of pebbles, soil, and small boulders, and the voice merely a rumble of stone grating against stone. To a magus versed in the Elemental Languages, the rumbling was as comprehensible as English.

"I thank you for your regard, oh Earth," he replied gravely.

The mound shook slightly, as if shrugging. *"You are Second Man, and Earth listens. In all the countless eons, only you out of all the numerous legions of Man have been a constant, and for that as well as your assistance in restoring Primal Water to the Balance, Earth will grant a boon."*

It took over five minutes for Earth to complete those few sentences because its Language was the slow grate of tectonic plates. However, for an entity that measures time by geological events, the words practically tripped over themselves.

For Earth, the return of Primal Water to its just domain in the oceans of the world two years ago was a mere blink of an eye, not even the tick of a geologic clock. Even for Cain, who watched the mayfly existence of his fellows all around, it was hardly a breath ago. But big things can happen in a short time.

Cain looked at the gibbous moon and considered his request. The light shone down upon his face and the surface of the Rhymney River that flowed through Cardiff, Wales. The night was cool and peaceful, and as he always did when forced to move, he felt a sense of renewal. He had long since grown accustomed to loneliness, to the need for hiring new staff wherever he planted his flag, but the sense of change, of doing *something*, always comforted him.

He had left Omaha several hours ago and felt the first insistent tugging of jet-lag as well as worry for Michael, whom he had trained to the best of his ability. Hopefully the priest remained safe, because he reckoned that the Sicarii would take action against him sooner rather than later. Well, he had done what he could, called in old markers and made arrangements with those who even the Sicarii feared. He prayed that those arrangements would not be necessary and that if they were, they would not prove harmful for Michael.

The Language of Water floated to him, carried upon the slight breeze that whispered lightly in the Language of Air. Water talks. It was always talking, as was Air, but where Air laughed and gibbered almost inanely, Water told deep secrets in a rush of words hard to follow, even by someone as learned as he.

Behind him stood the mansion he had purchased many years ago and seldom used. It stood far enough from the city that the likelihood of collateral damage was low should the Sicarii choose to visit, but close enough to Water should he need to summon that chatty Elemental. The fields all around provided abundant opportunity to summon Earth, while the wide-open sky above and the near-constant breeze from the ocean provided a link to Air. All that was needed was a volcano and he would be golden. But he felt that fire was the one Elemental he did not need. Why?

He was surrounded by three, so the need for the fourth was not evident.

"Bind the feet and hands of those who would approach," he said to the mound. "Hold them fast that they may not escape. Those who dwell here now are exempt from this order."

"*So you ask*," said Earth ponderously. "*So it will be done.*"

Next he walked to the river, bare feet swishing through soft grass, then squelching through mud and water. He placed his hands on the surface of the river and gurgled in the Language of Water, summoning Elementals and bidding them to keep boats away from the shore. If any abandoned the boats to swim to shore, Water was to hold them fast, hand and foot. Water agreed, respectful of Second Man and what he had done to free Primal Water.

Next he whistled to the sky, the sound a rush of wind, the tickle of breezes and the flow of air through trees. Air responded, and he blew it full of flattery, cajoling, convincing foolish air Sprites that any who would approach his home from above be bound hand and foot and delivered unto Earth. By the Words of Air he commanded them, by the Word of Binding he held them to task, that they would obey until he left the boundaries of his home. Laughingly, they obeyed.

THREE DAYS OF WAITING. HIS SMALL security team of five stealthily prowled the grounds, weapons in hand, ready for any incursion. They were hard men who had seen too much, done too much, men whose souls were scarred by their actions, by the blood they had spilled and the horrors they had seen. There would always be men like this, who seek something or someone to tell them that there was a way to make their peace with God, and they gravitated toward Cain and his magic like filings to a magnet.

As for the world's oldest man, he strode into his mansion like a colossus, filled with the surety of eons' worth of experience that the Sicarii would come soon. They were, if nothing else, predictable. And impatient.

When things went pear-shaped, Cain was in the kitchen fixing his favorite meal: a bacon, peanut butter and banana sandwich, food fit for the King of Rock and Roll.

Elvis had gained serious weight off that sandwich. It had turned the svelte rocker into a roly-poly, rhinestone-studded lard ass with heart problems. For Cain, who could eat sugar cubes day in and day out for a year without gaining an ounce, the calories were of no concern.

The sandwich consisted of two pieces of plain white Texas toast, Skippy All Natural creamy peanut butter mixed with honey, two thick slices of thick-cut applewood smoked bacon, and apple bananas—also called Latundan bananas—spread thick and quickly grilled. Taken out of the pan right before the peanut butter turned liquid and dribbled out from between the bread, it was consumed before it had a chance to cool.

Cain was on his second one—washed down with a pint of Otley mOtley Brew from Glamorgan—and his stomach was feeling pleasantly full, not to mention a bit distended, when the front of the mansion disappeared in a ball of fire.

Before the world dropped down an endless well, just as his uncovered eyes caught a glimpse of a doorknob flying at his skull, he thought, *Of course ....*

Then the blackness took him.

Chapter Five

"For it is written, 'He will command his angels concerning you, to guard you.' "
—Luke 4:10

"**W**HO ARE YOU?" I REPEATED. "WHY did you kill him? We could have gotten information from him!"

The woman stared, almost disbelieving, and again her uncanny beauty struck me deeply. It had been a long time since a woman had affected me so, and the testosterone rushing through my system nearly choked me.

The corners of her perfect ruby lips turned upward slightly as if she could read my mind. "Let's save the introductions for later. Just know that I'm not a friend. I'm *he* one sent to guard you. *He* would've told you diddly squat." A slender and perfect finger pointed at Alvin's corpse. "He's been conditioned not to talk, as have all the Sicarii." The tiny grin turned into a miniscule frown. "Now, hurry up. I don't know if this pinhead had any backup."

Hurry up. I could hardly grasp her words, but some small part of me perked up, and I moved mechanically toward my office, the one I shared with Father Paul—God rest his soul—and Father Brendan. I crossed myself, grief finally constricting my throat. The movement felt stilted, almost wrong, and I suppressed a giddy laugh, a giggle, as the absurdity of the situation hit me. Once again I found myself ready to run, to speed off toward a destination unknown.

The woman followed and watched as I picked up the cardboard box Morgan had left for me. "What are you doing?" she asked, clearly anxious to get going.

"I have to bring this." My voice seemed to come from far away. Leaving behind the *Codex Infernales,* which included Morgan's story, was abhorrent. Too many had died, too many had suffered, and I had to know why. What was in the *Codex*?

She grimaced, and even that expression of disgust was beautiful. "Fine."

One last thing, a keepsake valuable to me and incomprehensible to others, a silvery cylinder seven inches long that I hastily stuffed into my pocket. I looked around. Everything seemed so small and alien, as if this aspect of the church belonged on a different planet that had no room for an aging priest named Michael Engle. That thought struck me as funny. I suppressed a giggle … maybe Alvin's mad laugh was contagious, infecting my brain with its ugliness.

"You done?"

Yeah, I was done.

As we exited the office, I stopped at the cross, staring up at Father Paul's bloodied face. His mouth was open and his bloated tongue stuck out like a fat worm. "We have to cut him down."

The woman shook her head. "Let the police handle it. We'll call them after we've left."

Every particle of me wanted to argue, but I was past that. All I could do was wonder how Alvin had lifted a one-hundred-sixty-pound man ten feet in the air and bound his legs to the arms of a wooden cross despite no sign of a ladder. I shook my head. Another mystery.

My eyes crept to altar and the odiferous pile decorating it. It seemed that Alvin had taken a dump there to show his Sicarii contempt. For a moment, unreasoning rage shook me.

The woman didn't miss a thing. "The church will have to be re-consecrated. Deschamps tore the holiness from this place like he tore the life from your fellow priest." She sounded almost sad, this woman who had calmly blown Alvin's brains out, consigning him to Hell.

I nodded dumbly and let her lead me away from the one place I'd ever really called home.

THE KOWASAKI PARKED OUTSIDE THE CHURCH had Illinois plates. I thought on that as I stared out the window of the private jet I found myself in. The motorcycle must have been Alvin's, his ride from Chicago to Omaha. A good, powerful vehicle—although not to my taste—nearly perfect as a getaway.

Below, jet-black darkness covered the face of the world. Above, the diamond stars stared down, making me feel small and mean and of little consequence. It's hard to be an egotist caught between Heaven and Earth.

"Are you all right?"

I flicked my eyes from the window to the woman who sat opposite. Still cool, calm, and collected. For a moment I envied her detachment, but realized that because of my own emotional numbness, I must have looked just as impassive, as deadpan as a boulder. I gave her a slight nod.

She poured two fingers of Jack from a pint bottle resting on the table between us and handed me the tumbler. "Have a snort. It'll do you a world of good."

"Alcohol is not the cure for what ails me," I said.

"And you're not sick. What you are is wound tighter than a cheap watch. This will help you relax, perhaps even sleep."

What the heck. It burned, and the acidity stung my mouth, but it did feel good. After the second sip, some of the tension that hiked my shoulders up to my ears evaporated. "Thanks."

"So you're the famous Father Mike." She said it without irony, without sarcasm. She was only stating a fact.

"Don't know about 'famous.'"

"You were kidnapped by the Sicarii, survived Boris the Bodyguard, exorcised demons, destroyed the Silver—good job, by the way—and held the Holy Grail in your hands, seeing it for what it truly is." For a brief moment her teeth made an appearance in something close to a smile. "Yeah, in certain circles you're practically a rock star."

"That wasn't me," I replied. *Sip, sip, sip* …. The Jack was having an effect, rendering me positively chatty. "That was God working through me."

She snorted. "And why do you think God worked through *you*, you big oaf? Because you're something special, that's why." A slender tongue moistened perfect lips. "Trust me, I'm something of an expert when it comes to special."

"Who are you?" Those darker-than-dark eyes captivated me. Not quite brown, not quite gray, they seemed to be a color not yet named by man.

"Minerva." She leaned back in her leather chair, crossing her arms under her breasts. Her leather vest did nothing to hide her spectacular curves, and I shook my head slightly to dispel lustful thoughts.

"Minerva what?"

"Just Minerva."

Right. Like Madonna, or Cher. "How come *he* sent you? Who are you to him?"

"You mean Cain."

"Yeah, Cain."

Minerva chewed on that for a moment, giving me a hard look before answering, "I'm an old friend of the Cursed and I owe him a favor from way back." I had a feeling that *way back* was one heck of a long time ago. "This is my way putting things square. Called me a couple of weeks ago, offered to cancel my debt if I watched over you after he left. I agreed." She blinked lazily, like a cat. "So here we are, me pulling you out of the fire and you safe as houses on one of Cain's private jets."

"You didn't quite pull me out of the fire. I had Alvin beat. You were late to that rodeo."

"Sorry about that," she replied, still staring with those uncanny eyes. "I was so busy looking for Sicarii SS teams that I let the one guy slip by. My bad."

No, not her "bad" and I told her so. Who would've thought that the Deschamps would send a notorious serial killer to off a priest?

"Mighty kind of you, Father Mike."

"Just Mike. Not feeling very fatherly right now. Bruised and battered, but not fatherly."

Laughter, beautiful and brief. "No, not with a few snorts of whiskey in you, I imagine." She ran a hand along my arm and I felt a strange sort of lassitude, the beating I took from Alvin seeming to fade into the background as the warm sensation of Jack Daniels surged to the fore.

The miles passed quickly in comfortable silence, the kind that's absorbed into your skin until it becomes part of you and your eyes wander to a fixed point far away. People call it the thousand-yard stare—the gaze of a person who's seen and done too much and his or her mind is seeking a vanishing point to lose itself in. Some say it's part and parcel of PTSD, but I think it's simply a way of shutting down for a while and letting life flow over and around you while you remain rock steady in the flood. So it was shutdown time for me and Minerva didn't seem to mind at all. She focused her gaze on a glass of whiskey, as if it contained some great mystery, and didn't come up for air until neon flowed close beneath the belly of the plane.

"Where are we?" My voice was a harsh croak and I looked at my tumbler in surprise. When had I finished the Jack?

"Dulles."

"Why?"

"Refuel."

"Where to after that?"

"Europe."

Okay, I wasn't built for monosyllabic conversation. "I don't have a passport."

That earned me a small smile. A blue booklet flapped my way and I caught it out of reflex. *Well, dang … a passport.* My face adorned the inside, handlebar mustache and all.

"You should shave."

"What?"

"Your face. Shave that thing off your lip. You look like a pro-wrestler cowboy. It's too distinctive."

Shave? I'd had this thing for years and years and years. Always neat and trimmed, never shaved.

Minerva sighed. "Mike, you might as well wave a flag and jump up and down for all the monitors to see, and believe me, the Sicarii have facial recognition software watching for you. You don't want them to know you survived the hit too soon. We need to be subtle, and brother, with that mustache, you ain't subtle at all." She paused. "By the way, how did you survive as long as you did against that psychopathic Sicarius? He was big … and well trained."

"I received a warning."

"What warning?"

I told her about the SOS transmitted by droplets of water, and my theory that it might have come from my friend, Morgan, who had, just before his death, become one with the great Elemental known as Primal Water. Needless to say, she was skeptical.

"I guess I need a shave." *Ouch, that hurt.* "But I also need some new threads." I wished for more Jack, while realizing that it was more trap than panacea, even though it might smooth me out some.

"There's a suitcase with a change of clothes, a shaving kit, and a variety of hair dyes, as well as a pair of Wayfarers." Minerva closed her eyes and rested her hands on her tummy. "We don't deplane in Dulles. Cain has our exit strategy from the U.S. all set, so get back to the loo and do what you need to do."

Back to the *loo* … funny word for a bathroom. Very British. Loo. Like *Skip to my Lou.* That rattled around and around in my head as I robotically obeyed her command. *Skip to my Lou, my darlin'.* I was certainly skipping to music, dancing to the tune set by Cain and the Deschamps and Minerva— the modern-day Xena—and I really didn't care. Too numb, I was still held in shock's adamantine grip, so I went back, and what do you know? There, on the last chair to the left, was a bundle of clothes, brand new and pricey, as well as all the necessary toiletries. *Skip to my Lou, my darlin'.*

The head—excuse me, the loo—was bigger than my walk-in closet and even had a small shower, which I used to remove the stench of blood and feces from my nostrils. As the spray hit me, I realized that it was only this morning that I'd tapped out Eddie, the up-and-coming MMA fighter. It seemed like the day had started a month ago.

The razor was sharp, the old-fashioned kind with a detachable blade sandwiched between two thumb-sized pieces of metal, like the Gillettes the men in my family used way back when. It cut through my 'stache in record time, slicing hair from my face, although one or two drops of red made it to the drain, due to an unsteady hand.

Next came the dye. Blond? Nah, wrong skin tone. Red? Not on a bet.

Finally I settled on a rich walnut brown, shades lighter than my raven black. The model posing on the box had beautiful, wavy hair that photographed perfectly. There was no way mine would look that good. *Skip to my Lou ....*

The plane lurched beneath me, the *thump* of tires hitting the runway. I grabbed the shower bar for support until the jet slowed.

Done. I toweled off and wiped condensation from the mirror.

Darn.

Not bad. Not bad at all. The hair was a hack job, splotchy brown with darker brown streaks at the temples and top, but the effect was strange and stripy. I looked considerably younger than my forty-five years, and the color youthened me up some more. I grinned and found a rocker/rebel smiling back at me. Gone was the sober man of God. Hello *Twilight* superstar.

As disguises go, it was good. No would look twice at me and think 'priest,' not in a million years. It seemed that simple was the key. I wouldn't have recognized me.

Minerva agreed. "You look like a weekend warrior."

I parked a black-leather biker jacket with all its zippers over one of the seats, sat, leaned back and put my feet up on the table next to the bottle of Jack. It was mostly empty. No way had I drunk that much.

Minerva closed her eyes and smiled.

That was one scary lady.

"You know the song 'Skip to my Lou'?"

She nodded.

"What does it mean?"

"It is an old partner-stealing song and dance from the American frontier. 'Lou' refers to the Scottish word 'loo,' which means 'love,' not 'toilet.' "

Yep, scary lady, all right.

As we waited for the ground crew to refuel the airplane, I began to sing:

> Skip, skip, skip to my Lou
> Skip to my Lou my darlin'.
> Fly in the buttermilk, Shoo, fly, shoo,
> Fly in the buttermilk, Shoo, fly, shoo
> Fly in the buttermilk, Shoo, fly, shoo
> Skip to my Lou my darlin'....

I thought Minerva asleep, but she joined in the next verse with a pleasing contralto, keeping her eyes closed:

> There's a little red wagon, Paint it blue,
> There's a little red wagon, Paint it blue,

There's a little red wagon, Paint it blue,
Skip to my Lou, my darlin'.

Hours later over the Atlantic, I couldn't sleep. Too hyped up, even with the Jack fizzing through my system. It felt like my skin was too tight, my mind too big, and I sighed and grabbed for the cardboard box beside me, lifting Morgan's journal to my eyes. Scanning the pages, I skipped those I had read two years ago. That part of the story I knew and remembered well. It was indelibly etched into my brain during a time of pain, and I could probably recite it word for word, from adolescence to adulthood, from the leading killer and magus of his Family to the wounded, emotionally scarred man he became.

There. New pages, crisp and clean and waiting for my eyes. Dated 2008, the passage started with a short note. I began to read:

Dear Mike:

Well, I assume that I'm dead or gone and that you've read my journal. Trippy, huh? Just when you thought it was safe to get back in the water ....

I encourage you to read this section before you flip through the *Codex*. It tells how I came to get my hands on the *Codex*, and it'll show you how far the Family will go to retrieve it. Unlike the Silver, the *Codex* is not magical, contains no Words that bring pain or death, although it does contain insight into the darker arts of magic that only the Family has access to. I wish you well.

Jude

I will not cry. I will not cry. Dang it, but the tears tried as hard as they could to burst from my eyes. Funny, the numbness that had encased my soul like ice cracked, then melted away in the heat of a letter from a dear friend dead and gone these past two years.

"What's wrong, Mike?" Minerva's lids were open just a crack, and I could feel her gaze on me.

I shook my head.

"Is that a letter from Olivier Deschamps?"

Her power of discernment was uncanny. I nodded. "But his name was really Morgan Heart."

"Morgan Heart?"

"The final name he used. His true name, I believe."

She snorted. "True names are ... overrated."

"Nevertheless."

"What does it say?" She leaned forward, eyes fully open, curiosity shining bright.

"He wanted me to … read his journal."

"You've read it already, haven't you?"

"Most of it." I held up a sheaf of papers. "All except this part." Heart aching, I stared at the ceiling, emotions finally beginning to overwhelm. A minute passed while I studied the ceiling. Then two. "Where are we going?"

"We are going," she began, "to meet some people who can take care of you better than I. Cain thought it would be the last, best chance you'd have to hide from the Sicarii."

"Why didn't he mention it sooner?"

"Because these people are dangerous."

Now *my* curiosity was piqued. "Then why?"

"Because it's your last option. Cain wanted the Sicarii forces divided, some looking for you while some tracked him."

"I don't understand."

She sighed. "Mike, have you ever wondered why the Sicarii haven't just taken over the world already? I mean, for hundreds of years they had the Silver with thirty terrible Words granted by Satan himself. Even though using those Words takes a toll on a magus, they should have been able bring about the rule of Evil on Earth. Yet they never have."

That was a good point. I'd always assumed that the Words were so onerous that few of the Sicarii magi could use them. Why hadn't they caused more destruction and chaos with the awesome magic of the Devil's silver coins, the original thirty pieces of silver given to Judas to betray Christ?

Maybe they'd tried. I mean, look at the horrors of Hitler, Stalin, Pol Pot, the Tonton Macoute, and Hussein? Bloodthirsty animals all, yet they'd been foiled, or rendered obsolete by time and circumstance. Either way, it came down to three little words.

"I don't know," I said.

Minerva heaved a heavy sigh and gave a shake of her head. Her shoulder-length midnight hair flowed about her shoulders like liquid midnight. "In this world, there has always been a balance between Good and Evil, Light and Dark. Where there are massacres by despots, there are also miracles by saints." She gave me a tight smile. "The Sicarii have enemies they fear, whom they try to work around. These enemies have foiled their plots for the past several centuries, and it is to them that we go."

"Isn't the enemy of my enemy my friend? Why would they be dangerous to me?"

"Because *fanatics* are always dangerous. Always. Although these people will probably greet you with open arms. A rock star, remember?" A slender hand with long fingers rose, palm toward me, forestalling any questions. She had quite the Queen of England attitude. "Enough. Get some sleep or read your letter. As for me, I wish to pass the rest of this little jaunt in silence."

Queen of England indeed.

So I found myself at thirty-five thousand feet above a dark ocean, full of unasked questions, heading toward a foe of the Sicarii who could very well be my foe as well, if what she said was true. I had no cause to doubt her, none at all.

I got to reading.

Skip to my Lou, my darlin'.

Chapter Six

<hr>

"And let us not be weary in well doing: for in due season we shall reap, if we faint not."
—Galatians 6:9

Pain was the first reward for awareness. It started at his toes and the backs of his forearms, an ache that reached deep into flesh. Tingling grew into throbbing that grew into full-blown agony. Fifty thousand years of discipline kept him from crying out. Pain was an old friend, so often visited that it was almost like donning comfortable shoes.

Voices intruded on his pain, harsh grating with syllables that rasped against his eardrums. German. They were speaking German, with its hard consonants and glottal brazenness. Beneath him he felt rhythmic movement.

The last thing he remembered was fire and concussive force, debris arrowing toward him and a crushing noise that drowned out the world. What had happened? Before he could stop himself, a small grunt escaped his lips through something hard jammed between his lips.

"Is he waking?" someone asked in a hard baritone from the right.

No! He was among enemies—that he knew as well as the beating of his heart, and he sought to put his body at peace. He sought stillness.

There was a discipline, one he learned from his giant of a father, Adam. "Son, attend me," he had said so long ago when he was a boy, when he looked upon his father in the same light he regarded God. It was shortly after the Banishment from the Garden. "There is a quietness, a stillness, in things." Adam had stared into his first-born son's eyes with a love that was palpable, a warm caress on a cold day. "You can seek the Stillness of Stones, but that is an unnatural thing for a man, for there is little breath and the heart slows to the point where it seems to stop. Animals are wary of things that do not move, that are *too much* at peace. They seem dead. The deer we hunt flee from dead things and that stillness sticks out in the forest and on the plains where nothing is truly still.

"When hunting, Son, seek the Stillness of Trees." Adam's dark-brown hair hung straight and long down his back, not a strand of silver or gray marring its luxuriant color. Even in his three-hundredth year, he'd been vital and strong, a man in his prime. The first men were long-lived and vibrant, as if too much life pulsed in their veins. They were strong and solid like the faces of mountains, like the Nephilim born to the short-lived people of Nod.

"What is the Stillness of Trees, Father?" Little Cain held on to Adam's work-roughened hands, unwilling to let go, and it made the older man smile.

"Look." Adam pointed to a tall pine with bluish green needles. "See that tree. Look at it … *really* look."

Cain looked. The boughs swayed slightly and the tree bent in small motions to the rhythm of the wind. The needles made small circular motions, as if waving to a young boy. "It's not still at all, Father."

"Exactly." Adam beamed. "Only rock is perfectly still, yet sometimes even rocks move. Nothing alive will be perfectly still and the living know this." He touched his breast. "All living things know this, consciously or no."

In the darkness behind his eyelids, through pain and nausea and the slow ooze of blood in his mouth, Cain sent his mind spinning inward for the lessons of his father, for the Stillness of Trees.

First: respiration. Slow, easy, even. A piercing pain in his chest threatened the steady cadence, but he mastered it with a will grown sharp and hard through countless centuries of discipline and heartache.

Second: small movements of the body. A twitch here, a slight shift there. All indications that the person is alive, yet unresponsive unless outside stimuli are applied.

In less than two seconds he established the near silent Stillness of Trees within his long frame, his body reacting normally as if there was no pain, as if it had not suffered indignities yet uncalculated.

A hard prod to damaged ribs threatened his peaceful state. "No, he's still out," said a pleasant tenor that came from the left.

From above and behind. "He doesn't look so tough." The lilting tones of a woman. Three people with him, most likely armed with automatic weapons and Words. The odds seemed grim.

"He's killed plenty in his time," said the Baritone cautiously. "Shame to take out the man many Dagger Men seek to prove themselves against."

"Dangerous for sure," replied the Tenor. "We should have used an RPG on him in Omaha where he was out in the open for the first time in decades. A sniper with a .50 cal to blow his head apart from a mile away would have worked as well."

The woman chimed in, "Blaine said no, that he was being watched by *them*."

"Fuck *them*." The Tenor's voice became ugly with hate. "We're so busy being afraid of *them* and this guy that we've become paralyzed. I'm sure the Patron wouldn't have minded a judicious assassination."

"The Patron plays the long game, so if you want to go against His will and Blaine's, be my guest." There was malicious laughter in the woman's vibrant tones, like a singer bound in razor wire. "I might even be sad … for the first ten minutes or so."

The voices droned on, talking about *them*—Cain had a good idea who *they* were—and the various things Blaine Deschamps would do to the legendary Son of Adam, most of which were as mundane and unimaginative as they were horrible.

Assessment time. Cain used the Stillness as a shield while his mind enumerated the multitude of hurts his flesh bore and the situation he was in.

One: he was in a vehicle of some sort. It jounced and bounced over a rough-paved road. The rumble of a powerful engine told him it was a truck of some sort.

Two: broken ribs, three of them. Fourth, fifth, and sixth on his right side. Not breathing blood, so no punctured lung. Easy to repair with a Healing, although casting a spell would alert those voices that he was indeed awake.

Three: missing ring finger, left hand. The indignity of it nearly shattered the Stillness. The absence of the digit was a gaping wound in his self-perception. Years upon years upon years he'd walked the earth with only slight damage to show for it. There was the missing toenail on his left foot—big toe due to an misunderstanding at Troy—but that had been it.

Now he was disfigured. He brutally suppressed the beginnings of a bonfire raging in his belly.

Four: something protruded from his left butt-cheek, hot and violent. It slowly leaked blood, pooling under the small of his back. It burned, and every jolt of the vehicle sent needles of pain up his back.

Five: broken right leg. Partially crushed, bone sticking through flesh, but not through the expensive though now worthless pants he was wearing.

Six: flap of skin loose on his forehead. *Drip, drip, dripping* into his ear. It was more annoying than painful, although the headache he was sporting was no fun at all.

Seven: cold metal circling his ankles and wrists and a gag in his mouth. Apparently this new crop of Dagger Men were not fond of taking chances.

Could be worse, he decided.

What to do, what to do? There were three of them and one of him. All three were armed, most likely magi and highly trained in hand-to-hand as well as bladed combat. And he was damn sure they had more than a few blades secreted upon their persons. As for him, well, all he had was a variety of injuries, some serious, his cunning, his hands—sans left ring finger—and his magic.

Hardly seemed fair at all.

How had they caught him in the first place? It took a second, but the answer hit him with the speed of a bullet. *Fire.* He had warded the mansion, called the elements to protect him and his men, but never called upon Fire for assistance.

Arrogance, he thought. *Pure arrogance.* The SS team had probably used an RPG or a large Fire Elemental to destroy the mansion, trapping him inside so he could be scooped up at their leisure. He should have seen it coming, should have known that Blaine would be as subtle as a thrown brick. That shortsightedness had nearly cost him his life. The blow to his ego was enormous.

For years he had hidden from the Sicarii, but every now and then one showed up to turn him into a corpse, and he wound up leaving theirs on the stony soil. Always a singleton would find him and always he would dispatch them quickly, bored by their predictability. Apparently this Blaine Deschamps was anything but predictable. So now that the Sicarii had moved past expected behavior, he had to react swiftly, ruthlessly.

The plan formed fully in his mind. From beneath the Stillness, he used a Word.

Morgan Heart had been a great magus, the best Cain had ever known—other than himself, of course. The young man had a way with Botanical Magic that was astounding, performing feats that took Cain's breath away. He drank in Words, instantly understanding their import and complexities. But there was one thing he did not know that Cain did—the real secret behind magic.

The Silent Word.

Words of magic were reflections, poor copies really, of the First Word used by God to create the universe. Like a copy that has been copied, and that copy copied until that Word of Creation was rendered into barely legible smudges poorly seen on tattered paper. Those smudges contained the power of the First Word, albeit in limited quantities.

Cain knew it was not the actual utterance of a Word that crafted the magic, but the *intent* of the person using the Word. One need not say *anything* aloud at all. When he had fought Julian Deschamps' enormous bodyguard two years ago, he used Shield to stop a ballistic knife from slicing through his neck, then silently used Break to shatter the thin blade. It happened so quick, no one was the wiser.

He used Heal first, bearing down with all his will. His flesh responded instantly, sending sweet relief through his mauled tissues. The smell of fresh-cut grass tickled his nose. Bones slid into place, and minor cuts and abrasions evaporated from his skin. The piece of whatever was lodged in his butt emerged with the low, slow scraping noise of metal on metal. Cain tensed, but the SS team was so busy with their banter on what tortures Blaine would employ that they didn't hear it.

Unfortunately, all that chatter did not hide the smell of magic.

"Shit! He's Healing!" Baritone sounded terrified.

Every Word carried a smell unique to each individual magus. For Purify, Cain smelled freshly sliced apples, for Healing, cut grass. Apparently Baritone knew Healing and could identify it.

Things went a bit wonky from there.

The Stillness of Trees was broken, and before his eyes opened the tiniest bit, Cain mentally shrieked a Breaking, flooding the area with the smell of rocks heating in a sauna. He focused on the tight metal wrapping his wrists and ankles and the gag in his mouth. There came the sound of an icicle shattering against concrete as metal turned into shards, flying away from his body. The gag in his mouth shredded like rotten cheesecloth and was gone.

He was free.

Everything became snapshots, stills of the world around as his mind processed the situation. Large man to his left, blond with a short-cropped dirty-blond beard. The Tenor. The Word of Force passed Cain's lips, accompanied by the smell of roses, and a disc of compressed energy slammed into the man, backed by cold fury. Tenor hit the side of the truck—fourteen feet of aluminum wall and lit by icy LEDs on the ceiling—with such force that blood splattered and the sound of snapping dominated the space just before thin metal tore. With a shriek, the SS man disappeared, extruded through a small hole to fall on the road with a greasy *splat*.

Burnt dust clogged his nose as Pain was screamed into him from the lady behind and above. One thing she had not counted on, much less thought of, was how accustomed to agony the oldest man in the world was. It danced across his nerves, each point a tiny, flaring node of anguish that sent his brain on overload, but he rode above the misery, letting it wash through and around him. At the same time, Baritone mumbled Strength, sending onion stench through the air.

If Baritone had known Force or Avoidance, he might have lived, but Strength is a base Word, useful in many situations but strategically weak. Cain knew this and did not bother with another Word; instead he rode Pain and torqued his hips, snap-kicking the man from a reclining position. Cain's long leg reached high enough to catch the sitting man at the throat, crushing cartilage.

Baritone, a swarthy man with a falcon nose, gasped and gurgled before collapsing, soon to become a corpse, forever devoid of strength.

Pain from above and behind. Again and again the Word slammed into his ears. The musky smell of furnace dust nearly made Cain's head swim, but he jumped to feet, the roar of wind in his ears from the shattered truck wall and the sight of a terrified woman meeting his eyes.

Clothed all in black—black helmet, black body armor and boots—she continued screaming Pain at him, her plain Jane face contorted in fear. It began to mount. Word after Word, it flensed his nerves. Salt and vinegar on an open wound, the kiss of a knife slicing skin away from pale muscle, the sting of superheated needles sizzling through the eyeballs and teeth torn from the roots of his jaw. All this and more hammered through his brain, but still he persevered.

He stood over the woman, the roof barely tall enough to accommodate his length, and spoke through the pain of shattered bone and the taste of blood. "Stop." The movement of his jaw sent flakes of crushed glass tearing through his lips.

She ignored him, continuing to holler the Word Pain over and over, and each time it scourged him without damaging flesh, tearing at nerves, or breaking bone.

But it felt like it.

Blood burst from both her nostrils as Backlash hit, and Cain smiled through the Pain. She could not keep the magic going. The piper must be paid.

"Stop."

The truck slowed to a halt as the woman muttered Pain over and over again. Each time the barbs dug a little less deep, and the knives cut shallower and shallower grooves through his nerves.

Through the hole in the side of the truck smeared with blood lurid as hooker-red lipstick, he saw the jagged shadows of night and thought Vision, adding cordite to the smell of burning dust. The darkness turned into a kaleidoscope of fantastical colors. Now he could really see.

Back to the woman.

Her eyes bled crimson tears that mingled with the blood-laced snot from her nose, and her ears gushed. Lips moved soundlessly while her face wore a mannequin's inscrutability.

Backlash. Fatal. No longer any of his concern. He shouted Force at the hole, widening it so it could accommodate his bulk. Vision showed him exactly where concrete ended and grass began. His feet hit the ground three feet from a man in black who immediately raised a 9mm pistol and fired.

The man's aim was good, but so were Cain's reflexes as he willed Shield into existence. The round leaving the barrel at 1200/feet per second was suddenly the world's smallest party favor as it came to an abrupt halt half an inch from Cain's right eye.

Cain responded with Force, hurling the Sicariius thirty feet through the cool night air, tossing him ass over back over head over ass over back over head and repeat until he lay motionless.

Another man burst from the truck's passenger door, firing an H&K G36 from the hip, shredding the air with sound and rounds, bright flashes strobing into darkness. When he stopped to change clips, a large pair of hands clamped on his helmet from behind and twisted his head 180 degrees with a wet *crack*.

Before the body had a chance to hit pavement, Cain was in the truck, a long knife taken from one of the SS held to the throat of a woman who stared at a nightmare face painted in black blood, soot, and grime, flashing a smile that would have been charming if not for the filth surrounding it.

His whisper hurt her ears. "It appears to me that you SS folks somehow evaded the good grips of stony Earth. I am understandably curious as to how a gaggle of psychopathic nincompoops managed such a heroic feat."

From the corner of his eye, he glimpsed a large black sedan a hundred yards away flip a *screeching* U-turn and head their way. More Dagger Men to contend with.

"Well? Hurry up, girl, time is running out."

Sudden fury blazed in her eyes. "Fuck you."

Cain sighed and plunged the long knife up under her chin, through the soft palate and into the brain. She twitched once, twice, then lay still.

"Although I dislike removing one of the fairer sex from the game board we find ourselves upon, I do have to observe that some of the most evil, insane motherfuckers who have walked upon the face of the Earth have been women." With a sigh, Cain exited the truck and picked up the dropped G36, his body awash in the lights of the approaching sedan.

He grinned. It was not pleasant.

Chapter Seven

—————⚬⚬⚬—————

"For we must all appear before the judgment seat of Christ, so that each one may receive what is due for what he has done in the body, whether good or evil."
—2 Corinthians 5:10

I STARTED TO READ, BUT REALIZED IT had to wait because sleep wouldn't. As we soared over the mid-Atlantic, my eyes closed of their own accord and I was sawing logs.

But before everything went dark, I ran through the day's events. Over and over, my mind went back to the same moment: the SOS at St. Stephen's.

Was it Morgan? Was his spirit out there looking after me? Watching and waiting for the day the Sicarii would make their move? Or was it Primal Water, that first Elemental that bonded to Morgan back in New York, who helped him destroy Mephistopheles? Perhaps it was grateful for my role in its rescue.

Sighing, I drifted off.

IT WASN'T THE FIRST RAYS OF dawn that woke me, but the sudden *thump* of wheels hitting tarmac as the jet landed.

Skip, skip, skip to my Lou.

Darn, I really hated it when tunes got stuck in my head. It was worse than infomercials.

"Good to see you awake. You snore something terrible, Mike." Minerva's eyes glinted with humor, and all I could manage was a raspy grumble in reply. Opening my mouth would let my appalling morning breath escape. My tongue felt like I'd been licking lint all night, and even with the comfy seats, I was sore, as if every joint was filled with sand.

My ribs protested as I stretched, and now that adrenaline was no longer a chemical factor in my system, all the hurts that Alvin had visited upon me were demanding my full attention.

A can of Coke appeared in front of my nose, as well as a couple of yellow tabs of ibuprofen. "Here, you look like you could use this."

Could I ever. "Thanks."

"You've got a nice mouse under your left eye. It's coloring up quite well."

I felt the puffiness there. *Ouch.* Yeah, tender and swollen, soon to be deep purple.

"Where?"

She knew what I meant. "Charles De Gaulle Airport." Two beats while she waited for a reaction. "That's in Paris." Another beat. "France."

"I've heard of it. Seen pictures, too." France? Is that where helpful fanatics waited?

Charles de Gaulle Airport, where the roof of the main terminal seemed to be one big skylight arching overhead, supported by thousands of girders. Tons of glass and metal just waiting for an earthquake to shake the whole thing down on the unsuspecting crowd of international travelers. Wasn't that a heck of thought as I walked beneath the dangerous roof?

Okay, I was not at my cheeriest, but you have to realize that I hadn't felt so horribly out of sorts since Boris decided to use my torso as a punching bag a couple of years ago. Time is the great eraser of memory. Pain fades and experience becomes almost illusory until you realize that even the memory of agony is a blurry, distant thing.

It wasn't so distant for me that morning. As we made our way through the throngs (Do you have anything to declare, *monsieur*? Yeah, I'm declaring that I hurt all over), and over to the rental kiosks where blue-blazered men and women wearing professional smiles greeted customers needing transportation.

Minerva gave me a look. "Speak French?"

I shook my head. *Ouch.* "I speak English, Latin, and Bad Spanish."

She sighed. "Americans."

"What are you?"

"Cosmopolitan."

It seemed we shared one language in common besides English—sarcasm. *Lovely.*

She approached a kiosk where a plastic platinum blonde with a perfect smile greeted us. "*Bonjour.*" There was an American flag pin next to flag pins from other countries: Spain, Germany, and Sweden.

Minerva's smile was every bit as polished as the other woman's. "English, please."

"But of course, *mademoiselle*, how can I be of service?"

"My brother and I would like to rent a motorcycle."

The woman—her gold nametag read *Emilie*—shook her head sadly. "I am so very sorry, but we do not rent motorcycles here."

"My name is Minerva Weaver." Pause. "My employer called ahead."

I whispered, "Thought you didn't have a last name."

"Only when necessary," she whispered back tersely. "Now shhh."

So I shhh-ed.

Meanwhile, Emilie had become paler by three shades. "But of course, *mademoiselle*, all arrangements have been made."

Within a minute, we had two keys and the necessary paperwork. No muss, no fuss.

"Let me guess," I said. "Cain?"

Minerva nodded. "It's good to be the boss."

Go figure.

A courtesy shuttle waited for us, the driver in a tight blue polo shirt shooing away tourists who needed a ride. "This is special transport," he said in fractured English to an elderly couple from the UK. "Go now, please." But his bearded face was all smiles as he escorted us into the shuttle.

"Why a shuttle?" I grunted as I planted my behind on the shuttle's barely padded seat. "Seems kind of Third World for a guy like Cain."

Minerva's strange eyes with their multi-colored specks grew distant. "Shuttles are low-key. If the Sicarii suspect we are in France, then they will expect us to use a limousine. Trust in Cain, Michael; he knows what he is doing. He has been hiding from the Deschamps family for nearly two-thousand years."

Well, when she put it like *that* ….

Ibuprofen didn't quite take the edge off. Stiff and sore and suffering from ten kinds of achy-breaky owies, I wondered if Minerva might have some Percocet stashed upon her person. I doubted it. All we had were our clothes, wallets, passports, and determination to get as far away as possible from the machinations of the Sicarii.

France was green. No one ever told me how green France was, and awareness of its lushness trickled through the filter of my pain. The airport and support buildings hid most of the green, but I could see tall grass and dark soil, straight trees and dew, all signs of the fertile land prized by farmers. Then I remembered the French specialized in growing grapes for wine and tending dairy cattle for cheese. That's what people think of France, right? Not just snooty waiters in romantic comedies, but a land of wine and cheese. Like

Northern California, and Northern California is as lush as it gets. Still, my ability to appreciate God's creation was severely curtailed by the indignities inflicted upon my frail flesh.

At the rental shop on Rue du Berceau, sitting all by its lonesome except for a blue-blazered minder with shoulders like a linebacker, sat a brand new, white MV Augusta F4 RR motorcycle, a shining sculpture of perfection in titanium and fiberglass that made me drool. I'd ridden Harleys, Ducatis, BMWs, and even an Indian, but this one left them all in the dust. It gleamed in the early morning hour like a promise of excellence and speed. Twin leather saddlebacks, custom designed, were attached to the rear flanks of the machine—storage for our cargo.

"Holy moly," I breathed, nearly in tears. "Are you kidding me?" My hand fluttered above the seat especially designed for two, something the manufacturer had never intended.

"You know your bikes, Mike?" Minerva sounded impressed as she handed the gentleman the necessary paperwork.

I nodded. "In the world of motorcycles, this is Superman." I flipped open a saddle-bag flap and set the box containing the *Codex* inside. On the other side I stowed the manuscript Morgan had left me.

She looked at the attendant and shook her head. "Americans."

He nodded, suppressing an amused smile, right before his head exploded.

Red, pink, and gray showered my new, clean clothes and warm chunky wetness splashed my face and forearms. I found myself gripped in momentary paralysis, but that moment passed before the man's body even hit the pavement. Old reflexes kicked in as I ducked. There was a faint *wzzzzzz* from the space I had just vacated.

"Sniper!" My powers of observation never ceased to amaze.

Gripping my arm hard enough to leave bruises, Minerva yelled, "Hop on!" She did her own hopping, inserting the key and bringing the bike to life, its engine a smooth, velvet purr.

I had barely planted my behind when the motorcycle took off just as another bullet whizzed past. I could feel its heat across my back.

"Hold on!" Minerva screamed as she weaved the bike between Renaults, Opals, and Fords, tires leaving black streaks on concrete.

Holding on wasn't the issue; the issue was not screaming like a ten-year-old girl. For most of my adult life I had ridden a motorcycle, but never in a hell-bent-for-leather style that Minerva showed me that hectic morning in France.

Spang! Fiberglass shattered, shards of cowling breaking off as another bullet nearly found us, Minerva desperately working to keep the speeding bike stable. My heart almost broke as well, seeing such beautiful craftsmanship pummeled into garbage.

"Watch your hands, buster!" Minerva yelled as she maneuvered the bike over a curb onto grass, which the rear tire spit out in clots behind us.

I removed my mitts from her round, soft bits, more than a little chagrined. "Sorry, my bad."

Before I knew it, we were jangling across train tracks, and only Minerva's expert handling kept us from becoming one with the rails. "Do it again and I don't care what Cain says—I'm dumping you to fend for yourself."

My cheeks reddened. "Got it."

Off the tracks and on pavement again, Minerva hit the throttle. The Augusta handled like a thoroughbred, zipping around other vehicles, their drivers offering us the near-universal sign of a single finger.

"Where to?"

"Paris," came the reply. "They reacted faster than I thought possible and sent someone to stop us. We can lose them in the city."

Sounded good to me, even though we made a kidney-jarring transition onto some major unpronounceable highway heading south.

Things went smoothly from there, the Augusta gliding through aggressive traffic with ease like a shark among minnows, slip-sliding around a host of early morning commuters shifting gears while drinking their morning coffees. I tucked my head down and let Minerva do the driving, trusting her ability to get us to safety. No problem at all.

Until we reached the city.

Thwap, thwap, thwap. A sound more felt than heard.

Thwap, thwap, thwap.

What? I looked around, startled by the noise, which seemed to tug at my ear bones.

What I saw nearly made me pee my pants. As we slewed around a blue Citroën, the city rising around us like the walls of a concrete canyon, the dark, menacing shape of a Black Hawk helicopter bore down on us from behind, blades spinning with cold fury.

Sicarii. Had to be.

"Must go faster!" I yelled.

My warning proved needless because Minerva was already on the case. The Augusta leapt forward, whipping my head back.

I thought we'd been zipping along pretty nicely before, but now the motorcycle showed me exactly why it was the premier performance vehicle of its kind, shooting forward hard enough for my grip to actually loosen on my companion's waist. Wind tore at my hair and cheeks as I did my best to hunker down. I blinked at my surroundings through wind tears and tried to ignore the complaints from my battered body.

Paris …. Eighteenth-century architecture peeking through the flesh of a modern city, surrounding the glass and steel core with antiquity. Wrought-iron and pale brick slapped against soulless concrete and rusting steel. Narrow streets converged with modern thoroughfares like streams merging with a river, but these rivers carried more traffic than their watery counterparts—honking, belching, smelly vehicles of makes and models unknown to my American eyes. I saw Deboras and Peugeots and a few others I had no name for, vehicles that bore more than a passing resemblance to their American cousins. Most were small sedans and coupes, but here and there was a smattering of minivans.

It was unnerving—the mix of old and new, the familiar and unfamiliar—but oddly enough, the one thing that did comfort me somewhat was the green and white sign bearing its mermaid logo. It blurred as we ripped past, and it soothed me to find that the U.S.'s favorite franchise coffee chain had roots in Europe as well. It somehow made Paris less alien to see that they liked their cup of joe as much as I did. We had that in common.

Contemplation of our surroundings came to an abrupt halt as the deep roar of a mini-gun overpowered the sound of the Black Hawk's rotors.

Concrete stung my legs as bullets powdered sections of the street ahead and to the left of the bike. Grit stung my eyes, and the harsh scent of concrete dust clogged my nose. I sneezed once to clear my nostrils. We zipped through more gray dust that hurt to breath in and I heard the sound of shattering glass as compact cars were violently perforated. It was by sheer luck that I held on when Minerva took a hard right into a dank alleyway between two tall apartment buildings that had seen better days. The walls to either side became nothing but a dark blur as we sped on, eventually slowing as we exited the alley to merge into southbound traffic.

"Any ideas?" I hollered through the testicle-shriveling fear that gripped me. The Augusta was a sweet machine, all speed and sex appeal, but it couldn't hold a candle to the Black Hawk/mini-gun combo. How the heck had the Sicarii arranged it? I half expected the city to be blanketed by Dassault Rafale fighter jets within a few minutes.

She shook her head, black hair whipping into my face. "I am open to suggestions," she replied, dodging a cyclist who smacked into an Opal in surprise. We left the cursing cyclist far behind as we weaved through traffic, dodging quarter panels and bumpers by scant inches.

"That's an SS team."

From behind, the *thwap, thwap, thwap* of the helicopter approached. The

Augusta was fast, but a Black Hawk had a maximum speed of 222 mph, easily faster than our motorcycle.

Another alley, then street, then alley again, all the while riding fast as possible without killing ourselves or surprised pedestrians. After a few harrowing minutes of dodging people and one angry poodle, we found ourselves in a narrow, trash-filled alley that smelled much worse than it looked. And that's saying something.

Minerva stopped the bike. "Of course it's an SS team, Mike. Who else would it be? The question is why expose themselves like this? Answer: they know you killed that sick fucker back at the church, and they're not taking any chances of you getting away. They must have really liked that serial killer."

I sat there, mouth open, as she continued to monologue, unable to find the energy to interrupt.

"Thing is, we have to find someplace to lie low. I was supposed to take you to Troyes, but that plan has been shit-canned." Minerva stroked her chin, strange eyes wide. "What to do, what to do?" Suddenly, her head swiveled and she fixed those orbs on me. "Quick, ask me a question."

"Wh-what?"

"*Pertinent* to our situation. Ask me a question pertinent to our situation."

I wiped the sweat from my upper lip, which was still red and raw from shaving off my mustache, and looked around. I could hear the helicopter, but couldn't see it. "Uh … how did they find us? The Sicarii, that is."

Minerva smiled, and I nearly lost myself in a rush of testosterone. "Good question," she said and focused on a point far away. "One of your parishioners came to church, saw the mess, and called the cops. The Sicarii were monitoring all communications relating to you and St. Stephens and realized you had escaped their little assassination attempt. Facial recognition at Eppley Airfield is a Deschamps exclusive program that flagged you and notified them that you were leaving. It was only a matter of time before they sussed out our destination and set plans in motion, including two SS teams, a Black Hawk, and a sniper." One beat, then two. "Yep, that's how they did it. Pretty good, considering the logistics involved and the limited time frame."

My mind flashed back to two years ago, when Morgan (then Jude) first showed me the truth about magic and Elementals. "You're a magus," I exclaimed.

She shook her head. "No, not me."

I gave her a good squint. "Sure?"

If looks could kill and all that.

"Okay." I threw up my hands in surrender. "Then where in Paris can we hide and be protected from the Sicarii?"

The smile that broke through the clouds of her face nearly made me faint.

"Now *that*," she said, "is a really *good* question." Once again, her eyes took a trip to the vanishing point, and after a few seconds she shook her head and put the bike in motion, barely giving me a moment to grab on. "Okay, Mike, time to go to church."

What?

And we were off, but this time she didn't bother with such things as safety and roads. Instead she burned rubber on every horizontal surface the bike could navigate, including parked cars, if the mood struck her.

Streets blurred by. Pedestrians were mere smudges of color on my retinas. Fear burned hot and coppery in my mouth, as if my lungs were filling with blood, and I kept a death grip on Minerva's waist. We sped along the sidewalk, knocking cursing pedestrians to the side, and I didn't have time to yell a quick 'sorry' before they were far, far behind.

It didn't take long for the familiar *thwap, thwap, thwap* to reach my ears. I risked a look and saw the Black Hawk zip past behind, then slew suddenly and give chase. The party boys were back.

Cars, trees, cyclists, and pedestrians ... all fell victim to the horrible clattering rounds of the mini-gun, blown apart into twisting ribbons of steel, flesh, bark, and rubber. Buildings that had survived Nazi occupation shed fragments of façade. Several of those rounds came far too close, but Minerva managed to keep up enough zigzag action through alleyways that for a moment we lost the helicopter.

Deeper and deeper we sped, into the core of the ancient city that was waking to the new day. Traffic grew heavier as the early-morning commuters emptied onto the roadways, slowing us down. Apartment buildings flashed by, then a pair of alleyways, then Minerva hit a street named Sebastopol and gunned the Augusta, heading straight down the middle between vehicles that could crush us in an instant. Twenty-foot-tall trees flashed by and motorists tooling on Vespas tumbled across the street like tossed Dixie cups in a effort to avoid us as the Augusta topped 150 mph. City noises were drowned out by rushing wind to the point that even the *thwap* of the helicopter was lost and my eyes watered and stung. The part of my mind that wasn't screaming in terror wondered why Minerva wasn't blinded.

In fact, that part of my mind also wondered why she wasn't on the racing circuit, because with her reflexes and instincts, she'd be a shoo-in to win every time.

Skip to my Lou, my darlin'.

The world was speed and wind and sudden movements of the bike that threatened to unseat me. It was the twitch of my shoulder blades that anticipated a small chunk of lead to end my life. It was the nightmare reality of my life that began with blood streaming down a cross in Omaha, macabre art sculpted by a madman whose patron was another madman in service to the greatest serial killer of them all. And through it all—the madness, the fear, the cramping of my hands and thighs as I struggled to hold on, the twitch, the shake, the sweat and the horror—through all that, I began to get angry.

It had been a long time since I'd been good and pissed off, righteous wrath burning through the skin as if it was gasoline, not blood, that flowed thin and toxic through my veins.

Enough was enough.

Chapter Eight

"Revenge is the only holy thing left to man."
—*Codex Infernales*

Reporters crowded the limo, but one look at the towering bulk of Blaine's bodyguard Alexander and they backed off, sharpish. Even dressed in suit and tie, he was a furnace of suppressed violence, ready to burn those who pressed too close. Blaine considered reporters to be the scavengers of the modern world who picked at the bones of society. They knew perfectly well when an Alpha predator hovered close.

Blaine Deschamps exited the vehicle with his patented smile, waving to the paparazzi and reporters alike. Where Alexander embodied mayhem and destruction held tightly in check, Blaine, moving with a rake's swagger, exuded confidence and cool practicality. With his long hair perfectly styled and teeth gleaming, he knew he cut a fine figure in his dark R. Jewels Diamond edition suit and salmon-colored power tie. At six-two and one hundred ninety pounds, he was a long lean form packed with solid muscle and firm, perfect skin the color of cream.

As he surveyed the gaggle around him, Blaine resisted the urge to punch one of the reporters holding out a microphone. One clean shot to the throat and he would feel the delightful give of cartilage under his knuckles that would vibrate up his arm to the shoulder in a rush of satisfying sensation. Instead, he continued to wave and smile and wink as Alexander plowed through the crowd like an icebreaker through the North Sea.

"Mr. Deschamps, Mr. Deschamps!" It was an idiot from BBS with a weak chin, his shrill voice razoring through Blaine's ears. "What do you think of the allegations that one of your companies, GeneLogistics, is to blame for the so-called SuperCholera outbreak in Somalia?"

It was almost too perfect. Blaine stopped and faced the reporter, his face schooled into a serious and compassionate expression he practiced daily in the mirror. He called it his Nice Guy CEO look. "I understand that the outbreak of SuperCholera is devastating a country already torn asunder by poverty and internal strife." The crowd hung on his every word as his eyes tracked to find the best camera. Only his good side for the evening news. "My heart goes out to the victims and their families. I am pledging ten million dollars of aid to the people of Somalia affected by the disease and ask my fellow CEOs across the world to join me in helping those who need it most in that beleaguered country." Now for Stern Resolve. He saw one woman bat pretty blue eyes at him from behind an enormous microphone decorated with the CBS logo. She was fine-looking filly in a green silk blouse, albeit in a plastic talking head sort of way, and he made a mental note to bed and broom her later. "However, that said, I must point out that GenicGlobal has also been active in the region, attempting to grow drought-resistant food crops. Although such a breakthrough would be a miracle for those afflicted by drought, I wonder what *their* involvement in this outbreak could be." He sighed, a sad, lonely sound calculated to tug at the heartstrings. "I have asked for the board of GeneLogistics to make all their files available to the relevant authorities, including Interpol and the United Nations, and I invite GenicGlobal and other companies working in the region in the area of biotech and related research to open theirs as well. You will find that the outbreak of the so-called SuperCholera has nothing to do with my family's company. My father, the late, great Julian Deschamps, always held the various enterprises under his command to strict moral standards and forced them to adhere to an unshakable code of ethics. I intend to see to it that they continue to operate in such a fashion."

"Mr. Deschamps, Mr. Deschamps!" hollered a reporter from NBC, holding his microphone a little too close to Blaine's face. "Do you think the death of your brother and father in that hotel fire two years ago affected investor confidence in your family's businesses? Is it possible that you being such a young head of the Deschamps' concerns is the reason GeneLogistics, DesTech, and PitCom have backslid while other competing companies have shown regular quarterly gains?"

Blaine didn't recognize the reporter and that troubled him. The man had been either lucky or clever enough to make it past his security to join the horde of approved so-called journalists. His willingness to ask such an impertinent question also indicated a high degree of ruthless ambition.

"I think you will find," Blaine said, "that the next quarter's earnings put to bed such foolish ideas." Time for a Forgiving Look. "The various businesses of the Deschamps family are in capable hands."

With a sincere smile, he turned away, marching resolutely up the stairs of the Deschamps International Building.

It was Fergus who held the door open. "Excellent speech, sir. Too bad GenicGlobal had nothing to do with the SuperCholera outbreak."

Gone was Blaine's charming smile, replaced by a small, ugly smirk. "As of this morning, our infiltration program has managed to insert the necessary memos, emails, and data incriminating GenicGlobal, including all the information about the correct antibiotic treatments. It is the reason I leaked my arrival to today's meeting. All the inserted data is carefully hidden, of course, but easy enough to find for a diligent bureaucrat. And I do want Miles to open all files to the authorities. There is nothing in them now that can implicate us." He paused. "By the way, who was that last reporter, the one with shitty goatee?"

"Sorry sir, don't know how he slipped past. He's from CNN."

"Hire him. He's obviously ambitious and cunning and I want him working for PitCon by the morning. Double his salary if you have to."

"And if he refuses?"

"Then kill him. Make it look like suicide. He either works for us or no one at all."

They passed the spacious lobby, heading toward a bank of elevators. There were no up or down buttons, just a blank, black-plastic rectangle. Fergus placed his palm against the rectangle and an elevator door *dinged* open, revealing a plush interior car done up in various types of wood and purple carpeting. Although large enough to hold twelve comfortably, the compartment felt more than a little claustrophobic for the two of them, with Alexander's bulk standing resolute nearby.

"Our agent within GenicGlobal will make sure that their files will be opened to the authorities, just like I suggested, and when GenicGlobal takes the fall, their stocks will plunge." The ever-present Alexander handed Blaine a plastic bottle of spring water. The young man unscrewed the cap and took a long swallow. "When that happens, buy them out. I want to own them lock, stock, and barrel."

"Sneaky, sir."

"Damn right."

"All that to buy out a rival."

"They are working on some cutting-edge ideas that are years ahead of our efforts. It took months for us to hack their computers without detection, and that was just the outer system, not their primary servers, which are so heavily encrypted they make the NSA servers look like Apple IIs. It also took our agents nearly a year to infiltrate their research division. I could have used a virus to wipe out much of their research, but that would just slow them down, not stop them." Blaine's eyes blazed. "I wanted that research and I wanted their scientists. Now I have them."

Fergus nodded, a small smile on his face.

The stood silently as the car rose, while hidden speakers regurgitated a Muzak version of "Girl from Ipanema." It was the only song that was ever allowed to be played in the elevator, and it never, ever went away, repeating over and over again *ad infinitum.* It set Blaine's teeth on edge and made him want to kill someone slowly with a spoon, but the Patron had been adamant about keeping the tune. Said it amused him terribly.

Blaine's mouth barely moved as he said, "Are they here?"

"Aye," Fergus replied, laying on the Scottish brogue. "Waitin' for ya like ya asked."

Pause. "You only talk like that when you expect me to be violent."

Longer pause. "And …?"

"Nothing. Just an observation."

The elevators opened onto the thirtieth floor, showing a hallway carpeted in deep blue pile. A few twists and turns later, the trio stopped at a set of double doors made of dense white oak and banded with iron. The wood had darkened with extreme age to a light coffee-with-cream shade and the iron was pitted from hard use. It looked like a prop from a Hollywood movie.

"Fergus."

"Aye?"

"Is there anything I need to know?"

The older man closed his eyes for a moment. "Etienne is gonna be a right pain ta ya."

Blaine cast a hard look at the Scotsman, but Fergus simply stared back impassively. If he was nervous or unsure, he did not show it. "Right."

Through the doors was a room large enough to qualify as a concert hall, with load-bearing pillars faced in Italian marble spaced at regular intervals. The drop ceiling contained bright fluorescent lighting embedded in state-of-the-art white acoustic tile. The floor was also white, no breaks, no lines, as if it had been poured from liquid latex and dried smooth. There were no windows, nowhere to look but the violently white walls and no other doors— just one entrance, one exit. It was the one place in the United States where the board was allowed to convene, in an environment totally controlled by Blaine and totally secured from prying eyes or ears.

In stark contrast to the room's sterile-white modernist look, assaulting the eyes with a blunt disconnect, was an ancient table placed smack dab center. Wood older than cities, stained black and scarred, drew the eye like a lodestone. Fourteen feet long and six wide, it seemed a crude joke. Its rough planks and crusty iron nails made it a setting more appropriate for a horror movie than the meeting place of the board.

Eleven men sat in office chairs so thickly padded their bodies were half hidden by brown lambskin. All age ranges were represented, from the oldest, Etienne at eighty-six, to the youngest, Bernard, at twenty-three. All were fit and trim and could out-fight, out-drink, and out-fuck any professional athlete you would care to name. And every single one had the cold, predatory eyes of a shark.

These were men at the top link of the food chain. CEOs of the major corporations dedicated to the goals of the Sicarii and the Patron. Some of the most powerful and ruthless men alive, sociopaths and psychopaths all.

And every one answered to the head of the Family, Blaine Deschamps.

He felt the force of their combined gaze upon his skin—greasy, thick, and abhorrent. He knew they constantly probed him for weakness because of his youth, because of his relative inexperience, and because each and every one believed they could do a better job.

It was his job, his duty, he felt, to show them how very wrong they were. They were all masters of manipulation and business, and each possessed the ruthless cunning of a Third-World dictator. Each one, given a fraction of a chance, would gladly see him in a pine box, and it was his mission to force them to toe the line or become part of the local geography.

Fergus took his seat with lithe grace, but Blaine did not bother to sit; instead he stood next to his plush chair and stared at each in turn, waiting for eyes to drop, for the first indication of shame or doubt or fear. There was none.

"Two teams," he began without preamble. "Two highly trained Special Services teams. What was their one job? Their single mission?" No answer. "Anyone?"

More silence. It was uncomfortable, but no one looked away. Looking away would show weakness, and that was never done unless one wanted to be forcibly retired with extreme prejudice.

Finally Fergus spoke up. "To kill Cain."

"To kill Cain!" Blaine jabbed a finger at the Scotsman. "Exactly right. To kill Cain. To murder the man, eighty-six him, deep-six him, grease him, blow him away, end his motherfucking life." Deep breath. "That being said, who the bloody fuck told those idiots to *capture* the world's most dangerous human being? To transport him in a fucking truck without doping or blinding him?" Pause. "Who's the fucking genius who came up with that brilliant idea?" He knew the answer; they all did. He just wanted the person responsible to 'fess up.

Hamilton, the head of the Family's arms manufacturing (*Fabrication des*

Armes Royales), spoke up, his voice dry and devoid of passion. "Possessing a trophy like Cain would have proven—"

"NOTHING!"

The shout, a fierce thunderclap that was more felt than heard, took the men by surprise. Alexander's eyes gleamed.

"It would have accomplished nothing, not a damn thing." Blaine began to walk around the table, each stride as graceful as a leopard's, full of repressed violence. "In the past, we could have killed him at almost any time, with a half-dozen teams and advanced weaponry, if we'd bothered to try. Hell, we could've dropped a bomb on him, and he would've been nothing but a greasy spot on the pavement. Why didn't we? Anyone? The short answer is that Julian and those before him thought Cain could be used to cull the overly ambitious among us. To rid the Family of those the Family Head thought would not fall in line. By the Patron, we had an *agreement* with the bastard." Faster and faster he paced, his brown A. Testoni Norvegeses *clacking* across the floor. "The Holy Grail of the Sicarii Dagger Men … the death of Cain, the most dangerous man in all history. Bagging him would have immortalized the assassin who accomplished the feat, and the person who achieved Cain's death would prove himself to the Patron as the leader of this Family by right of assassination." He shook his head in disgust. "What a fucking joke. The only result is the thinning of our ranks."

Continuing his pacing, Blaine raised his arms, every line thrumming with anger and frustration. "What are we? Bond villains? Do we have to capture him just so we can strap him into some absurdly slow torture mechanism?" Abruptly, he was behind Hamilton's chair, crouched inches from the man's ear. His voice slithered from between clenched teeth, "Whatever happened to two in the chest and one in the head?"

Chuff, chuff.

Two coughs, barely louder than mouse farts, but loud enough in the still air. Hamilton looked dazed, then bewildered as blood dripped from his thin lips. Blaine stood and raised his hand. It held a 9mm Ruger, a three-inch suppressor screwed to the barrel. Calmly, so everyone could take note, he had placed a bullet squarely between Hamilton's eyes.

The man's seat back became a wash of red and pink. He slumped forward, revealing twin holes in the chair, the off-white stuffing smoking gently.

"That is how you take care of a problem," he said matter-of-factly. To the rest of the group, "Do you understand?"

All save old Etienne nodded sagely, their eyes refusing to settle on the dead man. Alive, he was a power. Dead, he was just refuse.

"Two five-man SS teams. I asked for two teams chock-full of Words and staffed with the Dagger Men most experienced in Elemental Magic. What did our late brother here do? He sent only *four* magi, and minor ones that that, people who didn't have more than one Word apiece. *One-Word magi to capture that motherfucker Cain!*"

Etienne, straight as a stiletto and almost as charming, leaned forward slightly. With his snow-white hair and leonine good looks, he was the very image of an elder statesman. "Blaine, don't you think—?" He did not have time to finish because as the next word trembled upon his lips, a bullet tore it from him, shattering teeth and decorating the chair behind him with gore. Two more soft *chuffs* put twin holes in the center of his chest.

"Don't interrupt," Blaine said calmly over his smoking weapon. "It's rude."

The others merely sat watching him carefully, ready to act if the pistol was pointed their way.

As if sensing that he had used up his free shots and that further violence might actually put him in peril, Blaine handed the weapon to Alexander, who efficiently disappeared it.

"Two to the chest and one to the head. *That's* how you deal with an enemy; every true soldier on this planet knows that. Now, I understand that letting Cain live to cull the overly ambitious and foolish tickled our former Family heads no end, but they all have taken their final dirt nap and are no longer in charge. I'm the *motherfucker* in charge now and I say that Cain isn't to survive another year, another month, and Patron help me, another day. I want him dead right *now*. So the next order of business is to find out where that sonofabitch has gone to ground and have him killed. Is that clear?"

Nods all around. It was still far too dangerous for anyone to speak.

"Wonderful. Now some of you are probably asking yourselves why the fuck, if I have such a hard-on for Cain and the priest, I didn't have them killed in that shithole of a town in Nebraska. Answer: together they would have been nearly unstoppable, and I would've had to nuke the city. Apart they pose far less of a problem. *Capisce?*"

More nodding.

"Wonderful. Excellent. Good to know everyone is now on the same page." To Fergus, he added, "Tell Damien and Alistair that they have just been promoted. I want them in New York by the end of business."

"Yes, sir." With a nod, the Scotsman quickly left the cavernous room.

Blaine took his customary seat at the head of the table, carefully adjusting his silk power tie. "Now, gentlemen, I want to talk to you about Project Fallow."

What came next was more Family business—dull, brutal, and utterly ruthless. Human cost was discussed dryly, as if talking about money, although to Blaine, money was far more useful.

Before Blaine could finish speaking his piece on the current project, Fergus returned and handed the young man a tablet.

A few seconds of reading and the head of the Family rose, features set in concrete. "That is all for now. Stay in New York. There will be more business to conduct."

"Where are you going, sir?" Bernard asked while standing slowly so as not to alarm Alexander. His long, youthful face was as unreadable as his Desmond Merrion Bespoke suit. "If you don't mind my asking."

Blaine considered Bernard for a whole half-second, trying to detect some iota of disrespect. As part of the same B-series as the failed Burke, Bernard was birthed from a Middle Eastern woman and resembled the former Dagger Man closely. Half-brothers physically, if not emotionally. The only reason Bernard had not succeeded in assassinating Blaine years ago was his lack of Words. Of any kind of magic at all. So he'd been relegated to the humdrum life of business, never to know the secret thrill of using a Word or calling upon Elementals or creating magic.

He almost felt sorry for the guy. Almost. Such feelings were beyond his grasp.

"I am going to co-ordinate with our forces in France." He paused. "I have a priest to kill."

Chapter Nine

⸎

"And I tell you, you are Peter, and on this rock I will build my church, and the gates of Hell shall not prevail against it."
—Matthew 16:18

UNFORTUNATELY, ANGER ALONE WASN'T ENOUGH. AND it sure as heck can't stop a round from a mini-gun.

As we sped down Boulevard de Sebastopol, the Black Hawk fell farther and farther behind, until its mini-gun went silent and bodies and blood and clouds of shattered concrete ceased to appear. Only the wind streaming in my ears and the roar of the Augusta remained.

"The Black Hawk is disengaging!" I yelled over the noise.

Minerva nodded, not bothering to reply.

I was plenty angry, but it was the good kind of anger, one that focuses the mind, and mine was humming along faster than any computer. I didn't need Minerva to answer any questions; I knew them already.

"Ambush!" Through the noise, the shout was a thin, lame thing, but Minerva indicated she heard with a nod.

Too late, though.

Just as a river came into view—a gray/green ribbon barely seen and beyond tall buildings old and new—a new and alarming sight captured my attention. From either side just slightly ahead came two motorcycles gunning to cut us off.

Time became molasses-slow as adrenaline sharpened my awareness.

Both cyclists had large pistols in hand. Very large.

The Augusta sped toward them, a streak of white through the morning traffic.

Closing in on each other, they almost blocked the street. The riders, all in black with black helmets and darkly tinted visors, raised their pistols, a slow-motion threat. The clips of the weapons extended far below the grips. Large capacity magazines.

All I could see was *flash, flash, flash* as the weapons barked, but the sound of it was lost to terror, anger, and the high-pitched roar of engines. I imagined lines of heat passing by my skull as rounds pierced the air. Bullet casings flew in a nearly unbroken arc from weapons altered to fire on full auto, and my lungs seized up with fear.

And … we were through. Minerva expertly steered the screaming Augusta between the two riders with only inches to spare. Then I caught a glimpse of several more black-clad bikers on those side streets, all hightailing it our way.

Gravity shifted, or perhaps we did, as the bike slewed to the left, laying a black streak of rubber along pavement. My body dipped sharply, and I felt the cuff of my jeans scrape the road as we became almost horizontal. I winged a quick prayer, certain I was about to wind up a long, red smear.

And … upright. My neck near snapped as my body tried to fly off the bike, now facing perpendicular to Sebastopol. For the briefest moment we stopped, the river to my right, only a few feet away and down below the level of our street.

Six gunmen lined up behind us on motorcycles painted dead black, raising weapons, ready to send more bullets our way. But Minerva gunned the Augusta and we sped off again, my arms tight around my companion's waist.

A hot poker was dragged across my back, a slice of fire that was all too familiar.

"*Arrrgghh!*" I kept most of the scream behind my teeth, but some leaked through. Minerva swung her head to see what was wrong, but I freed one hand to wave her forward. Too many guns behind to worry about. A sticky wetness began to flow from the wound.

Over the river, we sped along a bridge filled with tourists jumping out of the way, the Augusta spitting dark smoke from a couple of holes beneath shattered fiberglass. The bike had been hit, and I never knew, never even *felt* the rounds that wounded the beautiful machine.

"Sorry!" I hollered at a small Renault that slammed into the guardrail in an effort to dodge the bike.

Thwap, thwap, thwap.

Not again! We were far too exposed and motoring along at a stately sixty miles per hour due to pedestrians. From the noise, the Black Hawk was still far enough away not to engage with the mini-gun, but that wouldn't last.

Best guess, we had maybe fifteen seconds. A quick glance back took in our pursuers, six people on bikes, all armed to the teeth, all having no qualms about killing innocents to get to us. Revised estimate: ten seconds, and then we would be meat.

It was more than enough time for Minerva and the failing Augusta.

A hard left and Minerva sped toward a large open space paved in rose-gray cobblestones, filled with people who scattered like pigeons when we sped up. I noticed them only peripherally. What caught my attention was something more important, something that dominated the large cobblestone square like stern headmaster did unruly schoolchildren.

Notre Dame. *What the …?* "Are you kidding?" I screamed.

"Off … now!" Her shout shook my bones and I did as ordered, vaulting off the bike as it skidded to a stop and hitting the ground at a dead run. Minerva's boots hit cobblestones a split second later.

The valiant Augusta careened into a five-foot wrought-iron fence ten feet from the famous cathedral, tearing through two bars before flipping up and over to land in a crash of ripping metal and tearing fiberglass. More tourists scattered, screaming. As for me, my feet took me all the way to the iron fence and its spiky top. I raised my hands, using what strength remained in my cramped arms to prevent my guts from being impaled. The pain of impact against the ornate bars sent sharp spikes from my palms to shoulders, but my stomach hit the fence top lightly, the spikes bruising instead of piercing. As for the graze across my back, more blood flowed, drenching my shirt.

Rebounding from the fence, my gaze went up. And up. And up again and beheld a sight for sore eyes.

It was the Galerie des Chimères, the gallery of chimeras that links the two towers above the façade. Both square, ornate towers loomed two hundred twenty-eight feet overhead, the south tower the seat for Notre Dame's largest and most famous bell, Emmanuel.

An iron hand on my collar hauled me away, cutting short my brief moment of sightseeing. "C'mon."

Minerva did the driving, and I was the passenger, unable to tear myself loose from her surprisingly strong grip. A small black pistol appeared in her right hand, waving at a gate attendant who gabbled angrily at us in French. Seeing the weapon, the attendant shut up quick and showed us his back and elbows.

"What?" My brain hadn't quite caught up with the situation yet.

Minerva pulled harder, a force of nature in one pretty package. "Inside!"

More attendants, guides, whatnot, in white button-down shirts and tan slacks melted away from the grand double doors of the entrance when they saw a crazed couple—an impossibly beautiful brunette waving a pistol and a large, ragged man with stripy punk-rock hair. The look on her face told one and all that she had no compunction in using violence.

Ahead of us, the west portals of Notre Dame. Six doors in groups of two—left, right, and center. Minerva took us to the center two doors.

"Oh my," I breathed while being dragged like a naughty schoolchild. "The Portal of Last Judgment."

"Not now, Mike," she growled, face tight.

It was the sight of the Augusta that stopped me cold, causing Minerva's grip to finally slip. The motorcycle lay at an angle on the inside of the iron fence, one of the ornate spiked tops piercing the fiberglass cowling. It looked beaten, defeated, and I nearly cried at the loss of such a beautiful machine.

"Dang it," I cursed as realization hit me. The saddlebags. Quickly popping them open, I found that the ancient box was mercifully intact, along with all Morgan's notes, and I thanked the Lord right then and there they hadn't been perforated by the hundreds of rounds that had flown our way. Stuffing the box and papers under one arm, I signaled Minerva to proceed. She tossed me a look of disgust, which bounced off the shield of my indifference, and led the way to Notre Dame.

I couldn't blame her for being tense, because right then the Black Hawk entered the airspace above the plaza, accompanying our six pursuers on their motorcycles. Not that I could argue much anyway. Her death grip on my collar was almost strangling me.

It was a moment I had hoped to live out in quieter times, without the fear of taking several rounds to the butt. Notre Dame Cathedral was on my bucket list, right up there with Saint Peter's Basilica, the Vatican Archives, and Legoland. For years I dreamt of walking through those doors. Carved in the stone all around was the representation of the Last Judgment as described in the Gospel of Saint Matthew.

As we approached, my eyes found the lower lintel where the dead were being resuscitated from their tombs. Above that on the upper lintel, the Archangel Michael looks down with stony resolve, weighing souls according to the lives they led on earth and the love they showed man and God. The fortunate are led to the left, toward Heaven, and the not so lucky are led to the right by a demon to be sent to Hell.

Next came the tympanum, the triangular decorative wall surface over the entrance bounded by the lintel and arch. On it, Christ is seated on His throne, a reminder of His sacrifice on the Cross to save Mankind. His face manages to look both soft and wise, and it sent a shiver down my spine. There are wounds on his hands and side, and two angels are stationed on either side. The one on the left bears the spear that pierced His side and the nails of the Cross. The one on the right is holding the Cross itself. My eyes began to water …

probably allergies. Near to the angels, kneeling, are John the Baptist and the Virgin Mary.

The twin russet doors towered over us, the right-hand door open, and we ran inside.

Another attendant rushed up, an older man wide in the middle with thick white hair. His face was red with anger and his hands twitched. Eyes blazing, he jabbered something in French, pointing at the door.

Minerva jabbered back in liquid syllables and waved the gun under the angry man's nose, releasing my collar and pointing to the open doors. He yelled back, seemingly unafraid of her pistol, so she raised the weapon and fired off a round. The flat *crack* echoed around the stone walls and pillars, bouncing to and fro. It seemed to get the man's attention and he ran to the doors.

"Told him to lock us in," Minerva explained. "Buys us some time."

If I hadn't seen Elementals and demons and evil magical assassins before, standing in Notre Dame with a coldly competent ... whatever she was ... would have freaked me out. Oddly enough, I was calm and breathed evenly, as if my emotions were detached. "What now?"

Crack! The sound slammed into my ears and I ducked, twisting to look behind. Moreharsh cracking sounds resounded as holes appeared in the portals shedding stone dust and wooden splinters, the morning light streaming through in bright spears.

"Now you have to ask the right question!"

Oh, brother, not this again. At the far-left portal, the angry attendant danced a bloody jig as bullets tore through ancient wood and stone to rip him apart. It was the sight of that poor man dancing his death at the hands of the Sicarii that rekindled the anger inside.

"How do we defend ourselves from the Sicarii?" I bellowed over the constant *crack, crack, crack* of bullets shattering wood and powdering stone.

Minerva stared, her eyes not quite focused on me. A bullet tore through the door and impacted on the tile next to her hand, sending marble chips flying. I scurried across the floor and hid behind the dubious protection of a wooden bench.

"Faith," she said slowly, mechanically, amid the racket. "You have to have faith. Pray, Mike, pray."

Prayer? That I could do, all part of the job description, but doing it from behind a bench splayed out upon the floor didn't seem right at all.

Sudden inspiration gripped me with the power of absolute conviction, and I scrambled to my feet and ran deeper into the cathedral.

Describing the artistry of Notre Dame would be like explaining a baby's cry to a person born deaf, or the works of Van Gogh to a person born without sight. There's just too much to include: the one hundred twenty-four-foot vaulted ceilings, the numerous pillars escorting parishioners deeper inside, or the *twenty-three hundred* statues adorning the structure, works of priceless art celebrating a nation's faith.

My footfalls followed me as I ran down the aisle, the altar seeming a good country mile away. I seemed to gain no ground. It was like a nightmare where you run and run, feet encased in lead or molasses or mired in mud, and you never go anywhere no matter how fast or how hard you run, no matter how your lungs burn or how much sweat coats your skin like an oil slick, greasy and thick.

The noises, the horrible noises, the screams of the wounded and dying, the *cracking* of tortured wood and stone, all served to propel me faster and faster, my feet slapping against Egyptian marble. It seemed to do no good. The altar was still so darn far away.

Minerva was counting on me. So were the poor people we put in harm's way. It was up to me and my faith. That had been unshakable for years now, but fear and doubt always crept in, because in spite of God's perfection, I was a far ways away from being perfect. It's completely normal for even the most pious, most devout to harbor doubt. Not about God, but about our ability to be worthy of His love and attention. That's what trips up us poor humans into failing Him. Failing ourselves.

I had plenty of faith, but it's not like a keg of beer you can tap in to for a good time. Faith is a living thing tied to your heart and soul. It's infinite, but carried by finite, flawed beings and as such is infrequently, imperfectly accessed. Even with my faith, with my surety of God's existence and His infinite wisdom, it wasn't a sure thing that I had enough faith at *that* time and at *that* place. Such is the nature of doubt; it creeps up on you at the worst times.

Almost before I knew it, as if by magic, I was there, at the altar, and it took my breath away. Christ before the tomb in gilded bronze. The two angels to either side in all their glory with the cross in between, but I didn't see them, not really. I knew they were there—Christ and the cherubs and the angels and Mary and the intricately carved marble—but all I really took note of was the Cross and the steps I took to reach the altar, ignoring the six ornate candlesticks, the flowers on the dais, and the kneeling statues on either side of the bronze angels. They weren't relevant. All that mattered was that from behind what remained of the Portal of Judgment, something burst inward with a mighty roar, and I heard Minerva's scream and the echoes of her firing a pistol, a sound sharp as knives. Someone yelled at me in French, but I was too far gone, too winded and wounded and lost in the moment to pay any attention.

Falling to my knees, I stared at the Cross and felt the same peace I felt in that small church in Omaha all those years ago on the day I found my calling.

"Dear God," I prayed, hands clasped before me, "deliver us from this evil. Save these people."

I heard an explosion from behind, a visceral *whump!* that shook my insides like Jell-O, but I remained kneeling, eyes on the cross, praying with all my might.

Minerva screamed.

Then there were more screams. Many more.

Chapter Ten

⚬

"Strife is natural, even desired."
—*Codex Infernales*

WHEN PEOPLE THINK OF BUNKERS, THEY think of dank, smelly, concrete tunnels poorly lit by sputtering bulbs and coughing fluorescent tubes. Bunkers are supposed to be safe places for VIPs to conduct business. A place of order against the chaos outside.

For Blaine, the Bunker was the top five floors of the Deschamps Building in New York. Accessible by two elevators and a well-guarded stairwell, it was as safe as four hundred fifty feet could be, considering the hidden and very illegal Vulcan cannons, surface-to-air mini-missiles, and external armor plating covered in building fascia. Not to mention a bevy of air Elementals swirling outside ten-inch ballistic security glass that served as windows. Given the Family's history with the capricious nature spirits, it was a small miracle they'd agreed to serve as invisible guardians, a feat Blaine was happy to take credit for.

Thanks to the lessons of Cain's assault on the Sicarii hotel two years ago, the only rooftop access was by a heavily guarded access shaft while Earth Elementals prowled the foundations to prevent other Earth Elementals from shaking the building apart.

No underground for the head of the Family. No fake subway exteriors, abandoned subway stations, cow tunnels, crypts, and hidden bowling alleys. Sewer gas, mole people, rising waters, insects, mold, under-city explorers and after-hours subterranean raves; Blaine wanted to avoid them all. Besides, the Metropolitan Transportation Authority was carving new tunnels into the bones of the world, and even he didn't have the authority or means to halt the progress. Although, with his vast influence, he'd managed to stall the project's completion by five years.

The Bunker was actually a ten-by-fifteen-foot room that contained a mix of hideously expensive ancient art and modern furniture. Said art would have looked more at home in the Louvre or the Guggenheim, and for all Blaine's sensibilities, would have been more appreciated. He cared more about monetary value than artistic value. Outside the room were living quarters for the Twelve and their assistants, a fully stocked kitchen, and enough supplies to last through a nuclear winter.

Currently, the head of the Family sat in a brown-leather recliner, holographic keyboard on his lap and a drink in a built-in cup holder at his elbow. Facing him, looming large on the monitor that encompassed the entire wall, was a stocky brunette in the uniform of a *capitaine* of the French *Police Nationale*. She was seated at a cluttered desk with a large shuttered window at her back.

"What happened, *Capitaine*?" Blaine's voice was deceptively mild, his eyes hooded.

"*Monsieur*, it is difficult to say. There is much confusion at the site. My men are dealing with ambulances, crowds of locals, and terrified tourists." Her English was flawless, with only the slightest trace of a French accent. "I will have more information as the afternoon progresses."

"What about the survivors, Claudette, the ones *inside* the cathedral?"

She shook her head, face dispassionate. "No reports, yet."

"Find out as soon as you can, *Capitaine*. You know how generously I reward efficiency."

There came the slightest of cracks in her icy exterior, swiftly hidden. "Yes, *monsieur*." The large screen went blank.

After taking a sip of his beer, Blaine tapped the appropriate keys on his virtual keyboard and an aerial view of Notre Dame appeared. Flames scoured the west fascia of the building, thick black smoke obscuring the large plaza. Dozens of police at the edge of plaza held crowds back while photographers blazed away with their cameras.

There were scattered … *things* littering the ground, too small, and the view was from too far away to see clearly, but Blaine thought he spied a pulped head only a few yards from the crowd.

What the fuck happened there? he wondered for the umpteenth time.

Bzzzzz.

Pushing another virtual button caused the door behind him to open. Despite the Monet hanging dead center on the left wall, the thick burgundy carpeting, the city spreading out beneath him, the green of Central Park and the majesty of other skyscrapers, he felt no sense of awe or appreciation. He had no eye for beauty. What occupied his attention was far too dire to acknowledge the world around. The fates of the priest and his companion were still in doubt, and on the list of things he hated most, doubt came right after humility.

Fergus stepped in, adjusting a green Ferragamo Primavera tie, tablet in hand. "Sir, you must see this." He tapped a few icons, and a new image appeared on the wall.

The priest, caught in the act of rifling through the saddlebags of a ruined motorcycle. His companion, an almost ethereal beauty, stood to his left, seeming to urge him on. To Blaine, the priest looked anything but priestly in his T-shirt and leather jacket combo. His splotchy, stripy brown hairdo was definitely un-priestly as well.

"What am I looking at, Fergus?"

The other man tapped an icon and the picture zoomed in on the object in the priest's hands. "That, sir."

For a moment Blaine was tempted to raise his voice and curse his right-hand man for being obtuse, but what he looked at finally sparked the fires of recognition. "*Fuck me,*" he breathed, "is that what I think it is?"

"Analysis indicates a ninety-nine point six percent probability, sir."

"Olivier, that motherfucker. Had to be. This is his doing."

"That is likely. It disappeared from Seattle over a decade ago. Until now we assumed it might have been *them* because our facility there was utterly destroyed, but with the involvement of the priest, it seems certain that the culprit was Olivier."

"You know what this means?"

Fergus raised an eyebrow. "I am afraid I do not."

"It means—"

"It means," interrupted a deep voice, "if you pardon the vulgarity, that you are up shit creek."

Both Sicarii started, Blaine's hand reaching for the pistol holstered under his armpit. There, smiling down like a less than benevolent god, was Cain, face rendered in millions of pixels, dominating the enormous monitor.

Blaine was flabbergasted. Things like this *just did not happen!* "How?"

"Did you imagine that with the vast wealth and influence I have accumulated these centuries past, I could not find those with the expertise and requisite skills to infiltrate your computer systems, despite the wonderfully elegant and sophisticated encryption you employ?"

Fergus sat heavily on an eighteenth-century settee and rested his face in his hands. "Wonderful."

As for Blaine, he furiously tapped his holographic keyboard, but nothing happened.

"No matter how much effort you expend, Mr. Deschamps, your private communications system dances to the tune I so merrily play. Only by my leave will you and yours once again regain control, and I will it not."

"What do you want, Cain?" Blaine snarled in frustration, hate distorting his features.

Cain pretended not to hear; instead his uncanny brown-rimmed, white irises focused on the other man in the room. "And who are you, Sicarius with the flame-touched hair? By your coloring, I would hazard an educated guess: you swim in the gene pool that touches upon Ireland, or perhaps the Scottish Highlands? Which one would it be?"

"The name is Fergus."

"Scottish? Excellent. Your countrymen make a most wonderful beverage fit for monarchs."

Blaine had had enough. "You going to shit or get off the pot, Cain? What do you want?"

"Ah, yes … to the point it is. How very American. Rush, rush, rush." Cain laughed merrily, obviously enjoying himself immensely. "Never ones for the fine art of conversation."

"I'm becoming bored."

"Very well, then. Do you know why the Sicarii and my own humble self have *not* been at odds for the past few decades? The fountainhead of our mutual wariness and detente?"

No answer. Instead Blaine stared at him with almost palpable hatred streaming from his eyes.

"No?"

Finally, "The Cain Accords."

From where his face rested in his palms, Fergus sighed.

Blaine held silent, still smoldering.

Cain merely smiled, staring hard at the head of the Sicarii.

Finally, the young man broke. "An agreement between Cain and the head of the Family before Julian, grandfather Gustav."

Fergus looked puzzled. "What agreement?"

"A written agreement, signed in blood and bound by fearsome oaths, one that forbid the Sicarii from taking overt action against my own humble self, excepting a few misguided lone wolves seeking to acquire a more fearsome reputation, and myself from directly initiating hostilities against the Family." All joviality fled from Cain's face as he spoke. His manner seemed mild, but the two Sicarii could feel the righteous indignation that boiled beneath the calm façade. "You have overstepped your bounds, boy, and that will cost you."

"You fucking liar!" Blaine was on his feet in an instant, fists clenched. "It was you and the pussy Olivier who attacked *us* and killed Julian!"

The two stared at each other for a long moment fraught with menace, neither man willing to look away first, but it was Blaine who lost the battle, rattled by Cain's eerie eyes.

A small smile appeared on Cain's face, not quite gloating, but definitely a jab at the younger man. "It is my suggestion to you that you peruse the Accords once again."

Fergus' tablet beeped. An icon appeared—a caricature of Cain's smiling face. The Scotsman tapped the icon and a file appeared.

"Sir," he said after a moment, "it seems that the Accord has been sent to my tablet."

Cain smiled. "Actually, I have caused it to appear on every tablet in the possession of the Sicarii, so I am relatively certain that your Twelve are perusing it as we speak so they can gaze upon "

"Still, you broke the Accord first." Blaine regained a measure of composure, standing in front of the large screen and sipping his beer. Gone from his cheeks were the twin spots of color and from his neck, the flush of red. Once again he was the very model of a cool, collected businessman.

"I must disagree with you upon this point, young Sicarius." Cain shook his head. The screen split, with his olive-skinned face on the right and the words of the Accord streaming on the left. "Please give note to Article Three, subsection C, and you will understand that the late, unlamented Julian Deschamps violated this clause by carrying out a most heinous act of aggression against a member of the holy clergy, a vessel for the Lord our God, specifically one Father Michael Engle."

Blaine sneered. "He destroyed the Silver and he killed Dagger Men. And you aided in an assault on one of our hotels. The footage of those golems tearing our men apart made that perfectly clear." Frost seemed to rim Blaine's lips.

Cain shook his head, as if admonishing a child. "You do not comprehend the meat of the matter, Blaine Deschamps, for actions taken by members of the clergy matter not in these circumstances. It clearly states that all men of the cloth are to be left in peace *at all costs*." Cain let that sink in for a second before continuing, "Even if he had taken out an op-ed in the *Washington Post* naming Julian Deschamps a pedophile, it would not matter. All clergy are to remain unharmed. I have not taken action against your people ensconced in the Vatican, and the Sicarii must not interfere with clergy of any faith. The language of this document leaves no ambiguity. Julian was the first to violate the Accord, and therefore it was incumbent upon me to take action. To the letter of our agreement, I am blameless. Add to this most grievous violation the continued violent actions against members of the true faith by the notorious criminal dubbed The Atheist." Cain chuckled at Blaine's look of surprised fury. "Did you conceive that I would not ascertain the identity of that notorious person and his relationship to your diseased bloodline? Because of such detestable actions, the Accord fair resembles rubble rather than whole boilerplate."

"Fuck. The. Accord." Each word was bitten off sharp and clean, Blaine's whiter-than-white teeth snapping. His words and tone were angry, but he kept his features impassive against the tornado that raged within.

"That is your response? 'Fuck the Accord.' "

Fergus adjusted his tie, green eyes sharp and hard. "Sir?"

Blaine raised a hand. "Not a fucking word, Fergus. This is between me and Methuselah."

Cain showed his teeth in something that was not even in the same hemisphere as a smile. "Methuselah was an interesting fellow and a friend, despite being a chronic masturbator. I assure you I am far older."

"Whatever. You came against the Family and you have to pay."

"That is the full extent of your rebuttal? 'Whatever'? And here I thought your infernal employer possessed good sense and sufficient judgment in his horned head to choose someone with a modicum of intelligence to lead your family of dysfunctional nitwits." Cain shrugged dismissively. "While your Family is a living, breathing affirmation of Darwinism at its finest, I must grieve at its enormous failure to produce sufficiently capable offspring if you are the genetic apex of the Deschamps Family tree."

"I am more than you could ever expect." Like two junkyard dogs, teeth bared and hackles up, neither backed down or let weakness show. "However," Blaine added suddenly, "there are many concerns I must oversee. I am a man with a lot on my plate, so I will give you and your choirboy priest a pass. Call it a new and improved Accord." The expression he offered as a smile could have frozen entire lakes. "Know this ... you are still subject to lone wolves out to make a name, just as in the original Accord, but in this new, revised edition, you have lost all New York and Geneva privileges forever. You enter those cities, you are *mine*, no ifs ands, or buts."

"New terms so swiftly given make me question the giver's veracity."

"I don't give a good flying fuck whether you believe me or not. Take it as you will, but I am telling you, enter Geneva or New York City and I will send all my Dagger Men equipped with the latest armaments and legions of Elementals ready to tear you apart. I will pull out all the stops, level the city, *both* cities, if that's what is required to take you down. You want a war, I'll give you a war like you won't believe."

Blaine's speech was delivered in the same dead monotone as if he were reading from a particularly boring expense report, but the look on Cain's face said he believed the young man. The Son of Adam possessed cursed eyes, eyes that struck fear in the hearts of everyone on the planet, but Blaine's were dead and cold as twin blue marbles, bereft of anything approaching human feeling.

"Very well, young Sicarius, I will do as you say. Although it surprises me that you do not seem to fear the third party in this planetary drama of ours."

"Oh, *them*?" Blaine waved a hand dismissively. "The problem with the Sicarii leadership in the past was that they feared for their own lives; they were unwilling to jeopardize all for the Family's greater good. Much like Congress today. I, however, have no problem getting my hands dirty, no qualms about a scorched-earth policy. That's why I'm such an effective leader. That is why I win." His voice lowered to barely a whisper. "I *always* win."

A red dot began to flash on and off at the corner of the screen. "It seems your countermeasures are well on their way to blocking this transmission," Cain interjected, "so further discourse is no longer possible. Know, however, that I will brook no violence against Father Michael Engle. Beware, lest the full brunt of my wrath fall upon *you*. As for the 'lone wolf' members of your horrid fraternity, I can only quote a Mr. Jesse Pinkman from that most wonderful of television series, *Breaking Bad*." The screen filled until Cain's cursed eyes dominated the wall. "'Bring it, bitch.'"

The screen went blank.

Blaine's smartphone rang. "Yes, I know, our communications and outlying systems were compromised. If you can't place an impenetrable firewall around our entire network by this time tomorrow, consider yourself fired." He hung up without waiting for a reply. "Stupid fucks," he muttered.

Fergus stepped forward, eyes sharp on the other man. "Are you really letting the priest go?"

"Fuck no. That man has the fucking *Codex* and it belongs to the Family. If word gets out that the single greatest Family treasure next to the Silver is in Engle's hand and I'm not doing everything in my power to retrieve it, the board will take it as weakness, and within a week, I'm tits up somewhere in the Everglades."

"What about Cain? He's bound to be watching over Engle like a mother hen."

"What about him? Let him worry about the priest. The closer he gets to Engle, the easier it will be to eighty-six them both." Blaine stroked his chin, face hardening to granite. "But if I find Cain, I'm going to drop Armageddon on his ass. Maybe a fuel-air bomb. No more losses, no more Mr. Nice Guy. I don't care how much collateral damage there is, he's dead."

Fergus smiled slightly. "Interesting, dropping a thermobaric weapon. Very droll."

"I'm serious as a heart attack." Blaine straightened his jacket and tie. "I'll acquire a suitcase nuke and a suicide bomber if I have to."

The other man's fair skin paled slightly. "Yessir." He turned to leave.

"Fergus."

The Scotsman stopped. "Yes?"

"Ready the Oracle."

Fergus closed his eyes. "Oh shit."

Chapter Eleven

<hr>

"If I whet my glittering sword, and mine hand take hold on judgment; I will render vengeance to mine enemies, and will reward them that hate me."
—Deuteronomy 32:41

Most people think priests spend quiet days of reflection thinking about the Bible or God or the sublime profundity. That's silly. Priests are people just like you, and we think about the same things you do: showers, food, a movie seen a week ago, and whether or not there's enough money in checking to cover the month's bills.

But that's not what I reflected upon as I sat in a leather recliner sipping wine and listening to the burble of water. No, I thought about the events that had occurred in Notre Dame just two days earlier. I rubbed the small scratch on my cheek, the scab crusty and hard. It seemed like ages ago, the crazy blur of events and emotions messing with my time sense. The itching along my back where the bullet grazed me was annoying, but I was dealing with it.

It's funny how such things can shake you. I've seen Elementals, magic, demons, and even a Duke of Hell up close and personal, but what happened at Notre Dame ....

I heard screaming, not from inside but from the grand plaza. Shrieks and pleas for mercy, surprisingly loud considering the thickness of the cathedral walls, as if there wasn't a huge stone structure in the way. The *thwap, thwap, thwap* of the helicopter came through loud and clear as well, along with the staccato rhythm of gunfire. The answer was merely a glance away ... the Portal of Last Judgment had been reduced to little more than a pile of French toothpicks, even the stone pillar separating the doors had been shattered into pebbles and dust. The sight of the destruction tore at me—ancient artistry reduced to so much detritus in less than two minutes. Any person near the portal would have been pulverized into a fine red mist.

Minerva. The thought galvanized me. I prayed she was okay.

I beat feet down the aisle, my breath loud in my ears, and saw my companion rise to her feet, left arm a bloodied mass of torn cloth and muscle that hung in strips. The wound didn't seem to bother her much.

"What's happening?" I somehow managed to keep my voice steady. My heart trip-hammered and my head pounded with adrenaline.

She pointed with her good arm. "Look outside. Should be safe ... well, *safer* for us now." I could see bone where the flesh of her biceps had been literally blown away, pink and gray bone shining through the blood and meat.

"You're hurt," I said. "Let me help."

She turned her body from me, hiding her damaged arm. "Go, look outside." Her tone brooked no disobedience.

Outside ... where the screams came from. Where the helicopter and mini-gun waited, ready to rip me to shreds. Where the corpse of the Augusta smoked and smoldered, impaled on a four-foot iron fence. For a second I was paralyzed. It was crazy to even think about; I must have been out of my mind to want to pass through the shattered remains of the Portal of Last Judgment, but my feet decided to disobey my will and began to head toward the ruined entrance.

More screaming assaulted my ears, harsh and desperate. Men and women howling in pain and fear and the barking of gunfire. The all-too-familiar stench of burnt propellant irritated my nose, something I never grew accustomed to during my tour in the first Gulf War. Daylight stung my eyes as I moved woodenly outside, stopping a few feet from the iron fence and the tortured, twisted remains of the Augusta. What I saw shouldn't have surprised me.

Winged creatures of dun stone, gray stone, and black stone, flapped, flew, and crawled around the plaza, hundreds of them. Each movement, large or small, came with a subtle *creak*, high-pitched, that pierced my eardrums and skittered across my nerves. Horned, beaked, and gnarled, bird faces, monkey faces, reptilian, goat-like, cat-like, and devilish. Faces both fanciful and fierce snarled and yowled and howled, slashing with beak, tooth, and horn. Blood flew in great gouts, decorating many of the stone creatures, coating them in red as Sicarii were torn, bitten, ripped, and crushed.

I saw one black-garbed assassin sporting a black motorcycle helmet fire a Mac-10, spraying an eagle thing that shrugged off each bullet like a horse twitching away biting flies. It swooped down upon her and smashed her flat in a spray of blood and guts that spattered the iron fence. Paving stones shattered and cracked underneath the beast, chips flying and dust billowing. I could feel the impact of stone on flesh on stone through my feet. The eagle thing's head snapped forward, crunching through heavy plastic and bone to snip the woman's helmeted head from her shoulders.

Another Sicarius squared off against a squat, ape-like creature with a single horn protruding from its forehead. The man holstered his weapon, choosing instead a telescoping steel baton. One swing, two, and chips flew from the beast, who didn't try to duck or dodge. Instead, the large wings on its back flashed forward, crushing the man between, forcing both eyeballs out of their sockets with sickening *pops*.

A third assassin, a woman without a helmet to contain her long blonde hair, was set upon by at least six lion-like beasts with muscular, human arms. She disappeared in an instant with a small, forlorn cry. Then came the horrid rending of cloth and flesh and the monsters tossed bloody pieces high into the air. One landed on the white cowling of the Augusta with a *splat*. It looked like a kidney.

More stone things flew through the air on twenty-foot-long wings, disengaging from their perches on the cathedral's face, swooping and diving, snatching armed Sicarii from the ground to drop them from a great enough height to burst organs and shatter bones. Not a single one uttered a sound other than high-pitched creaking.

Gargoyles. They were the gargoyles of Notre Dame, thousands of them in a variety of sizes from small as terriers to large as motorcycles. More and more stretched wings and took flight, while many clambered down the cathedral's façade in waves, thick, relentless, and remorseless—a tide of stone and fury no being of simple flesh could withstand. The Sicarii, never many, were overwhelmed by the ruthless horde of stone.

The Black Hawk hovered over the plaza, mini-gun chattering, and one unlucky griffin gargoyle was blown apart by hundreds of high-caliber rounds. Stone shards rained down upon the plaza, and a good-sized chunk fell square onto a hapless Sicarius, smashing through his plastic helmet and crushing skull and vertebrae.

All of a sudden, every gargoyle was focused on the aircraft, their regard terrible to behold. One second, two seconds passed as they studied the vehicle with its roaring mini-gun before every winged gargoyle took flight, arrowing straight for the aircraft, wings flapping.

There was a convergence of stone and metal as lightning-fast gargoyles momentarily obscured the helicopter in a blur of stony bodies. Rotors met rock in a shower of sparks and a squeal of rending metal that set my teeth on edge. Flame burst from between a squirming ball of stone bodies with a *whumph*, and a moment later the creatures flew away, the ones who weren't powdered by spinning rotors. What was left of the Black Hawk hung momentarily in the air before twisted fragments of metal and burning debris fell from the sky to land in a fiery heap on the plaza.

A small piece of metal whizzed by my head, but I hardly noticed. My eyes and mind were too busy with the thousands of gargoyles that covered the sky and ground, pecking and clawing at bloody bits and pieces of the Sicarii SS teams. Eventually the last of the them, a large man with a Desert Eagle, was killed, ripped open by the horns of a goatish flying gargoyle, his guts slapping to the ground. His shrieks were lost in the fiery crackle of the burning helicopter.

Air whooshed and swirled around me as an another horned, ape-like gargoyle (or perhaps it was the same one) landed in front of me, wings stretched wide, casting shadows across my face. It gazed solemnly at me with blank, stony eyes before nodding once and flying away to land far above on the face of the great cathedral. Seconds later, the plaza was empty, save for a burning helicopter belching black smoke and the tattered dead.

"Oh, my Lord," I whispered, both awestruck and horrified by what I had seen. Shock enveloped me in a smothering embrace, and I summoned the will to fight off its numbing touch.

A tide of people, slack-jawed, staring, and hunched with fear, slowly crept toward the plaza, irresistibly pulled by the horror strewn about and the miracle of the defense of Notre Dame. Not that I blamed them. Even knowing what I know, I still forced myself not to fall to my knees in prayer.

Inside, Minerva was talking animatedly on a cell while churchgoers and tourists huddled far away among the pews, terrified. To my right, I saw the crumpled remains of the attendant who had locked the portals.

My heart constricted as I knelt at his side. The mini-gun rounds had torn his torso to shreds, and his right arm was held on by only one thin strip of meat. I closed his sightless brown eyes and words came to me unbidden, flowing from my mouth in a wave of sorrow. The Sanctification of the Rite:

> O Holy Hosts above, I call upon thee as a servant of Jesus Christ to sanctify our actions this day in preparation for the fulfillment of the will of God.

The Invocation was next and my voice gained power and resonance:

> I call upon the Great Archangel Raphael, Master of Air, to open the way for this to be done. Let the fire of the Holy Spirit now descend, that this being might be awakened to the world beyond and the life of

Earth, and infused with the power of the Holy Spirit.

Time for the Dedication of the Soul. My heart was breaking as I stared upon the dead man I'd never known. If not for me, he might yet be alive; it was my presence that drew the Sicarii.

Oh Lord Jesus Christ, Most Merciful, Lord of Earth, we ask that you receive this child into your arms that he might pass safely from this crisis, as thou hast told us with infinite compassion. Let not your heart be troubled. In my Father's house are many mansions: if it were not so, I would have told you. I go prepare a place for you. And if I go prepare a place for you, I will come again, and receive you unto myself: That where I am, there ye may be also. And whither I go ye know, and the way ye know.

It was almost too much. Tears blurred my vision, but I kept going, "So let it be done."

It was time for Absolution and Purification, but I could not take his confession. As I raised a hand to lay it upon his head, another appeared in my vision holding a clear glass bulb. Inside was a transparent, thick, slightly greenish fluid I knew to be olive oil.

I looked up. A priest in full vestments knelt by my side, an older man with sparse white hair and a kindly face behind thick horn-rims. I smiled slightly as I took the bulb.

By this sign thou art anointed with the grace of the atonement of Jesus Christ.

My voice broke and my throat felt constricted by an enormous lump. With my thumb, I drew the sign of the Cross on the dead man's forehead. First the vertical line from top to bottom, then the horizontal from left to right.

And freed to take your place in the world He has prepared for us.

I faltered as tears coursed down my cheeks. I was overcome by emotion. The kindly priest took over, his deep voice ringing in the air as he offered the Prayer of Universal Thanksgiving in heavily accented English.

I listened, letting the words slide through me, around me, and over me, finding comfort in the message. When the lump in my throat finally dissolved, I managed to join the other priest in the Benediction—I in English, he in

French. Two languages far apart yet blending together in a message of love and peace.

> And thus do I commend thee into the arms of our Lord of Earth, our Lord Jesus Christ, preserver of all mercy and reality and the Father Creator. We give Him glory and we give you into His arms in everlasting peace to be prepared to return into the denser reality of God the Father, Creator of all. Amen. Amen. Amen.

I finished with "In nomine Patris, et Filii, et Spiritus Sancti."

"You are a priest," said the other in Latin. Not a question.

I nodded.

He took the glass bulb of olive oil from my hand and tucked it inside his vestments. "You knew this man?"

"No."

"Yet you cry for him."

"He is dead because I came here. To Notre Dame. Had I let the men who fired upon the cathedral have me, he would still be alive."

A slightly withered hand found its way to my shoulder. "Look at me, my brother."

His voice compelled me to obey.

Kind eyes stared into mine. "These men wanted you dead?"

"I believe so." It was hard to breathe through the guilt. "Forgive me, Father."

The slap was gentle, but firm, his hand surprisingly hard and callused. A man used to manual labor. Had he wanted to put mustard in the swing, the back of my head would have been bruised. "There is nothing to forgive. All men are welcome in the church during times of trial. Even priests." Another small slap.

I tried on a smile. It didn't fit right. "Even priests."

Another small slap. "This is all the punishment you deserve. Although that hair is an affront to good taste."

It bubbled up like a cool clear spring. Laughter, a healing peal that burst from my lips. The priest joined me a second later. It was a good laugh that helped a lot, despite the body on the ground next to us.

The slaps to the back of the head seemed familiar, then it hit me. "You watch *NCIS*, don't you?"

The priest's eyes twinkled. "My favorite show."

"Are you all right?"

It was Minerva. She stared at me—the both of us—as if we'd lost our minds.

I nodded. "Yeah." My eyes wandered to her arm, where the tattered remains of her shirtsleeve failed to hide her biceps, which appeared to be whole and unblemished. "Angel."

Those uncanny eyes widened slightly. "What?"

"Angel," I said, rising to my feet. My spine and knees popped. "It's what you are, an Angel. Or should I say—one of the Fallen."

She didn't utter a word, only narrowing her eyes in cold calculation.

Before she could unload a denial, I said, "It was easy to figure out. When you get Cain talking, it's really hard to shut him up. He told me how they were the basis of the old Norse Gods. Not too much of a stretch to realize that other Fallen could and have represented themselves as, say, the Roman or Greek Gods." I gave her a good long stare. "Not very subtle naming yourself Minerva, which was the Roman equivalent of Athena, Goddess of Valor and Wisdom. Couple that with your suddenly healed arm and strange talent of knowing things when put to question … well, safe to say it wasn't a stretch."

"I didn't know you knew about the Fallen," she conceded. "I would have used another alias."

"Who were you?"

Her face shuttered, becoming an impassive mask.

"You realize I am going to keep after you about this."

While her eyes blazed at me, the older priest moved away, comforting both tourists and parishioners. "Atheniel," she said finally. "I was Atheniel."

I nodded. "Thank you … Atheniel. Athena … Minerva."

She fixed me with a steady glare. "Any other questions, Father Mike? Because I don't want to talk about this anymore, but I have a feeling you aren't going to be satisfied until I'm more forthcoming. So, if I answer your question, can we get this show on the road?" She crossed her arms under her breasts and I had to force my eyes to meet hers. Darn testosterone.

Hmm …. She knew me well. "Of course. What was with the questions you had me ask? And who were you talking to on the phone?"

"That's two questions."

"Only one of them personal. No one gabs on the phone during a firefight for personal reasons."

"Okay, question one: I was Atheniel, Angel of Wisdom, so I have access to much knowledge unknown to man. In order for humans to access that knowledge, they have to ask me a question. Much like typing a question into Google, but the results are better."

I didn't mention the irony of an Angel of Wisdom picking the wrong side in the Rebellion against the Throne, but from the look on her face, she knew what I was thinking. "Don't you mean 'knowledge'? Wisdom is something different, more like having the experience and knowledge to make good judgments."

There was a long pause as she considered her next words. "A … long time ago, when mankind was in its infancy, wisdom was equated with arcane knowledge, information that was not normally accessible.

"Think upon the old stories, in particular the one about Odin and the Mimir's Well. You know it?"

I shook my head, unwilling to interrupt her.

"Under the root of the great world tree, Ygdrassil, was the Well of Wisdom guarded by Mimir, an Aesir of great wisdom because he drank from the well every day. Odin wanted wisdom, so he agreed to pay the price for it, his left eye. When he drank from the well, he saw all the trials and tribulations that would befall mankind and the gods, and he saw the purpose for those trials, that they would forge mankind into a weapon that would defeat evil once and for all." She smiled softly. "A story, of course, cute fiction, but the underlying truth is that Wisdom has always been equated one way or another with knowledge not normally attainable by humans."

"And the part where I have to ask you a question to get this wisdom?"

She sighed. "You are a pain in my left butt cheek, Priest."

That was one of the nicest things she'd said to me since we met and I told her so.

A snort and a shake of her head, but she did answer. "All Angels have special abilities, such as my ability to heal." She held up her unblemished arm. "We also have a Quality. For example, Azrael is the Angel of Death, and Barakiel is the Angel of Lightning, so Death and Lightning are their Qualities. My Quality is Wisdom. However, that wisdom can only be bestowed when I am asked a question, and it is up to me whether to share that wisdom. Before the War in Heaven, my duty was to live on Earth, to walk among mankind and answer the questions of those whom I judged worthy. A divine encyclopedia, as it were."

"All right," I said, staring at her beautiful face. "Thank you for that." Smiling, I asked, "Are you sure that story about Odin was fiction?"

"Quite sure."

On to a different subject. "What can you tell me about the gargoyles?"

She shook her head. "More questions." Her eyes of unknown colors grew distant. "They were sculpted by Victor Pryanet during the restoration of the cathedral between 1843 and 1864. In reality, the flying ones are a combination of Air and Earth Elementals, while the non-flying gargoyles are simply bound Earth Elementals. They were created specifically to protect Notre Dame and can only be summoned to action by someone with true faith." She paused. "In this case, that someone is you."

I shook my head in wonder. "How … how …." The words just didn't want to leave my mouth, but I managed to force them out. "How is that possible?"

"The artist Victor Pryanet was, in reality, Cain. He has a soft spot for this cathedral, and during its restoration he wanted to ensure it survived any attack by the Sicarii, should they decide to destroy it. He knew the Sicarii would gain greater and greater power and feared a time when they would out themselves and take to eradicating those works that honor the glory of God. In all, he created five thousand gargoyles."

It took a moment to wrap my mind around a task so monumental. But I didn't think five thousand would be enough if the Sicarii really had a bug in their ear to do serious damage. One thing about us humans, as good as we are at creating masterpieces, that ability pales in comparison to our capacity for destruction. Maybe that was one of our Qualities. "It surprises me that an Elemental would consent to be transformed into a statue."

"He asked. Nicely."

Of course. Very few beings ever said no to the son of Adam.

"Now, Mike, let us go before the reporters and police start to arrive. We'll have some help from Cain, a place to hole up."

Cain's help was the guided tour of the catacombs of Paris—not the famed ones located at Place Denfert-Rochereau, but farther east, deep in the bowels of the city. Not the shallow depths of the tourist catacombs, but deeper than anything any French citizen could imagine.

With Minerva at my side, I snuck out of the cathedral while everyone pointed and gawked at the remains of the Sicarii—just two more tourists escaping a "terrorist" nightmare, at least that's how I figured the Family would spin the whole situation. Over a bridge to the south and then east, past morning crowds heading toward Notre Dame in an attempt to catch a glimpse of some bloody spectacle.

Later, after a mile passed beneath our feet, we entered what appeared to be an abandoned building and descended a crumbling stone and iron staircase down, down, down into a basement devoid of light. A small, red aluminum LED flashlight held in Minerva's slender hand popped to life. A blue/white spot of illumination guided us to a far wall and a rusting steel door.

"What is this?" I breathed, watching the air from my mouth steam in the sterile light.

"The boss's hidey-hole," she replied. "Now hush."

I hushed and watched as she tested the knob, turning it three times to the left, then four to the right, then two to the left again. There came a sharp *click* and the door eased open an inch. Minerva completed the process and I saw a small room. It took me a moment to realize it was an elevator.

"Who the heck would put an elevator down here?" I asked, then shook my head, realizing who. "Never mind ... Cain. Hidey-hole. Right."

Minerva snorted and gestured for me to enter, which I did. There was only one button, plain white with no markings. My companion shut the door, closed an accordion gate, and pushed the button. Immediately we descended.

A long, long way. Far enough down that I began to grow nervous. Enough that I started fidgeting, and I'm not prone to such things. Through the accordion gate, smooth-planed rock passed by, then concrete wet with condensation. As we descended, more moisture appeared on the concrete, soon to become a constant trickle. Would we end up underwater?

When the elevator stopped, it was enough of a surprise that I almost stumbled. Minerva shot me an amused glance and opened the accordion gate, revealing another steel door as rusty as the first and coated with water.

Creeeaaak. The door protested against Minerva's hand, but she was stronger than its will to remain closed. On the other side was a short, concrete hallway lit by bare bulbs hanging from the ceiling. The smell of mold and stagnant water was heavy, but the concrete was dry.

"What is this?" I whispered. "And don't say 'a hidey-hole.' "

Minerva stopped and stared at me for a good long moment. "The catacombs were created from the old limestone mines over a thousand years ago. This place was originally created by Cain as a resting place for his descendants."

At my look of surprise, she smiled. "Oh yes. His descendants, the last of his line who settled here in 400 AD. Fashioned by Earth Elementals, its breathable air supplied by Air Sprites and the local aquifer and held in check by Water. Warmth supplied by Fire. It is a safe haven for him when the world proves too much. Even he needs to vanish every once in a while to take a breather. Lost in nostalgia and regret, he sips wine and ponders his mistakes." The last sentence was said in a hushed whisper, a voice thready with sorrow.

"I'm surprised you answered the question using your Quality," I remarked, awed by her display of raw emotion.

Minerva nodded. "I wanted to know myself." She shook her head. "It wasn't worth it, you know, using the Quality to find out."

"What do you mean?"

"Using the Quality for Wisdom often means I *feel* what others feel. I have felt Cain's misery and pain and loss." Her voice again fell to a whisper. "It was almost more than I could stand."

I kept silent, awed by her ability to remain composed while assailed by the emotions of the world's oldest man. Not wanting to stand there in uncomfortable silence, I strode down the hall until I reached a modern wooden door with a gold-colored knob. Minerva remained a solid presence at my back.

The door opened into a simple room, ten by ten and lit by a soft CFL bulb hanging from the ceiling. A cubical Franklin stove crouched against the opposite wall and an overstuffed recliner sat nearby.

It wasn't the drawing-room coziness that stunned me. It was what comprised the walls from floor to drop ceiling.

Skulls.

Slightly yellowed, pitted, and grinning, skulls stared hollowly at me as I entered. All set in neat rows in almost perfect symmetry. I couldn't help myself, I let my feet take me to the right hand wall, sneakers swishing through gray wool carpeting, and I set a hand on bone.

Cool, not cold, and smooth, almost slick. Each exposed bone seemed to be coated by a thin, clear substance like lacquer or some sort of polymer. Perhaps to seal water away, perhaps to keep bone from degrading. Whatever it was, the overall effect was beyond macabre.

The soft gurgle of water drifted to my ears, as if a river flowed behind the hollow eyes of the skulls. It was oddly comforting.

"Cain said that down here you will find what amenities you need," Minerva said. "Doors are hidden on the opposite walls—one for a bedroom and bathroom, one for a kitchen."

I didn't bother to look at her. "How do I open them?"

"Just push."

"Where are you going?"

She grinned slightly as she closed the accordion gate to the elevator between us. "Cain wants me to obtain aid. I'll be back."

I'll be back. Classic Schwarzenegger line, one that didn't set me at ease.

So when Minerva left, I settled in front of the Franklin stove with Morgan's papers in hand and began to read. I had prayed for Morgan's soul, prayed for Cain's safety, prayed for my friends and parishioners.

What new evil would I learn from this manuscript? What fresh hell awaited my curious eyes? Whatever Morgan needed to tell me, I'd listen.

Part Two

The Codex

Chapter Twelve

"You can always count on Family."
—*Codex Infernales*

Dᴇᴀʀ Mɪᴋᴇ:

By now you've read all about the Family and the truth behind the world, the magic that can be seen by those whose eyes are not veiled. Trippy, huh? You've read the whole sordid story, about how I grew up in a Family where assassination and treachery are held in the highest regard. Where the goal is nothing short of global domination and the elevation of Satan to the position now held by God. Needless to say, Christmas wasn't a big event in our household.

By now I've spent a few years in Omaha, and although it is considered backward by most, it's not without its charms. Not the least of which is you.

I can't tell you how much your friendship means to me, a sinner by anyone's standards. Friendship was something I thought would never be available to me, but you took me in and accepted me, despite not knowing what I had done and where I came from. Although I was born to evil, for the past few years I have been trying, trying so hard, to be good.

I know forgiveness is part of the job description, but we're only human, so I wouldn't blame you if you can't forgive me. Something tells me, however, that you will. You're just that kind of guy, far too good for this tired old world.

If you have the stomach to continue (and I think you do) this is an appendix to my little story, a sort of epilogue. It's a story of the *Codex*. If the Silver is the Might of the Family, then the *Codex* is its Heart and its Will. It's the one thing besides the Patron that drives the Family forever forward.

This is the story of how I laid hands on the *Codex*. It may not look like much, but neither does the Bible, and yet people commit violence and murder to uphold the words contained within—at least their interpretation of them. So consider the *Codex* as the Deschamps Family Bible. It contains the innermost secrets of the Sicarii, and they will stop at nothing to retrieve it. It is more valuable than the Silver. Hopefully you've read my story by now, the part that pertains to the Silver. If you haven't, then I suggest you do so first, although you can follow this one regardless.

I am so sorry to have laid this matter at your feet, but there isn't anyone else I trust with the *Codex*. You are certainly tough, capable, and smart enough to decide what needs to be done with it, and no matter what your decision, I have faith that it will be the right one.

Man, I hope you have your belt fastened and your tray table in an upright and locked position, 'cause it's gonna be a bumpy ride.

In 1998, facial recognition programs were still in their infancy, but growing more and more sophisticated by the month. None was more sophisticated than that used by the Family, which were years ahead of the NSA. Piggybacked on software employed by most airports, this program hindered my movement, so if I wanted to travel, it needed to be by bus or car. Not that I hate to drive, but it's boring as hell. So, my desire for a trip to the Big Apple found me traveling via transportation most unusual for a scion of the wealthy: on a cross-country bus to New York City.

For the past couple of years I'd been looking for artifacts that would help me destroy the Silver. The best way to destroy an artifact is with another artifact, although not all artifacts are created equal. Some are far more powerful than others. For example: the Spear of Destiny, the spear used to pierce Christ's side while he was on the Cross, is more powerful than, say, the Ring of Solomon, which was used to summon demons. One was forged to command otherworldly forces while the other tasted the blood of Christ, analogous to tasting the blood of God. God trumps demons every time. If the two were ever to be pitted against each other, I believe the Spear would cleave the Ring in two.

I could go on and on with the dueling artifacts scenario, but you get the gist.

During my self-imposed exile, I had spread a lot of money around in my search for the strange and unusual, and it had finally paid off. A contact in New York emailed my Hotmail account informing me he had a line on a very unusual artifact:

O:

You will be delighted to know that your quarter-million USD investment has paid off. Archeologist Jennison Archer's discovery of the Akkadian Stone has not received much attention, considering its controversial nature, but thanks to the skepticism of the scientific community and his heroin habit, your ready supply of cash has purchased that curiosity and it has arrived safely here in New York.

O, I cannot tell you how excited I was when first I held the item. It is authentic, the real thing! Who would have guessed when first I read of its discovery that it was truly the item you surmised it to be? Besides yourself, of course. I still do not know how you learned of its existence, this Akkadian Stone. Testing has confirmed it is over seven thousand years old.

I would dearly love to plumb your sources. How did you know about the stone? Would you tell me if I ask?

It awaits you and I await the promised payment. Meet me at the place whose owner has resisted temptation time and again.

Regards,

A

The message was etched deeply into my brain. Damn, I was so excited—heart pumping, pounding in my ears. My hands shook slightly as I stared out the bus window at the hills of Pennsylvania lush with the green of summertime. Just a few more hours and the stone would be mine.

If you've never been on I-80 through the Keystone State on a Greyhound bus that smelled like refried armpits and moldy polyester, you'll discover new record highs oflows. Lows like utter, complete boredom .... There are only so many trees a body can look at before the sight of a forest becomes tedious. By the time the bus chugged past Pittsburg—the city was just a dirty smudge to the south—I was starving for the sight of steel and glass, plastic and concrete.

Next to me, a young man of perhaps twenty snored, his dark-blond hair greasy and lank. His hoodie was dirty and torn, his nails untrimmed, and the scruff on his cheeks hadn't seen a razor in a while. That was the companionship afforded me for this trip.

In the past I would have been on a private jet, drinking champagne, and flirting with pliable flight attendants, all while a personal masseuse rubbed the day's tension from my shoulders. Had I remained in the Family, my life of opulent privilege would have continued, and comfort would have been my companion. That is, until some clever relative managed to slip a knife between my ribs or poison my merlot.

I didn't miss that life one bit.

The kid's soft snores didn't bother me, not really. The rumbly bus with all its interesting smells didn't bug me, either, nor the endless tedium. No, what really began to chap my hide was the stiffness. Stiffness in my joints, in the large muscles of my legs and my shoulders. It wasn't so long ago that such ailments were never a concern. I could party, fight, and screw all night long and still be bright-eyed and bushy-tailed come morning.

Age was starting to catch up with my body.

Not since I'd lived in the house in Geneva with Burke, Henri, and the twins (Julian II and Philip) had I felt the icy grip of mortality. Back then, I had to be on the alert day and night for assassination attempts. Long life in the Family meant surviving those members you grew up with, shared a table with, and sat next to during lessons. If you could do that—make it through the ultimate Darwinian test—then you were in.

The assassination attempts stopped—mostly. (They never *really* stopped. I think assassination attempts are my Family's way of staving off boredom.) At that point, I was assured of a permanent role in the Family hierarchy. Most of the time growing up was spent with fear as your constant companion, and that fear gave you a keen sense of mortality.

Now I had stiffness in my joints and a crick in my neck to remind me that I wasn't the Apex predator anymore. Nope ... time is the greatest hunter of them all, the ultimate assassin. No one gets out alive.

Somewhere during my maudlin musings, I fell asleep, only to wake when the bus pulled into the station. Finally ... New York City. Dangerous as hell, literally, but my contact wasn't about to travel to Omaha. No, for this I had to come to him.

Knees protesting, I stood and followed the kid with the ratty hoodie off the bus, trading the stale smells of the bus for the big-city smells of New York: diesel and gas, hot metal and concrete, all overshadowed by smog and the musky reek of millions of people living far too close together.

Damn, I loved it.

Hailing a cab was no problem, with thousands to choose from. The very first lesson I learned when visiting a few years ago was *never ever* drive your own car into the city. Not if you want it to leave in the same condition in which it arrived. A hooker in an all-male prison has less chance of being molested than your Honda in New York City.

The cabbie's ID read Bao Nguyen. "Where you want?" he asked in passable English. There was a purple birthmark shaped like a dolphin next to his nose.

"Barstow Bill's on Third Avenue near—"

"I know, I know," said the cabbie, hauling the taxi into traffic. "Is long way off. You got money, yes? Credit card?" His eyes in the rearview mirror stabbed at me.

I held up a roll of bills. "Yes."

"Good, good. You need anything, you call Bao. I will take care of customer."

Sure you will, my man, I thought. *What you see is a tourist with a fat roll.* I shook my head, slightly angry at my pessimistic attitude. I had to learn the trick of thinking the best of people. That's what you do, Mike, think the best of people right off the bat. It still isn't something I've mastered. Perhaps someday.

Barstow Bill's is a somewhat classy bar/restaurant near Central Park, just south and east of Lenox Hill. An Upper East Side joint that serves food good enough to attract repeat customers in an atmosphere comfortable enough for families and singles alike. If you dig fifteen-dollar bacon-coated burgers and seventy different kinds of microbrews, you'll love Barstow Bill's so much that you'll leave only when they throw you out at closing.

The owner, Nate Williamson, was known to the Family. Time and time again, one member or another wanted to buy the place, even offering six, seven, eight times its value, but with each offer, he simply said "Not for sale." Thus my contact's allusion to the place whose owner resisted temptation. Again and again.

It never stopped Family members from trying. Legitimately, too. I think buying the place without resorting to dirty work was seen as a sign of superior business acumen, a way to prove that you were better than your brothers and sisters. "So you collapsed the French economy. *I* bought Bill's."

My Family has some pretty fucked-up priorities.

Sorry about the language, man.

Where was I? Oh, yeah, Bill's. The AC hit my skin just right as I entered. Not cold enough to make you swoon and gentle enough that you barely felt the breeze. Like many places in Manhattan, it was much longer than wide, a skinny aisle of a place with small round tables and plenty of booths for pseudo-privacy. Along the right-hand wall was the bar, which ran the length of the wall and offered dozens of taps with decorative handles proclaiming the flavor of amber fluid within. Most of them saw brisk business.

As usual, Bill's was full of people, and the blended noise of their babble was enough to make my ears want to shut down.

"O!" The voice came from the second booth, where a swarthy man with black hair waved at me.

I sat and shook his hand. "Ricardo," I said softly. "You look like shit."

Dark circles under dark eyes in a round face paler than I last remembered. Hollow cheekbones, receding hair, and blue veins spidering under thin skin. He looked as if Death had one bony hand clamped firmly on his shoulder. "The cancer is worse?"

Ricardo Deschamps nodded. "Yeah, cousin. Not too long now." He paused. "Unless you intervene."

"You have what I'm looking for, then?"

His easy, very white, smile slipped a bit. "Most of it."

Dammit! I resisted the urge to lash out at my cousin, but a few years in your company, Mike, had softened me somewhat. "And here I was about to make your dreams come true, Ricardo. Looks like I've made a trip to for nothing."

A painfully thin hand gripped mine. "Please, Olivier."

"Not here," I hissed. "Not now. Not *ever*."

The hand quickly retreated. "Apologies, Cousin, but I am desperate."

That much was obvious. The cancer that gnawed at his bones would give any person pause. "One minute," I said. "Choose your words wisely."

He explained quickly, feverishly, eyes bright and teary. "All right, I lied. I admit it, I don't have the stone and I'm sorry, but I was afraid you wouldn't come if you knew the truth." My expression must have frightened him, because he began to speak faster and faster. "The stone was sold to a collector in Chicago, a man by the name of Munakata. Mori Munakata. He's rich, almost as rich as Family. A real-estate man whose factors purchased the stone from the disgraced archeologist before I could approach him. I tried to buy it from Munakata, but he refused, and there was nothing, no amount of money at my disposal that would sway him …. But there is good news, I swear it!"

I could practically smell the desperation boiling from his skin, a foul whiff of musky acid. "So, spill with the good news."

"As you know, I oversee one of the largest security companies in America, although it is small compared to other Family concerns. Munakata is one of my customers, his security system one of mine, his vault purchased from me years ago." He paused and licked his lips. "Like all my systems, the one Munakata purchased has a back door known only to me. For the past year I have kept tabs on him and the stone through an inventory program devised by the company. Every time the stone is removed, it is tracked and recorded, so I know where it is at any given time."

"You've known of its whereabouts for a year, man?"

"Don't be angry, O. I had to know if it was valuable, if Munakata held it in high regard. I can tell you that wherever he travels, no matter near or far, the stone travels with him." He leaned forward. "It *must* be magical, or the man is obsessed. And I have the codes to his home, his safe, and his private vault. They're yours."

Either explanation was plausible, yet I felt hope that the former was true. I had searched for so long, spent so much money to find a magical artifact capable of destroying the Silver. The thought that my objective was so close at hand and yet out of reach taunted me.

I gazed at the man next to me as he slumped and wallowed in self-pity, which was dangerous when dealing with Family. "You know, when you found me two years ago, I was afraid I would have to kill you."

That was shortly after I set up in Omaha and had spent a good three months traveling around the country placing spookers (caches of money and false identities) in hard-to-find places. I had meandered my way to New Orleans when I ran into Ricardo at a little dive bar off Bourbon Street. I recognized him from several training sessions with Master Cheng, one of the many martial arts instructors the Family employed to train us unruly kids.

The music from the juke was loud, all '50s and '60s classic rock played on real vinyl, and even though the place looked like the kind frequented by cheap gumshoes from a Bogart movie, it served high-quality booze. My eyes strayed to the mirror behind the bar as I sipped from a tumbler of Jack on ice then flitted across to where Ricardo was sitting at a table alongside a cute blonde with big tits in a dress that looked as if it had been applied with a paintbrush. High-end call girl was my best guess.

One thing you should always remember: don't let your eyes land on the target. Let them slide off like oil on glass because if you make eye contact, it's over. My eyes passed right over Ricardo, through him and beyond without a flicker, even though my heart skipped several beats and I felt a light sweat dampen my upper lip. Unfortunately, my nonchalance proved insufficient.

His eyes were burning into me. He saw my reflection in the mirror and I knew he had me dead to rights and that any minute he'd make his move. It turned out his move wasn't what I expected.

I slumped my shoulders, pretending to relax a bit, and took a good long pull from the tumbler. Swishing the Jack around in my mouth before swallowing, I kept Ricardo in my peripheral vision. He still looked the same—hair black as midnight, olive skin, aquiline nose, and a sprinkling of acne scars on his cheeks.

Any minute now.

It took two.

He stood, kissing the hand of his female companion, and casually strode toward the rear of the bar as if heading to the men's room. Because I always scout out the location of the places I frequent, I knew there was an exit in the rear. He was making his move.

A twenty dropped on the scarred wood of the bar, and I was out the front door, feet flying as I raced down the side alley toward the back. I heard the creak of hinges and the *thud* of a steel door slamming shut.

Thirty feet away and Vision, the aroma of pears and apples, caressed my nose. The night became a riot of colors as darkness fell away from magically enhanced eyes. Ricardo looked up from the cellphone in his hand, startled. He'd smelled the magic I used. Good, that meant he wasn't dialing.

He shouted Vigor and the odor of peanuts flooded the alley. I smiled in anticipation of a fight.

Twenty feet.

I didn't want to kill him, but I had no choice. He would rat me out in a heartbeat.

Then he took off running, as if hellhounds were nipping at his heels.

Damn. I used Vigor as well and gave chase. Why hadn't he drawn down and fill me with holes?

I have to give Ricardo credit; he was fast, zipping through the alley and across the street, jumping over a slow-moving Mercedes like a champion hurdler. I cleared the same car a second later, leaving the driver honking angrily.

In another alley, he was only a few short feet away, the slap of leather of his Berlutis ringing against the alley walls. I grinned—he had the wrong shoes for a footrace. My own Nikes ate the distance between us and I shouted Strength just as my fingers snagged his suit jacket. Ten thousand dollars worth of cloth ripped as his feet flew out from underneath him.

With my magically enhanced strength, I was able to slam him into the brick walls on either side to soften him up a bit. Time was I would've enjoyed myself, reveling in the rush of victory, relishing the snap of bone and the tearing of flesh. That was before the Angel, before my second chance. Before you, Mike.

"I'll make this quick, Ricardo," I grunted as he fell to concrete.

"Please, Olivier," he sobbed. "Please, I'll do anything." A hand filled with the strength of desperation clutched at my jeans.

What? Where was the old Ricardo Deschamps, the man who laughed as he broke bricks with his bare hands? Where was the proud magus and businessman swiftly climbing the Family hierarchy? What lay at my feet was a broken thing, a man at the end of his rope, clutching at denim in desperation.

It hit me suddenly … he was far too thin. His expensive suit might have been the hand-me-down of a bigger man. The hand clutching my pants was thin, almost skeletal, and his skin was sallow, strung tight across bone.

"What's wrong with you, Ricardo?" I asked.

Soft brown eyes became despondent. "Cancer. I have bone cancer." His lips quivered.

Bone cancer? Magic can cure a lot, but some things were beyond the capabilities of the Twelve Words. "What are you doing here?" Botanical magic could help, but it would take a true savant to stave off bone cancer.

"Business. This is where the Family's security firm is based. I'm the CEO."

Well, shit. If I were still Family, I would have pulled the Beretta from the small of my back and put two between his eyes. But I remembered your lessons, Mike—how we all have to at least try to make the right choices. How God gave us free will to choose between Good and Evil.

Thou mayest. Right, dude?

In the back of my mind, an Idea began to form.

"I AM VERY GLAD YOU DID not kill me, O."

My mind tracked back to the present. I smiled. "Oddly enough, Ricardo, I am glad as well." I pointed a finger at his chest. "Although you would have sold me out to the Family in a heartbeat had we not reached an agreement."

"Speaking of that, O … is the information enough for you to … help me out?"

He smiled. It was ghastly. His face looked like a skull draped with wet, flesh-colored toilet paper. Nodding, I reached into a pocket and pulled forth a small, four-ounce steel flask and held it out. Ricardo snatched it from my hand.

"Is this it?" he asked, eyes glittering feverishly.

I nodded.

"How long?"

"Ten years."

His lips trembled and tears flooded his eyes. "Ten years," he whispered. "Ten more years of life. Ten more years of no pain, of feeling good for a change."

"Only the once, Ricardo, only a one-time deal. Most of the ingredients are fairly common, but the last I could only obtain through sheer dumb luck, the rarest flower in the world. And thanks to my ability to steal things, there are only two left in existence."

I was talking about Middlemist Red. Originally found in China, it has been wiped out there, and the only two remaining were in New Zealand in Great Britain. The third, the one that went into Ricardo's cancer potion, had been obtained from a man in California whose son suffered from ALS, or Lou Gehrig's Disease. As with Ricardo's cancer, I could cure the disease, but only for a while, two years tops, and only with great effort. It was enough for the owner to give me the flower and to keep his mouth shut about the transaction. That temporary cure for ALS cost me three months of research, fifty grand of cold, hard cash, and six months worth of preparation. The flower was history, but for the man whose son would have a little more time to play in the sun, the price was happily paid.

Eyes still fixed on the flask, Ricardo reached into his own pocket and produced a small, rectangular device. I recognized the Crystal Drive straightaway. Years ago, I stole the plan and the first prototype from one of

American's largest tech billionaires. This one looked to be developed to fit into one of those new USB ports that were all the rage.

It was light and much smaller than the original. "Nice."

"Thought you might like it. A study in irony, no? The regular market will unveil these next year, but they won't be as powerful. While theirs are measured in megabytes, the Family's are moving beyond terabytes."

"Thank you."

"No, thank *you*, O. Without you, I'd be dead in two months. Now … now I have ten years."

I stood, fingering the Crystal Drive nestled in my pocket. "This is the last time we meet, Ricardo. Good luck."

Chapter Thirteen

"Present a fair face lest the world see the real one."
—*Codex Infernales*

Back to Omaha. I won't bore you with the details of the return trip except to say the route was indirect in case Ricardo actually managed to grow a pair and sic the Family on my butt. Suffice to say that through all the bus changes and taxi rides, I managed to get a little sleep, thank goodness. The Crystal Drive burned a hole in my pocket the entire way, though.

I could've gone straight to Chicago, but I wasn't sure how long the mission to retrieve the stone would take and I had to take care of the Silver.

If you've read the story of the Silver, you know the dangers of that bag of coins. I won't repeat that here.

I'd purchased my little white house on 61st Street recently for cash at a very reasonable price, and ever since moving in, I'd been looking for decent furniture. Currently I had a few plain but serviceable pieces from Nebraska Furniture Mart, but had recently gotten a line on a little old man who was a wizard with his hands. Soon I would have a nice bed and armoire.

In the basement, behind a carefully crafted fake wall, was a space just large enough for a ten-gallon fish tank. It was filled to the brim with holy water, and dangling from the lid, secured with silver chain, was a black-leather bag the size of a large egg.

The Silver.

Thirty pieces of silver, thirty *talents* paid by the Romans to Judas for the betrayal of Christ, imbued with the power of Lucifer manifested as thirty

Words so terrible, so potent that using them did … unfortunate things to the magus wielding them.

What did Judas think when he realized those talents had become so much more than mere coins? Did he use those horrible Words to his advantage? Or did he hold them in reserve for his Family? I have a hard time thinking that Judas Iscariot, betrayer, son of Lucifer and founder of the Sicarii assassins had any warm, loving feeling for his offspring.

Judas. The Founder, my direct ancestor, the first Sicarii assassin. I still think that his greatest achievement was to make the world believe he died shortly after the crucifixion. Good trick, that, one worthy of a Las Vegas primetime magic show.

I had always wondered why the Words weren't used more often, but realized that they must have been used during the entire two thousand years since their creation. Think about it …. You have the Fall of the Roman Empire, the Anarchy, the One Hundred Years' War, the American Civil War, more military conflicts than a person can count in one day. The October Rebellion, WWI, WWII, Korea, Vietnam, Pol Pot, Tonton Macoute, the Russian War in Afghanistan, etc., etc.

Look at all the bodies, the blood, and the misery. Look at the orphans and the widows, the grieving and the angry and ask yourself, Mike, why would the Sicarii indulge in all that death and destruction?

Forget all that malarkey about the Voice reveling in the mayhem, forget the Book of Revelation, because I guarantee you, Lucifer can read and learn from that particular prophecy and adjust plans accordingly. No, there is one thread that can be pulled by all those conflicts, the single motive that has always driven the Family. Money.

Money is power, and power is what it's all about for the Family and the Voice. And war is good business, *very* good business, if you are on the right side of events. The Silver can easily ensure that is the case.

For centuries, the Family has been earning big bucks through conflict thanks to the Silver: weapons, armor, food, logistics, intelligence, and transportation—everything needed to run a war. Everything needed to come out on top.

I'd come to realize that the Voice and the Family didn't want the Four Horsemen, didn't want the third part of the seas to become as blood. Everything I'd seen of the Family business, all the machinations, backstabbing, corporate deals, and covert operations indicated to me that the Voice definitely wanted to rule the world, but more in the manner of a corporate takeover than through apocalyptic war. No use ruling scorched earth when you can lord over a garden.

Still, there was the issue of the Anti-Christ. That aspect of the prophecy churned my stomach. I was half a step from becoming the Voice's mortal vessel in this world, the being who would allow him to indulge his senses, to really *feel* for the first time in millennia the splendors of the world all around. It looked like I had been slated to become the finger puppet for a being grown too fat with evil to press his true form onto our reality.

Small wonder I decided to distance myself from Family.

I disposed of the unholy water and refilled the tank, closed the fake wall, and left with a few necessary supplies. It was time to catch a bus, and I won't bore you with the details except to say that the company was better: a twenty-something brunette with a pixie face off to visit her mom and dad in Joliet. She had a rocking bod and we flirted shamelessly. However, one-night stands aren't really my thing, so I shook her hand at the station and said goodbye.

She was pretty damn cute, though.

From the station, I made my way to the nearest car-rental kiosk, where I flashed some cash and my fake ID and rented a seriously ostentatious ride—a Toyota Land Cruiser. It was the perfect vehicle for my nouveau-riche-wannabe disguise. After all, my destination was Winnetka, some fourteen miles north of the city. If you've never been there, let me say this: it is one of the top ten Richest Neighborhoods in America. Yeah, not too shabby.

Munakata's place was a five-thousand-foot affair on Prospect Avenue close to Lake Michigan. Close enough, in fact, that I could smell the water and feel the moisture on my skin. The sun was high overhead, blazing down with all its summertime warmth.

One thing about rich neighborhoods is there are no cars parked on the streets because there is enough garage space at each house for a fleet of automobiles. As I turned onto Prospect, I realized how clean everything was. No tagging, no garbage blown out of overfilled cans, nothing that would spoil the Stepford-like perfection. It irritated the hell out of me. Too much time away from Geneva, too much time in middle-class America had desensitized me to names scrawled in spray paint and beer bottles broken on sidewalks.

The door opened after only one ring of the bell. A small, dark, and extremely pretty Asian lady appeared. She wore too much makeup and her teeth were whiter than anything produced by Sherwin-Williams.

"Yes?" There was no suspicion in her eyes—the neighborhood was *that* safe. And why would she be suspicious? My hair was freshly cut and styled, my eyes hidden behind wire-rims, and I was clad in a new pair of beige Bermuda shorts and a forest-green Hilfiger polo. No danger here, thank you, just a refugee from the local golf club carrying a duffel bag.

I shifted the half-full duffel so I could free up a hand. "Mrs. Munakata?"

"How can I help you?" Her voice was soft as a cotton ball and faintly musical.

I dipped a hand into my shorts pocket. "Is your husband here?" There, a small, plastic tube with stoppers at both ends. I used a thumbnail to carefully remove both stoppers without spilling its contents, all the while trying to appear nonchalant. Not as easy as it sounds.

She shook her head. "No, he is at work. Are you a client of his?"

I nodded, bringing my right fist to my lips. I blew a sharp breath between the loosely tightened fingers and a puff of whitish powder hit her square on the nose. I caught her before she hit the floor, holding my breath in case any trace of the magical powder still floated in the air.

It was a mixture of dried agrimony, elderberry, meadowsweet, and valerian, mixed together in the light of a full moon. A bit of talc had been added in, not enough to weaken the formula, just enough to add a sweetish smell.

Once inside, I closed the door behind me and set Mrs. Munakata on a black-leather couch where she'd be comfortable. I had an hour or so before she woke, logy and with only the slightest of headaches—plenty of time for me to do what I needed to do.

Thanks to the Crystal Drive, I had the blueprints to the house and the codes needed to bypass Ricardo's security systems. What I was looking for was downstairs, in the basement, a private vault, a small room used to house Mr. Munakata's most valuable possessions. If the stone proved to be as valuable as I thought, he wouldn't take it from the house during normal business hours, only when he felt its magic was needed.

There were those I thought of as subject to the Gollum Obsession, a condition whereby the owner of a valuable item is so enamored of it that he doesn't let it out of sight for an instant. Good thing Munakata didn't suffer from such a malady, or this was going to be harder than expected.

I found the door to the basement and flicked the light switch, illuminating gray-painted wooden stairs that led into a large cinderblock room with a Nautilus on one side and a large steel door on the other. The door had a spoked wheel in the center next to an electronic keypad. Bingo, the vault.

Five, six, six, seven, three, one, nine. Each button lit briefly, a greenish glow that shone dull against the latex gloves I'd donned after entering. There came a muted click from the door and I spun the wheel, opening the vault.

It was a five-by-ten room lit with eye-watering fluorescents that immediately caused my head to ache. Six three-foot-high pedestals dotted the floor, silvery cylinders that supported the treasures Mr. Munakata had spent years acquiring.

One pedestal supported a sword, a large blade called a hand-and-a-half or bastard sword. It rested on its tip, supported by a sleeve of clear plastic that balanced the blade perfectly. It looked brutal and efficient, with a worn, darkened leather grip and a large black sapphire on the pommel that winked wickedly in the harsh light. As interesting as the weapon was, I didn't bother to examine the intricate etchings on the blade, although I did take a pic with a digital camera. Never know what you might find, right?

There it was, the stone. Or should I say, a stone tablet. Roughly three feet tall and two inches thick, it rested on the largest pedestal, obviously custom-built for the occasion. The tablet was crafted from tan-colored rock and etched with crude letterings I had never seen before. My education was extensive, better than most. I spoke six languages and read half a dozen more, including Hebrew and Arabic, but this language wasn't like either of those. The symbols were oddly angular, like Viking runes, and they contained peculiar, angled marks that intersected the middle of many of the letters. Each symbol was clearly defined, as if cut into the stone yesterday, without the wear that time would bring.

My gloved fingers ran over the markings, and a faint tingle at the back of my skull told me that the artifact was definitely magical. *Bingo*.

Heavy plastic grips held the tablet in place, but a few flicks with the molecular knife parted the high-grade material and the stone was mine. Once again that piece of stolen Deschamps tech proved useful, and I grinned happily as I slid the cylinder into a pocket.

Damn, that tablet was *heavy*, and it felt strangely warm, as if it had rested near a heating register.

Ammonia tickled my nose.

Imagine every hair on your head standing on end at the same time and a creepy, crawly feeling skittering over your skin as your balls shrivel and goose bumps sprout like weeds. You know the feeling, Mike … fear. Naked fear. That's what I felt because I knew what had just happened. It wasn't the odor of disinfectant that had me fighting panic.

No, someone had uttered a Word.

Most magi wouldn't be able to smell a spell through multiple walls and a floor, but I'm a twelve-Word magus and far more sensitive than your one- or three-Word man. In fact, not meaning to boast, I am probably the most talented magus the world has seen in centuries. Perhaps even better than da Vinci, although no one knows how many Words he truly possessed.

"Dammit!" I cursed, carefully laying the tablet on the floor and opening the duffel. Out came a Walther P99 and five plastic vials. Each vial held a potion of various potency. Each had taken me several days to concoct and cost me hundreds of dollars in ingredients. The best part was, when used, they produced no smell to alert a competent magus.

I reached into the duffel and pulled two Velcro tabs. A tug or two later and the duffel expanded, growing large enough to accommodate the tablet. In went the tablet and I was good to go.

Duffel strap over my shoulder, gun in hand, I exited the vault, closing the door behind me.

Up the stairs I went, my sneakers whispering over wood, the Walther proceeding me by an arm's length.

Movement, just the barest flicker of black cloth, and the Walther barked twice. Blood, bone, and black cloth fragmenting, flying ... only to be stopped by a knock-down textured wall.

The figure lay bleeding just above the basement stairs, brown eyes behind knitted ski mask staring sightlessly. A Mac-10 lay next to the body.

Black clothes, machine pistol ... Dagger Man.

Ricardo, you bloody opportunist! He had to be the one who snitched to the Family.

Peanuts, bacon, and ammonia. More spells, magi readying themselves with Vigor, Clarity, and Strength. Looked like the Family had brought out the big guns.

"Olivier," crooned a hateful voice.

Oh shit. I felt my stomach boil with the acid of hate and fear.

Burke.

Of all the Family members, why did it have to be him? It was Burke who had almost killed me during winter training, and if it hadn't been for the Angel Harachel, the Angel of Knowledge, I'd be worm food. I supposed it was too much to ask for a second gift of divine intervention, no matter how dire my straits.

"Olivier, I know you are there, on the stairs. I can smell your fear."

I sneaked a sniff of my pits. Not *that* rank. Not yet. Still, I was plenty afraid. Burke was the bogeyman from stories, the monster under the bed, and I feared him like I feared the bubonic plague.

Down the stairs ... softly, quietly, using all my training to remain a ghost, a shadow flitting hither and yon. I was almost out of sight from the door when a black-gloved hand appeared holding a Mac-10, which sprayed bullets into the basement.

A line of fire across my thigh and a sharp punch in the gut as I dodged. Ricochets drawing blood and slamming deep into flesh. I spoke the Word of Healing, feeling bullet fragments work their way out of muscle tissue in a spurt of blood and the familiar itch of quickly knitting flesh.

"Gotcha!" Burke screamed in triumph.

He must have smelled the Healing, which meant he was close. Of all my close relatives, only Burke had anywhere near the amount of Words I possessed. Six, if I recalled correctly. Six Words too many.

Where to go? I looked around. Not up the stairs. My eye spied a window well, narrow, a tight squeeze at the best of times. No, too tight, wouldn't be able to get the duffel through.

More bullets pattered off cement as the Mac-10 stuttered again and ricochets came perilously close to perforating me again. No more time. If Burke had a grenade, I was toast.

Facing the window well, I shouted out Force, ignoring the smell of burning insulation. A disk of energy hit glass, cinderblocks, and rebar with all the power I could give it. The well, along with seven inches of surrounding wall, blew outward in a roar that shook the six inches between my ears.

I scrambled up and out the window well, climbing, barking both shins and knees and drawing blood from all four as I choked on cinderblock dust, eyes stinging. The duffel bumped my legs, bruising calves, but I didn't care. There was danger behind and escape in front. What was a little pain compared to that? Sunlight met my face as I flopped onto the grass and scrambled to my feet. Freedom and fresh air. What more could a man wish for?

A sudden burst of pain along my side and my muscles convulsed painfully and my brain switched off for a while.

Chapter Fourteen

<hr>

"Place trust in thyself, not in others."
—*Codex Infernales*

DARKNESS. COMFORTING AND WARM. JUST WHAT the doctor ordered. What the doctor *didn't* order was the sharp pain piercing the velvety blackness. It radiated from the web of skin between thumb and forefinger, up my arm, and to the base of my skull. I resisted for a while, but the pain built and built and built until I swam up out of the darkness into … more darkness.

My eyes were open, but the only thing to see was black and lots of it. Dull aches around my wrists and ankles, a hot throbbing that told me of torn skin. The feel of steel around my extremities indicated that my limbs were bound, possibly shackled. My mouth tasted like a dirty sock bin, dry and tacky with the foul flavor of stale sweat and dirt.

It was hot and humid, and I could feel the sweat dribbling down my skin. I tried moving my head; the result was prickles of pain at the base of my skull that spread throughout my neck.

Maybe I was a bit logy from whatever had knocked me into the land of unconsciousness, but it took a while for me to realize I was on my back and that my spine was pressed hard against an unyielding surface—metal. It was cold, stealing warmth from my body and offering only aching muscles in return.

"*Mmfh,*" I gurgled through the obstruction in my mouth, trying for Strength. Nothing. In a big way.

"Nice try." The voice was oily and contemptuous.

I felt my testicles start to shrink. Burke. "*Fufh ufh.*"

A soft step somewhere behind as Burke drew close. "You will not be able to employ any Words, Cousin." A deep, amused breath. "Your wrists and ankles are bound, and I even offered one of my own socks as a gag to stop up that odious mouth of yours."

Burke's sock. Gross. Vomit clattered at the back of my throat.

"Enough, Burke." This voice belonged to an older man, deep and full of confidence. Family, no doubt.

"I should be able to have a little fun with the little shit, Mason."

Mason. Mason. The name was unfamiliar.

"I allowed you to gag him with your filthy sock and duct tape; now let the grownups have their turn."

Mumble, mumble ... Burke's words were better left unscribed here. Safe to say they implied that I'd had strange relations with a diseased goat. His speculations on the anatomical details of my sex life continued as he moved away.

"Apologies for Burke," said Mason, not unkindly. The gentleness of his words grated on my nerves. My Family was a far cry from gentle and kind. Not even in the same zip code. "As you have no doubt deduced, my name is Mason. I am one of the Twelve."

Holy shit. One of the twelve CEOs of the Family businesses, the most powerful men in the world (no women among the Twelve—my family is *that* misogynistic), controlling billions of dollars. Although often chosen from amongst the Wordless, any one of them could collapse a small government with a mere flick of the wrist and the casual movement of assets.

After we scions of the Founder are tested for Words, the Wordless go into business, toddling off to the cutthroat sector of money-making and world-shaking. From there, they compete in an organization that makes the Dagger Men look like the participants in a Cub Scout jamboree. If one is brilliant, then advancement to CFO or COO is granted, but if one surpasses all others in corporate villainy and legal piracy, then he will become one of the Twelve— the most cutthroat bastards on the face of the planet. If a Family magus shows prodigious business acumen, then he is also given the opportunity to become one of the Twelve.

Julian was a magus ... three Words and the ability to use the Silver, or he'd had that ability before I stole it after inflicting some serious bodily harm on him and his bodyguard Boris. But being a magus wasn't a requirement for running the Family. No, the ability to use the Silver was. As far as I knew, Julian knew only one of the Terrible Words housed within the Silver. Julian's father, my grandfather Marcel, knew none of the normal magic Words but had access to three of the Silver Words. With those Words he did great and horrible things. Don't believe me? Ask the Kennedy brothers. That is, if they could speak from the grave. Who was that man on the Grassy Knoll? Why did Ruby assassinate Oswald? What about the Magic Bullet?

Marcel exhibited cold, ruthless efficiency all his life, a perfect human predator right up until the time Julian killed him.

Do I have a messed up family dynamic or what?

"By the subtle tensing of your shoulder muscles and the perspiration accumulating upon your brow, I gather that Julian has filled you in on the Family hierarchy. That is well; I tire of long explanations. Safe to say that you fully understand the lengths to which I will go to achieve your full cooperation." Mason's voice vibrated with the confidence of a man who had vast experience in achieving his goals and plowing any opposition under hard earth.

Shit.

"*Ylth*," I mumbled. *Yeah.*

He seemed to understand. "Good. Now we can begin. As you may have ascertained, you are bound to a steel table. Cuffed, actually, made steadfast so all attempts at escape will be in vain. Your head is wedged between padded bars bolted to the table, held immobile by copious amounts of duct tape. There are heavy gauze pads over your eyes, and as you already know, there is a rather disgusting article of Burke's clothing taped inside your mouth." He laughed, a surprisingly gentle sound. It scared the shit out of me. "Boys will be boys, you understand." His voice suddenly became diamond hard. "Now, I will remove that sock, but if you attempt a Word, the consequences will be dire. Do you understand? Grunt once to signal your comprehension."

Grunt.

"Excellent. I call this progress." Steady fingers gently picked the tape and gauze from my eyes, adhesive stinging flesh where it was pulled away.

Light speared my eyes, causing them to tear up fiercely. I blinked several times as fingers removed the gag. The sock was black and crusty looking and I nearly threw up as it was lifted from my throat.

A cool rim touched my lips, and sweet water flooded my mouth. I drank greedily, swallowing every drop I could.

When I was done, I asked, "Why so gentle?" I still couldn't see well. The light directly overhead was *blinding*.

"Julian wants you alive and whole."

No words had ever put so much fear into me. I'd faced death, been healed by an Angel, and had risen in the estimation of the Patron. Heck, I even threw down against *Boris*, but now I felt a fear so gut-wrenching and intense I was rendered speechless.

"Alive?" It was Burke. Apparently he hadn't gone far. "Whole? What kind of nonsense is that? For a one-Word magus not worth a piss?"

I almost laughed. When I was younger, before I escaped the Family's clutches, I had let on that during the Reading (the process of learning one of the twelve Words) thatI had comprehended only one—Healing. I suspected that Burke saw through my ruse, but it warmed the cockles of my heart that it had indeed worked. I'd fooled the high and mighty multi-Worded Burke. It was *delicious*.

"Don't be an idiot," Mason said. "Olivier has all twelve Words and is unmatched in both Elemental and Botanical magic. He is the strongest magus the Family has ever produced and there is no way we are letting him slip away." Mason paused. "One way or another, he is coming back to us."

I really wished I could have seen the look on Burke's face. My eyes fluttered open, and I detected two blurry shapes. "Ha ha, Burke," I taunted. "Looks like you aren't the big shot you thought you were." Was it mean of me to poke fun at my cousin? Of course, but I'm only human.

Hot pain exploded against my eye, fierce and corruptive to my tissues. It stunned me so that I couldn't even scream.

"Burke! Enough!" Mason barked, a man quite used to obedience.

"Don't worry, sir, he is still whole. Just a little bruised." I felt his hot breath against my cheek and his whisper slithered against my skin like an oily snake. "It must kill you that Annabeth chose me over you." He paused to let that sink in. Annabeth. My cousin. My lover and my betrayer. It still stung that she had not only chosen Burke, but helped him in his assassination attempt, which would have worked but for divine intervention.

I thought that she might be the one for me, the woman I would start a whole new line with once Julian was no longer in the picture. Turns out she had different plans, and they didn't include me.

Yeah, not a highlight in my life. The pain still squirmed in my guts, bilious rejection.

As though the agony streaming through my tortured eye somehow dragged me into clarity, I realized that we had been speaking in Romansh, one of the four official languages of Switzerland. Although the Family had no real centralized location of authority, Geneva was the closest thing. Julian always had a soft spot for Switzerland; in fact, the Family owned the country's largest bank.

Romansh is derived from the Latin spoken in the Roman Empire, although it is heavily influenced by German, French, and Italian. The Family has always been partial to Romansh because of their fondness for the latter half of Roman history. Had it not been their influence on emperors such as Elagabalus, Commodus, and Caracalla (the latter secretly a *member* of the Family), the Empire would have lasted for at least another five hundred years. The most notable example of the Family's handiwork was the use of the Silver on Emperor Diocletian, who, although he stabilized and improved Rome's economy and military, became the greatest persecutor of Christians in history, almost singlehandedly wiping out the growing religion.

Yeah, my Family is a cluster of dickheads, natch.

"Been a long time since I spoke the language," I croaked through my semi-parched throat in English.

More water .... I needed more water.

A light slap to my forehead. "I detest English," said Mason disapprovingly. "Please speak in a civilized language."

Right. Romansh it was. Each Family member spoke several languages. I spoke six. "All right then."

"Wonderful. Now ... look at me."

Eyes stinging, I gave the blurry shape, the one on the left, a good hard squint. The blur resolved into a man in his forties with a cleft chin and slightly Native American features. Or perhaps Middle-Eastern. That was not uncommon, the Family having originated in Judea.

It was a handsome face, confident and avuncular, filled to the brim with both knowledge and compassion. It said to the unwary: "Trust me, I know what I'm doing and you will be well cared for."

I didn't think I could be more scared. I was wrong. The worm of fear turned heavily in my belly as I stared into his dark-brown orbs, certain that even though Julian had given orders to have me delivered whole, my reunion with dear old dad might be marred by a total lack of sanity. All thanks to Mason.

"You know what I want."

I nodded. "The Silver."

"Yes. Tell me where it is."

Burke snorted. "Please don't."

The Silver, the most powerful artifact in the world next to the Ark of the Covenant and the Holy Grail. Created by Lucifer for his Family to work his terrible will upon mankind. Although it wreaked horrible havoc upon the wielder, it was responsible for some of the most dreadful events in human history. The thought if it back in the Family's clutches scared me more than the pseudo-kindly expression on Mason's face.

"It's long gone," I said with more calm than I felt.

Burke smiled.

Mason sighed. "Please, Olivier, no games. The Silver cannot be destroyed by any means known to man, and that includes the tablet you liberated from Mr. Munakata's vault." His eyes glittered with good humor. "By the way, thank you for that. It saved us from having to do the heavy lifting."

"Damn Ricardo," I grumbled. "He sicced you on me, didn't he?"

Mason's smile was beatific, while Burke grinned with sharp malice.

"Never trust Family, especially those who owe you." I tried not to sound bitter, but how could I not be?

"A lesson I thought you'd have learned by now. You should have killed him."

"I'm trying to turn over a new leaf."

He drew closer. "And how is that going for you?"

"Well, it depends on your perspective."

"Enough of this. It is my turn." Burke's face grew large in my sight, and everything went white as muslin was pulled tight across my face.

Momentary confusion was followed quickly by realization as the first splashes of water doused the cloth.

So … waterboarding. Let the fun begin.

In the history of torture, waterboarding ranks up there in the top ten simply because it messes with the mind as well as the body. It simulates drowning and can cause extreme pain as well as oxygen deprivation. Simply place a wet towel on your victim's face and pour water onto the cloth, and it will be almost impossible for them to breathe. After a few seconds the victim's lungs start to feel full of cotton as they begin to fail. It's called dry drowning, and it sucks the big one.

I gagged and struggled, the cuffs cutting into my limbs as water crept into my nose and mouth. My struggles delighted Burke, who laughed as he kept pouring water onto the cloth for what seemed like a good chunk of forever and a day. I could feel skin tear under the cuffs held tight to my wrists and ankles and blood begin to flow.

Mason said something, but I was too busy gasping, lungs raw and bloody, screaming for air. Copper clogged the back of my throat, and a few drops of water made it past to irritate my lungs. No matter how much I wanted to cough, there wasn't enough air in me to do it.

The cloth was whipped away and air, sweet air, flooded me. I was finally able to cough out the water, along with a certain amount of phlegm. Hot pressure boiled up from my diaphragm as I gasped then choked, gasped then choked.

After an eternity, Mason's voice drifted into my consciousness. "Now you know how this will go, Olivier. Burke is looking forward to your resistance, and eventually you will break. Everyone breaks. No human can withstand what we have in store for you, so it would be in everyone's best interests if you told me now where you hid the Silver."

Everyone's best interests? Not mine. No, I had a sneaking suspicion that if I spilled the beans, Mason's next move would be to deliver me to my father for tortures yet undreamed of at the hands of Boris, or (more likely) I would be drugged and reprogrammed. Brainwashing was a long-established, well-researched Family practice. When I emerged from my mental readjustment, what would be left would no longer resemble the man I had become, Jude Oliver. No, what would remain would be the empathy-blinded killer I used to be. My free will would be stripped away. I mean, after all, it was not likely that Julian would waste a twelve-Word magus.

Thou mayest. You said those words to me, Mike, as did the Angel who saved my life, but where the Angel saved my flesh, you saved my soul. At least, I hope you did. The jury is still out on that one.

Thou mayest. Before I met you I had never read the Bible, not required in the standard Family education. I had no knowledge of Abel, just Cain, who has been the Family boogeyman for the past two thousand years.

Thou mayest. In Hebrew it was *Timshel.* The words God had spoken to Cain after the murder of his brother. *Thou mayest* choose between Good and Evil—a sign that God had blessed man with free will. Good and Evil not as cast-in-iron fate, but as choices given to mankind. Words more powerful than any magic ones.

And Mason would take all that away from me.

No way. Giving them the Silver would ring the bell, throw in the towel, forfeit the game. You wouldn't do it, Mike, no matter the cost, and if you wouldn't concede defeat, well then, neither would I.

My voice emerged as a whisper. "Burke."

He loomed in close. "Yes, *Cousin.*" The word was a curse flung from the bastion of his teeth.

"One day we will meet one on one, on equal terms, and then I am going to kill you."

His smile was radiant. "I doubt that."

"I don't. Do you want to know why I'll win?"

"Do tell."

"My back won't be to you."

The muslin obscured my sight and everything became agony and rue.

Chapter Fifteen

SUFFOCATING PAIN BECAME MY WORLD, SLEEPLESSNESS my personal galaxy. At irregular intervals, so I couldn't gauge the time that passed, Burke would treat me to a round of waterboarding. Mason would ask me where I stored the Silver, sounding like a kinder, more reasonable version of Lawrence Olivier's *Der weisse Engel* from *The Marathon Man.*

Is it safe?

That's what I substituted in my head, those three simple words, when Mason asked, "Where is the Silver?" Three words for four. Fiction for fact, entertainment substituted for torture.

Is it safe?

Then darkness, but no sleep. Speakers blared clanging noise like a dryer full of nickels. It chased my drowsiness away, and if I managed to ignore the hideously tinny clamor, lights brighter than the sun flared to life. Light so intense it seemed to bypass my eyes altogether and shine directly onto my brain, frying neurons. Brain Flambé.

The food given to me was spicy, mostly Mexican and Indian, hot enough to hide the taste of the stimulants laced throughout. Every meal—served at odd times, no need to give me a sense of day or night—brought the jitters, my heart racing like Seattle Slew at the Kentucky Derby. The cell I occupied was barely habitable, the size of a small broom closet with no space to lie down and with a ceiling a good five feet above my fingertips if I stood on tiptoe. It was cold, slightly damp, and made of solid steel. There was no evidence of a door. When Burke came to collect me, a wall would simply slide off to the side and rough hands would wrestle me to the steel table, where I would be bound again for another fun session of waterboarding.

Is it safe?

Magic Words were strictly *verboten*, as I discovered to my chagrin. The second I attempted Force against one of the walls, I found myself juddering and jittering like a spider on a hot plate as thousands of volts of electricity were sent through my steel prison. It was the first and last time I attempted magic.

I chewed on hard misery for many days, huddling on the cramped floor next to a coffee can that was my primitive toilet. After a while I learned to ignore the thick fecal smell along with the sharp, musky scent of stale urine. Needless to say, I only accidentally spilled my crude chamber pot once— during my electric convulsions after attempting Force.

At least they left me my clothes.

My Bermuda shorts and forest-green polo had seen better days, though. No dry cleaning for the tortured, and my sandals were nowhere to be found. That sucked. Inside the soles, in carefully concealed special compartments, were a pair of tough, plastic vials containing potions—potions that would have helped tremendously.

Time was a blur and sleep but a distant memory. Moments were chopped up into sessions with Burke, as I was handcuffed to the steel table. He took great delight in torturing me. Sometimes Mason didn't even bother to show; instead he let Burke Pose The Question.

Where is the Silver?

Is it safe?

Sometimes he didn't bother to ask, rather he let me choke, spit, scream, and gag while he chuckled in my ear, his foul humor tickled with mad joy.

My nerves became pregnant with misery, the dense tissues of my bones started to feel rubbery, and my eyes were scratchy and dry. Swollen with dismay, my tongue lay in my mouth all fat and lazy while I tried to drink the water they'd left me after a session of torture. But the joy of drinking was gone. My sinuses were raw with sneezing, and the memory of dry drowning had quashed any desire to fill my stomach. I was racked with cramps and nausea, my mind slowly unraveling to a *tabula rasa* fugue state.

Is it safe?

I had all but given up. The answer they were looking for was on the tip of my tongue. But three words kept the others at bay.

Is it safe?

When the wall slid aside behind me, spilling my slack and dirty body out of its confinement, it wasn't Mason I saw. He had transformed into *Der weisse*

Engel, the White Angel from the movie, pink pate like a baby's butt shining over a snowy fringe of hair, gold wire-rims glinting in the harsh light.

Is it safe?

I think I laughed.

"He's almost ready," said Lawrence Olivier in his kindly, grandfather's voice.

"He looks like shit," came the reply. I tilted my head to see Peter Janeway, played by the actor William Devane. Seemed like the whole cast was going to attend. I really wanted to meet Dustin Hoffman and tell him I forgave him for *Ishtar.*

How funny. "You sound like my cousin Burke, man."

Devane snorted. "He's lost his mind."

Nope, I know just where it is ….

It's safe.

Lawrence Olivier shook his head. "He is ready."

"I hope so. This has gone on long enough."

Der weisse Engel's eyes grew frosty. "That is not for you to say, boy. Shut your mouth and lift him to the table."

Damn, the White Angel sure had a plateful of anger issues. I giggled as Devane's strong arms lifted me almost effortlessly and set me unceremoniously upon the cold steel table, my ankles and wrists once again cuffed. The raw skin there burned, but my mind was far, far away as I watched Devane strap my head between the padded bars of the restraints. For some reason William Devane looked pissed, which I supposed wasn't too off the mark. Angry was his standard look in whatever movie he starred in.

"What's wrong, Bill?" I slurred. My mouth felt uncoupled from my brain, as if the messages I wanted to send had to be forced through some thick filter. "You look really put out, man."

"What is he babbling about?"

"He's hallucinating," Lawrence replied almost sadly. "His brain functions seem to be severely impaired. Cognitive loss, hallucination, desensitizing of neurons to serotonin, and lack of neural repair due to loss of REM sleep. Soon he might have severe memory loss, risk of stroke, heart failure, and other physiological ailments."

But it is safe.

"Damn. I thought we were supposed to bring him in whole."

"We are, no worries there yet. He has not reached any critical failure points. His health is excellent. Muscular, bone, and vascular scans show that he is still well within the norm. It's only his brain that is currently affected. Once he tells us what Julian wants to know, we can let him sleep."

Man, Lawrence sure was chatty, although the poor sod he was talking about sounded pretty fucked up.

It is safe.

"Can you hear me, Olivier?"

Strange … Lawrence Olivier was either talking to himself or talking to some dude named Olivier. Still, it was pretty funny and I couldn't stop a chuckle or two.

A light slap, barely a tap on the cheek. "Stop laughing."

"You talking to me?" I tried for De Niro, but it came out Buddy Hackett. That made me laugh even harder, and I made a mental not to thank Mike for introducing me to *The Love Bug* and other cinematic masterpieces.

"His mind is gone." William Devane didn't sound disappointed. In fact, he sounded rather happy.

"No," replied Lawrence Olivier. "He needs a stimulant."

"What?"

"A stimulant. To focus his attention. I give you permission to enter my room. On the side table is a valise with the appropriate medications, which I did not think we would need at this juncture, but medicine is an inexact science. Bring it to me."

"What about him?"

"He is harmless. I doubt he could summon enough magic to light a fart."

Is it safe?

"Hey, Lawrence," I giggled. "Did you just say 'fart'?"

William Devane snorted and said, "I see what you mean." He gave me one last pissy glare before walking out of sight.

Lawrence Olivier continued to secure my head to the padded restraints, a look of detached concentration on his round face. His eyes were bluer than in the movies.

"Mr. Olivier," I began, "got to tell you that I really loved you in *The Boys From Brazil.* Hey, I thought you died in 1989." Strange, why would he come back from the dead just to torture me? The bright light overhead stung my eyes as Mr. Olivier tightened the straps. "Let me tell you the big flaw with the movie … it wasn't that Guttenberg blinked during his death scene." I tried to shake my head, but it was clamped tight. "No, I can forgive that. It's the whole cloning Hitler thing. The technology for successful human cloning wasn't perfected until 1991 by München Genetik." I lowered my voice to a stage whisper. "One of my father's companies. Problem is, although the clones are perfect physical specimens, they have no mental faculties. You wind up with drooling idiots, which isn't too far off the mark where Hitler is concerned.

"You see, the real power behind the Third Reich was Helmut Von Eichel, who was in reality my grandfather's brother." Recalling Family history was like pulling barbed wire through a brick—difficult at best, the memories didn't want to come—but I kept pulling and pulling, reaching back far into the dim recesses of my mind for any relevant tidbit. I was desperate to use Clarity to help me focus, but the Word didn't want to surface.

Is it safe?

"Do tell, Mr. Deschamps," Lawrence Olivier urged placidly while wrapping a blood-pressure cuff around my left biceps.

"Mr. Deschamps … that's my father. You can call me …."

The hands on my arm were businesslike, but I sensed the anticipation in the air. Alarm bells went off. "Yes?"

I sang … and it hurt. "'If you'll be my bodyguard, I can be your long lost pal ….'"

Bless you, Paul Simon.

It is safe.

Disappointment radiated from Britain's greatest actor, but I didn't let it get me down.

"Anyway," I continued, "dear grand uncle Helmut was really Jean-Paul Deschamps, who worked behind the scenes during Hitler's rise to power. It was his use of the Silver that had that German pinhead and his cronies dancing to the Family tune. It was actually dear old grandpappy who came up with the idea of the Final Solution and it was Jean-Paul who forced it upon the Reich." I sighed. "Not that he needed to do much forcing. By the time they broke ground on the first camps, the German people were so brainwashed by the High Command that if Hitler told them to search for leprechauns, the entire countryside would have been teeming with people carrying sacks and flashlights. Still, the use of the Silver turned old Jean-Paul into a cripple." It became easier and easier to remember as I continued to talk, as if the waters of recall were starting to flow downhill a little faster and faster as I added to them. "By the time 1944 rolled around, he was a shriveled shell of a man, barely able to feed himself. It was a kindness, actually, when grandfather had him put down. *Put down.* Nice way to say *killed.* Terminated. Put to grass, greased, blown away, and eighty-sixed. That's what the Family does, Larry. It kills anyone who gets in its way or is no longer useful. You know that?"

Is it safe?

"Yes, Olivier, I know that." The blood-pressure cuff began to inflate as Lawrence squeezed the little rubber bulb.

Of course he would. "But I know a secret."

The cuff stopped inflating. "Do tell?" Was that a spark of interest in the thespian's eye?

Is it safe?

"Come a little bit closer," I sang. Bless Mike for introducing me to Jay and the Americans.

Larry O moved a little bit closer, a warm expression on his seamed face. "Yes?"

"You want the secret, Larry?"

A whisper. "Of course, Olivier. What is the secret?" The air was thick with anticipation.

Strength suddenly roared past my lips, unbidden, unlooked for, but welcome. Filled with unnatural potency, my muscles moved as if with a will of their own and metal parted with soft *pings*. Flesh tore, bones bruised, but that didn't matter because my hand was around Larry's throat, cutting off wind. A big smile sliced my face. My teeth felt like tombstones.

Then came Vigor. Suddenly I wasn't so tired and the light above, that hateful bright shining, became a bare, hundred-watt bulb. Tape tore apart as I hoisted myself into a sitting position, still holding on to the struggling Larry, who was turning a startling shade of lavender.

Clarity.

As soon as that Word left my mouth, life became a little less confusing. Larry morphed into a quickly purpling Mason while peanuts, ammonia, and bacon smells vied for my attention. Sometimes the ability to smell magic really upsets the stomach.

I leaned in and whispered into Mason's ear as his hands clawed at my forearm, "It is *safe*."

Man, I was bleeding from wrists and ankles, the cuffs shiny accouterments to my tattered wardrobe. Not a fashion statement likely to catch on.

A light slap took Mason out of the picture. Not much time before Strength failed and I didn't know how much of a personal reserve of energy I had left. I could blank out at any moment. Sweat stung my eyes. Mason hit the floor at my dirty, bare feet as I took a gander at my surroundings.

It was a basement. A large one with brick pillars at regular intervals. Shadows danced along concrete as the bare bulb swayed slightly. Despite Clarity, my head swam to the silent twist of the light.

I spied with my little eye something that began with "my little prison." "Well, well, well … what's all this then?" It was a rectangle of metal standing on the small end placed smack dab on some thick, black material that covered the floor for several inches around the box. The top of my former prison rested only an inch from the nine-foot-tall ceiling. Two of the prison walls were constructed to move, to allow access to the interior, and several micro-cams—each the size of a pencil eraser—were placed in holes drilled in the metal, high enough to be safely out of reach of yours truly. Thin fiber optic cables ran from the tiny cameras to a small black box the size of a cigarette pack. I reckoned that was a transmission hub to monitors located upstairs.

"Sarky beggars," I breathed, "watching me all the time. Cheeky, really." Laughter oozed out like pus from a boil. The humor was obsidian and just as sharp and my perspective was skewed to the left, my mind fracturing off into wild tangents and strange, ungovernable regions.

One of those strange splinters of thought connected with another and an evil idea began to form. Lurching into motion before I could come to my senses, I moved to my former prison and what lay on the other side of its steely bulk. I had to get it in gear if Burke smelled the magic I just used.

It's called a picana, Mike, and it's a mean little device. Imagine a short wand with bronze tip and an insulated handle connected via a wire to a control box with a rheostat to raise or lower voltage. Connect that control box with a couple more wires to a car battery and you have an excellent torture device. That picana was wedged tightly against the steel prison box, the bronze connected to metal. A remote trigger was affixed to the wand's power button. My torturers didn't even have to be in the basement to send twenty-thousand volts up my ass; they could watch me on the insulated micro-cams and jolt me at their leisure whenever I attempted a Word.

Time for some table turning.

The whole shebang proved easy enough to move after another Strength was used. The first Word had worn off—I had uttered it hastily and with terrible enunciation. I took more care with the second so it would last significantly longer. Only a few minutes later, my everything was set.

Just in time, too. Footfalls sounded from beyond the basement door— shoe leather against concrete. I thumbed the rheostat to juice up the picana to max and pressed the button. A short, fat spark appeared momentarily where the bronze tip met door handle and a faint whiff of ozone floated to my nose.

The handle jiggled, then shuddered as if the metal became a living thing and the door jangled in its frame. A muffled gurgling came from just beyond, the sound of a throat filled with oiled pebbles, and I flicked the picana away from the knob.

Thud.

Well … good.

And there he was. Burke in all his glory, lying unconscious just outside the door with an alligator-skin valise clutched tightly in one hand. The other hand sported a nasty-looking burn mark that smoked ever so slightly.

I checked his pulse. He had one, more's the pity.

For a moment, Mike, I debated doing some serious dirty to dear old cousin Burke, fixing it so I would never have to worry about him again. A very long moment.

"You are so lucky, Cousin," I panted as I pried the valise from his grip. His hand was cold. "Trying to turn over a new leaf here, you know." *Pant, pant.* Vigor was fading, so I said it again and vitality flooded me, cutting off my deep breaths. Once again everything was right with the universe, although I knew that once Vigor wore off again, my body would crave sleep like a junkie craved heroin. "It's called turning the other cheek. Ever hear of that? Of course you haven't. Our lot isn't big on the New Testament. Heck, I didn't even know there was such a thing until a very good man introduced me." I leaned in, giggling crazily. "A *very* good man. Better than me, Cousin. Better than anyone I've ever met and it's because of him I am trying to change, trying to be better than I was. So I am gonna let you live, man. Perhaps you will find me again and we will square off and one of us will die, but not today."

Is it safe?

Chapter Sixteen

Free.

Well, freedom is relative. More like I was out and about without Burke and Mason waterboarding me until I puked. And no steel closet with interfering cameras and no picana wedged against steel to shock my ass if I tried a Word.

Good times.

I was almost whistling "Zip-a-Dee-Doo-Dah" as I made my way up the basement stairs, alligator valise in one hand and Burke's Ruger P90 .45 in the other, sweat beading on my forehead and running into my eyes. I blinked rapidly against the sting, weapon raised as I backed up onto a landing. Nothing there except a brown door above. No bad guys, no alarms. Not yet.

Is it safe?

My *Marathon Man* hallucinations had stopped with Vigor and Clarity, but lack of sleep kept teasing me with little trailers, snippets from the movie fluttering through my mind like cottonwood seeds drifting across the Midwestern landscape. When Vigor wore off, I was going to crash hard. There is only so much sleeplessness a body can stand before it starts to experience systemic failure.

Up to the brown door. Steel, heavily painted. The stairwell continued up, up, up at least seven more flights, but the first was the only one I was interested in. I needed out, I needed away. I needed sleep like you wouldn't believe.

Through the door, I entered a hallway, its white walls yellowed with age giving it an air of abandonment. The entire building smelled of dust and neglect. What the heck? This looked more like the desiccated remains of a building at the heart of an old city, a historic structure big companies would renovate and convert to tony loft apartments.

Linoleum floor, off-white and scuffed. I chose to go to the right, following my pistol, keeping a tired and wary eye out for others. It must have been a team effort to catch me, and I reckoned the team was still around. Where there was Burke, there would be more.

I sneaked up to a thick, wooden door with a thin, vertical window over a round steel knob. The glass was laced with wire. Peering in, I saw a tidy bed and footlocker. Further examination revealed nothing else. The room was Spartan, with greenish paint and fluorescent lighting.

Continuing, I stepped softly, my bare feet a whisper across battered linoleum. Next door, same setup and just as empty. People were sleeping here, but they weren't around for me to interrogate.

Next came a room the same size as the previous two—about twenty by fifteen—but empty, thick dust coating the floor. As with the other two rooms, the windows were boarded up with plywood.

With a sigh, I continued down the hall to the next door, and a trickle of unease rubbed against my mind. I stopped, trying to identify what was bothering me. Ears straining, I heard nothing. Eyes peeled, I saw nothing but the hard light of the bulbs overhead. Nose questing, I smelled ... I smelled ... food.

Immediately my tummy rumbled, the noise loud in the hall and startling in its intensity. I waited, fearing that someone had heard my errant stomach and its demands. Five seconds ... ten ... twenty ... nothing.

Thank goodness. Still, someone had food and I was hungry for anything not laced with amphetamines. *Starving.* My mouth threatened to become a waterfall as my feet followed the smell that so tempted me. I was on autopilot, directed by forces beyond my control, and my belly scourged my will, stripping away the tatters of my volition.

Another door, another thin, wire-mesh window. This time there was something to see.

It was Annabeth.

Good Lord, Mike, my mind went completely off the reservation. You know what she meant to me. Annabeth, my cousin. My lover. She betrayed me for Burke and left me for dead to rot in the winter snow of New Hampshire. The sight of Burke cupping her breast as I drowned in my own blood was as fresh as if it had happened seconds ago instead of years.

I still remembered her skin, the slightly musky smell of it and its soft silkiness. A chemical rush flooded my veins, hormones of memory, the recollection of slipping into her while showering, our tongues clashing in what was more war than lovemaking. I ached for her despite the betrayal that struck so deep I still bore its bleeding wound.

She sat at a table next to a spare bed eating pad thai noodles out of a Styrofoam container with a pair of plastic chopsticks. What looked like fried calamari with peanut sauce rested in the container at her elbow. A stray lock of midnight-black hair hung past her jaw line. A remnant escaped from the sensible bun at the nape of her neck.

Damn, she looked good.

She was reading a newspaper and slowly eating her noodles, full lips slurping bean sprouts and beef, her dark eyes intent. Behind her, another woman sharpened a K-bar with a whetstone, porcelain finishing sticks and small can of oil placed carefully on the bed. *Shhhhttt, shhhhtt, shhhhttt* went the edge against the fine-grained block of gray stone. *Shhhhttt, shhhhttt, shhhhttt* ... the sound as soft as a kiss.

At any moment one or both of the women could glance up and see me peering through the window with a vapid look on my face, but I couldn't move, couldn't twitch. I was at sea in a raft of my own impotence.

The other woman, a blonde with features hard as old oak, glanced up. Our eyes met, mine brown, hers a light hazel. For a brief moment that stretched out across space and time, we stared at each other in icy detachment.

Force blurred out of my mouth with the smell of burning insulation and the door, which normally swung out from the room, burst inward in a shower of splinters and droplets of glass. Those bits and pieces preceded the disk of Force I hurled, cutting into the hazel-eyed woman, each shard of wired glass and splinter of wood painful shrapnel.

She screamed as flesh was pierced, her cheeks shredding as fragments flew past just before Force, dissipating rapidly, hurled her against the back wall in a spray of blood.

I was in the room before my conscious mind could register the fact, gun up and trained on the spot between Annabeth's eyes. The memory of her staring coldly at me as I bled onto the too-white snow of New Hampshire enveloped me, but did not stay my hand or blunt my will.

Before the other woman could slump into unconsciousness, I said, "Still think I lack killer instincts?"

We stared at each other, her eyes deep pools of hate and malice, mine colder than midwinter. The moment stretched, then contracted as she lowered her head in defeat. The crack about killer instincts referred to one of the last things she'd said to me before Burke shot me in the back a few years ago. She'd thought my lack of sadism was weakness and so hitched her wagon to the dark star that was Burke. I threw the line in her face because it kept me from planting a bullet between her eyes.

What can I say? I was exhausted and running on fumes. My old habits were beginning to ooze up through the cracks in my control. Being a good guy was such hard work. No wonder so many didn't bother.

The answer to my question came in a surprisingly low growl. "You're dead, Olivier."

"Check on your comrade and don't try anything. I really have no qualms about shooting you."

Annabeth felt for the other woman's pulse and said, "She's alive."

Whew. "Excellent. Now … where is Mason's room?"

She glared, not answering.

And here I'd hoped it would easier than this. Pain slipped out of my mouth, low and calm with the smell of bleach. Just a trickle of magic, enough for her eyes to widen and her skin to pale from olive to bone white.

"Next time I use Pain I will shout it for all to hear," I said blandly, hiding the nausea that twisted my guts. A couple of years ago I wouldn't have blinked at the thought of torturing a member of my Family. People *can* change.

That's because of you, Mike.

"Now, to Mason's room."

"You will kill me."

"No."

She didn't seem convinced.

Sighing, I waved the gun in tight circles, never aiming far from her skull. "If I wanted you dead, I'd use Truth to get the info and be done with the whole sordid mess, but I am trying to walk a better path these days, Annabeth. A path that does not require killing everyone who happens to annoy." I leaned in close. "But my patience is not infinite, so get a move on and take me to Mason's room."

I can be pretty convincing when I want. She led me out into the hall, keeping a wary eye on the Ruger in my hand. We went back toward the stairs, but before she could open the door, a sharp cough came from behind and pain exploded in my left butt cheek, a furious heat that felt as if I'd been struck by a baseball bat.

My left leg decided that a stroll was not in the cards. It decided to fold, spilling me backwards as another harsh cough sounded. A buzzing passed over my skull as my spine met linoleum, and I saw an upside-down version of what was behind.

A man in black slacks and T-shirt stood holding a pistol in both hands fronted by a rather large suppressor that belched tiny tongues of flame accompanied by quiet coughs.

Pain exploded from my mouth, shouted at the man as the pistol tracked down to the point between my eyes. Green eyes flew open wide as agony racked his tissues and the heavy pistol flew from his hands to clatter upon the floor.

Breath exploded from my chest, and my ribs creaked alarmingly as the heel of Annabeth's shoe connected in a vicious ax kick. A knee followed as she knelt down hard, driving what was left of the air in my lungs out through my nose. Small fists, hard as stones, began to rain down on my cheeks and jaw. *Smack, smack, smack.*

Sharp agony ripped through my face as my nose *cracked* harshly, a casualty of one of Annabeth's pistoning fists. Copper and salt, tangy and thick on my tongue. The inside of my lips were shredded by my teeth as my cousin continued to batter me. I couldn't feel the Ruger—its familiar heaviness was gone from my hand—and I tried to raise my own fists, to defend myself from my enraged former lover, but they were too heavy, clumsy, and ineffectual, and my mouth was blocked with blood and gelid hurt that stopped any Words as firmly as if my lips were sewn shut. I knew, *I knew*, down to my bones, down to the quiet places in my heart that Annabeth wouldn't stop, not until my face was pulverized by her adamantine fists and my brains were leaking out of my ears.

Another blow to the eye sent a spear through my skull that threatened to tear it apart, and through the shower of sparks in my vision I caught the fleeting, smug smile that passed across Annabeth's face.

I bucked, or tried, in an effort to dislodge my attacker, but a bullet in the butt beat my ability to buck a brawny brunette.

Smack, smack, smack, the blows came faster and faster, and more and more stars began to shine in my fading vision. That's when fear really began to take root in my chest. Right under her pressing knee, in fact, an icy sensation like cold water poured directly upon my heart.

It is definitely not safe.

Perhaps she thought she was winning, or perhaps anger made her sloppy. Looking back, I really don't care. What matters most were the results, which were dramatic because I spied something in my fading vision that afforded me an opportunity to save my life.

For those whose eyes aren't veiled, the world is a wondrous place full of creatures both great and small, gross and minute. If the average person on the street could see the world as a magus does, their eyes would always be wide inconstant total amazement. What I saw, what gave me the impetus I needed, was not some grand and terrible demon, not some beautiful and astonishing golden Angel but something much more base.

It was an Air Sprite.

Sprites are the least and weakest of the Elementals—the greatest are the Primals, the ones from whom all others spring. Sprites have very little real power. These spirits of Air, Fire, Earth, and Water are mischievous creatures who love to play jokes on unsuspecting mortals. Of them all, Air Sprites seem to take particular delight in annoying humans.

No Words hissed through my teeth, not as such. What emerged was the Language of Air, which brought with it the smell of lemongrass and the sound of the wind through spiny trees. Of all the Elemental languages, Air was the easiest, and my battered lips proved no impediment as it rushed forth.

Annabeth's eyes flew open as she was lifted straight up to smack right hard on the ceiling, popping one of the inset bulbs with her rather shapely behind. Sparks fell on my face as I attempted to rise, my ass shrieking bloody murder. The perforated *gluteus maximus* drooled my life into my shorts, but adrenaline had me on my feet in no time, the world tilting at crazy angles thanks to blood loss and the indignities I'd suffered at the hands of Burke and Mason.

The man I'd hit with Force was slowly wobbling to his feet, a rather mean look on his face, so I launched another Force. It took him square in the chest and hurled him twenty feet down the hall. Then it was a Healing for me, followed quickly by another Vigor and Clarity, the spell odors assaulting my delicate nasal membranes.

"Damn," I breathed as spots flashed in my vision, the beginnings of Backlash. Any more magic use and I might find myself scraping my IQ off the ground. If Backlash didn't kill me, it might actually damage me to the point where I lost Words.

Nevertheless, the world around steadied and my split lips healed, my eyes de-swelled and my nose *popped* back into place with a solid wrench. Far more disturbing and distracting was the bullet in my butt spitting out from between the lips of torn yet rapidly healing flesh, a sliding, shifting motion that stung like acid.

"Once again … *damn,*" I groused as I approached the floating Annabeth. The Air Sprite swirled around her torso and arms, giggling like the whisper of wind through a keyhole. Its humor to those who could see and hear it was almost infectious.

"Keep her there, please, oh mighty one," I whistled to the Sprite. "Feel free to give her a squeeze or two if it pleases you." Air Elementals, especially the small ones, love flattery and respond to it like a Pekingese to bacon.

A tendril of air forced its way through Annabeth's mouth, ballooning out her cheeks. "This one amuses me," it said with almost musical glee. "It struggles and wiggles delightfully."

"Please keep it alive," I replied, feeling shagged out despite the Vigor.

Turning away, I caught a hint of movement at the doorway to Annabeth's room and I dove for the Ruger.

Blue steel met warm flesh and the heft of it filled my palm with surety. I hardly aimed, letting years of training take over. I was an automaton, a creature of pure reaction and pre-programmed moves that took place without conscious thought. Three bullets left the Ruger in short, flat barks that rang harshly down the hall.

The hazel-eyed woman, cheeks a ragged mass of red and pink tears, spasmed as each bullet hit, two to the chest and one to the head that entered at the bridge of the nose. It exited out the back of her head, leaving a hole the size of an egg. She sank slowly, blood streaming from her nostrils.

"Fuck me," I cursed, my heart aching in remorse. Not too long ago, killing her wouldn't have bothered me one bit, but now, as I stared into unseeing hazel eyes, it was all I could do not to throw up.

I made it to my feet without upchucking, however, and walked past the corpse to the man who had shot me in the ass. He lay on the floor gasping and groaning, twitching and holding his belly as if his guts were heaving hard to exit his belly button. The disk of Force I'd cast had been strong, stronger than necessary, but urgency and desperation don't allow for careful planning. I examined his face but didn't recognize him. The Family was large, perhaps larger than even I knew, and he came from the far side of the Family tree. Blondish hair and blue eyes marked the distances between our genetic make-ups. He looked Germanic, possibly Scandinavian, while I favored the old Middle-Eastern roots that were the source of the Family.

I manhandled him into a chokehold and put his lights out for the near future. Not the wisest course. No, the smart thing to do would be to put two in his skull from three feet away, but I had long since lost the stomach for that kind of wet work. Perhaps Annabeth was right in thinking I lacked a true killer instinct.

Right … speaking of Annabeth ….

Wow. If looks could kill and all that. The heat of her glare was enough to cook a twenty-four-pound turkey in two seconds flat. The little Sprite still had a tendril in her mouth, making her cheeks balloon comically. I whistled for the Sprite to vacate her mouth and replaced the Elemental with the barrel of the Ruger.

"I think you were wrong about the killer-instinct thing," I snarled as the blue steel chipped her front teeth, "don't you?"

"Funck 'oo!" she gurgled around the gun.

"Been there, done you," I said calmly. "Now, the Sprite is going to put you down, and if you don't take me to Mason's room, I'll simply pull the trigger and search for it on my own. I've already taken care of your team. There's only you left."

The widening of her eyes told me all I needed to know. "Ahh, so there are more." My smile wasn't friendly. "At least one more."

"Gldmnt!"

"Right. Whatever." A whistle, and the Sprite unceremoniously dropped Annabeth to the floor. There was a loud *snap* as her arm bent the wrong way and the sound of tearing paper as bone ripped through flesh, spattering blood on the dirty floor. Gray-pink and shiny, the jagged end pointed toward me like an accusation. Annabeth's eyes grew wide in shock and pain, and a low growl shot from her throat, sounding like a dull saw blade ripping through rotted wood.

Ouch.

"Heal me!" she urged through clenched teeth. Sweat beaded her forehead.

"After."

"After? After fucking what?"

"After you take me to Mason's room." I leaned down and grabbed the valise. I was ready to go.

The look on my face must have been enough to convince her of my seriousness.

Up the grimy stairwell, we climbed the many stories to the top floor. As Annabeth slogged up the last two steps, blood dripped from her torn flesh, her broken humerus a sharp punctuation of pain.

My eyes began to track randomly, the world around beginning to tilt to the left and right, up and down. Vigor was beginning to wear off, its efficacy leaking away as the relentless tick tock of time wore it down.

"Hurry up." My throat felt sandpaper raw.

She didn't bother to look around. "Fuck you, Olivier."

Mason's room was large, of course, and less water-damaged than the others. It sported a king-sized four-poster with the finest Egyptian cotton sheets colored cornflower blue under a thin, sky-blue comforter. Next to the bed was an armoire, no doubt containing several changes of clothing for a VIP like Mason. A mahogany desk and plush-looking office chair stood along the wall opposite to the bed. On the desk lay a closed laptop next to the stone I had liberated from Munakata. It was propped up, leaning against the wall with the butt end against the desk. The engravings, crude and harsh, ran up and down the length of the tablet, each symbol seeming to tease the mind with comprehension just out of reach.

"There, Olivier," Annabeth grunted, her head hanging, eyes half shut. "Heal me."

The words made sense, but they were stretched out and long in my hearing.

I was fading fast, but I owed her what I'd promised and touched her between the shoulder blades with the tip of a finger, all the while keeping the Ruger aimed at her head. I might have turned over a new leaf, but I wasn't going to be a fool about it.

Magic is a funny thing, Mike. Most everybody wants explanations of *why* and *how* it works. The mechanics of magic. Is it the manipulation of subatomic particles? The utilization of psychic energy to effect change on the material world?

Don't really care. Never looked too deep into it. Before my defection from the Family, I would've attributed magic to the Patron, how he works his will upon the Earth, but now I guess it comes from God. I reckon it is God who fuels—or is the fuel for—magic on this planet. But to the heart of the matter … I only care that it works. Call me callous or superficial, it doesn't matter. When your back is to the wall, all that matters is results.

Annabeth hissed deep, her arm suddenly straightening, the broken humerus withdrawing back into flesh. That flesh knitted quickly, the tear closing in seconds, leaving behind a thin, red line where her injury had been.

As she smiled in relief—as the sweat dried on her forehead and she shuddered with the ecstasy of respite—I clocked her a good one on the occipital. It was a calculated strike, one I had done before, but never while in such bad shape—sleep deprived and suffering the aftereffects of torture and borderline Backlash.

Still, it was successful. Annabeth dropped like a stone to the ugly pile carpeting and landed in an unconscious heap. Oh well, she already hated me, so what could she do to me? Kill me twice?

Somehow, knowing her, that didn't seem so farfetched.

In the armoire, I found my wallet—the fake Delaware driver's license identified me as Deacon Hope—and the several hundred dollars in twenties that used to be in my shorts pockets. Good, I'd need the cash to get home, but what really elevated my blood pressure and sent a wave of optimism roaring through my blood was the sight of my sandals lying next to a pair of brown Salvatore Ferragamo Tapas. As sweet as the $600 shoes were, my sandals were the lifelines I needed.

For the first time in my life, I prayed, Mike. I sure have seen you pray before, you and your parishioners. Always thought the practice was a bit hinky, you know, talking to a great big invisible deity who seems to know everything you do before you do it. I know, I know, it's all about faith and respect and love and such, but it still seems a bit dodgy, a practice to which I don't subscribe. Yet, when I saw those sandals, I winged a prayer to your God that Mason hadn't found my potion stash.

Apparently He heard me. The concealed leather plugs in the heels popped free and I teased out the small plastic vials. Less than a half-ounce each, they were not the most expensive potions ever brewed, but they'd required a fair amount of time and prep. I unscrewed the cap to one and downed it right quick.

Energy coursed through me, setting my eyeballs to vibrating in their sockets. Moving faster than the eye could register, I grabbed the stone and the laptop, shoving the computer into the valise and hauling the heavy tablet as if that thick stone weighed only a few ounces.

Goody, goody, goody, goody. I was speeding, humming along at velocities impossible for mere mortals. *Goody, goody, goody.*

Knotweed, mulberry, olive, pennyroyal, yucca, and just a smidgeon of saliva. Brewed in a copper pot during nights of the new moon while chanting in the Languages of Air and Fire. Four months per potion. Four months of exacting alchemy to produce the potion that coursed through my veins like a conflagration.

Through one of two large windows, I saw downtown Chicago spread out below. Across the street was a parking garage almost level with Mason's room. Roughly forty feet away and ten feet down. My humming nerves had me jittering in place while calculations spun with manic rapidity in my mind.

Hmm … if done wrong, it would be dicey.

I smiled. Piece of cake.

Furniture became airborne as I threw the armoire through the window. Jeweled daggers shattered against asphalt while the unlucky armoire became toothpicks for the Midwest's homeless. I followed quickly after. It never occurred to me to summon an Air Elemental to ferry me across. My humming nervous system overrode any vestige of common sense that remained after sleepless nights and days of being waterboarded.

The garage neared with glacial slowness as my leap carried me across the street, a white Chevy Suburban growing large in my sight.

The Suburban passed below and concrete rose to meet me at a velocity that would have been inconceivable had I not been buzzing like a speed freak on a hot load.

Impact. Both feet hit concrete and the shock sent a tsunami of anguish up my legs to nest firmly in my balls. Bones and flesh would have pulped, but the powerful efficacy of potion-toughened tissues resisted shattering, tearing, or pulping. Magic so mighty that it transformed human into superhuman kept my legs from becoming forty pounds of mush and blood. But being more than human didn't cancel the effects of momentum.

Bare feet struck and knees gave way, hitting pavement hard enough to split bone like balsa wood, but flesh held even though I tumbled end over end, trying for a roll. Skull hit concrete, followed by spine and curled legs.

The tablet flew from my hands as well as the valise. Fortunately a Kia Sedan stopped my roll, my torso crumpling the little Korean-made automobile's right front quarter panel.

Oddly enough, I managed to make it to my feet without a scratch to the paint job or a dent in my fender, although my Bermuda shorts and hideously overpriced polo shirt were a dead loss.

The stone tablet survived, although the Subaru Legacy it collided with sure wasn't going to be rolling again soon. I tugged the tablet from the front grill in a spray of green radiator fluid and snagged the valise. Inside, the laptop casing was cracked, one corner shattered completely, but I kept the thing anyway.

"Gotta make more of those potions," I enthused, although my super-high was beginning to fade at the edges.

I waved goodbye to the building across the street and the remnants and reminders of my old life.

Chapter Seventeen

"If one can profit by action, then that action should be taken."
—*Codex Infernales*

"MAN, YOU DON'T PAY ME ENOUGH for my genius." Rick handed me the laptop. "Although I really wanna know where you got this thing. It is light years ahead of what you can get at Best Buy."

"Ricky, my man," I said, handing him a fat roll of tens and twenties, "believe me when I say you don't want to know."

He tossed me a dubious look, eyes magnified by his Coke-bottle glasses. "Whatever, man. I ain't never seen an operating system like that before. It sure ain't Linux or Windows, so I figure it has to be an unreleased, private OS."

If he only knew. "You aren't paid to ask questions." The laptop's new casing gleamed in plastic perfection.

Hands flew up in surrender as he said, "I ain't asking nothing, man."

I stood quickly, the tiny trailer rocking slightly. "That's a double negative, so in fact you are asking the questions, *man.*" I tried the slang out, rolling it around in my mouth to get the taste. I'd used it a few times already and wasn't entirely comfortable with the flow. Maybe *dude*? Or *bro*?

I shook my head and snorted. *Americans.*

Ricky Eyes was the best hacker and computer nerd to graduate from the University of Nebraska in the past decade, although he looked more like a hobo. Five-foot-five inches tall and about five-feet wide, he ate Cheetos about as quickly as he wrote code, and his clothes were liberally sprinkled with orange dust. The flannel shirt he wore at present looked like it might be on the verge of developing language skills.

"Never seen that kinda tech before, Jude," he stated flatly, rolling his ponderous bulk upright. "I woulda worked on it for free, man."

"No bugs? No tracking software?"

He shook his head. "I removed the software during a secure boot and the tracking device was damaged when whatever happened to the casing happened, man."

"So it's clean."

"Clean as can be. Here." Ricky handed over a CD in a crystal case. "It had some ultra-cool encryption, but I managed to crack it and remove the password prompt. Start 'er up with this in the drive and you'll slip through the encryption like a hot knife through butter."

"Thanks, Ricky." I thought for a moment. "You didn't see any of the data on the drive, did you?" I was tempted to hit him with Truth then Forgetting, but such things were best employed as last-ditch efforts.

"Naw, man." He shook his head. "I know which side my bread is buttered on." The fat wad of money disappeared into his shirt pocket. "You pay for the best and discretion and that is what you get, man." There was no fear in his eyes. Despite his slovenly appearance, he was plenty sharp and dangerous. If he'd wanted to screw me over, he would have done so long ago.

"You lay that false trail?"

"Sure, piece of cake. As far as TransWays Bus Lines is concerned, Deacon Hope bought a ticket from Houston to Omaha to Chicago."

Excellent. Last thing I needed was for the Family to track me to Omaha. If they took the bait, Houston would soon be crawling with magi looking for the long-lost Olivier.

"Thanks."

Ricky ran a Cheeto'd hand through his thick brown mop of hair. "No, thank *you*, man. It's not often I get to tinker with great tech and unique software." He patted his pocket, expression content. "And you're never late with a payment, man. That says something."

The pudgy little computer nerd was venal, greedy, slothful (his housecleaning was amazingly atrocious—the little trailer looked like it had been decorated by winos using containers of rotting fast-food), and if the stacks of *Penthouse* magazines were any indication, lustful. Give him a few more years and he would be the embodiment of all seven deadly sins.

As I drove away from his beat-up place, I had to smile. Ricky was a find, a man of somewhat loose morals who didn't have a mean bone in his body. Upon arriving in Omaha a couple of years ago, I knew I'd have to employ a competent hacker to help me hide my electronic footprint and establish cover IDs. Fortunately, the criminal element in Omaha was small enough that it didn't take long—just a generous sum of cash—to find someone with the right skills. God bless the USA.

My house on 61ˢᵗ was a stone's throw from L Street behind a used car dealership. A quiet little neighborhood … for the most part.

The neighbors across the street were at it again, a husband and wife yelling at the top of their lungs.

As I parked my Honda in the driveway and walked to the door, I muttered, "Save me from the shirtless wonder." She was a large woman who wore a tent-like dressing gown that covered her to the ankles, but her husband stood there *sans* shirt and shoes as if the mid-morning chill didn't exist. I guessed the thick, black hair on his back kept him warm. His love handles jiggled and wobbled like Jell-O as he shook his finger at his wife. Meanwhile her curlers slowly came undone, her thin hair unfurling like graying capellini.

Tempted … so damn tempted to toss a Forgetting or Force or something at the two. I mean really, Mike, they square off on their meager front lawn, regaling the neighborhood with their trailer-trash lifestyle.

Okay … a bit mean, but they really get on my nerves.

Once inside, I retreated to the room in the back next to my bedroom. It was barely ten by ten, but it had everything I needed to continue my research—a desk, a brand-spanking-new iMac (its see-through plastic casing a pleasing aqua), and the tablet.

Let me tell you about the tablet, Mike: several somethings I found out in the two weeks since coming home to Omaha (I hitched a ride with a trucker who became extra friendly when I waved cash in his face).

One: it was over *seventy-five hundred years old*. Yeah, it predated the last known development of writing by a couple thousand years.

Two: it was magical. It oozed magic and that magic could only be accessed by touching the tablet, which allowed a person to read any written language. It even worked on computer languages such as Component Pascal and E. Trippy as all get out.

Three: this is the big one, Mike, so sit down or brace yourself against an immoveable object. Ready? Okay, here it goes. The tablet was created by and belonged to Cain.

Yeah, *that* Cain.

Which brings us to Four: the tablet was a letter. A letter to God. Yes, *that* God. From Cain to God. It was his apology for the murder of his brother Abel. I'd read the thing a few dozen times. The grammar was rudimentary, the syntax something awful, but just imagine the sheer *audacity* and imagination of Cain to invent writing in an attempt to apologize for fratricide. I wasn't sure whether to be stunned by his arrogance or impressed by his genius. Either way, it was quite the achievement.

When I first touched the tablet in the privacy of my home, I could read the writing. When I removed my hands, nothing, *nada*. Complete lack of understanding. Hands back on and *violà!* Instant translation.

Under the Pergo floor was a three-and-a-half by two-foot space where I hid the tablet. It was still there when I pulled the slab of faux wood aside. "There you are, lovely."

With the tablet on the desk and the laptop booting up, I rubbed my hands in anticipation. My palms were sweaty and tingling and I was hoping that Ricky's CD would work as advertised or else my investment was for naught.

I wasn't sure what I'd find on the hard drive—business details, a diary, or a recipe for fudge. My hope was that it was something I could use against the Family. Any edge would do. They had found me, actually *captured* me, and I needed to know if they were close to my Omaha hideout, or if I was safe for a few more years.

Perhaps it was filled with porn.

The welcome screen appeared, colored a happy blue with the Deschamps logo, a capital D in white Geneva font—you have to appreciate the irony— superimposed on the globe, smack dab in the middle. You can say what you like about the Family, but they are certainly unencumbered by modesty.

For a few seconds, the CD drive hummed along contentedly before suddenly ejecting the disk. On the screen, from top to bottom, appeared a mishmash of symbols and numbers that seemed to taunt me with their confusing array.

"Thought you'd cracked this, Ricky," I muttered angrily, regretting that all the money I'd paid him had gone to waste. "Now all I have is gibberish." The mishmash of symbols continued to irritate my eyes and I felt a rising anger heat the back of my neck. My options seemed limited.

Or were they?

The tablet translated written language, any language. Did encryption count? The standard definition of encryption is coding information or messages in a way that it cannot be read by a third party, unless the third party had the cipher key. As I stared at the letters and symbols flashing at me on the screen, I realized that language itself is a sort of code—only read by those parties with the correct set of symbol-translation variables … i.e., the ability to read. The ultimate cipher key.

I laid a hand on the tablet, staring hard at the screen. A tingle started at my fingertips and traveled the length of each finger like the pins and needles sensation of returning circulation. It continued to my wrist, moving past my elbow and up to my shoulder. When it reached the base of my neck, the symbols on the screen dissolved into comprehensible words, then sentences. My eyeballs began to itch.

File folders, each precisely labeled, dotted the screen, and with the click of a mouse I began to open each one and read its contents.

Three hours later, I sat back and blew out a deep breath, rubbing my eyes with stiff fingers. My mind was racing with what I had learned.

There were two gigabytes of hard drive, most of which was blank, but of the ten megabytes not allocated to the operating system, five were taken up by standard business programs: spreadsheets, humdrum reports and the like, but hidden behind a file labeled INTEREST COVERAGE RATIO was the only bit of information that really tripped my trigger.

Not that what I found didn't have some value if it made any sense. Much of it concerned a project called CENTURY, which seemed to be a major concern in Finland. That surprised me because the Family tended to shun the Scandinavian countries. Their governments were the least prone to corruption and their business dealings were relatively aboveboard. Not that you couldn't bribe the odd official or two, but those at the top of the food chain tended to place themselves on the side of the angels.

Whatever was happening in Finland ate up a lot of capital, but there were no real details except tonnage in freight and delivery estimates. There was a brief mention of a person named Himmel, but that rang no bells. The only other pertinent data was a notation that CENTURY was projected to be online by 2002.

From the spreadsheets covering his main area of interest (Globales Öl, or Global Oil as they're known in the States) I discovered that Mason was a clever monkey indeed. Which he'd have to be to sit at the table as one of the Twelve. Thanks to an extensive, expensive education provided by the Family, I was able to penetrate the thick legalese and creative accounting to discover that thanks to Mason, the Family's profits in the oil business had reached an all-time high. Enough so, in fact, that they had quietly taken over one of the world's largest oil companies a couple of years prior. Hint: the name has two X's in it.

Mason was a shark in a school of minnows, that's for sure. If Julian were to pass away, the most likely to succeed, by sheer volume of revenue brought in, would be Mason. Burke might be a total hard ass and a six-Word magus, but he didn't have the temperament to run the Family. At least Julian had a passing familiarity with subtlety.

The file labeled INTEREST COVERAGE RATIO was actually Mason's day planner, an account of his schedule—his comings and goings for the past three months and the next five. Personal notes, appointments, and an entire section devoted to the other members of the Twelve. Not surprising, really. If one had occasion to run for the head of the table, it would be a good idea to know your opponents' weaknesses.

Now, if I've given the impression that the Family is one big free-for-all to see who's King of the Mountain at the end of the day, let me lay that to rest. There are rules, very strict rules, laid down by the Patron on conduct within the Family. Although the Patron has a problem with authority (not too happy about anyone with authority over *him*, as you well know), he has no issues with swinging the big stick at others. Hypocritical? You bet, but who is going to tell *him* that?

The Patron loves structure, order, and strict discipline, but only on His terms. With every fiber of His being, Lucifer is a control freak and a micromanager. Very little is done without his direct supervision and input, one of the very things He advocated for in his argument with God. He said mankind, being so imperfect and finite, deserved only to be ruled, not shepherded. Commanded, not coddled. It was this intractable view that sparked the Rebellion against Heaven and led to the Fall. He never learned to compromise.

Of course, I never knew that before I met you, Mike. No, before my exodus from the not-so-loving arms of the Family, I believed the propaganda spewed forth by the Patron, that the "Lying God" thrust him from Heaven, a dreadful, cowardly attack while he was busy creating a Paradise upon earth. Ever since then, He has been trying to dethrone the Usurper and resume his rightful place in the Kingdom.

We scions of Yeshuda were kept ignorant of the truth, blinded to everything biblical, taught to see Christianity as a blight upon Earth, an abomination. Despite an education second to none, there were massive gaps as blinders were placed upon our eyes. Outside media was carefully screened, spoon-fed until we children were virtually brainwashed. My best guess was that the truth became known only when one rose high enough in the Family hierarchy.

And the higher up you went, the more the rules benefited you. Like politics.

Assassination of the Family head was unheard of, and any attempt to put one to grass would be met by the Patron with a punishment so dire as not to be contemplated. Think lakes of fire, chains of ice, boiling oil, and searing hooks tearing at your entrails. Worse than that by far.

Only with the Patron's permission could a Family head be removed, and to my knowledge, that hadn't been done in a while. The Family head is usually handpicked by the Twelve, or by the Patron if he thought intervention was warranted, and that was bloody well that. As long as the head of the Family was the bloodiest, meanest, sneakiest sonofabitch alive and achieved the results to back him up, he was sacrosanct.

Now, the Twelve was another matter. Though technically safe from assassination, they were not safe from *character* assassination. It was considered the height of business acumen to take down a member of the Twelve and that gave one a good chance to fill some large shoes, indeed.

As for the man who lost his position among the Twelve, well, he was retired, given a nice pension for service (just because the Patron is an asshole doesn't mean he turns his nose up at loyalty), and left to pass the rest of his life in whatever part of the globe he took a fancy to. We called these retired the Venerated, and they tended to live long, peaceful lives once forced out of the Family business concern.

Surprised that a Family dedicated to the evilest being in the universe would let the geezers live? Well, I can picture the confusion on your face, Mike, with your eyebrows furrowed and the wrinkles on your forehead all wavy and deep. But think of this: I said the Patron rewards loyalty, and he does. We live in the lap of luxury, people of privilege and education striding the world like colossi with whatever we desire at our fingertips. It helps spur us on, that great big carrot of a peaceful, nonviolent end to our lives when the time comes. Helps us focus our energies a little better. Satan knows how to reward his people, to wring the most out of them.

Besides, think of all the experience the Venerated have, the decades of business savvy that could be mined and put to use if necessary. Never waste a resource, no matter how old, decrepit, and marvelously bitter.

The Devil is in the details.

Everything in the computer seemed pretty straightforward and relatively boring—nothing of note except project CENTURY—but I wasn't about to go toddling off to Finland any time soon. I scrolled to the end of the file, where there was a interesting notation: "7/1 Seattle. Continue research of CI at ST."

CI at ST? Curious and curiouser. 7/1 was easy: July first. Now, to suss out the rest. Maybe I was tired, or my time away from the Family had dulled my edges a mite. Either way, it was a good five minutes before the light of understanding shone upon my poor gray matter.

SwolTech. One of the Family's biggest companies. The very best in computer hardware and circuitry. In fact, the Crystal Drive I'd stolen went to them for development and implementation for the various Family-owned corporations. SwolTech was the sparkling gem in the Twelve's crown of glory, producing more revenue than Global Oil and Halifax Armaments combined. They made Microsoft and Apple look like dilettantes.

After that little nugget clattered around the brain pan for a split-second, the second part of clue slid into place. There were no Family companies with the initials CI, but there *was* something, a rare object known of only by select Dagger Men and the higher ups. Something with those exact initials.

The *Codex Infernales.*
It was in Seattle.

CHAPTER EIGHTEEN

"If you can grasp it, it is yours."
—*Codex Infernales*

THE SCENT OF FRESH-CUT GRASS TAUNTED me as the Language of Earth rumbled off of my lips quickly, effortlessly. It was as familiar as my skin, the breath in my lungs, and the color of my eyes. Years upon years of practice and a natural facility for magic made me unequaled in Elemental Languages (or Elemental magic, if you prefer). Each Language consists of Words unique to each Element. You can't force an Elemental to do your bidding—that would make them slaves and they are far from *that*. No, the Languages are a Summoning that catches their attention, brings them to the magus, and after that it's up to the magus to plead with the Elemental for a boon.

Usually Elementals are pretty agreeable (although Air and Fire are particularly fickle) and perform tasks willingly. Perhaps they are starved for decent conversation. However, sometimes incentives are required, a little bribery to sweeten the pot such as magic herbs for Air, something to burn for Fire, or baubles for Water. Earth, however, never seems to want anything, performing tasks with minimal pleading on my part, which is why I prefer that Element.

Once my plea went out, I sat back on my heels in my little hidey-hole and considered the buildings before me, halogen lights turning the darkness near its walls into the brightest day.

Thick brush and trees curtained my presence, a screen against thermal imaging. I wasn't sure what defenses the Sicarii maintained around the buildings; no dogs or guards patrolled the perimeter, which had me nervous as hell. There were six buildings. Four three-story labs surrounded a four-story factory where the tech was assembled. The sixth was a ten-story office affair that loomed like a glass-and-steel monolith over the others. It housed the business offices for SwolTech and was the seat of one of the Twelve.

Last I heard, Vernon Deschamps ran the company. A capable, almost emotionless man, he was a cousin of Julian's and had zero sense of humor. I'd met him once, and his long, drawn face struck terror in my bones the second his washed-out, pale, pale blue eyes met mine.

Every now and then I remember those unsettling eyes, the breadth of Vernon's shoulders, and the strength of his handshake the first and last time I'd met him years ago just before the incident in Livingston, New Jersey, at Julian's underground lab. The recollection always gives me the shivers.

It was at this very site I met Vernon. The man was polite enough to personally provide a guided tour of the main factory, but he kept the labs and main offices off-limits. He was nice to me because I was Julian's son and a contender for Head of the Family, but secrecy is encoded into the Family DNA. Along with viciousness, sadism, and a capacity for evil that would make a Third World despot faint.

I stared upward, Vision piercing the darkness, enriching my eyes with a kaleidoscope of colors not found in nature. I could see with perfect clarity in all directions. Except up.

Up was filled with clouds.

Clouds were invented for Seattle. Every single time I have visited the Pacific Northwest, there were dense, gray clouds overhead, pregnant with rain and the promise of more gray days to come. If you like rain and don't suffer from Seasonal Affective Disorder, then Seattle is just the place for you.

Sprawling on the Washington coast in King County, it's known as "The Emerald City," "The City of Flowers," "The City of Goodwill," and "The Gateway to Alaska." Plenty of moisture and mild winters keeps the flowers blooming and the grass green. A nicer city you'll never find, assuming that you can live without sunshine for nine months out of the year.

With a population of approximately four million, the city is the hub of the Pacific Northwest and very kind to businesses, which is one of two reasons the Family bases SwolTech there. The other is anonymity. Who would expect that such ruthless, cunning, and downright evil entities would have a toehold in the middle of a Pacific Northwest forest? Most would think that New York, Chicago, Detroit, or Los Angeles would be more conducive to the business of the Sicarii. Too obvious. Evil often dons a pleasing mask.

A faint tremor touched the soles of my black sneakers. Earth was answering my summons, and a light sheen of sweat beaded on my upper lip despite the nip in the air.

In front of my eyes the thick forest loam began to rumble faintly, a near subsonic noise I could feel in the roots of my teeth. Pressure waves emanated from a small spot some three feet from my toes, very localized, each vibration dissipating before it reached me. At the epicenter, the ground began to bulge, leaves and twigs falling away from the swiftly rising apex. Excitement and apprehension warred for dominance within me and I took several deep breaths in an effort to calm my nerves. My fingers twitched, so I clenched both hands into fists so tight my nails bit deep into my palms. Cursing softly, I reached into my backpack, pulled out a pair of thin leather gloves, and quickly slipped them on. Now I was almost totally invisible, with black clothes from head to toe and black camouflage makeup darkening my face. The only parts of me that stood out were the whites of my eyes.

Higher and higher rose the mound of black earth until it reached five feet tall by five wide, a conical protrusion pointing at the sky. Even though there was no one side I could identify as "facing" me, no eyes to see or mouth to speak, I could feel its regard upon my skin like a subtle pressure pushing me back.

"*You have called, young Sicarius,*" said the mound of dirt in a voice that could only be described as subterranean, "*and I have come.*"

"*I thank you, Earth.*" The words felt like gargling with gravel. "*There is boon I would ask.*"

"*Ask. Earth will answer.*"

I pointed to the office building huddling near the behemoth of the factory. "*Will you take me to that building?*"

For a second the power of its scrutiny faded. A moment later it returned. "*It is normally within the power of this Elemental, but not at this time.*"

"*Why?*"

"*Earth guards this series of man-made mounds. No outside Earth or humans are allowed. Should I attempt to convey you beneath the surface, we would be challenged and detained by Earth much stronger than I. It is with regret, young Sicarius, that I tell you this because you, of all the Sicarii, afford Earth great respect, and for that Earth honors you.*"

"*I am no longer Sicarii,*" I said automatically, mind racing. This was a bit of a pickle. "*Will this honor allow the greater Elementals to let me pass?*"

A feeling of ... sadness? regret? radiated from the mound. "*Earth has taken duty and will not relinquish it until called upon to do so. Earth is not Air or Fire to be fickle and capricious. What Earth has said will be done.*"

A rueful smile appeared on my face at the Elemental's disdainful tone. Earth was the most patient and steadfast of all the elements, measuring time in geologic ticks of the clock. Fire and Air were lightning quick compared to stolid Earth, flibbertigibbets with no sense of decorum. Earth moved at its own stately pace, slow to anger, but quick to action when roused.

To Earth, mankind has been chugging along for about five minutes. We could blow ourselves to Hell and back, scorch every city in a nuclear frenzy and Earth would barely take notice. Nothing mankind can do could match the fury of a fully roused Earth. Don't believe me? Ask the Javanese about Krakatoa, or the Italians about Vesuvius. Or the people in the Valdivia-Puerto Monti area of southern Chile when in 1960 the largest earthquake ever recorded devastated the region and caused tsunamis that hammered the coastline from Lebu to Puerto Aisen. In Hilo, Hawaii, waves reached thirty-five feet in height, causing sixty-one deaths, and in Honolulu, eighteen-foot waves destroyed 1600 homes and killed 185 people. Damage also resulted in Easter Island, California, Samoa, and the Philippines, and that was just Earth shrugging its shoulders.

Earth fully roused could destroy all civilization on our planet.

"It would be wrong of me to expect Earth to break its word," I said. Then an idea hit. *"What about the other buildings? Can you take me to one of them?"*

"Earth is warding all this area," came the reply. *"I cannot approach without challenge."*

Damn. Earth was a no-go. *"I thank you."*

The Elemental did not respond; instead the mound slowly shrunk until there was nothing left but a level patch of slightly disturbed soil.

All the security plus the presence of greater earth Elementals keeping others away from the buildings only cemented the fact in my mind that the *Codex Infernales* was inside the SwolTech compound.

"Okay, Mr. Deschamps," I whispered, staring at the compound. "You have an IQ of 158. You're not the sharpest knife in the drawer, but no slouch in the brain department, either. So … think this through." My eyes investigated each building with the preternatural gift of Vision. Factory with attached warehouse and loading bays, office building and labs all surrounded by an innocent-looking chain-link fence. "What about above, Mr. Smart Guy? What about above?"

Air Elementals, be they simple little Sprites or one of the big ones (called Gales) look pretty much the same: a strange displacement that shimmers slightly around the edges and bends light oddly through their beings. To normal folk, they are invisible, but to a magus who sees the world as it really is, they are as merely difficult to distinguish.

Squint, squint, squint.

Nothing. Even through my mini-binocs, I couldn't find a Sprite in the sky, which in itself was somewhat odd. Perhaps what SwolTech was hiding was underground, hence Earth Elemental defenses.

"Okay, Vernon, let's see how this all works out." I began to whistle a tune.

Actually, it was the Language of Air, a quiet summoning of low-power Sprites. All I needed was one, perhaps two at the most. Lemongrass graced the slight breeze as the Language passed my lips, indistinguishable from the rustling of leaves and a soft wind through tall grass. Soon my lips began to ache slightly, then a few minutes later started to burn. Seconds later the pain was almost too much to bear. A stubborn streak kept me going even though my lips felt like they had been dipped in battery acid. Something was blocking the Summons, a haze of magic that caused the pain radiating across my cheeks and chin.

Each language has two parts, Summoning and Denial. The latter was used to keep Elementals from being called by creating an area where Elementals cannot be Summoned. To ward against the Elements, each Language had to be used. There was nothing to stop me from Summoning Earth, but SwolTech and the surrounding area had been Denied Air.

This, more than anything, confirmed the presence of the *Codex*. Elementals don't like to be Denied—it isn't natural. All the elements exist in harmony on all areas of the planet. Even in a desert there is Water, and in the middle of the ocean there is Fire existing as heat or light. Water penetrates deeply into the earth. The surface world was designed for the balance of all the elements. For an area to be Denied of even one of the elements takes at least *three* magi with incredible talent in Elemental magic working in concert to cast a Denial, and the element affected by the spell will constantly attempt to break the magic.

Even Julian hadn't used a Denial to protect the Silver, it being an artifact so powerful that the Patron could track its emanations.

Tears formed in my eyes and streaked down my cheeks, scarring through my features in details of pain. My mouth wanted to squirm off my face as searing worms writhed through the delicate tissues of my lips. The big muscles at the corners of my jaws began to cramp, the pain streaking to the crown of my head, and a little wisp of a thought worked its way to the fore.

Quit. Stop. It was seductive, that thought.

No.

I raised the pitch on the Summoning and the lemongrass smell became stronger.

No.

My lugs began to hurt, the air rushing though my nose and grating on my nasal membranes.

No.

Each breath became a burning coal in my chest, my lungs charring from Denial, and each curl of air from my lips was a lick of flame.

No!

With a sickening *wrench* that sent a spasm of nausea through my guts, I lost the thread of magic, the Language disappearing from my lips. My head suddenly swam with dizziness and I fell to the ground, sweating and swearing, my eyes staring, unfocused, at the clouds.

Damn, but I was worn out, totally drained. My limbs felt leaden and I had the logy, head-filled-with-cotton feeling of someone rudely awoken from a deep sleep. Despair and fatigue warred within me and I continued to swear futilely.

It began as a susurrus from just beyond my weary legs pointing into the depths of the forest, a soft sound like the papery rustle of dry leaves. Too exhausted to move or utter a Word, I could only wait with fear gnawing at me as the sound grew. Was this it for me? Had my stubbornness finally undone all my sacrifices? Why had I tried to break a spell it took at least three magi to cast?

Before regret and apprehension could erode my sanity, a voice trickled into my ear like silk rendered to air. *"Thank you, Sicarius,"* it whispered. *"You have torn a small hole in the Denial and I slipped through. I await your plea."*

Air! It was Air! Relief surged through me, adding a little vigor to my body, and laughter tried to bubble up out of my lungs at the Sprite's indignant tone. *"Thank you, magnificent one, for answering my call."*

"You did rip through the Denial," it said grudgingly. *"Answering was the least that a Lord of the Skies could do."*

Gee, why did Sprites have to be such raving egomaniacs? Oh well, it made them easier to manipulate. *"It is humbling to be greeted by one such as you."* Flattery will get you everywhere.

"You crave a boon. It will be granted and one more because of your piercing of the Denial. Air owes you a debt for your deed. Forbidding Air from this place is the greatest insult that Air has suffered in a long, long time."

"Good to know, great one. There is a way you can repay part of that debt."

I WAS A BLACK BLUR RUNNING THROUGH the forest, my breath flowing evenly, steadily through my nose and mouth. The little Sprite with the big ego swirled around my shoulders, cackling in breezy glee. Trees flashed by as I let slip Avoidance, leaving the scent of industrial disinfectant in my wake. Avoidance would keep me from magical detection, but as for electronic detection, only speed and a generous helping of luck would do the trick.

Next came Strength and the smell of ammonia, followed by Vigor. My destination was rushing in close, the too-bright halogen lights hitting my shoes an instant before enveloping my black-clad body. My recon had discovered no motion detectors, but I was pretty sure cameras were everywhere and that the fence was electrified. Good thing I didn't intend on touching it.

Actually, as plans went, it sucked. I had had no idea who I could call upon to handle this kind of job. 1-800-MERCENARIES? In the past, if I needed assistance with wet work or a little industrial espionage, I'd have a large pool of Family members to call upon. Not so much anymore. I had to make do with what little I had. And the stakes were very, very high.

There are artifacts galore associated with Christianity and Judaism: The Spear of Destiny, the Ark of the Covenant, the Staff of Moses, and the Grail, to name a few. For the Sicarii, there is the Silver and the *Codex*. The Silver receives its power directly from Lucifer, Words so appalling that using them inflicts various debilitating effects upon the wielder. The *Codex*, however, is about as magical as your average tree stump. To the best of my knowledge, from what tidbits Julian fed me over the years, it contains the true history of our Family.

I know what you're saying, Mike. I can hear it as if you were right next to me, chowing down on pizza at Big Fred's. "History, schmistory," you're saying. "Nothing is worth your life."

Most times I would agree. My life is certainly worth more than a collection of sentences strung together to form paragraphs to form chapters that form books. A lot more and a bag of chips thrown in. But the *Codex* isn't any mishmash of words forming sentences, etcetera, etcetera. No, think of it as the Sicarii version of the Declaration of Independence, with a generous dollop of biblical texts, and the lost writings Count Cagliostro. But that's not all ... Julian hinted that the True Secret (note the capitols) of Yeshuda the Founder lay within the text, the mystery most cherished by the Sicarii.

Stealing the *Codex* could very well take the heart right out of the Family, like the theft of the Mona Lisa from the Louvre would shred the soul of the artistic community and permanently shame the French. Stealing the *Codex* would be second only to the destruction of the Silver in its effect upon the Family. That is, if I could ever figure out a way to destroy that deadly artifact.

All this is to say that I felt a sense of urgency, a need to act and act soon in order to cripple the Sicarii's morale. I had to steal the damn thing before Mason could move it. Now, if only I could keep myself alive long enough to do so ....

At forty feet from the fence, I felt the Sprite tense around my shoulders. It was the smallest I'd ever seen, not near buff enough to lift me bodily into the air like the one that manhandled (should I say Airhandled?) Annabeth. However, with a little help ....

Twenty feet and my Strength-enhanced legs flexed, propelling me into the air. There came a sudden tug at my armpits as the Sprite strove to carry me into the night sky, and I became airborne.

Chapter Nineteen

❧

"Good and evil are merely masks to justify doing what you wish."
—*Codex Infernales*

THE FENCE PASSED QUICKLY BENEATH MY toes as the little Sprite pulled me up and over with all its might, aided by my Strength. What would have been a three-foot vertical leap became ten, giving me two feet to spare.

Fear momentarily took control of my insides, which threatened to eject the turkey panini and fried calamari I'd eaten for dinner, but training kicked in and I kept the too-pricey food down. A second later my legs flexed, absorbing the impact of the soft compound grass as I landed at a run. Immediately the little Sprite's presence around my shoulders disappeared and blood rushed back to my armpits.

No alarm sounded. I sped on, no time to worry as I rushed toward the big office building with the heavy pack on my back bouncing against my spine. It almost hurt, but any discomfort I might have felt was overshadowed by the need to get indoors. I was on autopilot, my body moving as if of its own volition while my mind slipped into a state of peaceful stillness.

I was at the building. Although ten stories doesn't sound like much, when you're at the bottom looking up, it's bloody *intimidating.*

I knew what needed to be done. Going through the front door on the other side of the building where parking spaces surrounded the factory was out. Breaking through the doors would be loud, and the lock was undoubtedly electronic. So, the best solution was up where the windows began, on the second floor.

Time for Potion Number One. Might have to take a second if things went south.

It's always a bit dodgy to be on more than one potion at a time, unless you are an experienced brewmaster such as myself; then it becomes a matter of knowing which potion reacts ... badly with another. It wouldn't do to find yourself exploding violently because you didn't pay attention in Botanical Magic class.

In the role-playing game *Dungeons & Dragons*, if you want to fly, there is a spell for that—fairly easy one—but in the real world flying is out. Only an Air Elemental can give a body the power of flight and the little guy I'd summoned wasn't up to the task. Good thing I knew Botanical Magic better than most in the Family. So, I managed to cook up the next best thing to a Superman impersonation.

Levitation. To rise and float in the air without visible agency. Not quite flying—you're not moving anywhere except up—but it sure comes in handy. The potion was relatively easy to brew, but the mixture of eiderdown, yarrow, saffron, and mace has to be simmered in amniotic fluid for full efficacy, and that's not something you can nip off to the local drugstore for.

Tastes foul, too.

Beginning a mental countdown, I willed myself to rise and felt my feet leave the ground. Up, up, up, quicker than I would've imagined possible until I reached the second-story window. I willed myself to a halt and studied my reflection a foot from my nose. Forty-five more seconds.

Potion Number Two, but this one I didn't drink. Some potions are imbibed, some are slathered onto the skin like Vaseline, and a rare few are applied to inorganic surfaces. I flicked off the cap to the steel vial and splashed the glass in front of me.

Thirty seconds to go.

Crrrrhhhhkkkk .... Where the liquid touched the glass, a white sheen appeared as if it had been scarred by hoarfrost. The white stain spread, accompanied by a high-pitched grinding like fingernails against a chalkboard mixed with a sandy grating. It ground against my eardrums and sent the muscles at the corners of my jaws a-bunching. My eyes narrowed to slits as the false frost spread rapidly until the entire five-by-three-foot pane became the white of freshly fallen snow.

Fifteen seconds to go.

It started with a single flake, the smallest, barely visible particle that disengaged from the mass and began its slow, stately descent to the ground a dozen feet below. Within a second, the entire pale pane disintegrated into flakey drifts and bits of glass dust. I closed my eyes for a second to protect them from the irritating crumbs.

Five seconds to go. Plenty of time. Gloved hands reached through the hole and pulled my floating body inside the building. I lay there for a split second as a brief thrill of accomplishment shivered across my spine.

"Am I good or what?" I whispered.

Enough self-congratulation, time to get a move on and see what's what. Vision and Clarity were still working, and I could see the second floor was filled with cubicles, the kind office drones find themselves spending too much time in. It was neat, tidy, devoid of decoration or personalization, and completely depressing. It was the perfect Family workspace—no innovation or free thinking allowed.

Again I was reminded why I was doing this. If the Patron managed to win the Big Fight and impose his sense of what's right on the universe, this was what the planet would look like—a bunch of sterile cubicles and billions (or perhaps millions, if he decides there are too many of us scurrying about, mucking up the place) of people stuck in dead-end jobs. A world of perfect order where everything and everyone would have its assigned perfect place where no questioning or creativity was allowed. It would have the regimented order of an ant colony, and we would all be the drones, mindless workers toting that barge and lifting that bale. A tedious existence of beige sameness as each life proceeds with the perfect sterility of a freshly scrubbed surgical tool.

Our lives would be divided between working for Lucifer and being forced to praise his greatness. Each person would be required to pledge his or her soul to the Little Horn, the Dragon in the Darkness, the Beast of the Abyss … pick your moniker. No morefast track to Heaven, only the express train to Hell, a one-way ticket for everyone. With the Voice (my name for the Morningstar), there are no take-backs, no do-overs and the real hell of it, the thing that would grind each person down just a *bit* more, was the knowledge that existence was futile, that nothing would ever matter anymore. Even death would provide no peace for the Devil's subjects. Faith would the first casualty after Heaven fell.

I thought about everything I'd been taught, that God was a liar who betrayed Lucifer and exiled him to Hell in a fit of jealous rage. The Patron, the Voice, Satan, whatever you wanted to call him, had been wronged, and it was our duty as his descendants to assist him in an attempt to retake the Throne or die trying. Part of that duty was to await the coming of the Redeemer, the Anti-Christ, the vessel into which the Voice could pour his awful might. A finger puppet extended into our world.

"You know what to do," I whistled. "Please get to doing it."

"It will be done," the Sprite answered as it flowed across my shoulders and around my neck. It was time for the second phase of my plan. *"What you ask is not much. Air will still owe you a boon."*

"Good. I will collect."

A deep breath later and the Sprite was out of sight, but not out of mind. My stomach fluttered, queasy with trepidation as I considered my plan. It was risky, perhaps stupid, but great risks offer great rewards. The problem was if I was wrong, then I was seriously shit out of luck, and this would be the last day of my life.

Through the cubicle maze, I noted off-white walls as high as my sternum, each space containing a desktop computer, a scanner/printer/fax combo, IN/OUT trays, and the ever-present Swingline staplers. I envisioned myself sitting at one of these desks, typing away while staring emptily at a monitor. The lack of personal touches made each little slice of Hell even more sterile. Abandon All Hope Ye Who Work Here.

Elevators. Good. Somewhere nearby would be stairs and *there*, there it was—a plain white door with a six-inch square plastic plate on the center containing a pictogram of a man descending stairs. Nothing else, no signs, just a stick figure in white heading down into the unknown. Just where I wanted to go.

Sweat stung my eyes, but there was nothing for it but to try the door. What do you know? It was unlocked.

"No, this is not creepy at all," I whispered just as Vision gave way and the building went dark. I cursed and uttered another Vision to chase the blackness away and entered the stairwell.

Gray concrete and gray metal tube railing and stairs leading up and down. My black Converse sneakers hardly made a sound as I descended carefully, keeping a weather eye out for motion detectors or other alarms.

One flight of stairs, then two with no exits, just stairs heading for the foundations of the building. My heart beat crazily in my throat. Closer and closer to the answers I sought. Although I'd planned for what I hoped was every contingency, plans had a way of falling straight into the outhouse once enemies appeared.

Three flights and a door. The steel knob was unlocked, and I slipped through quickly and quietly. The hallway beyond was well lit by fluorescents that reflected off the blindingly white and perfectly smooth linoleum floor. Far down at the end was a door with a numeric keypad and a hand scanner. Six doors lined the long hallway, three on the right and three on the left, white rectangles marring the white finish of the walls.

I eased my way forward, each step carefully taken, my hand tight around the grip of a matte-black Glock drawn from my pack. My eyes flicked this way and that, but there were no cameras, which I found odd. Well, more than odd. Alarming, actually.

Halfway to the door at the end and my Vision and Strength faded. I muttered another Strength, ready for the rush to hit my muscles and the feeling of invincibility.

I got nothing.

Chills rippling down my spine, I tried again. Nothing, no smell of ammonia, no super strength.

Impossible. *Impossible!*

The door at the end of the hall opened. "You didn't think that I was going to let you use magic now, did you?" said Mason as he stepped through, a big shit-eating smile plastered on his handsome face. Once again he was impeccably dressed in a hideously expensive suit, pin-striped and dove gray.

"I thought this seemed a little too easy," I said quietly. "Good trap."

He smiled wider, obviously titillated.

I raised the Glock. "How did you nullify the magic?"

"Look up."

So I did. At first there was nothing but the annoyingly bright fluorescent humming away, but when I squinted, I saw a small red sigil like *pi* with a second tilde at the bottom. A small reddish-brown dot was painted in the center of the rectangle between the two tilde.

Something stung the back of my neck and my hand slapped at a hard object affixed there. I tore it free and held up a small dart.

"Oh damn," I breathed.

"Like I said, Olivier, Julian wants you alive, and alive is how you'll reach him."

With a muttered curse I collapsed.

"I HAVE TO HAND IT TO you, Mason, he fell for it like you said he would."

"Torture works well, but sometimes a bit of craft proves more effective."

"How did you know he would come here?"

My mouth was filled with cloth, and steel hoops encircled my wrists. This was all depressingly familiar. I remained still and continued listening. At least where I lay it was soft, not like the small cubby where I'd been kept last time. My sneakers were gone, but my captors had allowed me to keep my nifty black outfit.

"How could he not? His psychological profile indicates he will do whatever he can to stick a finger in Julian's eye and I left plenty of breadcrumbs. It's all in the profile. The lad just can't help himself." There was a pause and I heard heavy breathing, as if someone was exerting himself. "Truth be told, he arrived sooner than expected. He must have had help cracking the encryption."

"Either way, it's a miracle he *is* here. The smart play would have been to stay where he was and resurface later."

Mason snorted. "Then he would have missed his opportunity to grab the

Codex. No, he's young, arrogant, and foolhardy. This was the best opportunity for him, and I knew he would take it."

"Well played, then. Although we are no closer to finding the Silver. He did manage to elude you in Chicago."

"He merely moved faster than anticipated and we lost track of him. Remember, he is a more than capable magus. While nested in the bosom of the Family, he was considered to be a real up-and-comer, one to keep an eye on. The only twelve-Word magus in centuries, if you recall, Vernon." Mason paused. "Either way, I took a chance in Chicago and it paid off. After all, he is here, is he not?"

I'd heard enough. Time to get the ball rolling. My eyes cracked open, and I finally saw where I'd been deposited. It was a cell, a four-by-six painted white, with padded walls and a pallet on the floor where I lay. Bars made the far wall, also painted white, my own private jail.

On the other side stood two men staring at me as if I were a specimen in a Petri dish. Mason I knew, and the other guy with the gnarled purple/gray scar across his forehead had to be Vernon, the head of SwolTech and a member of the Twelve.

"Mumph, dglmt." Not me at my most eloquent, but I was gagged so I had an excuse. The rest of me was securely bound with cuffs chained to steel rings affixed to the bare concrete of the cell floor.

Mason's eyes glittered. "You are far too predictable, boy," he said, not taking his eyes from mine. Hate sparkled there. Hate and a good dose of anger.

Tick, tick, tick, tick, tick. Each stab of Vernon's finger against the cell's doorplate brought forth a flat metallic tone like a paperclip tapping against a steel cup. The door clicked and slid to the side.

"I am going to remove your gag, Olivier." Vernon's voice was high-pitched, almost melodic. I bet he was a terrific tenor. "In case you're tempted to use a Word or three, I suggest you look at the wall behind you."

I craned my neck and saw drawn on the sterile white of the padded wall the strange *pi*-like symbol I'd seen earlier. From a distance of six inches, I could see that it had been drawn in blood, which still looked somewhat fresh, having had not quite browned.

"What you are looking at is one of the best-kept secrets of the Family," said Vernon as he loomed over me. "Blood magic."

"Mff?" I grunted.

He smiled. "When you reach the lofty heights of the Twelve, or you have proven yourself to the Patron beyond a shadow of a doubt, you are tested for the ability to use Blood Magic." The head of SwolTech nodded toward the rune. "That is a Blood Rune, a very specific Blood Rune at that. It negates the power of the Twelve Words."

"That's different," I said, mouth dry as Vernon removed the gag. "Blood Magic? Julian's been keeping secrets." And here I thought I knew everything there was to know about the different types of magic.

Vernon's eyes were fever bright with something that looked like … lust? "It is called Blood Magic because it requires blood to empower the runes. The blood of the line of Yeshuda. Innocent blood at that."

"When it comes to Family," I spat, "there's no one who is innocent."

He smiled. It wasn't pretty.

With realization came nausea and horror. I tried not to vomit on Vernon's brown Barker's and his brown Saville Row suit. For a second I was tempted to let spew, but there was so much bile in my gut that it would have burned my vocal cords. "Children."

A nod. "Infants, actually. The most innocent blood. You have to drain one like a champagne bottle to achieve the blood's full efficacy."

I've heard some sick shit during my time in Family, but this took the cake. "You sick fucks," I said to them both through teeth clenched with disgust. "You sick, pathetic asswipes. *Infants*?"

Vernon laughed and I nearly snapped.

I looked at Mason, who stood in the doorway with arms folded, impeccably turned out in his suit, and for the first time since Burke had shot me in the back, I felt absolute hate. Blind, searing hate that started at the crown of my head and ran throughout my body like a rampaging virus. For a split second I nearly gave in to that hate, let it consume me like Lucifer's hate had consumed him. How sweet it would be to destroy Vernon, rip his head off, play in his fountaining blood, and revel in his death.

But that way lay damnation. More damnation, actually. My soul has plenty of stains, thankyouverymuch.

"You are going to die, Vernon. Very soon," I ground out as I flogged my rising temper into submission.

"Doubtful," he replied calmly, still staring at me like a garden snake stares at a mouse. "You fell for Mason's little trap. We couldn't track you to where you lay your head at night, so we'll have to try torture once again."

"Mason," I said, dismissing Vernon as irrelevant, "you eased up on the drugs in Chicago, allowing me to escape just to track me to where I live. You took a heck of a chance."

Vernon's scar flushed a deeper purple and he stood, striding past Mason to take up a stand next to the exit, another door with an electronic keypad. Mason shook his head. "I learned much about you while subjecting you to torture. You said quite a bit, although not enough to reveal your new home or where you hid the Silver." His smile held no warmth. "You've developed an aversion to killing, which made the prospect of letting you escape less onerous. The only thing I did not take into account was Annabeth's desire for your death. She nearly killed you and that would have been quite embarrassing.

"There was a high probability you would search for your possessions, which I conveniently left in my room, along with my laptop and the Tablet of Cain." He laughed at the startled look on my face. "Yes, I know all about the tablet. It's depressingly easy; all you have to do is touch it while staring at the writing. It came to me that you wouldn't pass up a chance to steal it, so I placed it next to my laptop in an attempt to lure you into a twofer. With the tablet you could break the encryption, or you would do it yourself; it wasn't that complex."

"Complex enough," I stated flatly.

"But you had the tablet and you took the bait, coming here to Seattle to infiltrate SwolTech."

I nodded.

"There you go, then. All tied up in a bow. The only glitch was not finding the potion you used in Chicago. That did put a spanner in the works, but thanks be to the Patron, you still came back to me. Now you have no potion, no Words, no magic to help you escape."

"Let me guess. In Chicago you had hidden cameras recording everything, all my movements."

"Yes."

"Two questions, if you don't mind, before you start torturing me again."

"Enough of this twaddle!" Vernon shouted, the sound partially absorbed by the padding on the walls. "The sooner we start, the sooner it will be done."

Mason raised a hand. "Patience. I've a mind to grant the boy's request."

I dove in, not wanting him to change his mind. "First, why the electroshock? You could have used Blood Magic to keep me from using Words."

He shrugged while Vernon made a rude noise. "No access to Blood Magic. I'm not a practitioner. Nor did I have access to a supply of Sicarii infants, for that matter."

So offhand, so casual about the murder of children. I had decided to let him live. Not anymore. "And I don't suppose the *Codex* is actually here, is it?"

He hesitated before answering, weighing his words. "Yes, as a matter of fact. Close by, on the other side of yon door. It is Vernon's turn to safeguard our Family history and secrets, including the runes used in Blood Magic."

I laughed derisively. "Wasn't sure you would risk it like that. What if I'd succeeded in sneaking in?"

My laughter was met by his, Mason's clinical expression finally giving way to genuine mirth. We both continued to laugh for a while, but it was Mason who stopped first as he realized that my humor was genuine, not bitter or ironic. He shook his head, dismissing my words.

Ribs beginning to ache, I stifled my laughter enough to squeeze out a few words. "Earlier you called *me* arrogant for attempting this, but in *your* own arrogance you failed to realize one important thing."

Mason replied, "What?" just as Vernon's leaped forward. No slouch that one; he knew something unpleasant was about to happen.

"I knew this was a trap." The last word was a cough as the Sprite that had been nestling in my lungs burst free. My whistle directed it at Vernon, who raised his hands in a warding gesture, but to a creature composed of Air, flesh was hardly a barrier. It flowed through and past fingers and slid into Vernon's nostrils.

The effect was immediate and rather drastic. Back arching, Vernon stood on his tippy-toes and whirled around as if suspended by wires, his face becoming mottled and bloated with fearsome internal pressures. Capillaries around his nose and lips bulged obscenely and burst, flooding his countenance with scarlet pain. Abruptly, he stopped his mad twirling and stood there, balancing on the toes of his expensive dress shoes, eyes rolled back, exposing quickly reddening whites. With soft *pops*, both orbs burst from his skull and I was sprayed with aqueous humor. A yellowish blob of tissue bounced off my forehead and onto the floor. It was roughly 10mm in diameter, ellipsoid and biconvex in shape, and I realized I was looking at the lens from Vernon's eye.

Yeah, that was gross.

"To the other one," I whistled. "Don't kill him yet."

The Sprite exited Vernon's corpse, which collapsed into an eyeless heap—blood, bile and bits of tissue dribbling from his mouth. Before the stunned Mason could blink, the Elemental slipped between his teeth and entered his lungs. He immediately began to hack and cough.

"You know," I began as Mason sagged to his knees. "It was obvious that this mess was a trap. I mean really, dude, leaving the tablet next to your laptop? How gullible do you think I am? For a Family as paranoid as ours, that was your biggest mistake, not to mention having Burke leave us two alone." I reached two fingers into my mouth and felt around a back molar. *There*, a bit of string tied around the tooth, one end vanishing down my gullet.

Carefully tugging on the thick thread, I felt a response from inside my gut, a wormy, slithering feeling as something began its journey upwards. My fingers left my mouth, dragging with them the thread and a hard object rubbed against the flap of my throat. I had to repress the gag reflex. Still, a tiny amount of bile flooded my tongue, along with a small metallic cylinder. I spat it out into my waiting palm.

"See?" I remarked, holding up the tiny vial. Mason didn't seem that interested, as he was spending most of his time not choking to death. "I reckoned you'd search me, but not perform an X-ray. Holding a vial in your gut by a string is not something one of our Family would think of. Not dignified."

I unscrewed the cap on the little vial and downed the contents.

Oh, that felt so *good*. Strength flooded my tissues, and the cuffs around my wrists and ankles became so much junk jewelry as my suddenly amped body tore them apart.

"That Blood Magic may work on Words, but it doesn't do diddly-squat against Botanical Magic." I stretched, reveling in the feeling. "You see, I took an anti-drug potion before I leapt the fence, a little cocktail of avens, horseradish, parsley, and peppermint that kept the drug in the dart you shot me with from taking effect. I've been awake the entire time."

I knelt next to the thrashing Mason, easily capturing his flailing arms. *"Please leave his body, oh mighty one."*

The Sprite reappeared, to my unveiled eyes appearing like misty vapor from Mason's mouth. He gasped and inhaled madly, desperate for more oxygen to feed his starved tissues.

"You did not allow me to take his life," said the Sprite, sounding peeved.

"I believe you killed one of the magi who crafted the Denial," I replied, pointing to Vernon's mottled corpse. *"Your service is no longer needed. I thank you."*

The little Sprite floated to a point some six inches from my eyes. *"The Denial was a serious offense."* For the first time I heard a grave note in the voice of a Sprite. It blinked at me with airy eyes. *"Air still has not repaid you for tearing a hole in that foul magic. Soon greater ones will come to tear it apart completely. Yet a debt is owed and must be paid."*

"You owe me nothing."

"That is false. Debts must be paid. Ask for another boon and Air will grant it."

What more could I ask of the little guy? He'd already nestled in my lungs so I could sneak him in, my secret weapon. I was pretty sure that a magus wasn't going to check my chest cavity for Elemental smuggling. *"Then I will wait to ask, as I need nothing at this moment. I will collect what is owed in the future."*

An vaporous scowl marred the Sprite's *face. "I mislike waiting, but it will be as you say, young Sicarius. Farewell then."*

And like *that* the little Elemental was gone, quick as a wink.

"You know, Mason," I drawled, "you fell for one of the classic blunders, the first being 'never fight a land war in Asia.' "

He stared at me with panicked incomprehension.

"No? Not even a hint? That's a great movie reference, one of the best. Rent *The Princess Bride* sometime. Do you have a Blockbuster membership?" I leaned in so all he could see were my hard brown eyes. "The second blunder is failing to realize there is always someone sneakier and cleverer than you." I poked him in the chest. "*That* you should have learned while growing up." *Poke, poke, poke.* "Now, is the *Codex* nearby?"

No answer, just a malevolent stare.

"You may fear Julian, Mason, but you should fear me more. Much more." I spoke softly, using a soothing voice designed to relax the listener. "Tell me and you will live. Heck, Julian might not even kill you. He may cast you from the Twelve, but you'll be living when he does so. I am asking again ... is the *Codex* near this room?"

Still more staring.

"Mason," I said reprovingly, "if you don't tell me, I will slowly twist your head around a full three hundred sixty degrees. However, I give you my word that you will leave this building alive if you talk. Now, is the *Codex* nearby?"

"Yes." It looked like the admission hurt.

"Wonderful. Close by?"

A nod.

"Where?"

A long pause while he stared at me, measuring my intent. "Three doors down on the left."

I leaned in, squeezing his shoulders just enough for him to wince. "More."

"A safe behind the bookcase," he grunted. "Vernon had the combination."

All I needed. "Thank you, Mason. Like I promised, I won't kill you."

I broke his legs.

And his arms.

Hey, Mike, at least I didn't kill him, but I sure as heck didn't need him to raise the alarm. When the screaming was over and he lay sprawled semi-conscious upon the floor, I searched him and Vernon for weapons. I retrieved two pistols and my wallet (with fake ID, of course) and tried on both pairs of shoes the men weren't using at that moment. Mason's pinched something awful and Vernon had the tiniest feet I'd ever seen on a man that big. Briefly, I wondered about the old adage about the relationship between the size of one's feet and the size of the twigs-and-berries, but I wasn't eager to find out. Instead, I settled on being shoeless Jude Oliver for the rest of the night and headed out to find the *Codex*.

Chapter Twenty

"Birth is pain, life is pain, everything is pain. When this truth is truly accepted, the scales fall from the eyes."
—*Codex Infernales*

No door could withstand the magical strength that flowed through my body, and that included the door to the little annex I shared with Vernon and Mason. While the former just lay there leaking vital fluids, the latter writhed with a slightly used gag immobilizing his tongue. I reminded myself to send help … eventually.

One door, two, then three doors down. They all looked the same—white with electronic keypads straight out of an old sci-fi movie where everything is so sterile that a single germ would die of loneliness. There was nothing special about the third door, no plastic plaques bearing Vernon's name in Times New Roman font or any other sort of identification. Just a white door that looked like all the others.

A good, old-fashioned kick sent the door flying inward, and only my magically enhanced reflexes allowed me to avoid having my head blown off. As the door banged open, I caught a glimpse of a pump-action shotgun five feet away, and my hyper-speed kicked in. The gun went *boom!* and I performed my best imitation of the Flash. The door banged against the inside wall and rebounded, briefly cutting the assassin and me off from each other. Good thing, too, as I was busy hugging the floor and contemplating my next move.

Said move turned out to be diving through the door before the shotgun wielder could come through and cut me in half. My shoulder hit the door low and the door hit the assassin high, flinging him back and sending the shotgun flying across the room. Score one for the good guys. Well, the *better* guys. Not too sure if I qualified as 'good' yet, but I was trying.

I landed in a tuck-and-roll just as the potion's effects wore off. All of a sudden I was human again, with all the human weaknesses and frailties I was born with. Gone was the sense of potion-granted invincibility and cockiness that comes with great power. Being normal sucked, and the timing couldn't have been worse. I managed to stop in a crouch next to the desk, aiming one of the pistols that had been tucked into my waistband, a Desert Eagle—a little over-the-top for my tastes.

Soft, deep-green rug over hardwood floor. A desk with a Tiffany lamp and bookshelves behind an overstuffed office chair. The images hit my eyes, but at the time, I was assessing them purely for their value as objects that could be used for my defense. The shotgun was nowhere in sight.

An all-too-familiar voice spouted from the man rising to his feet. "You still remember your training, boy."

I felt my balls start to shrivel. *Sarge.*

Sarge was the Family wet-work instructor and a prolific serial killer. With a body count of over three hundred, he maintained his freedom from the authorities by exerting iron control over his base desires and never choosing a particular "type" of person for his next victim. He also never took trophies, never collected anything that could tie him to a murder, all of which ran contrary to the normal pathology. Of course, nothing about Sarge was normal. He looked like a kindly grandfather, avuncular and wise, proof that looks can be deceiving.

And there he stood, all five feet eight of him, grayed and gnarled, not looking a day over sixty-five, but fit and trim and lethal as hell. He was the best of the best, able to kill, gut, and clean a person in less than five minutes. His weapon was pointed in my direction, the barrel so wide in my eyes that it looked like a tunnel straight to Hell.

I went for Vigor, then Strength, but nothing happened. I risked a quick look but saw no Blood Runes.

Sarge caught my hasty search and knew exactly what my eyes quested for. "Blood magic has been cast throughout this level of the facility." He raised his arms and his smile sent a shiver down my spine. "I was asked to remain here in case you escaped, an event Mason thought unlikely, more fool him." A stubby finger pointed to a spot next to the door. A flat-panel monitor mounted on the wall showed Mason twitching feebly on the floor of the jail room. Sarge had been watching all this time and waiting for me to arrive so he could cut me in half with the shotgun.

"I hope it was entertaining." It was a miracle the words were comprehensible because my mouth was dry as dust. I feared Burke (although I'd never tell him that) but Sarge scared me spitless. Even at his age, he was more than a match for any one Sicarius, and even Boris, Julian's bodyguard, would hesitate before tangling with the likes of Sarge.

"That it was, boy," replied Julian's favorite psychopath with his terrible smile. "Now let us finish this, man to man. Drop your weapon."

That sounded so ludicrous I almost laughed. "We seem to be at an impasse, Sarge, because what's to stop you from plugging me the second this weapon hits the floor? Not that I don't trust you, but you haven't been a successful killer for the past forty years by taking unnecessary risks."

"Boy, I once sliced off a woman's tits, cooked them with a bit of olive oil and basil, and force-fed them to her husband, but not once have I lied, not even to my victims. I may be a monster, but I'm a truthful one." His eyes shone oddly. "So if I tell you I will not shoot you if you disarm yourself, you can take that to the *bank*."

Strangely enough, I believed him. I'd known Sarge for years and couldn't recall a single instance where he'd fibbed. If he gave his word, it would be set in bedrock. "So tell me then, Sarge. Give me your word."

Laughter like sandpaper over raw flesh hit my ears. "Very good, Olivier." Gone was the contemptuous *boy* appellation. "I give you my word that once you are disarmed, I will lay my weapon on the desk. Julian will reward me handsomely for returning you only slightly damaged."

I studied his face. All planes and angles with only the hint of softness provided by advancing years. There was cruelty there, if you looked closely, and a seething madness kept tightly reined. It smoldered deep within those gray-blue eyes, a hot mess of insanity bubbling and ready to burst forth and spew molten lunacy the second he lost control. Sadism and paranoia, loathing and an almost demonic fury—it was all there if you knew what to look for, and I'd known Sarge long enough. Too long, actually.

Fear of Sarge warred with my fear of finally landing in Julian's clutches, because no matter how tough you are, how noble your intentions and how great your faith is in a higher power, everybody breaks eventually. The human body and mind can't cope with mankind's torturous inventiveness. I knew that if Sarge managed to best me (which was likely) then Julian or Boris or even Sarge himself would eventually make me talk. They would recover the Silver and you'd die, Mike, and I wasn't about to let that happen. No way, no how.

Not moving my eyes from his, I carefully set the big gun on the desk next to the blotter, just under the Tiffany lamp.

Sarge took a step closer. "The other one. I saw you take two."

Damn. He chuckled at the dismay on my face, the wind from his mouth barely stirring his neatly trimmed gray moustache. I reached for the second pistol tucked in the small of my back, a 9mm Glock, much more my style. It *thunked* heavily next to the big .44 and I sighed, half expecting Sarge to shoot me in the kneecap. Disabling, but not fatal.

"Take a step back," he urged. When I did, he reached over and opened the center desk drawer, sweeping my two pistols inside. He laid his inside as well before shutting the drawer. "Now, Olivier, let's see what's what. Care to take a shot at the title?"

I was fast, fast as I'd ever been while not magically enhanced and my fist came nowhere near to striking his face. All he did was move his shoulders a fraction and my jab hit air.

"You'll have to do better than that," he taunted, reaching behind his back and drawing forth a knife.

And, oh, what a knife! Long and curved, fat at the pointy end and thin where it met the handle, it was eighteen inches of razor-sharp lethality. Made famous by the Gurkha soldiers of Nepal, it was both a chopper and a slicer, and judging by the size of the monster, it could hack through a man's neck with one swing. I personally didn't want to be that man.

My stomach felt queasy. "Thought you were going to bring me in only slightly damaged?"

"*Slightly* is a relative term," he remarked with a wicked grin. "But I do plan on bringing you in alive."

Joy, oh joy. Images of me pummeled into a human pillow flared through my mind just as the kukri leapt forward.

Ouch and dammit! My black shirt now sported a long, thin slice with a bit of red leaking into the cloth. It wasn't deep, but it bled and I'd hardly seen the man *move.*

Adrenaline pumped through my veins in reaction to the fear that flushed through me. My skin pebbled and my hair felt like it was standing on end as every nerve and fiber became hypersensitive.

The knife flashed again, but I wasn't there to greet it. Instead I leapt to the side, my arm swinging, palm hitting the Tiffany lamp. It flew off the desk and hit Sarge square in the face with a solid *thud,* accompanied by the tinkling sound of breaking glass. Blood spurted from the older man's nose as he swept the kukri back and forth wildly in an effort to keep me at bay.

"Good one," he gurgled painfully, eyes watering. In another hour he'd be doing an impression of a raccoon. "Won't happen again."

I believed him. Instead of answering, I stepped in with a sweeping hand in an attempt to grab his knife arm, but Sarge hopped nimbly away, weaving the kukri in a figure eight.

Blood ran steadily from his nose across lips and down chin to drip, drip, drip on the seriously expensive green throw rug. He ran a hand across the flow, smearing blood across his face and staining one cheek and the corner of his eye.

"Your nose is going to look like a mangled potato soon there, Sarge," I taunted in an effort to tamp the fear back down into a dark, distant place.

Sarge gifted me with a crimson smile. "Not going to work, boy. I've had better men than you try to get my goat, so don't bother."

My reply was another jab that earned me a shallow slice across my left forearm. It was instantly followed up with a short stab in the right pec and another shallow cut, but this time to the left shoulder.

The crazy was starting to leak out onto Sarge's face as the smell of my blood reached his nostrils. It excited him, ate at his carefully crafted will and discipline, and that translated to a slight tremble in his hands along with a tic at the corner of his eye. A pink tip of tongue flicked out and lapped at the blood oozing from his nose.

As we dodged and wove around each other, striking and blocking so fast that the eye could hardly follow, I realized that, although I was a pretty damn good martial artist, Sarge had me beat cold. Another cut, this one to the ribs, deep enough to grate against bone, punctuated that fact.

I blocked a savage chop that would've buried the knife deep into my shoulder and landed an overhand right to the cheek that sent needles of pain through my fingers. I danced back before he could bury the kukri in my chest, but his stiffened fingers struck my throat, causing me to gag as a numbness that stopped the breath in my lungs radiated from the affected area.

White light exploded against my cheekbone, and a searing line erupted across my chest, running from right shoulder to left hip. Hardwood met the back of my skull with stunning force. Harsh reds and yellows replaced the white as stars pinwheeled across my eyes and lethargy gripped my flesh in cottony talons.

The world was beginning to fade and lose cohesion as my mind circled the drain. It was almost peaceful, relaxing. I could just let go and everything would stop hurting. The hot wetness leaking from my skin would cease to bother me and the sting of parted flesh would dwindle down to nothing. *Nothing* sounded pretty damn good to me, and I *reached* for it, the center of the maelstrom in my mind, the eye of my psyche's storm. When I hit that eye, I would cease and it would all go away. *Nighty night.*

Or not. The voice that pierced the whirling storm in my head seemed to anchor me to painful reality, and that really sucked because reality *hurt.* "No, you don't, Olivier, not now." A harsh chemical smell invaded my nostrils and caused my eyes to sting.

"That's it, come on back now. You put up quite a fight. Took me by surprise with that lamp. Good move. I haven't been startled like that in a long time."

What the flying fuck was he talking about? I needed to go bye-bye and he was yammering on about lamps. My eyelids fluttered and light pierced my eyeballs. *Ouch.*

"There you go, Olivier, there you go." A palm made of velvet-covered granite slapped my cheek. "Wake up, soldier. Time to answer some questions."

I moved, or thought I did, but my body felt encased in wet cotton. Something stung my fingers. Something small and hard and sharp as hell. I felt more of my precious bodily fluids ooze from the fresh slices in my fingertips.

Let me tell you about the advantages of a private education in the Family versus American public schooling … nix that, there are too many to go into now. Let's just say that I instantly knew, thanks to Geology that was pounded into my skull at age eight, the potential of the glass shard that lay under my fingers.

Glass is an amorphous solid, lacking long-range order in its atomic structure; instead there is local (or short) order with the tetrahedral structure of oxygen atoms around the silicon atoms. What does this mean? It means that if you ever felt an obsidian blade, you'd know that glass can be shaped, or broken, into incredibly sharp edges that put the finest scalpel to shame.

The glass bit that sliced my fingertips was *that* sharp, having drawn blood with only the slightest pressure.

All this normally wouldn't have even traveled the painful route to my conscious mind thanks to the severity of the thrashing inflicted upon me, but Geology had been my younger self's favorite subject (next to Botanical Magic). Months of devouring texts on the subject gave me an almost reflexive recall, and that recall pierced the fuzziness of a mind not quite in tune with reality.

Another slap from the velvet-covered granite palm, this time harder. It stung fiercely, bringing heat to my cheek. "Wake up, Olivier," Sarge barked in his command voice. "You and I have much to discuss."

What was with the hitting? Seemed like everyone kept wanting to take a chunk out of me. Slowly I began to fight against the maelstrom. Pain and Sarge's insistent voice provided the anchor points for my wandering mind. A slight sting on my fingertips and I knew I'd cut myself yet again.

"Come on!"

My eyelids cracked a fraction, just enough to let in the sight of Sarge staring down at me with moustache bristling and the deep lines at the corners of his eyes furrowing further. He looked pissed.

Fingers slick with blood latched on tight to the sliver of keen glass, and I held on to the texture, the sting of the shard, using it to further focus my mind until I was almost fully back. I let my eyes open a tiny bit more, enough for Sarge to notice, and he smiled, seeming to relax a fraction.

That was enough for me. My arm shot up and out and I swiped my fingertips at the old man, brushing across his throat in a move that was far faster than I'd thought possible.

Sarge bolted upright with such force he knocked the desk over in his attempt to regain his feet. His face, twisted in shock, became paper white as a small pink line appeared against the wrinkled wattle of his throat. That pink line suddenly burst open wide to release a sharp spray of red that jetted across the air before subsiding to a trickle that once again became a ferocious stream.

Hands flying to his throat in a futile attempt to halt the arterial spray, Sarge glared his hate at me. I could feel the heat of it scorch my skin. In those eyes were the lives of all those he had devoured over forty years as a predator—every life he'd snuffed out screamed from those washed-out orbs—and I fancied I could hear his soul shriek as he caught a look at what waited for him on the other side. He died with a face full of fear.

"Ouch," I groaned, eyes blurry with pain. Electric currents of agony were radiating from each spot on my body that had been subjected to Sarge's fist, and blood still flowed from cuts both shallow and deep. All I could smell was blood, metallic and musky. I knew I had to patch myself up or the game would be over and the next thing to happen to me would be a flight to Geneva to meet dear old poppa Julian.

Using the overturned desk for leverage, I muscled myself upright, leaving red handprints on mahogany. As I became unsteadily vertical, my eyes spied a reddish-brown something scrawled onto the underside of the desk, on the central desk drawer.

It was a rune.

Without even thinking about it, I punched it dead center, driving splinters into my knuckles. The reaction was *not* what I expected and incredibly painful. An explosion is defined as a violent release of energy resulting from a rapid chemical or nuclear reaction. Simple, huh? When you watch the old footage of the first nuclear tests on water, you can *see* the pressure wave radiating out from the center as water is instantly turned into steam. What happened when I destroyed the rune wasn't quite so intense, but my body sure as hell didn't know that.

It wasn't noise nor was it a pressure wave exactly, but a relentless force of nature, like gravity, that flung me back, clipping the doorjamb on the way out, breaking my femur with a loud *crack*. Of course I didn't hear it, in that I was busy being flung about like a rag doll in the hands of a five-year-old on a sugar high.

Face hit hall wall, then linoleum, and I tasted blood—well, *more* blood.

For a few seconds it was lights out.

Chapter Twenty-One

~

"Revenge is good only if you live to enjoy it."
—*Codex Infernales*

Jangling alarms brought me out of my near-coma, a jarring, metallic *breep, breep, breep* so annoying and high-pitched that I'm pretty sure it irritated dogs all the way to Delaware.

My eyes were gummy with drying blood, my face slick with sweat and snot. I fancied I could see my reflection on the highly polished linoleum, although a widening pool of blood obscured much of it. The gears of my mind churned, slipped, then caught again, rumbling and rattling before engaging fully.

Time for an assessment: left leg a goner and my right arm no better. Both felt like ground glass had been thrust under the skin deep into the meat of the muscle, shredding my nerves. Every twitch was a stab, and every breath sent pulses of agony from shoulder to neck to back and down along my spine to lodge in my lumbar vertebrae. I'd been shot, pummeled, electrocuted, waterboarded, and tossed about like a crazed schnauzer's chew toy, but this flesh-tearing, bone-splintering, nails-through-the-eyeballs agony left all the rest in the dust.

Without my even realizing it, Healing popped right out of my mouth, low and croaking, the Word bouncing past my teeth, flung by my tongue out into the hallway.

The effect was immediate and not a little brutal. In fact, it felt like French-kissing a light socket while lying in a tub of salt water. My damaged arm suddenly popped back into its socket with a heavy *crunch* and my leg straightened, the jagged ends of my femur grinding together before hastily remodeling.

Again with a Healing, this time louder, my voice echoing as I put more will into the Word. Sliced skin knit at blazing speed, running together like melting wax before healing smooth and scarless.

I was upright, though a little wobbly, not to mention dizzy and nauseated. Moving gingerly, I took two precarious steps toward the doorway without falling on my face. Now I was better able to assess the damage the explosion had caused.

Nada. Okay, that was more than a little confusing. Then I took a moment, leaning against the doorjamb for support, to consider the situation. Fist into wood ... rune splintering ... white light and incredible force. All the classic signs of an explosion like that of, say, plastique.

Except it wasn't. Take Semtex, for example. When detonated, the blast wave travels at a rate of roughly 1700 feet per second, which is plenty to jelly any person foolish enough to be standing close when the thing cooks off. If the desk had been wired with plastic explosives, the blast wave should have ripped my arm out of the socket instead of dislocating my shoulder. The second and far more pertinent result would have been that my internal organs should have burst like water balloons dropped off the Sears Tower. *Ker-splat!*

I should've been deader than dead. Deader than Disco, as you like to say, Mike, but I wasn't. Thanks to Healing, I was fit as a fiddle, if a bit tired from being pummeled and then exploded. Even though my brain was jumbled, I tried to puzzle my way through the destruction of the rune. I closed my eyes and pictured my fist striking the desk, which had been an almost reflexive action, the secret to Blood Magic still a horror in my mind. I'd wanted to wipe that rune off the face of the earth, erase the evidence of innocents sacrificed for the Family's ambition.

White light had emerged from the fractured, splintering wood, the rune flash so intense I was blinded even through closed lids. I was picked up, almost gently, but my right arm was violently pulled from the socket. The pain hadn't registered—there was already too much stimulation and it overloaded my merely human senses as my brain desperately tried to impose a sense of order.

I remembered flying back and my leg hitting the doorjamb as I was flung through, the terrible crunch of bone failing. I hadn't felt the pain of that, either. The irresistible force continued to push me into the hall and I hit the wall ... hard, but not hard enough to imbed into drywall. Why not? I squeezed my eyes shut tighter in an effort to recall each instant of the ordeal.

Rewind .... Fist hits wood, wood becomes an explosive device, and I am propelled through the air as if tossed by a giant. Rewind again, hit play, fist connects to rune and it all happens again.

Nothing. No explanation of why the force of the exploding rune didn't kill me and left the office intact. Maybe magic detonations are ... softer than chemical.

Breep, breep, breep.

Right. The alarm. Guards might be on their way. First things first: the bookcase. It wasn't screwed into the wall, in fact it slid to the side rather easily, exposing a medium-sized wall safe about five feet from the floor. No electronic keypad, just a dial and a lever. Right. Since I didn't have the combination and Vernon wasn't about to tell anyone anything for the rest of forever, I blasted out a Strength and gave the lever a good, solid yank.

The handle didn't budge and neither did the door, but the safe sure made itself known as drywall and wood splintered and tore apart, practically dumping itself into my lap. Thank goodness for Strength or I would've dropped it and broken every bone in my foot. As it was, the wall released the safe so suddenly, I nearly let go and let it sail out the door into the hallway. Bits of two-by-four and sheetrock were attached to the safe by long screws.

"Shoot," I muttered. "Don't have time for this nonsense." I stared at the safe in my hand. "They should've used union labor to install this thing."

Sighing, I exited the office, the safe in one hand and the recovered pistol in the other, ears perked for security, puzzled by the fact I hadn't seen them yet.

Sometime later, at the building's main floor, I found out why security was suspiciously absent. I cast Vision so I could see and when I exited the front doors I got an eyeful.

Air Elementals, from Sprites to Gales and all in between, were *everywhere*, flying in a frenzy of airy destruction. Gone were the halogen lights and most of the windows as well, although the Sprites were doing their level best to put paid to what glass still remained whole. In my magical sight I saw an Elemental the size of a house, one of the biggest Gales I'd ever seen, pick up a man in uniform, a security guard, and casually rip him in half as if he were made of tissue paper.

"*It is glorious, is it not, Sicarius?*" said a familiar voice. "*The Denial is broken and Air teaches those responsible never to attempt such a thing again.*"

"It is ... something," I replied, shocked at the violence. A medium-sized Air Elemental burst from the factory in a shower of concrete, and a good section of the wall collapsed. The Denial was obviously history and probably had been the second I had the Sprite kill Vernon, since Mason possessed no ability at Elemental Magic. The violence in the movements of the Elementals was more eloquent than any story.

"*Away with you, little one,*" said a voice I could feel in my bowels. It was the rush of air through an empty house and the deep roar of a tornado, albeit a little toned down. "*I will have words with the Sicarius.*"

"I am no longer one of the Sicarii," I responded automatically, turning to see the mother of all Gales loom over me. It could have used the office building as a footstool and the factory as a doormat. My neck craned back, my eyes tracking up, up and even farther up. Before my vertebrae popped I finally saw the top of the Elemental, saw the immensity of the Gale and I was in *awe.*

Imagine a tornado given … a personality, a fierce will and a purpose as well. Give it a, well, not a head exactly, but a wide, flattish spot near the top where the force of its gaze can be felt against your skin as a subtle pressure like sunlight, only cool and somehow threatening.

"Of the Sicarii you were and of them you remain," it said. *"And a great debt is owed. Air knows that it was you who were responsible for removing the Denial and Air must repay that debt."*

"You owe me nothing. The Sprite has repaid any debt. You owe me nothing."

Its disapproval hammered against my skin and I tried not to flinch. *"That is not so. The Elements were made by the Creator to exist in harmony, everything in balance. Fire, Earth, Air, and Water, each has its place in the rhythm of the world. Denials are a grave insult because they create imbalance by forbidding that which belongs. If Air cannot flow, even over such a small area such as this place, that imbalance threatens the greater balance, which can have drastic consequences for the whole."*

Chaos theory. The Gale was speaking of highly sensitive initial conditions, which can widely affect and yield broadly different outcomes on larger-scale systems. It's commonly known as the *Butterfly Effect.* A butterfly flaps its wings in China and a week later there is hurricane in the Gulf. If I was reading the large tower of sentient Air correctly, a Denial could have that same effect, only so much worse.

That thought was more than daunting, it was terrifying and implied that Elementals had a broader effect on our world than we had ever imagined. It was a measure of the Family's arrogance that they never inquired about such a thing. Said something about mine as well.

"I did not know that."

"It is so. Now … Air owes a debt and debts must be paid. What would you request of Air?"

Good question. I glanced at the safe in my hand. Strength would fade soon, and the increasing strain of carrying it would mean I'd have to cast another very soon. Once again craning my neck back, I said, *"I could use a lift."*

I KNEW AIR ELEMENTALS WERE FAST, BUT damn, that Gale had me back in Omaha in a matter of hours, just before sunup. It was a smooth ride all the way with the Gale keeping me warm and comfy and hauling the safe along as well. Wrapped in a toasty cocoon of air, I even managed to doze along the way. The only thing missing was the bonus miles on my credit card.

"Air still owes a debt," said the Elemental as he dropped me off in my backyard. The sun was a promise in the eastern sky and I hoped no neighbor of mine was awake or they'd get an eyeful of me doing a Superman impression.

"You have done so much, but I will call if needs be," I replied.

"Fare thee well, young Sicarius. Know that Air holds you in the highest regard."

AND THAT'S THAT, MIKE. MY STORY in a nutshell. Although the incidents in Chicago and Seattle happened many years ago, it still feels like yesterday. The pain of my encounters with Mason, Vernon, and Burke are still fresh in my mind.

Of course, the *Codex* was in the safe, the ancient wooden box somewhat battered but whole. Of course, I used Cain's tablet translate the *Codex*, which is some seriously strange reading. Some of the ancient idioms and metaphors, being so culturally obsolete, don't translate worth beans so I added my own equivalents. As for Blood Magic, I didn't bother with that section of the text. Instead, I burned it. I am under no illusion that destroying the passages dealing with Blood Magic will end the practice; if I know Julian, he has his own copy.

Should you decide to read it, the *Codex* will shock to your core and challenge your worldview. It sure had that effect on me, but you are made of sterner stuff, my friend. In the past decade you have taken me under your wing and showed me a world much wider than I could have imaged. I only hope that I haven't killed you.

Why did I send you the *Codex*? Easy … I trust you. Destroy it, keep it, use it to wrap fish in, I don't care. Your judgment over this past decade has been indisputable (except for your tendency to pick up strays such as *moi*) and I know you will do the right thing, make the right choices.

Timshel, right?

Thou mayest.

Jude Oliver, 2008

Chapter Twenty-Two

"And ye shall know the truth, and the truth shall make you free."
—John 8:32

I SAT THERE IN THAT LITTLE ROOM, surrounded by unseeing, ochre skulls, heartsick and profoundly lonely, the pages of Morgan/Jude's manuscript falling from numb fingers to litter the floor like leaves of a dying tree. Tears I hadn't been aware of while reading dripped from my chin, and I wiped at them absently, lost in thoughts that swirled sluggishly in my head.

It took a goodly while for me to realize I was mired in self-pity, an emotional state I'm not prone to, but fatigue, stress, and emotional overload has a way of taking the starch out of your shorts quick-like. I missed Morgan, and instead of being happy that he was in a better place (I truly believe he'd earned the right to ascend to Heaven), I felt sad because he wasn't here.

"Don't be so pathetic, Ranger," I muttered, feeling the first faint threads of anger at the edge of my mind. The younger version of myself would've kicked my butt for such maudlin, self-absorbed reflection. "Snap out of it."

Easier said than done, but a good way to wash away sorrow is to take a long shower so hot that skin tries to crawl off bones. At least, that's what my mom always said. Memories of mom were hazy; the only clear ones were the times she comforted me or offered a pithy saying. Her favorite was the old chestnut about finishing your food because there were kids starving in China. At one point I'd replied that I'd like to join them if it meant not eating her famous, or infamous, risotto. That earned me a cuff to the ear and no allowance for a month. Not my finest moment.

I stank to high heaven, perhaps literally, thanks to an action-packed day of almost getting killed, so I exited the little skull room through one of the hidden doors and entered a bedroom filled nearly wall to wall with a queen-sized pillow-top bed and an oak armoire. This room had skull walls as well. Briefly I wondered how Cain expected me to sleep with all those empty sockets staring at me when the lights were out. I imagined bony jaws opening wide and fey lights shining through empty sockets, but realized that if a body is tired enough to easily sleep in front of a live audience, a dead one would be a snap.

Fortunately, the bathroom shone white with small ceramic tile instead of bone, which eased my mind somewhat. It held a toilet and bidet (never used one, wasn't about to try), a marble sink, a medicine cabinet filled with all sorts of handy prescription products ranging from painkillers to sleep aids, and a glass shower stall.

Just what the doctor ordered for shoulders with muscles knotted so tight it felt like there was gravel stuck under my skin. There were even some nice, white, fluffy towels labeled HAMPSTEAD HOTELS ready to dry my worn-out body. Within a minute I was down to my birthday suit, luxuriating under water so hot that my skin turned lobster-red in seconds.

Dang, did that ever feel good. I guess Mom was right after all. Not surprising. As kids we tend to think our parents are full of bullsquirt, but as we get older we realize that those old fuddy-duddies might have actually been on to something, might have had a few grains of wisdom in their aging heads.

Kids are jerks.

Although I'll never have kids (not part of the job description), there are those young ones among my parishioners who think old Father Mike has no clue, that it's been too long since *he's* been a kid and is out of tune with what's what.

When the truth finally hits them (especially little Anthony Hillibrand, whose fingers roamed when at the local department store), I hope they remember some of what I counseled and realize even a priest can be right every now and then.

In a way, I envied them their sense of invulnerability and the endless possibilities that lay before them. The young believe they are immortal, feeling totally fearless and flawless, and it's only the harsh scrub of experience that wears away the lacquer of false notions. But for a while we're all filled with the glaring light of our own promises. Robert Frost said it best: "Nature's first green is gold, Her hardest hue to hold." Stay gold, Ponyboy.

> Cows in the cornfield,
> What'll I do?
> Cows in the cornfield,

What'll I do?
Cows in the cornfield,
What'll I do?
Skip to my Lou, my darlin'.

I couldn't sing worth beans, but at least I bellowed with enthusiasm as I used a fresh bar of Dove soap to remove the last few ounces of grime from my chest. As the final *darlin'* slipped past my lips, I felt a strange sort of gelatinous pressure against my calves and I looked down to see that the water, all two feet of it, wasn't heading down the drain like proper and decent water should. Instead, it seemed to have solidified a little just below my knees, taking on the consistency of corn syrup. Brown streaks of soapy dirt marred the otherwise perfectly transparent treacle-like water, giving it a muddy/moldy look as if it were diseased.

Before my surprise could register to the animal parts of my hindbrain, the thick water flowed *upward* along my body. I tried to thrash, squirm, make a break for it, but the semi-solid liquid was too fast, trapping me firmly like a fly in dirty amber. No matter how hard I tried, the solidifying water held me fast. With a gasp of horror, I realized it was aiming to cover my head, the warm fluid cresting my jaw line and covering my ears, dimming the sound of the showerhead that was adding more liquid to its bulk. Within seconds I was completely covered.

Panic, raw and coppery, flooded my flesh, along with a serious amount of adrenaline, but there was nothing I could do, and to my surprise and disgust, the water *wriggled* past my lips and down my throat.

Oh, heck no! I redoubled my efforts at thrashing, but the jelly water wasn't having any of it and all I accomplished was an even greater panic. Black and yellow spots danced in front of my eyes.

In that moment I flashed back to when Boris, that giant Russian bodyguard who'd slit the skin along my side to expose one of my ribs. He did it so he could take a pair of pliers to the bone. The pain, the violation had been *indescribable,* the feeling of helplessness robbing me of my senses and the fiery agony robbing me of my dignity.

It was all there in full 3D and Sensurround, the remembered hurt and the terror and the utter certainty that I was going to die because Boris' eyes were pitiless pools of sadistic amusement and my mind was nowhere near rational—it was long-gone, bye-bye, sayonara Ace, it's time to die and my world was nothing but a spot of wiry agony centered around bloody bone. The only thing I knew was that Boris was going to take his sweet time killing me.

The jelly water was at my throat and down into my lungs in less than a second.

Skip to my Lou ....

What kind of last thought was *that*?

[PEACE.] The voice intruded from all sides, deep and musical, like a whale song translated into speech.

It was more felt than heard, that word, but there was no peace as I continued to struggle.

[Peace.]

What? My lungs burned.

[You breathed water for months before you were born; your body will remember how].

It hurt, it burned, but I held off taking a breath. My lungs felt scrubbed by sandpaper.

[Peace.]

No, nononononono!

As spots of color exploded behind my eyes, I breathed in deeply, fully expecting to drown.

[There you go.]

The first hit of jelly water felt like I'd inhaled metal filings, all sharp and pokey, and my lungs rebelled against the pain, but I couldn't help the second and third; my diaphragm needed to pull air into my body.

And I breathed. It was difficult, like trying to force air through a flattened straw, but I managed.

[Peace, Michael Engle.]

How?

[I have you safe in a cocoon of water, Michael Engle. Do not fret. All is well. The water is hyper-oxygenated.]

Apparently whatever had a hold of me could access my thoughts. Hot panic still speared my chest, but I struggled to master my flailing emotions because I sure couldn't do much else. Still, flashes of Boris threatened to undo my cool. *Who or what are you?* I managed while willing my muscles not to twitch and bunch.

[We have never been formally introduced. I am Primal Water.]

Hold on.

Primal Water? Last time I came close to the first of all Water Elementals was when my friend ... *bonded* with it and became water. With the power of Primal Water he was able to control all water, making it do things I wouldn't have thought possible.

What do you want with me? I asked, trying desperately to control myself. My head still swam, but now that I was breathing (or something like that), I was beginning to calm down. The murky jelly water around my eyes didn't impede my vision at all. I could see perfectly, as if the substance was air, although there appeared to be a gray tinge to everything.

[For countless centuries, I have existed to keep the Balance along with the other Primals, and we have been content, for it is as the Creator wills. However, when Olivier Deschamps *drank* me, I was given a rather unusual gift.]

There was nothing to do but listen. I appeared to be a captive audience. *Do tell.* Each slightly stinging breath brought more calm.

[A perspective not my own.]

?

[I already possessed sentience, albeit not a human one. My world was the flow of rivers, the rushing of creeks, deep currents, and the slow, sluggish movement of waters buried within the earth. It was a symphony for one and I was both conductor and orchestra. All that has changed. I now possess a uniquely human point of view and all that that entails. I understand fully the hasty, brutal, noble, and temporary nature of life.]

Not sure I understand.

The gelid water began to flow faster, caressing my skin with a touch softer than silk and it tickled.

[Imagine you are a dog thinking all your happy dog thoughts like chasing rabbits and wondering when you will eat next. All you know is what your nose and ears tell you and that you love the master who lavishes attention upon you. Then you wake up one day, thinking human thoughts, possessing human knowledge along with human emotions. The world as you knew it is gone. You now see the canned food you used to salivate as nothing more than disgusting, half-rotted beef by-products that only an insane or starving person would eat and that the master who gives it to you is a cheap prick who beats you now and then not because you've been bad, but because he has had too much to drink. Everything you thought you knew with your little doggy mind is as nothing compared to the complexity of human experience, yet you are trapped in a dog's body. That is what I am trying to tell you—the situation I find myself in. I can remember making love, but do not have the anatomy or hormones to appreciate it.]

Enough. Anger robbed me of composure just as the jelly water had stolen motion and now I finally rebelled, my fury an incandescent ball in my belly. *I appreciate your newfound dilemma, but LET ME GO!* My lungs, although drawing oxygen from the water, were still burning, and my diaphragm felt the first needle pains of cramping. I had to move, had to do *something* because panic was still at the edges of my vision and claustrophobia began to nibble at my mind.

[Very well, although I suggest you do not thrash around. We must continue our conversation.]

Movement, freedom thrilled through me as the jelly water once again became just plain old water, and I flailed briefly, trying to orient myself. The shower remained full of water, from drain to ceiling, and not a single drop leaked through the seam of the shower door. And now it was clean, totally devoid of all the dirt and grime and soap that had clouded it earlier, giving it an almost crystal clarity so pure that my vision was untrammeled by the liquid. Although my lungs and diaphragm still ached, I floated calmly in my watery coffin, waiting for the Primal to start gabbing again as I stretched my tired muscles. Although still achy, I felt the pain in my diaphragm begin to recede.

It didn't take long before it continued. [Forgive the rather drastic circumstances, but this is the easiest way for me to communicate with your kind.]

I can imagine. Is this how you communicated with Morgan? Sudden hope surged through me. *Is he here? Can I talk to him?*

[I am sorry, but he is gone. When our business concluded after the death of Mephistopheles' host he ... departed to where spirits go when the flesh dies. To the Creator or the Adversary, I am not sure. It is not for me to know such things.]

So he really was gone, gone for good. If my eyes hadn't been so full of water, I would've cried. *Thank you for that, I guess. Was it you who warned me about the killer in my church with the SOS?*

[It was.]

Why?

[Before he left, the man you called Morgan asked a boon of me, which I was quite willing to grant, having just learned the concept of gratitude.] The deep voice trailed away.

And ...? I urged.

[He asked me to watch over you, and I have done so for the past two years. Quite easy, actually, since I can expand my consciousness to include all water.]

Why SOS? Why not just intervene and suck the juice out of the killer like you did Mephistopheles?

[I was busy with larger matters, such as the Balance. Maintaining that Balance is a full-time job that I had forgotten for quite some time while I slumbered in the Arctic. When I abandoned the world those many years ago to sleep, to get away, I failed the Creator. I failed my purpose. The world became unbalanced and I have been working to correct my grave mistake. Such things require delicacy and precision. It is time-consuming. Besides, I'm can't do everything for you.]

So, what now?

The Primal took his sweet time in answering while I floated in a world that usually would've been inhospitable. My heartbeat had finally returned to something approaching normal, so I tried to enjoy myself as I did what no one has ever done in their adult lives—breathe water and not choke. Sure it was uncomfortable and disconcerting, but fascinating as well. Too bad no one would believe me. Even priests aren't exempt from being involuntary committed to a psychiatric institute.

[As one blessed by the Creator,] the Primal said, [you are a vessel for his might and therefore worthy of His grace. That alone would earn you some consideration not usually bestowed upon normal people. Add to that the depths of human knowledge granted me by Morgan Heart, a different way of expressing myself, and what is owed for my freedom, and you have only to ask a great boon and Water will grant it.]

My response was immediate, like the sudden flare of hope I felt. *Help me defeat the Sicarii.*

[How would I do that?]

Good question. I don't know. Somehow I had a feeling that this wasn't going to be as easy as the Primal made it sound. Being granted a boon was one thing, knowing what kind of boon I wanted was another.

[I suggest you find out, because I do not plan on doing all the heavy lifting myself. I promise a boon, not to be your panacea.]

How quickly can a person's dreams deflate? As quickly as they are born. I should've known better because the Bible teaches man to think for himself as well as providing a moral code to live by. Relying on the Primal was, in fact, counterintuitive, considering my profession. *So what now?* I asked again. Self-reliance, but I'd store that boon away like a miser hoards gold with the notion that I'd call in the marker when the time was right.

[I leave you to your planning, to your hiding, and to your self-reflection. If your need for me is dire, speak near water, any water, and I will hear and respond.]

And suddenly I was alone in the shower, completely dry and shivering, all water having disappeared in less than a second. Down the drain, I suppose. No feeling of sudden suction or flow of liquid over my skin, no swirling vortex as the fluid spiraled down and out of sight. Nope, it vanished as if suddenly, quietly, and invisibly turned into vapor, but without the violence of a rapid state-change.

"Whoa," I breathed, eyes wide. "That was trippy."

No need to towel dry, although my hair was flat and blotchy from the cheap dye job I'd given it on the plane. It looked like a blend of cheetah and punk rock—swirly, spotted, and striped. Not quite a clerical fashion statement.

I took my sweet time getting ready for bed, despite being tired to the bone. So much had happened recently, and my mind was slowly shutting down in self-defense. The Atheist, the flight and Minerva, Notre Dame and a note from the past, and now Primal Water. I wasn't sure how much more I could take before I blacked out from sheer information overload, not to mention the weirdness factor. The human mind has great capacity for learning, but few people are resilient enough to withstand the week I was having.

A little over two years ago, I had been a simple parish priest in a sleepy Midwestern town filled with salt-of-the-earth types and I felt content … happy. A good life with good people who shared with me a faith in a God who loved us. That was enough for me. Then a friend took me on a journey that not only rewarded my faith with proof, but also allowed me to hold in my hand one of the greatest artifacts of Christ's love—the Holy Grail.

But all that came with a price, which was terror, pain, and horror beyond what mere words can convey. A price that apparently I was still paying and would continue to pay for some time yet. How could I resolve this? What needed to be done? Who could I rely upon when the Deschamps came a-calling? Other than Primal Water, that is.

Perhaps Minerva? She seemed a little distant, perhaps scared …. I shook my head. No, not her. She was too emotionally distant and would avoid doing what needed to be done unless pushed to do so. Minerva would pay her debt to Cain then disappear as if she'd never existed.

Speaking of Cain, I knew he'd watch my six, but his was a game played deeper than I could imagine. Compared to him, I was a man blind from birth learning how to play three-dimensional chess.

Thinking on that, I remembered the manila envelope Cain handed me before he departed and I rushed back into the small living room where the *Codex* lay in its ancient box, unmindful that I wore nothing but a pair of oversized black boxer briefs I'd found in the armoire. My hands shook as I emptied the contents of the folder on the overstuffed chair.

It took a moment for me to understand the pieces of paper that flooded across the seat. I'd never seen the like before except on television, and comprehension was slow in coming.

Bearer Bonds. I counted the denominations quickly. About twenty million worth.

"Sweet Lord," I muttered. "What is this for, Cain?"

The answer was simple: don't worry about it right now, get yourself to bed and let tomorrow take care of tomorrow. No reason to worry about the kind of money that could finance a small war. Time for shut-eye, and wasn't that the best idea I'd had all day? Even those blessed by the Creator can succumb to exhaustion. When my head hit the pillows on that queen-sized four-poster

I slept deeply and without dreams, only an errant thought to accompany me into darkness.

Skip to my Lou, my darlin'.

Chapter Twenty-Three

"Use what you can, discard that which is not useful."
—*Codex Infernales*

It was a long flight from New York City, and Blaine felt like three kinds of crap. He hated traveling long distances, but the price paid in jet-lag would be worth it if the Oracle could provide insight into the whereabouts of the *Codex*, Cain, and the meddling priest. Cain he wanted dead in the worst way—it was an itch he longed to scratch—but the priest really chapped his hide. How the hell had he defeated Alvin the Giggler? Obviously there was more to the man than indicated in the dossier kept on the Crystal Drive buried in his jacket pocket.

The thought of the priest's preserved head floating in a jar of pickle brine comforted him as he exited the corporate jet onto the runway of a private airstrip that would have had the locals buzzing if they'd known about it. The land for miles around belonged to the Family, which afforded them the luxury of privacy in a world where Big Brother knew the color of your BM ten minutes after it hit the toilet.

A dark-blue Porsche Panamera 4S screamed to a stop not more than ten feet away, bringing with it the scent of burning tires and hot exhaust. The sun winked merrily off chrome and glass, the sleek perfection and power of the German automobile obvious in every line. Blaine watched blandly, one hand in the pocket of his dark Saville-Row suit, the other clutching a tablet computer Apple would kill for had the corporation known it existed.

"Hello, sir," said a cheery voice in Romansh. It belonged to the short, dark man in a black suit who exited the driver's side door of the Porsche. His eyes were hidden behind mirrored wraparound shades, and a subtle tension in the shoulders indicated a readiness to violence. "It is good to see you again, sir."

Yeah, right, Blaine thought wryly. He knew quite well that he was less than beloved by his fellow Family members, but he kept up the pretense and pasted a small smile on his face. "You, too, Carlo."

Carlo's answering smile was bright and white and a killer. As a four-Word magus, he was at the top of the Sicarii food chain, a leader among the Dagger Men assassins, one of their best and brightest and most successful. Although his dazzling smile showed nothing but bonhomie and joy, to those who knew him well it was the grin of a mako shark just before it struck and filled the water with blood. "And where is Cousin Fergus?"

You mean 'Brother' Fergus. Blaine shrugged. *Or half-brother Fergus? If you only knew.* Only the board understood the tangled genealogical web, a secret the Family preserved zealously. The moment Blaine took control of the Family, Julian's sperm, his father's seed, had been disposed of and replaced with his so that the next generation would bear his genetic stamp, relegating Julian to grandfather status. "Fergus is taking care of business in America," he replied softly, almost absentmindedly. "Keeping an eye on things until I return."

"Then we'd better head out, sir," Carlo said in flawless English, correctly guessing Blaine's preference in languages. He moved to the rear of the Porsche and opened the door for the head of the Family. Blaine tipped him a Spartan nod and entered.

"How long until we're there?" he asked as Carlo set the car in gear. "I want to get this show on the road." There was business to conduct and people to kill. Work, work, work.

"Not long at all, sir."

Whenever Blaine heard the word *sir,* he mentally substituted *fuck you* in its place. Every smile of deference hid derision, every obsequious bow a middle finger flipped in his direction. No one was exempt from hating their betters and those thoughts kept any sort of compassion or kindness at bay. "Well, let's get there, then."

The luxury sports car squealed off, leaving a streak of steaming black on hot pavement.

Driving across the countryside so far from a major city offered Blaine a scenic view of unspoiled nature, a sight wasted on the young businessman. In fact, such sights were more suited to less jaded eyes, eyes that housed far less contempt and indifference. Instead of drinking in the wonders of massive conifers and snow-capped mountains, he busied himself with his tablet computer, pecking away at expense reports and keeping half an eye on the Stock Exchange. Blaine knew full well that the verdant scene around the Porsche had no power to inspire him to rapture. Quite the opposite, in fact. What it did inspire was a desire to level fields and trees to make way for man-made structures such as shopping malls and post offices, things that offered mankind more than nature could supply. To him, nature was sloppy, uncoordinated, needlessly brutal, and of no value unless harnessed and bent to the will of someone capable of using it properly.

His was not a Family of tree-huggers.

"How are the Dagger Men taking my ascension," he asked suddenly, not bothering to look up from a profit-and-loss statement from UnexxOil.

When in doubt, lie, but when dealing with someone as powerful as Blaine Deschamps, handpicked by the Patron himself, fibbing more often than not proved to be an excellent route to a quick and messy retirement. Carlo, no slouch he, chose the wisest route with the fewest speed bumps. "They're not sure of you yet, sir," he said honestly, not taking his eyes from the road.

Blaine didn't bother to raise his eyes from the tablet. *Damn*, UnexxOil's profit margin this quarter had fallen short from the previous quarter. He made a note to have those responsible fired. Or killed. "What do you mean?"

Carlo frowned slightly. He did *not* like it when the boss asked uncomfortable questions. "You're an American and the majority of the Dagger Men were trained in Europe. Because of that, they have a very European attitude toward Americans."

"You don't say?" Blaine's voice was studiously neutral. With the tap of a finger he'd acquired the majority shares of CentexComm, not much of a company by itself, but combined with UnexxOil's distribution, the share prices should triple within eight months.

"Most Europeans think Americans have thick Southern accents, are rude, pushy, provincial, opinionated and are generally the world's greatest assholes. This is evidenced by European films that portray them as such, sir."

"And my European relatives think this of me?"

"Only the stupid ones."

"And you?"

The reply was instantaneous. "You are an eleven-Word magus with the finest education the Family can provide. If you were that kind of American, you would've been killed before you turned fifteen, sir."

Blaine's cold, cold eyes met Carlo's in the rearview as the car hummed along, hugging the road in a fine example of German engineering. The two stared at each other for a good long while, Carlo somehow keeping to the road without watching. Just when it seemed that an accident was inevitable, Blaine give him a miniscule nod of approval. Carlo nodded back and resumed not crashing the Porsche.

A small smile made a rare appearance on Blaine's face. He was impressed.

Not everyone would have the stones to lock eyes with the head of Family without looking away. Then again, Carlo was an accomplished Dagger Man with dozens of kills in his professional career. According to his file, which Blaine accessed on the tablet, Carlo was suspected in the death of all *five* of his crèche and a crèche sister. His brother Arnaud died choking on a fishbone, Everett of an aneurysm (Blaine, for the life of him, couldn't figure that one out), Bartholomew of a heroin overdose, Miles spent the last few days of his life screaming as his body was devoured by a flesh-eating bacteria, and Lyman's pet Doberman had torn his throat out in his sleep. As for the sister, Margaret, well, safe to say that her death gave Blaine a momentary stab of indigestion. All assassinations were as flawless as they were creative and perfectly executed, leaving no evidence whatsoever that could incriminate the survivor. Blaine made a mental note to keep an eye on the man for future use.

The Porsche turned into a thin asphalt road that wound through a densely wooded area. Carlo steered through maple and beech, the light becoming sparse and dappled as pine needles fractured the rays. In less than a minute the Porsche reached a clearing with a modest cabin in the center. The main floor housed the living area and kitchen while a cramped second floor contained a tiny bedroom.

Lounging on the front porch, sitting on a rough-carved oak rocker with his heavy brown boots resting on the front railing, was a bearded man wearing a red flannel shirt and jeans. He sipped lemonade from a frosted glass and stared languidly out into the forest as if the trees harbored some great secret he longed to learn. The arrival of the car was met with sublime indifference and a long drink.

Blaine didn't wait for Carlo to open his door; the excitement of the moment was heady wine in his blood and he couldn't wait to meet the famed Oracle for the first time. Looking at the man, one might think him to be a particularly laid-back lumberjack with a well-trimmed beard, but Blaine knew that the man posed more danger than all the Sicarii's enemies combined. He was also their greatest asset, used rarely because of the unusual nature of his ability.

In the past, various Oracles had parsed out granules of knowledge that had to be examined carefully in order to ascertain their veracity. Every oracle from the Oracle of Delphi in Greece to the Akashvani of India offered riddle-laced prophecies, but not the Oracle in service to the Deschamps. Instead their Oracle offered incomplete knowledge, claiming that God-given visions were dimly seen, only the fraction of a whole. More than once a foretelling ended with the deaths of many Dagger Men.

The Oracle who gently rocked in the chair didn't bother to look up. He seemed to find his boots fascinating. "So you're the famous Blaine Deschamps, the new head of the Family." The voice emerged smooth and silky, an orator's voice. Surprisingly, he spoke English, not Romansh, although Blaine could detect a slight Scandinavian accent. "Been expecting you."

"Of course you have," Blaine said. "You wouldn't be much of an oracle if you weren't." He stepped up on the porch and took a second chair, also made of rough-carved oak. It was surprisingly uncomfortable. Carlo remained by the car, his left hand hovering near the Glock tucked into his waistband.

"Have a seat," the Oracle directed drily.

"Don't mind if I already fucking did."

The two sat in silence, one staring at the other while the second merely regarded his boots as if the stitching contained the secrets of the universe. Blaine drank in the Oracle's appearance: straight brown hair falling to the shoulders, full beard, olive skin with eyes so deep brown they almost looked black, and fine, chiseled features, although the nose was a bit too hawkish for his taste. He looked Middle-Eastern, but Blaine knew his family lived in Oslo—a wife, three kids (two boys and a girl) and a border collie named Bjorn. It was all on the tablet, everything he needed to know about one of the Family's greatest secret assets, including careful instructions on how to control him.

"What did you think of Julian?" Blaine asked softly, still studying the Oracle.

"I didn't."

"You must have had an opinion."

"I did. I just don't think it's relevant." The Oracle took a sip of lemonade, the condensation dripping onto his flannel shirt where it beaded briefly before being absorbed.

"It's relevant to me."

"He was like all the other Sicarii I have met—smart, cruel, and efficient."

"That's it?"

For the first time, the other man's eyes met Blaine's and the young Sicarius felt a thrill of fear skitter down his back. His balls wanted to shrivel, his stomach gave a slow roll, and he almost succumbed to nausea. It took all his will power to keep from throwing up, although there was nothing grotesque or obscene about the other man's eyes. They did, however, hold a nearly unfathomable wisdom in their dark chocolate depths, a vast intelligence and compassion Blaine found repellant.

"Don't look at me!" he barked. Standing by the Porsche, Carlo had his Glock half-drawn, ready to start shooting at the slightest provocation.

The eyes veered away, studying the water marks on the flannel shirt.

It took a few minutes for Blaine to regain his composure, an unfamiliar feeling for him. It was unsettling and he didn't like it one bit, no sir. In fact, his loss of face in front of the oracle was a weakness that planted a kernel of hate in his heart that was already full of loathing, and when he next looked at the Oracle, a plan of action was already cemented in place. He would show the Oracle what's what and damn the consequences.

"Don't you dare," whispered the Oracle with a low heat that seemed to blister the air all around. "Don't you even think about it." There was such a rage in that silky voice, wrath that could shatter mountains.

Blaine felt his newly hatched plan wither and die before it fully maturated. "What?"

"You kill one of my family, you break the Compact and lose me." That deep gaze returned, pinning Blaine to his uncomfortable chair. "*Forever*, your best source of intelligence. That is the true consequence of your decision." Then the kicker. "What would your Patron say?"

"How did … never mind." Blaine shook his head. Mention of the Patron was a surefire way of taking the starch out of his shorts. "All right, I won't touch your family. Okay, Mr. Sensitive?"

A nod. "That's all I ask."

Blaine nodded to himself and resolved to school his temper. He'd read in Julian's journal (all Family heads were required to keep one) about the dangers of dealing with the Oracle, but encountering the man in person really brought home the perils. Despite his anger, he knew it would be a while before the next Oracle matured enough to replace this lumberjack-looking motherfucker.

At the age of thirty, the prospective Oracle was gathered and put through what was referred to as "The Crucible," a forced month-long stay in the most remote, hellishly hot desert on the planet, the Lut in Iran. With a max temp of 159 degrees Fahrenheit, it was the Family's go-to spot to activate the clairvoyant ability that lurked deep within the genetic code of the Oracle's family tree. For the past three centuries, the line of Yehuda carefully watched, protected, and ultimately harvested the Oracles when the time was optimal, which proved to around thirty years of age.

Three years ago, upon the death of the old Oracle, the Family had promptly snatched the Oracle-to-Be from Norway and thrust him directly, without any explanation except that the lives of his family depended upon his survival, for thirty days in the Lut. No contact with others who might happen upon the unfortunate man and no attempt to escape the desert. Any attempt to circumvent these orders would come at a price too high even for the most hardened soul. Needless to say, every prospective Oracle readily agreed to these demands.

Blaine understood that each Oracle, once their powers were activated, suddenly knew full well whom they were to work for and that it would be a lifetime gig. They also knew the fate of their family: the eldest boy would be groomed to become the next Oracle, and their spouses and secondary children would be held hostage to ensure cooperation. But with that crystal clarity came the knowledge that there was zero they could do to alter the situation. Once their clairvoyance came to the fore, they were shipped out to the cabin and held prisoner for the rest of their lives, which usually meant until their oldest son turned thirty. Any attempt to escape brought swift and terrible punishment to the Oracle's children and spouse. The Family never bluffed, never lied (an Oracle *always* spotted fibbing), and never failed to live up to a promise. It was their only way to deal with someone as awesome as the Oracle.

Not that the Oracles complied willingly. They made the best of a bad situation by supplying only the information asked for, no more, no less, and they stayed silent unless the correct, specific question was asked. Theirs was a *caveat emptor* relationship with the Family, one that had burned the Sicarii badly on more than one occasion.

The last such occasion was when this particular Oracle told Julian that the way to capture the wayward Olivier was to capture the priest Michael Engle at a Catholic church in Terrabonne, Oregon. He said that if the priest was held prisoner, Olivier would attempt a rescue and be vulnerable. What he didn't mention was that he would be bringing backup. It was Julian's last mistake.

"I need information," said Blaine.

The Oracle took another sip of lemonade, ice cubes clinking softly against glass. "Of course you do; that is the only reason you Deschamps ever visit." A pause. "Except for your Dagger Men minders hidden in the woods with their rifles and Tec 9s."

"They are for your family's protection in case you get jittery and lose all your marbles."

"I know why they are there." There was no sadness, no melancholy or anger in the Oracle's voice, only a dispassionate, analytic tone that Blaine appreciated.

"Where is the priest Michael Engle?"

"Ah, him."

"Yes."

"The one who got away."

"Not for long."

The Oracle said nothing, finishing his lemonade and refilling the glass from a pitcher tucked beneath his uncomfortable chair.

"Tell me," urged Blaine.

"Sure you don't want one?" asked the Oracle, holding up his glass. "You Sicarii do know how to keep me well stocked out here in the back end of beyond. Do you prefer Deschamps or Sicarii, since they're both one and the same anyway?"

"Doesn't matter."

"Deschamps, then. I like names better than titles."

"About the priest …."

"What about him?"

Blaine kept his temper in check. "Where is he?"

"I don't know."

"Don't lie."

The wise wells of the Oracle's eyes flicked toward him, and once again Blaine felt their caress on his skin before they returned to regarding the red flannel shirt an instant later. *Fucking lumberjack-looking motherfucker,* thought Blaine angrily. *A fucking backwoods, Canuck type of seer.*

"I don't lie, Deschamps." The Oracle sounded amused, as if the thoughts whirling in Blaine's head were broadcast loud enough for him to hear. "That is part of the agreement I made with Julian after the Crucible. You can, as you Americans say, take that to the bank."

This was a complication—if the Oracle was telling the truth. "Why not?"

Another sip of lemonade. "Not sure. Best guess is that God doesn't want me to know. My clairvoyance is not some sort of perfect radar that allows to me to see that which I want at any time. Sometimes what I do see is cloudy or out of sync with what is really happening. My vision sees but darkly. This is why, throughout the centuries, you Deschamps rarely relied upon the power of the Oracles. It is a tiger-by-the-tail at the best of times." A gust of a sigh escaped his lips. "Want a cookie? I made some killer chocolate chip raisin the other day and I have a few left."

Through clenched teeth Blaine replied, "No."

"Too bad. I may be a good Oracle, but I am one heck of a baker."

"What can you tell me?"

"Nothing. Nothing at all unless you ask. And only the right question. That's the deal made between your Family and mine."

If Fergus had been there lurking and listening at the edge of the porch, he might have smiled in satisfaction; there were few things that would have caused him more glee than the sight of Blaine Deschamps meeting his match. Oh, the Oracle was the Family's captive, held there by the threat of terrible things that could be done to his children and wife, but it was a little like sitting in a cage with a drugged lion. You *think* the animal is harmless, too logy to move and too domesticated to lash out, but at the point of maximum complacency, you realize you've just lost your arm to slashing claws, and that ivory daggers are flashing toward your exposed throat.

Julian knew the risks, as had the previous Family heads before him, and possessed the cool, almost analytical forbearance of a spider in the middle of its web. Blaine, however, had the wine of youth running through his veins, an intolerance of having to bide his time, and that was a weakness the Oracle knew full well how to exploit.

In a flash Blaine was on the other man, one arm raised with a large fist ready to rain down some serious pain, the other on the Oracle's throat, squeezing hard, not quite crushing cartilage. Time seemed to stop as the two men regarded each other, the Oracle's calm, loving eyes shining from a face swiftly turning purple and Blaine, blue eyes blazing with cold fury, ready to kill, ready to maim, to hurt this man who dared defy him. It was galling, the way the Oracle seemed to know how to push his buttons, and intolerable. He'd destroyed men for lesser offenses and this piece of shit had no *clue* whom he antagonized.

Or did he?

With movements glacially slow, the arm dropped, and the strangling hand, cramping, the tendons standing out like piano wire beneath pale skin, let go, allowing air to be sucked back into lungs and blood to resume flowing.

"You're fucking with me." Blaine's voice didn't betray the violent tremors twitching his fingers. "You want me to hurt you, to kill you, to break a centuries-old agreement between our Families."

The Oracle's deep eyes observed Blaine serenely, and the young man felt another shiver, but this time he held the gaze, steeling his mind with discipline and self-control. With the faintest of smiles, the Oracle nodded.

"You bastard," Blaine said matter-of-factly.

Not answering, the Oracle went back to sipping his lemonade.

The younger man sat down slowly, marshaling his reserves of control, and leaned back in the ugly chair. "I think I will take some of that."

"Under your seat."

And yes, there it was, right under the chair where it must have been resting all this time—a glass of lemonade, ice cubes mostly melted. Blaine took a sip. *Yep, pretty good at that.*

"You were testing me."

The Oracle shook his head. "I had hoped you would end all this, break the agreement; then your boss, the Fallen Angel you call Patron, would have to keep his word and destroy you … as per the agreement." A regretful sigh. "He lacks imagination, but when Lucifer makes a deal, he sticks to it, come hell or high water." The Oracle chuckled.

Fear lanced through Blaine's gut as he realized that he had just avoided a very messy death by a mere fraction. Had he killed or beaten the Oracle, the Patron would have taken his anger out on the offender, and after millennia, there was a whole big patch of anger built up under the Patron's prideful skin.

"You take some mighty big risks," said Blaine. "Got yourself a pair of balls. Big brass ones."

"Back atcha, Deschamps."

They sat there for a while, drinking lemonade, each refilling his glass until the pitcher was empty. Blaine took that time to reflect upon what just happened. He'd come to this cabin expecting to shake down the Oracle in the same manner he shook everyone down, by sheer force of personality, the threat of immanent violence, and an iron will. For him to lose, not to have the upper hand, was as alien to him as the surface of Mars was to a goldfish. He'd never met a man he couldn't break, a soul he couldn't dominate.

But the Oracle seemed to be made of sterner stuff. Blithely contemplating his boots, the man had nearly caused him to break a centuries-old vow, and that was a horse of a different color, indeed. Soft-spoken, gentle, he nevertheless knew (by agency of the Lying God or natural ability) how to get under the skin and *twist*.

For the first time ever, Blaine felt regret. Not for almost breaking the agreement, but for not fully reading Julian's notes on dealing with the Oracle. That was a mistake he would not make twice.

"Cain."

The Oracle sighed and seemed to deflate a bit, his eyes drifting from his feet.

"That's the right question, isn't it?"

No reply.

Jackpot. "You know where Cain is, don't you."

A nod.

"Spill."

Lips barely moving, and with great regret, the Oracle said, "The Valley of the Moon."

Blaine smiled.

Gotcha.

Chapter Twenty-Four

"Do not be unequally yoked with unbelievers. For what partnership has righteousness with lawlessness?"
—2 Corinthians 6:14

THE COFFEE WAS GOOD, BETTER THAN you could find at most franchise coffeehouse chains, and it perked me right up. If I have an addiction, or vice, it would be caffeine. I can't help it. Ever since Desert Storm, when all that kept you alert was a good cup, or a bad cup, of joe, you learned to down the stuff by the gallon until you peed brown.

Just outside the window of the small shop lay a white-sand beach, and beyond that, the blue/green water of the English Channel. Thrust out from the beach, dividing the water, was a long pier, and at the end of the pier stood a small, white lighthouse surrounded by tourists and gulls.

The sky was as blue as I'd ever seen it, a bowl covering the world with the white orb of the sun shining down fiercely. The beach, a long strand of sand in front of a bustling hotel, had its fair share of tourists as well, and I sighed, wishing I could be down there on the sand, lying on a blanket and soaking in some rays, but my fate was no longer my own. No, it was tied to others.

"What's wrong?" asked Minerva. She had a croissant and her own cup of java in front of her. The pastry looked yummy, but my stomach didn't want anything but coffee; it was knotted tight and burned slightly. Her eyes, still that disquieting color-without-a-name, narrowed as I studied her.

Where once her hair had been straight and black enough to drink in light, now it was blonde, almost white, and frizzy—a halo around her head, pardon the expression. She still looked like a million dollars, but was a different kind of pretty. In place of finely chiseled features, she sported an upturned, slightly puckish nose sprayed with freckles and her chin, still strong, was dimpled deeply in the center. Her lips were fuller, too. Not Angelina Jolie huge, but full and kissable. Not that I dreamed of kissing her, understand. My profession and her eyes put paid to that notion quick enough. It was a different face she wore, and a slightly different body, and normally I would've said that was impossible, but I guess for Fallen Angels, impossible was part of the job description.

Hey, a couple of days ago I'd witnessed flying statuary, so I guessed the word *impossible* was officially obsolete.

As for me, my looks were a far cry from a few short hours ago.

After waking from my dreamless sleep, all logy but refreshed, I hit the head and proceeded to get dressed. I'd just put on a pair of clean boxers (thanks again to the armoire) when I realized I had an audience. Minerva stood in the doorway, arms crossed and a faint smile on her perfect face.

"Jeez, Louise!" I yelled. "Trying to give me a heart attack?"

That smile grew wide, showing plenty of teeth. "I like a man who stays in shape."

I slipped on a plain white T-shirt as quickly as possible. I'm not a prude, but I wasn't used to being half-dressed in front of a woman. Hadn't had that pleasure in a couple of decades. What made the experience more unnerving were the blank stares of the skulls as they silently watched in judgment.

"Don't bother with pants or a shirt. I brought some."

Instead of arguing, I followed her into the small living room. The elevator door gaped open like a metallic maw, and there lingered in the air the faint odor of cinnamon. Before I could open my mouth, a bundle of clothes hit me in the chest, and I fumbled awkwardly to keep from dropping them.

Minerva's smile still stretched her lips a little. "There you go."

"What the heck?" I muttered as I examined the white shirt, a simple, black three-piece suit, and a long, black cloth jacket called a *rekel*. A black homburg hat and shiny black shoes completed the outfit. A strange feeling of recognition sparked somewhere between my eyes as I caught sight of the twin spirals of dark hair glued onto the inside of the hat, and I knew that when I wore it, the two locks would frame my face.

"You want me to impersonate a Hasidic Jew?" I asked, stunned. That was old-school religion, while I tended toward the new.

What I thought was another article of clothing flew through the air and smacked me in face before flopping down upon the clothes in my arms. A long, dark-brown false beard. "Now I do," Minerva said, finally breaking out with a bark of laughter. It was brief, almost harsh, but musical—the sound a calliope would make if it could laugh.

I didn't need to be told why I had to wear such a ridiculous outfit. There were CCTV cameras in Paris and there was absolutely no doubt in my mind that the Family was running facial recognition software. That software could pinpoint me in a heartbeat, though the wide-brimmed hat and beard should throw it off some. What about Minerva? I asked her what her disguise would be.

"Watch," was all she said and shook herself like a wet dog. Instead of shedding water, however, she shed light. Little droplets of liquid-seeming radiance burst from her body in a thick, slow-moving cloud. Thick enough, in fact, that she was obscured for a moment, just a fraction of a second, before fading away.

The woman who stood there no longer resembled Minerva in any way, shape, or form. A little curvier in all the right places, shorter, but still a knockout that strained my vow of chastity.

"Wow." All I could say. I didn't have the energy to form more words.

Minerva turned around like a runway model. Even her clothes had changed to hug her more than ample endowments. "Not bad, huh? I haven't done this in years." She shook the blonde mop of her hair. "I do prefer being a brunette, though."

"How?" I cleared my throat. "Another one of your Qualities?"

She tapped a finger to her even shapelier lips, the smile disappearing. "No. Angels, even fallen ones, have bodies, but they translate poorly in the mortal realm, which is why we appear golden and winged. Although my wings are long gone." These last words were uttered with a faint trace of sorrow that tore at my heart. Atheniel still hurt after all these years, I could tell, and those eyes hid a wealth of regret and shame. "But we can take mortal form using the base matter of this universe, fashioning any likeness we choose. Even animal." One perfect blonde eyebrow arched upward. "Of course you've heard the story of Leda and the Swan?"

Greek mythology. I had a passing knowledge. "Yeah, Zeus turned himself into a swan to mate with Leda. Not my favorite story. Zeusiel, right?"

"No, his name was Zuriel and he was a horny bastard."

My turn to raise an eyebrow. "Was?"

"Even Angels can die, Mike." The remark was as brutal and final as a fatal gunshot wound. Obviously a sore subject. "Get dressed."

So there I was, sipping coffee at a tiny little shop that also sold croissants, one hundred forty-seven miles from Paris, our little white Renault rent-a-car baking in the late summer sun while I watched tourists gather around a distant lighthouse that looked incongruously like Calais was flipping England the bird.

Perhaps it was.

Minerva took another bite of croissant and me another sip of the slightly nutty coffee. Black and thick and rich, it slid down my gullet warmly, taking up residence and sending blessed caffeine through my veins. I closed my eyes in appreciation and gave voice to the question that had been sitting at the back of my mind for a couple of hours.

"Will you tell me about these mysterious allies we are waiting for?"

Mysteries surrounded by enigmas and shrouded by riddles. For too long I'd waited to see what's what, telling myself that patience is a virtue and that I should try to be as virtuous as possible because virtue is part of the job description. Enough of that. I was tired, the fake beard itched, and I was hot as heck in the extra cotton padding next to my skin that made me appear forty pounds heavier. Frustration warred with hard-earned discipline accumulated during my Ranger days when following orders from the ranking officer was the only course of action available.

And of course that thought brought forth images of Iraq, of Bush Sr., and the liberation of Kuwait, and we found ourselves supporting Delta Force's SCUD hunting operations in places where the heat hit over one hundred degrees. We acted as a blocking force for them, giving quick reaction and reconnaissance against the Iraqis, and oddly enough, when I look back at the heat and my mind conjures the screams of the wounded, I kind of think of those times as my salad days when things were fresh and fun. Not because I loved killing or even firing my weapon. No, it had to do with my brother Rangers, the camaraderie, and the absolute trust you place in the guys standing to the right and left. They watched my six and I watched theirs, and for a brief moment we were perfect, life seemed perfect, and when the job was done, it became more perfect at the realization that we still lived, still loved, and were loved in return.

We took a communications facility near the border with Jordan, destroying an enormous 350-foot microwave tower, eighty-sixing the facility, and taking prisoners. It was the farthest a light infantry unit found itself in Iraq during the whole shebang. The memories were both cherished and repugnant, a dichotomy I have coped with for years. Brotherhood and death, friends and foe, laughter and screams and horror. Could I have the good without the bad? No, not in a time of war when you fought terror with camaraderie, faith in your brothers with hatred of the enemy.

Salad days.

The screams of my men swirled behind my eyes as Minerva looked up, and I swear she flinched, as if she could see the ugliness intertwined with the beauty in my mind. "I will let them introduce themselves—it is better that way," she murmured, not meeting my eyes.

"So ... no information."

Her perfect face once again regained its serenity. "All I will say is that they have been fighting the Sicarii for nearly a thousand years in one way or another and have blackened the eyes of the Family on more than one occasion. They're the only ones besides Cain that the Deschamps truly fear, and they are your only hope, I believe, to live through the next decade."

"That's helpful."

"Do you really have a choice?"

She had me there. "What about you?"

"What about me?"

"You're going to be part of this, aren't you? As a favor to Cain."

The temperature suddenly dropped. Usually that would be a metaphor, but my breath steamed and roiled in the air and my coffee developed a thin layer of surface ice. That cold entered my lungs and seemed to freeze my lungs solid. Fear and the cold stilled me, clenching my muscles to the point where I couldn't even blink.

It was a good long while before Minerva finally broke the frigid silence. "I believe I have paid my debt to our mutual friend, and when I am done handing you over to the enemies of the Sicarii, I will be on my merry way, all accounts settled nicely."

While she spoke, the ice melted in my chest and I took a deep breath, choosing my next words carefully. "It seems I am being handed off to these 'fanatics,' " I made air quotes, "so I can join up and be part of their group opposing the Sicarii." I had mulled over the situation while donning my disguise earlier and wasn't entirely thrilled by the prospect. "All to keep me relatively safe, but considering the use of the word 'fanatic,' my guess is that I'll be dealing with a religious group of some sort." A mirthless chuckle burst forth. "Not that I'm against religion, but religious fanatics can be just as bad as the evil they fight."

Minerva nodded, eyeing me solemnly.

"So," I continued, "despite their religious fervor, Cain wants me to either join them or ..." my voice trailed off as a new thought hit me with the force of a sledgehammer, "assist them somehow, perhaps to provide military or organizational aspects they now lack."

"Yes."

"What I'm really wondering is, if I'm being dropped into the middle of these fanatics, why wouldn't you come along? We could oppose the Sicarii together. Cain earned a measure of forgiveness. Perhaps you could, too."

Wrong thing to say, and I mean in a huge way. The cold came back with a vengeance that shocked my skin into goose pimples, and the voice that emerged from her throat almost froze the juice in my eyeballs. There was nothing human in what issued from her throat. Imagine the low rumble of thunder from the bottom of a well and mix in the shriek of ripping metal and the cries of lost souls. Something like that, yet not quite. All I know is that I never want to hear it again, and I pray I never do. "I have sinned against the Throne, performed the ultimate Treason, followed the Adversary in his quest to storm and take Heaven, the City of Light, and destroyed my brothers and sisters with savage weapons. There is no forgiveness for my sins, so don't try quoting the Bible to me and talking about returning to the state of grace I used to enjoy. That has been lost to me forever. When the stars burn out and the universe collapses in on itself to start Creation all over again, I will still be an outcast—unforgiven and alone. That is what I deserve." She shook her head slightly. "No, I am going to leave, head back to a place where I can keep my head down, where it's quiet, where I can live out my exile in peace and quiet. Alone."

Alone. Is there a more terrible word in the human language? The priest in me wanted to argue, to comfort, and to teach, but the regular guy side of me rose to the surface and sawed back on the reins. "Fair enough. No more preaching from me."

I could see that set her back on her heels, and a look of gratitude flashed across her face.

So ... I was to be handed over like a football during the Sugar Bowl, or a hot potato, and I wasn't too thrilled about the prospect. "This is a partner stealing dance, isn't it? And it just keeps going."

"Lost my partner, what'll I do?" she sang softly and my rough bass joined her.

"Lost my partner, what'll I do? Lost my partner, what'll I do? Skip to my Lou, my darlin.'"

The shop's lone barista, a tired-looking teenage girl with thin, black hair and a cluster of pimples on her chin smiled at the crazy Americans.

"I wish you would tell me who these people are, use your Quality, and give me the intel I need."

Eyes with that nameless color narrowed, focusing on something beyond the window. "I don't use my Quality willy-nilly, only at need, and you don't really need to know ... not yet. Besides, you're about to get your answers."

Answers. That would be good. I followed her gaze outside to the sight of a motorcycle pulling into the coffeehouse's small parking lot, and for a second the motorcycle was all I could see.

A Harley Davidson 1200 Custom, orange fenders and tank, gleaming chrome and the standard loud-as-possible Harley noise. Its rumble deepened then died as it pulled to a stop. Two black-helmeted riders with dark visors dismounted, clad in heavy black leathers and chaps. For a moment they stood in the sun, large figures next to a large bike, and I felt a stab of jealousy. I used to have a Harley, a fixer-upper I'd sold a couple of years ago soon after my return from New York to replace my old Corolla that had been lost thanks to my adventures with Morgan. The sight of such mechanical perfection set my heart aflutter. The riders were mere optional extras to my eyes next to the glory of that motorcycle.

Besides coffee (and the occasional Toblerone) my holdover vice from my pre-clergy days rested out on the lot looking sleek and dangerous and shining in the sun. Briefly, I wondered if the mysterious *them* would allow me to take the bike out and give it a good shakedown cruise. Perhaps if I asked nicely?

Looked like I was going to have my chance, because the two mystery riders strode to the door and entered the shop without taking off their helmets. I stood, adjusting my long coat, while Minerva, also standing, moved slightly ahead. With a start, I realized that she had reverted to the form she wore when I first met her. I guess in my fascination with the motorcycle, I missed the light show that came with the transformation back to her previous self.

From the ample curves, I realized that one of the riders was a woman, while the other looked to be a big man, even larger than myself, with shoulders so wide I was surprised he made it through the shop door without having to turn sideways.

The big man removed his helmet, revealing ebony skin and a shining, almost glossy pate where hair used to be. High cheekbones framed his handsome, almost feminine face and eyes of green were set deep beneath thick supraorbital ridges. All in all, the face was striking enough to grace a fashion magazine or *GQ*; he was almost too good looking.

"I take it you are Minerva," said the striking black man, green eyes sparkling. They turned to me. His English held a trace of a French accent. "And this is the principal?"

Before Minerva could reply, the other rider removed her helmet, letting loose a cascade of long blonde hair. "Beneath all that fake hair, Renaud, this principal is an old friend." The woman's voice held laughter and smiles.

My heart raced with joy. "Maggie?"

Big dimples flashed in a wide, rawboned yet pretty face. "Hiya, Mike. Long time no see."

Chapter Twenty-Five

"For God did not give use a spirit of timidity, but a spirit of power, of love, and self-discipline."
—2 Timothy 1:7

A THOUSAND MILES EAST OF SONOMA VALLEY, California (also known as the Valley of the Moon), a UAV (Unmanned Aerial Vehicle), called a MALE (Medium Altitude, Long Endurance), or Tier II drone, cruised along at fifty thousand feet above the eastern plains of Colorado, powered by a TP-331-10T rear-mounted turboprop. It carried with it three thousand pounds of death.

"Flight status normal, systems nominal. Everything is looking good. Our dedicated satellite link is stable."

"Military?"

"All military satellites and radar have been compromised. As far as the United States government is concerned, this Reaper does not exist."

"And our target?"

"Still stationary and likely to stay that way at this hour."

Blaine drank from a ceramic mug, enjoying the near scalding Kona coffee. The shot of tequila he'd added gave the brew a medicinal edge. He hid his smile, but his bright blue eyes betrayed his joy to the other two men in the room, one the drone operator, the other a computer programmer who was keeping the Reaper invisible to prying eyes. "Excellent."

* * *

AMONG FRAGRANT GRAPE VINES THAT STOOD in ruler-straight rows all along the floor of the Sonoma Valley, near a small white house that crouched all by its lonesome in the middle of a clearing, two men lay comfortably on soft California dirt beneath thick thermal blankets.

One was tall, taller than most except for professional basketball players, and even by that standard he loomed. Olive-skinned and shaggy-haired, he stared unblinking into the night with magically enhanced vision that turned the dark scene around them into a riot of kaleidoscopic colors. Black jeans, boots, and T-shirt camouflaged his long body while a pair of handguns rested in holsters beneath his armpits.

The second man seemed almost a midget in comparison. At a hair over five feet, he was short by most standards. With his broad shoulders and defined muscles, he evoked the surface of a rock face and radiated the intractability of a pit bull. Fair-skinned with charmingly freckled, he also sported black outerwear that hid him in the darkness, all except the fall of wavy blond hair that was gathered into a two-foot ponytail that hung between his shoulders.

"Verily," said the first man, Cain. "My acute senses can detect the rumble of your thoughts, Apprentice mine. Pray, do tell what disturbs you so on a night such as this, which has graced us with the glory of Heaven above." He waved at the blanket of twinkling stars above, hardly dimmed by the scant light pollution of the Valley.

Pale blue eyes like chips of ocean ice regarded the ancient man, the legend from days so far removed from history that most considered him myth. The young man, Lincoln Hannock, shook his head ruefully, still surprised after three years as an apprentice magus that Cain could read him so well. He shifted under the dirt-colored blanket, careful to expose as little flesh as possible. "Three days, boss. Three days sitting out here while Elementals above and below keep guard over the house. Still no signs of the Sicarii and I'm pretty sure I swallowed a bug a few minutes ago."

"That extra protein has untold health benefits, no doubt."

The young man snorted in disgust. "I know I'm not supposed to ask, but I'm starting to get cramps in places I didn't think I could get 'em and I'm tired and hungry. Even an apprentice deserves answers to some questions, so I'm asking."

Eyes as pale as glacial ice turned and regarded Lincoln sagely, and the young man felt the full brunt of millennia of wisdom and loneliness in that pallid stare. He squirmed a bit, the toes of his boots digging into the rich soil. "You have a canny knack for magic, Lincoln," Cain said slowly. "One that I have always been able to ken in my apprentices. That is how I am able to make the wise choice in whom to teach the ancient arts of the magi. You have served as an apprentice for three years only and have earned two Words. Normally I would disclose only that which I feel you have a necessary right to, which is little to none."

Lincoln opened his mouth, but it snapped shut with a *click* when Cain raised a hand. "No, speak not yet, Apprentice, but let me instead impart some much-earned wisdom upon your delicate, shell-like ears. For two thousand years the Sicarii have, in various fashions, launched assaults upon my person in an effort to extinguish the flame God has so kindly bestowed upon this crude clay vessel." Cain smiled, but it didn't reach his eyes. "Every locale where I have endeavored to lay my head, every home, hostel, hotel and hearth I have owned has been found out with amazing alacrity by the enemies of God, the Sicarii, and I am in a quandary as to how that could be. But it has happened. No matter how distant a land I lay claim to, I am found out, and I like that not one bit."

"They got spies on you, boss?" Lincoln asked.

Cain's laughter was rich as chocolate and soft as silk. "Would that it were that simple." He shook his head. "Mortal spies prove quite easy to evade, and no Elemental would attempt to locate my humble self because of their respect for me and my lineage. No, there is more to the contumely of the Sicarii than can be easily explained, and I find myself well and truly irked.

"They will come for me, and soon, because young Blaine Deschamps is an intemperate sort of fellow who possesses not an ounce of patience in which to plot and scheme. No, this young man manufactures a plan and is most quick to set the machine of his desires into motion. He will strike, and soon. He will strike with great force and furious intent, no doubt sending in several SS teams to extinguish our lives with extreme prejudice. I fain feel it in my water. He is a blunt instrument and will employ tools of equal dullness, such as RPGs or tanks. All that is incumbent upon us is to bide our time until the agents of young Deschamps signal their intent by assaulting my domicile." He gestured toward the small house, a hundred yards down the gentle slope.

Lincoln peered with eyes enhanced with Vision. He almost pitied the ordinary folk who had ashes in their eyes, blinding them to the real world all around. To his unveiled vision, Air Elementals from the tiniest of Sprites to the mid-level gusts of Air the size of Hondas floated around the tiny house in a chaos of seemingly random motion. Earth Elementals, subtle and slow, humped through the vineyard in motions so delicate that ordinary people would chalk it up to the rustle of leaves or the soft patter of loose soil sliding gently downhill. Lincoln knew that Water Elementals lurked deep underground in the silent waterways known only to Earth and in the water pipes and the sprinkler system that ran throughout the valley.

The only Elemental that seemed to be missing was Fire, but Lincoln knew that to summon that destructive force, Cain would need to light the tiniest of sparks, which might burn every vineyard to ash and cinders. Fire Elementals always scared him awful, even though he was powerful enough to summon one or two at a time, because the mercurial beings cared only to devour, and their unceasing greed unnerved him. Only Cain's presence throughout the past few years had steadied him while he learned the four Elemental Languages that gave him the ability to communicate with the creatures.

The past few years, he mused. *More like seven, to be exact.* Strange how he had yet to feel that itchy, ants-in-your-pants sensation that all those who worked for Cain claimed to experience in their second year of employment. How many had approached him wringing their hands in concern, confiding their growing revulsion of the man most knew as Forrest Evers? Dozens of fellow apprentice magi had developed itchy feet after two years, and he couldn't understand how they felt, couldn't understand what drove them to abandon their master, the man who considered them worthy of Words.

He'd known Cain for seven full years and toiled under the great man's tutelage for three of those, and all he wanted was to learn more, become the best magus possible. He wanted to learn all about the wonders the world has to offer and see the secret places that held amazement. He knew that if people could see what he saw, they would be walking around in a state of absolute wonder.

But for him, it didn't start out that way.

Home was Colorado Springs with his mom and dad and high school drama and dreams of separating Stephanie McCallister from her underpants after the Freshman Homecoming dance. He'd wasted so much time thinking about that soft, sweet spot between her legs that the world could've gone to hell in a hand basket and he wouldn't have known, or cared. Such was the power of a young man's testosterone.

One summer Dad had finagled him a job as janitor (he hated the PC Custodial Engineer title on the back of his coveralls) at the small, private airport where he worked as a mechanic. The work proved tedious, boring enough to make him want to stick needles in his eyes just for a change, but the money was okay, enough for him to buy a new iPod.

The midsummer sky blazed in the blue bowl of the sky as he swept the hangar where his father, Wilson, serviced the Lears and Gulfstreams owned by the rich, making sure that their next flight wouldn't be their last. His father hoped that his son would earn enough for a down payment on a car, preferably a Toyota so he wouldn't have to borrow the Subaru all the time. The rest would be financed with Dad as a co-signer so Lincoln wouldn't have to settle for a rusted-out hunk of shit. Wilson believed in giving kids enough money to do something, just not enough to do nothing, and that was a point Lincoln was slowly coming to appreciate the summer Cain came into his life.

Shhhhht, shhhht, shhht, went the broom across smooth concrete as Lincoln listened to Daughtry sing "It's not over" on his iPod. *Shhhttt, shhhhtt, shhhtttt.*

"I merely wish to ascertain the state of repairs upon my vehicle, my good man." The voice intruded upon the segue between Daughtry and Johnny Cash, who was singing mournfully about that old familiar sting. It was a powerful voice, deep and velvety and used to issuing commands and being obeyed. It pierced right through his Skull Candy earbuds and demanded his attention.

"Mr. Evers, like I told you, it'll only be another hour or two." That would be his father, a medium-sized man with a high forehead, close-cropped blond hair and forearms like Popeye's. He wore faded blue coveralls and carried himself with the casual ease of a former boxer who could still handle himself if necessary. Hard work and regular workouts in the fourth-bedroom-turned-home-gym kept him fit, and the years from stealing too much vitality.

"Understood, Mr. Hannock, and I do not question your competence or your diligence, but merely wish to observe you in your element. I find that there are always new wonders to be discovered and I wish to acquire knowledge not previously encountered."

Wilson Hannock's voice rose an octave. "You want to learn how to fix the landing gear of a Gulfstream?"

And *that* incredulous tone caused Lincoln to raise his eyes from the dusty concrete floor of the hangar and catch his first glimpse of the man called Forrest Evers.

Big dude, was his first thought at the sight of the man who towered over his father. *Like really freaking scary big. Nice shades, though.* The second thing he noticed were the Air Elementals.

Ever since puberty he'd been able to see what others couldn't, the strange wispy shapes in the air, the odd currents in water, the quick dancing of flame that didn't seem normal, and the sluggish movements of earth. He'd quickly learned to keep his trap shut about it after telling his mom, because the first thing she did was to take him to St. Luke's and have Father Steve give him a good once-over. That and the queer looks Dad threw his way for months afterward. Last thing he wanted was to have Wilson call the big guys with the butterfly nets to fit him with a jacket with wraparound sleeves and settle him into a room with padded walls. But that didn't stop him from looking. On sunny days, he'd stare at the big blue trying to catch a glimpse of flitting Air Elementals, some small and some so huge they seemed to take up half the sky. He would stare for hours and hours at the gamboling beings, and at times he could almost understand their breathy cries.

The ones that swarmed three feet over Mr. Evers' head were the size of hummingbirds. And there were dozens of them swirling around in a pattern so intricate and graceful it took his breath away.

Of course Forrest Evers noticed Lincoln's rapt attention.

"And who is this young gentleman with the rather amazed look on his face?" asked the billionaire with a small, knowing grin. His dark skin, a mixture of suntan and natural olive, was stretched tight over heavy bone, his curly hair falling to his shoulders in a thick mop. There was something about his gaze shielded by an expensive pair of sunglasses that spoke of ancient wisdom and hard experience. This was a man heads of state would listen to closely and heed.

Wilson shot his son a look that was equal parts irritation and affection. "Over here, son," he barked in a voice that sliced through Lincoln's fascination. He trotted over, leaving the push broom behind. "This, Mr. Evers, is my woolgathering son. Bit of a dreamer, but don't you fret, he's a hard worker for all his fantasies."

Shaking Mr. Evers' big hand felt like gripping a handful of road flares. He was sure that the man could have crushed his bones into powder with very little effort. "Please to meet you, sir," Lincoln said softly, eyes still glued to the frolicking Elementals above.

"It is mine, young man, to be sure." The big man offered a wide smile that was all brilliant white teeth, but since Lincoln couldn't see the eyes hidden behind the dark-tinted glacier-style sunglasses, he couldn't rightly gauge the other man's sincerity.

"If you want to get to Chicago before dark, I have ta' get to work," Wilson said. "You can watch all you want, but I have ta' ask you to keep the questions to a minimum."

"Go, my good man, go. I wish to converse with your fascinating son," Evers said mildly. "If you, of course, do not mind and he has no urgent need to resume sweeping."

" 'Course not." To Lincoln, Wilson added, "Trash in Hangar Three needs emptying when you're done, Son." With a curious backward glance he walked away.

"They fascinate the senses, do they not?" Evers said when Wilson was out of earshot. "Those little Elementals provide a wondrous vision."

Lincoln started, eyes widening. "You see them?" he whispered in awe. "You know what they are?" The idea that someone else could see what he saw cut the underpinnings from his reality.

"Indeed," the big man said, grin widening to show all his nearly perfect teeth. "And it is within my power to teach you the means to communicate with yon flighty beings." He paused to let that fact sink in. "Would such a prospect be of interest to a young man of your capabilities?"

Of course it was.

Forrest Evers became a fixture in Lincoln's life after that, hiring Wilson as his personal aircraft mechanic at a ridiculous salary that enabled Mr. Hannock to send his son to the University of Denver. It also allowed Evers access to the young man, to evaluate his potential and eventually (after he graduated with a degree in Geology) to recruit him as an apprentice magus. It was an offer Lincoln didn't hesitate to accept.

"What fever dream occupies your mind, Apprentice?"

Lincoln brought his mind back to the present and answered, "Just thinking about the Sicarii and Mr. Mike the priest, that's all."

"You never had occasion to meet the good clergyman."

The young man shook his head.

"Then why the sudden curiosity about the aforementioned father?"

It took a good minute for Lincoln to consider his response, which he delivered carefully. Cain was not a harsh master, but he didn't appreciate being second-guessed. "Not to question your intentions, boss, but although you're the richest guy in creation, the Deschamps are richer by a good bit and seeing as how you were caught flat-footed last time at your house in Wales, why go so far to protect one lone priest who's in the Sicarii's crosshairs? There are a lotta priests out there worthy of our attention and help."

Cool, brown-rimmed wolf eyes regarded Lincoln sternly for a moment before they softened. The young man was an oddity, an apprentice who'd stayed with him far longer than God allowed others to tolerate. For that to happen, young Lincoln must be a special man indeed, and Cain intended to find out why. After seven years, he had learned to love the young man like family, like a nephew, and that was as much a surprise as the brown ring around his irises that was proof of God's forgiveness. He'd had family in the past, all dead and gone with a goodly amount of them decorating the deep rooms of his hideout in Paris. The pain of their passing exacted such a toll upon his soul that he'd long since given up on having any more to call kin. It was with some surprise that he recognized his feelings for the young man. Somehow, during his long apprenticeship, Lincoln had snuck into his heart, and that was miraculous.

Either that, or loneliness had made him susceptible to the persistent vagaries of human emotion.

"Father Michael Engle is a man particularly blessed by the Almighty," said Cain slowly. "I feel that God harbors in His heart special designs for the good father, as evidenced by the holy power lent to him in the past. So there is, in my heart of hearts, a desire to protect father Michael Engle so he may fulfill what heavenly destiny awaits him. Besides, young Blaine Deschamps craves an end to the good father, and I mean to see said desire thwarted." He paused for effect. "Even if the effort of doing so costs me my life.

"And be aware of this: although the Deschamps may have wealth unimaginable, much of it is not in a liquid state, while mine happens to be and is therefore readily disposable." His voice, his demeanor, turned hard and glacially cold. "They have caught me unawares on one occasion, but I assure you that it is not a situation that bears repetition. My sole mission now is to chip away at the small force of Dagger Men Deschamps possesses, and I thank the Lord for the Darwinian orgy of competition that decreases the numbers of that hateful family. Whittling away at the Sicarii will weaken young Deschamps with the Board and his infernal Patron, and *that*, my dear apprentice, is when he will succumb to a grievous error that will allow me to strike at their beating heart."

"But they have mercenaries, security personnel that aren't Family."

"Men for hire do not have access to the most sensitive areas held by the Family, and therefore are of no consequence." Cain chuckled. "Fear not; there are still plenty of Dagger Men and Women to kill. You shall soon have your fill of death."

* * *

"WE ARE AT ONE THOUSAND FEET and closing fast on the target."

"Are they in the house?'

The drone pilot nodded. "Satellite imagery shows two human-sized, human-shaped heat signatures in the residence as well as several smaller ones in the surrounding areas. Most likely rabbits and foxes and such."

"Two heat signatures?"

"Yessir. On opposite ends of the building. Apparently lying in bed."

"Do you have a lock?"

"Yessir."

Blaine smiled. "Take them out."

"Yessir."

Chapter Twenty-Six

———

"Both of these will overtake you in a moment, on a single day: loss of children and widowhood. They will come upon you in full measure, in spite of your many sorceries and all your potent spells."
—Isaiah 47:9

"WHAT'S THAT?" LINCOLN ASKED, HIS FACE screwed up tight, eyes shut. Cain glanced around, careful not to expose too much of himself from beneath the thermal blanket, but saw nothing. "What's what?"

"Shhhh," Lincoln said, raising a hand. "Listen!"

A few moments later, Cain said, "Listen to what? I hear nothing."

"I do, boss. A kinda mechanical whine or drone."

At that moment, a small Sprite the size of a robin flitted down, shrieking, "From above, from above, something approaches!" in its breathy voice. It extended a length of itself to point at the sky.

The two magi looked, and what Cain saw curdled the bile in his stomach. A smoke trail headed by tiny black dot raced toward the little white house where he had set his decoy golems, a pair of crash-test dummies carefully draped in electric blankets. Cain suspected that the Sicarii might use heat-seeking tech to set their targets, but certainly didn't expect them to employ what was speeding to the house with the inevitability of death itself.

A Hellfire thermobaric missile (AGM-114N) utilizes a metal augmented explosive. It's designed to cause greater carnage than the blast fragmentation or standard warheads when deployed within a building. It contains an aluminum powder sandwiched between the explosive and the warhead casing in many layers.

All this raced through Cain's mind with the speed of a supercomputer as he hypothesized the kind of armament the Sicarii would use against an occupied structure. Thanks to his extensive knowledge of arms manufacturing (his firm was the third largest in the United States and had been awarded the contract for the new Harvester drones), he also realized that the two of them were well within the warhead's two-hundred-foot kill zone.

An instant before the missile tore through the asphalt shingle roof, he snatched his young apprentice, clutching him hard against his broad chest, stuck his hand out toward the house, and screamed a Word with all his might.

The 108-pound, five-foot missile reached the center of the house, a small living room with a brown corduroy sectional heaped high with comfy tan and brown pillows. The charge inside the warhead detonated and the aluminum mixture dispersed, burning rapidly at temperatures that could crisp flesh from bone in seconds. The pressure wave tore the small structure to flinders, shredding drywall and wood and turning anything metallic into lethal, superheated shrapnel. The wave tore through the surrounding grape vines, flattening the resilient plants, which were flash-fried by the heat bloom that followed. By the time the first plant caught fire, the wave had reached the two men.

It was Shield that Cain shouted with all the magic at his disposal, a three-foot diameter invisible barrier with a durability and impenetrability directly in proportion to the force and will of the magus casting the spell. Cain blasted out the Word with every erg of energy in his lungs, backed by a will turned adamantine through millennia of hardship and pain. He was the son of Adam, with strength and capabilities far beyond those of modern man, and he put all that ability and determination into that Word, holding a heavily muscled arm out, fingers of his hand spread wide, willing the Shield to hold against what was coming.

It was almost enough.

The two men lay perpendicular to the house, and at the perfect angle for the Shield to deflect a massive amount of energy, but it was of limited size, not big enough to fully blunt the wave that crashed into it. For a fraction of a second the Shield held, weakening the wave, forcing it around and over the two crouched men, but no magic is unlimited, and although Cain's force of will and the well of his magic was vast, the Shield crumpled like an aluminum can in the fist of a giant.

Instantly they were engulfed in sound that was less an auditory barrage and more like a physical blow that tore at ears and eyes and mouths with blunt fingers, a hard slap of noise that drowned out everything.

The wave picked the two men up like a child would a pair of Hot Wheels and tossed them end over end to bounce them up the gentle slope of the valley. The burning detritus of thousands of grape vines followed the two as they rebounded over and over off the soft soil. Invisible hands plucked at Cain's clothing and tore at his skin, but he managed to keep hold of his young apprentice, clutching at the young man as if letting go was to lose all hope, to lose the very essence of his soul. Up and over and through vines that shredded his flesh, broke his bones, and pierced his skin. More than once, he bounced off one of the older plants, venerable bushes thick around as his ankle, but his muscles still remained locked iron tight around his young apprentice. Had the space between the rows been narrower than twelve feet, he would've left his brains upon the dirt. As it was, bone after bone broke and tore through skin with every bounce. Healing passed his lips over and over again, although the roar of the explosion kept the Word from his ears, but the effects were felt as his flesh knit. Bone pulled back into flesh from where it had burst, to join together seamless, only to break once again. Desperately, between bounces, Cain aimed a Healing at the limp bundle in his arms, praying that it would be enough, because he felt the heat bloom beginning to eat at his flesh with blunt teeth, blackening his clothes and setting his hair afire. The pressure wave threw them far, but the heat followed close behind.

When he finally came to a juddering, shuddering halt, it was on his back, amid a shower of piercing pain and oceans of burning agony. Warm, sticky wetness flowed into his eyes, and smashed lips were barely able to move as he mumbled more Healings through shattered teeth. Relief was slow in coming, so he cast Healing again. And again.

With amazing speed, torn and burnt flesh mended, running like wax until not a blemish remained. Broken bones moved like scurrying mice beneath Cain's skin to set with faint *popping* noises and knit together until straight and true. Once-shattered teeth straightened and became whole. Debris was forcefully ejected from healing flesh and blood briefly spurted from ragged holes before they suddenly closed. His back arched, only his feet and shoulders touching the ground, as his spine realigned and became whole.

All the while his arms still cradled Lincoln close, muscles tight. He *screamed* with release and relief as pain swirled away from abused flesh and then he collapsed, his newly healed body still holding the younger man like an infant while all around flaming debris floated to the ground. Soon the smell of fresh smoke began to permeate the area.

"There we go, lad," whispered Cain when the dizzying relief allowed him some semblance of coherent thought. The words felt fresh and new to ears made recently whole. "Let us see what we can see, shall we?"

No answer.

"Lad?" Cain slowly sat upright, still cradling the unresponsive Lincoln. He peered closely at the young man, Vision still active, and saw something that turned his stomach.

Lincoln looked relatively unscathed, just a few abrasions on his face and hands, but it was the unnatural angle of his neck that struck the son of Adam through the heart.

Tears blurred magical vision. "Oh, lad," he moaned, knowing Lincoln was well beyond any sort of magical healing. "Not you. Oh, please Lord Almighty, not you. I cannot stand it. It is beyond me." Lincoln's face became a blur as Cain wept, the hurt a weeping sore upon his old heart.

Fifty-thousand years can build up a lot of calluses on the soul, making a man hard and sere, drying the soil of his spirit, but Cain's particular curse was many-faceted. When God curses, it is as thorough and complete as the Flood that Noah endured within the Ark. The main ingredient to the curse, besides immortality, was a crystal-clear sanity that allowed total, perfect recall, as if events from a thousand centuries ago happened only yesterday. No blurring of memory, no steady retreat into madness, not for the oldest man in the world. His punishment lacked the finality and relative swiftness of a lingering death and had more soul-wrenching desolation than the loss of a child. It held on like the soft grasp of gravity itself. Each death of a family member, each passing of a loved one was a new wound that bled eternally. No passage of time blunted or healed those lesions. The total recall God granted Cain meant that his memories would be fresh until he took his final breath, and thanks to the complexity of the curse, suicide was not an option. The curse was not only within the Mark, the uncanny blue/white eyes like those of a wolf, but upon his heart as well.

"Whatever will I tell your dear father, lad?" crooned Cain softly. His head tilted toward the night sky and the stars sparkling therein. "I know he is not truly dead, Lord, only that his fragile flesh no longer houses his immortal soul, but what shall I tell his father to ease the pain? What will ease my pain?"

That was the hell of it. His pain would never cease. Some injuries never healed, and perfect recall was definitely not a blessing.

From up the slope came the harsh *slam* of a car door and the deep rumble of an engine firing to life. The sounds had no impact upon Cain, at least not for a few seconds; then, while his tears rolled down Lincoln's cheeks, he realized what they meant. Years of experience taught him to keep a corner of his mind clear so that not even the most explosive emotions would completely fog his faculties.

"An explosion and someone *leaves*?" Quickly, yet lovingly, he set Lincoln to rest amid the burning shards of grape vines and stared toward the noise, which was now a hard roar growing steadily fainter. Whoever drove the vehicle was in a particular hurry to move away from the site, and Cain could think of only one reason someone would rather hightail it out of the valley than stick around to see what's what.

"*No*," growled Cain, spitting out Vigor a moment later. With long, graceful strides, he began to run, long legs blurring as he chewed up the distance from the vehicle.

* * *

"ASSESSMENT." BLAINE'S VOICE BETRAYED NONE OF the excitement that coursed through his veins like alcohol.

"Satellite shows complete destruction of the residence."

"Any signs of life?"

A shake of the head. "Right now it looks like the entire vineyard is catching fire. You could hide an army among the flames and I wouldn't be able to give you an answer. Too much heat, too much wreckage. If Cain was within two hundred feet of the explosion, he's dead. Nothing human could survive that."

Blaine's eyes glittered with madness or delight or both. "Good. Bring our bird back."

"Yessir. Climbing to fifty thousand feet."

"And contact our spotters, tell them to come home."

"Yessir."

* * *

SPEED. IT WAS A WORD CAIN rarely used, because with his longevity, going anywhere fast seemed trite. However, if needs be, he had no problem letting the Word rip.

Wild clover hit his nose, but he left the smell far behind as the world blurred around him, his legs pumping at such a furious pace they were almost invisible, like a hummingbird's wings. Within seconds he found himself on a paved road, the baleful red glare of receding taillights far ahead.

"No, you don't," Cain muttered, putting forth more effort. The twin red dots stopped dwindling and slowly started to draw near while his Reeboks began to smolder, leaving acrid smoke in his wake.

"Come on, come on, comeoncomeon*comon*!" The words floated on every exhalation, a demand, a plea to the Divine, although he considered any prayer to God to be a sign of arrogance on his part, not to mention ironic. Cain was no fan of irony, even if he could appreciate it when applied to others.

Whoever was driving decided to obey the rules of the road, and the taillights flared bright as the vehicle slowed to a stop at a red light. The wind whistled in Cain's ears as he neared, and Vision let him see that it was a large black SUV. Strength flew from his lips, pumping energy into his muscles.

Closer, fifty yards.

Thirty.

Ten.

The SUV accelerated hard from a dead stop, tires squealing the moment the light turned green. The rear window starred around a quarter-sized hole that suddenly appeared and Cain felt the air from a bullet pass close to his head. He grinned with anticipation, a red mist flowering across his magical Vision.

The Sicarii, the bullet a speeding confirmation.

Two more holes sprouted in the windshield before it collapsed in a shower of tempered-glass hailstones that bounced and *tinkled* on Highway 12. The shooter was mostly concealed by one of the rear seat headrests. Then Cain was right *there*, at the SUV, and the savage stings of bullets tore at his stomach and his arms. Each report was accompanied by a muzzle flare that revealed a long, harsh face filled with fear, but Healing put paid to those assaults upon his flesh and he did the only thing he could to even the odds. Some bright penny might come up with the idea to run him over, smearing him into the pavement. He slammed into the side of the large vehicle, and with his enhanced strength, *heaved.*

The tires on the driver's side left concrete, and for one crazy moment the SUV balanced on two wheels, jiggling and swerving slightly, before falling on its side at fifty miles per hour. Metal *screeched* and tore, lighting the highway with a shower of sparks while glass shattered amid the terrified cries of those inside. The SUV slid and slewed before coming to a shuddering crash in a soggy ditch.

The rear door couldn't withstand Cain's Strength, the metal screeching before parting like taffy as he ripped it free from its moorings and flung it across the highway.

"Ahh, there you are," Cain enthused, head throbbing with adrenaline and magic.

Two men in Sicarii black lay tumbled among the seats, one with a neck canted at an odd angle against the B-pillar between the opposite doors, eyes staring into infinity. The other was held fast in the driver's seat by his belt. Cain ripped the driver's door free and tore the seatbelt apart, hauling the groaning man out.

"Oh, look at you," crooned Cain with awful mirth. He shook the Dagger Man like a rag doll. The man came to when Cain hit him with a Healing. Struggling proved futile and Cain's grip on his arms too strong, his big body pinning the Sicarius to the side of the vehicle. "You shall divulge what you know," panted Cain, "and your answers are to be succinct and truthful lest you regret securing yourself to your seat with that now-useless belt. Have we reached an understanding?"

"Fuck you," the man spat in Romansh, blood running down his chin. His terrified eyes belied his defiance.

Cain had to give the man high marks for bravery, even if it was fueled by stupidity. "Oh, how I was hoping that would be your reply."

Chapter Twenty-Seven

"For if they fall, one will lift up his fellow. But woe to him who is alone when he falls and has not another to lift him up."
—Ecclesiastes 4:10

WE WERE THIRTY-FIVE THOUSAND FEET ABOVE ground, forty miles from the target zone.

"There are no Elementals at our destination," Maggie shouted over the sound of the engines. "At least, none that the Sprite I summoned earlier could detect."

I nodded, licking my lips and absently adjusting the oxygen mask that was plastered to my face.

"Nervous, Mike?" she asked, voice only slightly muffled by her own mask.

"Who, me?" My smile felt a bit shaky. "A little. Been a while since I performed an HAHO jump." High Altitude High Opening jumps were only used for covert insertions into enemy territory, and although I'd flushed the nitrogen from my system with oxygen so I wouldn't get the bends (nitrogen bubbles forming in the bloodstream), accidents do happen. Such as hypoxia, when the body is deprived of an adequate oxygen supply ... another reason to have the oxygen mask and bottle handy. Also, if, let's say, something happened to my breathing apparatus such as a hole or the seal failed, I could black out in an instant and miss the whole thing. Most likely I'd die before I hit the ground, which wasn't a comforting thought.

Maggie dimpled prettily behind her mask while the other seven jumpers merely offered thumbs-up. I was glad to see that they were so confident, but one of the perks of advancing age is a growing respect for things like gravity, something lost on the young. "You'll do fine. You're in great shape for such an old guy."

I snorted. "Thanks, kiddo. Guess I'll just have to race you to the ground. Loser buys dinner."

"You got it, boss."

Boss. Me. It still hadn't quite sunk in that I was leading a motley crew of Sicarii haters who were willing to die just to give the Deschamps family a black eye. They all looked at me like I was the Last Coming. Pardon the expression.

A man opened the hatch on the fuselage and thin air screamed into the plane. It was time. One after the other, they jumped. The last to go was Maggie, who tipped me a wink before she disappeared into the night sky.

The plane flew high enough that I could see the curvature of the earth, a dizzying sight I wished I could study, but time was ticking away and my allies were swiftly falling away.

I jumped.

Thirty-Six Hours Earlier

"YOU'VE GOT TO BE KIDDING ME." I rubbed my face, not tired, but a little frustrated. At least I was able to ditch the disguise because there were no cameras with facial recognition software in Maggie's apartment.

The lady in question sat opposite in a black office chair and crossed her arms beneath her prodigious bosom. "Sorry, ace, but it's true." The tall, pretty man, Renaud, puttered around in the kitchen, fixing us a little something to eat, but he paused long enough to add an affirmative.

Minerva, looking bored, sat next to me on the black leather couch that dominated the little apartment. I'd asked her nicely to come along for the ride, to be there when Maggie debriefed me. Not that I felt I needed the Fallen Angel's Quality to assure me ... no, more like I had a sense she was still needed. Whether it was divine inspiration or just gut instinct, I didn't know, only that I needed her near me.

I tossed her an inquiring look, and the one she threw back was filled with wry amusement. Yes, Maggie was on the up and up. Not that I had much doubt.

Two years ago, after the battle at the Deschamps hotel and my subsequent rescue, Maggie had followed Cain and me back to Omaha. Morgan's death had hit her hard. They call it "love at first sight," something I really don't subscribe to (more like 'instantaneous lust'), but she seemed to have fallen for my friend in an amazingly short span of time and found herself adrift in sorrow. Nothing I said helped; nothing Cain could teach her could mend the hole in her heart. She was damaged, sad, and lonely. Instead of seeking solace in the Lord, she'd chosen to hop on a motorcycle and find meaning on the open road. Instead of answers, she'd found some significance in life with the mysterious *they* or *them*, the group of fanatics who for nine hundred odd years had battled the Sicarii. I had to admit she seemed happier, smiling and laughing. All trace of the sullen, sad woman had vanished, so perhaps this group of comrades did offer some solace. And what a group they were.

The Knights Templar.

Imagine my surprise. "But they were disbanded by Pope Clement in 1312."

Maggie shook her head. "No, Clement announced their dissolution to put the Sicarii at ease. They continued as a covert force acting against the heirs of Judas. They voluntarily abandoned their financial business, stopped wearing their white tabards decorated with a red cross, and started working for the pope in an unofficial capacity."

Of course, why not? "You mean a medieval secret police?"

She nodded, eyes hooded as she gauged my response. "Exactly so. You see, one of the leaders of the Sicarii at the time was Philip IV of France, the king. He was deeply in debt to the Order and covertly started a campaign of misinformation that led to distrust of the Templars by the other royals of Europe. Many members were arrested and tortured into giving false confessions, then burned at the stake. With such pressure mounting all over Europe, Clement 'disbanded' the order, took over their financials and had them work against the Sicarii in secret. What began as an overt attack on the Dagger Men became a shadow war that has lasted to this day."

"So why are you with them? I thought this mysterious 'them' were all fanatics, and the definition of fanatic is someone who adheres to a belief system (not necessarily religious, could be political, etcetera) with extreme zeal, often bordering on madness." I took a deep breath. "I don't know you *that* well, Maggie, but it sure doesn't sound like your thing."

AT THIRTY-THREE THOUSAND FEET ABOVE GROUND, forty miles from the target zone, I checked my watch. It was time to deploy the chute, so I pulled the ripcord. Normally I'd wait until twenty-seven thousand feet, but forty miles is a long way to glide and I wanted as much air time as possible. Above me the airfoil deployed with a harsh *crack* that I couldn't hear thanks to my helmet. Oxygen flowed into my lungs, and I tried to keep my breathing even as the world became still all around with a dense cloud layer a few thousand feet below my position. Somewhere in the cold night, the others floated and glided gently among the clouds, steering their way toward the rendezvous point forty miles away.

That's the brilliance of an HAHO jump. Due to a drawn-out canopy time, a person could travel forty miles and beyond. It was perfect for sneaking up on the bad guys.

A GPS was strapped to my left arm, the screen barely larger than that of a wristwatch. A bright-red blip marked my landing point while a blue blip marked my current location so I wouldn't get lost. As if a Ranger could ever forget the training received at Fort Benning. While staring down at the clouds, I found myself muttering under my breath, the words falling rapidly from my lips:

"Recognizing that I volunteered as a Ranger, fully knowing the hazards of my chosen profession, I will always endeavor to uphold the prestige, honor, and high esprit de corps of my Ranger Regiment.

"Acknowledging the fact that a Ranger is a more elite soldier who arrives at the cutting edge of battle by land, sea, or air, I accept the fact that as a Ranger my country expects me to move farther, faster, and fight harder than any other soldier.

"Never shall I fail my comrades...." The words kept coming, the creed slipping through my lips effortlessly as it had over twenty years ago.

"Gallantly will I show the world that I am a specially selected and well-trained soldier ...." A lovely peace settle upon me. I was smiling behind my oxygen mask.

"Energetically will I meet the enemies of my country ...." The ground rushed toward me, but I was too lost in my recitation to care.

"Readily will I display the intestinal fortitude required to fight on to the Ranger objective ...."

It was a bit surprising when I realized, as those words passed my lips, that instead of a prayer to Almighty, it was the Ranger Creed I relied on at that moment for comfort. For a man in my profession, it was a bit of a *faux pas*.

But that realization didn't stop me from adding:

"Rangers lead the way."

Thirty-Six Hours Earlier

"It was Cain who told me to find the Knights," Maggie said calmly. Now that her black motorcycle jacket was off, I was able to get a good look at her as she leaned back in her chair, crossing her arms. She was leaner than she'd been two years ago. Leaner and stronger, her muscles sharply defined and facial bones pushing harder against her skin. Where there had been softness, a slight padding that blurred the lines of her musculature, there were now well-demarcated sharp lines showing every hard strand of muscle beneath her fair skin. Time had hardened her, and judging by the look in her eyes and the lines on her face, not just physically.

I shook my head in wonder. After all that had happened in the past few days—an attack by a psychopathic assassin, a deadly motorcycle chase through Paris, seeing gargoyles brought to life, and being whisked away to an underground lair that would give Batman chills—why was the continued existence of the Knights Templar disturbing me so? Maybe I was beginning to overload. I fancied I could smell the sharp, acrid smell of mental circuits frying like bacon. "Why would he do that?"

"Because over a decade ago he lost contact with the Knights, and it wasn't until shortly after Pope Francis was elected by the College of Cardinals that he received some intel on the whereabouts of the Templars. He sent me to contact the Knights, to find out why they'd been out of touch for so long."

"And …?"

The big man came into the living room holding a small plate. A grilled cheese sandwich by the smell, although instead of cheddar, some ultra-stinky variation had been thrust between the slices of baguette. He offered half to Maggie, who shook her head. Calmly, as if this kind of conversation happened every day, he answered me around a mouthful of hot sandwich. "The Knights have been operating independently from the Vatican ever since a Deschamps assumed the papacy several decades ago." He swallowed the big greasy lump. "When His Holiness rose to power, the remnants approached him carefully with the assistance of one of our longest serving Knights, Cardinal Binacello, in hopes that he was untainted. That proved to be the case."

"Remnants? Untainted?"

"Untainted by the Sicarii. Uncorrupted," Maggie said. "Not a stooge or another Family member." She took a deep breath, her eyes darting to the side. "As for 'remnants ….' " She gave Renaud a hard look, which he blithely ignored while taking another huge bite out of his cheese sandwich, acting as if the fantastical tale of a near-mythical papal organization was a humdrum occurrence. Who knows, maybe it was. "There used to be a couple hundred Knights all over the globe combating the Sicarii wherever they lurked, financed by one of the world's biggest corporations, the Vatican." She sighed. "Fanatics, true believers, the Knights Templar were the bastion against which Satan and his minions raged."

I noted the past tense. "Were?"

She smiled ruefully. "There's only a little more than a dozen active Knights left. The rest are dead."

AT TWENTY THOUSAND FEET ABOVE GROUND, thirty miles from the target, I thought, *Damn, it's cold.* Even through the polypropylene knit undies and heavy clothing, I could feel the chill seep into my flesh and my teeth began to drum together. At current altitude, it was around negative forty degrees Fahrenheit. Clouds below, blackness above sprinkled with a field of shining white dots.

Despite the terror of potential death at any second, it was beautiful, awe-inspiring. Was this how astronauts felt when they went EVA on the International Space Station? The wonder of the universe and the planet below mixed with a heady frisson of fear, knowing that the first mistake would be the last.

The GPS continued blinking, and I pulled on the steering cords to alter my vector. The airfoil above responded quickly. I made an adjustment for a slightly steeper descent to pick up speed and I wasn't too worried about falling short of the mark. There was altitude to spare.

Oddly enough, that wide smile still creased my cheeks beneath my facemask. This was fun. Crazy and dangerous and all kinds of uncertain, but I felt the juices flowing through my body, and my muscles thrummed with anticipation. Better than the Mamba roller coaster ride at Worlds of Fun in Kansas City, that's for sure.

Before I became I priest, I was a soldier and a darn good one, the kind of man others could depend on when the lead flew and the blood began to flow and that old feeling, the grim competency, came to the fore as the man I used to be replaced the priest I'd become. A heady feeling, drinking the wine of violence, and I knew that if it wasn't Godly, it was at least part and parcel of my humanity.

It's not easy reconciling such to divergent aspects of one's personality, but somehow I achieved a balance within myself, with the killer and the priest, with the hard and soft sides of my nature, a dichotomy that normally wouldn't mix. But somehow it did. The oil and water of my natures and the precarious equilibrium made me a much more dangerous person than I had been before. Only on the dagger's edge can we truly see both sides of the blade.

Strapped to my belt was a MAR (Micro Assault Rifle) or Micro Galil, a weapon produced by Israel Military Industries, Ltd., and a favored weapon of soldiers around the world. It fires a 5.56x45mm NATO round and is tough, accurate, and dependable. It was a gift from Maggie.

Thirty-Six Hours Earlier

"IT WAS 9/11," SHE CONTINUED BEFORE I could express my surprise. "You see, the Templars still dabbled in high finance, enough to keep their operations against the Sicarii well-funded." A loud *plop* came from behind as a large drop of half-melted, stinky, whitish cheese fell from Renaud's sandwich onto the floor behind her. Maggie spared him a sharp look as he hastily bent to clean the offensive dairy product from the beige carpeting. "Templar operations are mobile because for the past few hundred years the Sicarii have always managed to locate stable bases of operations and shut them down, no matter how well hidden. While mobile bases remained untouched. The arrival of the electronic age assisted the Knights in keeping their operations ambulatory and that ability allowed them to stay one step ahead of whatever magic the Family used to track them." She finished, gazing at me impassively.

What could I say? I had no reason to doubt her word or the story. The one thing I'd learned from my travels with Morgan is that history is never what you thought it was. There was always something new right around the corner ready to challenge your world view. "Why did so many Templars need to attend?"

"We're a pretty democratic group." Maggie shrugged. "All are joint shareholders in the various companies we own and the meeting of the shareholders is not only mandatory, but required for the votes that are on the docket." A slight shake of the head. "But that's not important. What is important is that the majority of the Templars were in the World Trade Center when the planes hit."

After a minute of mulling this over, I said, "So … 9/11, huh?"

She nodded.

"What happened?"

"Like I said, there were votes to be made regarding the future of our companies that would land the Templars an extremely large amount of capital. It was the height of the economic boom, and those decisions would have ensured the financial stability and expansion of the Knights for the next three generations. Necessary moves considering that, at the time, they were operating without the full economic might of the Vatican."

"What were these institutions?" I asked.

"Matsumoto Bank and Stanley Coopersmith."

I whistled. Big players indeed. One of the world's biggest banks and one of America's largest investment firms. Enough cash flowed around those two to finance any three small countries. Maybe more. "What was the deal?"

She shook her head. "I don't know. Those answers died with nearly three thousand people, two hundred of whom were Knights, the core of the Templar brotherhood and their security detail. Needless to say, the whole terrorist plot was engineered by the Sicarii. They somehow knew of the meetings happening on that fateful day. They played the board like Bobby Fischer and managed to capture most of the pieces."

Not too darn surprising. Not at all, but I looked to Minerva for confirmation and she tipped me a slight nod. That was enough for me. I crossed my arms. "So what happened after that?"

"The remaining Knights, the remnants, almost literally fell apart." Maggie steepled her fingers. "You see, the Knights were ruled by the Elders, the oldest and most successful of the Templar order, and with their stabilizing influence gone, the hotheads went berserk. Each fanatical sonofabitch thought he knew best and split off from the main branch, forming splinter groups, which lashed out wildly at the Sicarii in several spectacular, often suicidal ways."

"For example?"

"For example, on January third, 2004, a Boeing 737-300 operated by Egyptian Flash Airlines crashed into the Red Sea after taking off from Sharm El Sheikh. One hundred thirty-five passengers, the bulk of whom were French tourists. What the papers and television never found out was that fifteen of them were Sicarii. Three were members of the Board, also called the Twelve, and their security detail of a dozen Dagger Men. The Twelve are the men who operate the entire Deschamps conglomerate from stem to stern. The twelve most powerful men on Earth. It was considered quite a coup for the Templars. Another thing the papers never mentioned because the media didn't know is that thirty of those on board were Templars there to kill the Sicarii. They weren't supposed to crash the plane." Maggie made a face. "I considered it fucking stupid waste of manpower. Pardon my language."

What could I say? She was merely echoing my own sentiments. During WWII, while the Japanese kamikaze pilots were initially effective, the long-term loss of pilots and materials (i.e., the planes themselves) took a toll on the Japanese industrial base. Eventually they were reduced to using inexperienced pilots flying severely outdated aircraft, which meant the effectiveness of the program began to tilt toward zero. All in all, of the 2,800 kamikaze attacks toward the end of WWII, forty-seven ships were sunk, 368 were damaged, 4,900 sailors were killed and over 4,800 were wounded.

Sounds like some big numbers, but look at some realistic totals: from 1938 to 1945 the United States produced ten battleships, twenty-seven aircraft carriers, 110 escort carriers, 211 submarines, and 907 cruisers/destroyers/escorts. Next to those numbers, forty-seven weren't near enough to blunt the U.S. advance upon Japan.

So I said the only thing I could think of. "What now?"

Ten thousand feet above ground and ten miles from target, everything moved faster and faster and I could see the ground under my feet. Kind of. Mostly the dark, humpy shapes of hills like the folds of the world's largest bed sheet. Here and there shone the occasional pinpoint of light that indicated a village, sleepy and unaware of the dark forms that glided above them like hawks. Far, far behind me shone the bright lights of Geneva, filling the air with luminescent pollution, dominating the smaller towns around Lake Geneva.

We were in prime Deschamps territory, the small country they considered their own, with banks that held billions of dollars in currency and billions more stowed in vaults, treasures looted from around the world, or so the Templars claimed. Secret Nazi hideaways, the greatest relics and artifacts hidden away from prying eyes.

Sure, the real-life Monuments Men (an allied group tasked with locating and retrieving art and other important items before their destruction by the Third Reich during WWII) saved millions in stolen art, but according to the Templars, *billions* worth were still out there. Maggie said all that loot was the singular obsession of the Templar Knights, or had been until 9/11 all but destroyed them.

Years of fragmentation and splintering had weakened the Knights further until only a handful of bitter men and women remained. And then along came Maggie. With Cain's connections, she was able to make contact, then join the remnants, quickly establishing herself as an up-and-comer. For the past year and a half she'd led small but effective raids against Sicarii targets: the MacDowell Pharmaceuticals plant in Glasgow, the *Noche Verdad* software firm in Madrid, and the bombing of NightLight Computers in Silicon Valley, to name a few. All her objectives were achieved with no loss of life, a fact that endeared her no end to the remnants.

Because of her magic and her savvy, she became leader of the Knights, initiated into the fold with sacred rites, rituals, and terrible vows—vows that bound her to the Templars for life. With all that on her plate, she hardly ever made contact with Cain anymore. That didn't mean he'd failed to keep in touch, which was why I found myself the new *de facto* leader of the Knights Templar.

Just when I thought life couldn't get any stranger.

Chapter Twenty-Eight

"All the days of Saul there was bitter war with the Philistines, and whenever Saul saw a mighty or brave man he took him into his service."
—1 Samuel 14:52

I WAS AT GROUND LEVEL AND A mile from the target. Touchdown. My feet hit soft earth a second before I would've slammed face first into the gnarly bark of a large tree. As it was, I came close enough to see every gnarl and whorl on the trunk. Still, the impact from landing traveled from ankles to knees to shoulder in a sickening wave of pain. I fell to one knee, disengaging from the harness before a gust of wind had me fighting the air foil all the way to Lake Brienzersee, a couple hundred yards away.

"Nice landing, tall-dark-and-priestly, but I won the bet."

Holy Mackerel. I nearly jumped out of my skin. Even with my eyes adjusted to the dark, I hadn't seen Maggie leaning on a chestnut tree just a few short feet away. By the crescent-shaped reflection of moonlight, I could tell she was smiling. "This clearing is barely as big as my church in Omaha," I whispered irritably. "I'm lucky to be in one piece and not smeared across every conifer in the area."

Seven other shadows emerged from the surrounding woods into the small clearing. Four men and three women, all tough as nails, all dressed in black like me—although it was warm enough that they had exchanged their warmer clothes for lighter attire. Each of us had a white patch painted on our left foot to differentiate us from the Dagger Men, who also had an affinity for all-black outerwear. After ditching my oxygen mask, I decided to follow suit. "Still no

Elementals at our destination?" I checked the GPS. A small green dot had appeared, indicating that our objective lay about a mile away.

Maggie shook her head. "Just conferred with a Sprite and an Earth Elemental, and they report that there are none to be found, which bugs me something terrible."

"Why does that upset you so, Maggie?" asked a lanky brunette named Amelie, a small frown on her narrow face.

I fielded that one. "Because it could mean that there's something worse guarding the cabin."

Amelie snorted in derision. "What could be worse than an Elemental that can burn flesh from bones, rip limbs apart, have the earth swallow you whole or fill your lungs with water?"

It was Renaud who answered. "That is what is so worrisome, *ma chérie.*"

Despite ominous forebodings, the entire team double-checked each other's gear with aplomb, making sure that when the feces hit the fan, no one would die due to inadequate prep. I always follow the 7P rule that my DI knocked into my head in Ranger School: Proper Prior Planning Prevents Piss Poor Performance. Some say it's a British Army adage, but I think it's common sense.

Twenty-Nine Hours Earlier

A FEW HOURS LATER, AFTER THE LITTLE debrief with Maggie and Renaud, I slept. Information overload aside, I'd been trained to catch winks whenever I could. Just because my mind was reeling and once again my perception of reality had been knocked on its butt didn't mean my body could go without proper rest.

Surprisingly enough, I awoke refreshed, bright-eyed and bushy-tailed. During sleep my mind must have come to grips with my situation, no matter how odd. It helped that two years ago the circumstances had been just as odd and I came through that more or less unscathed except for some epically unpleasant memories.

After a shower and a shave, I walked into the living room to be confronted by Maggie, still in the same all-black she'd worn that morning to the coffee shop. Her mouth quirked. "You look younger than I remember," she said.

"Not how I feel." Wide awake, yes. Young, no.

Minerva, who was reading a James Patterson thriller on the couch, looked up. "You still have the stripy coloring in your hair. A Catholic punk rocker look." Her voice contained just a smidgeon of humor.

Skip to my Lou, my darlin'. "You're still here." Part of me wanted to say "You're still blonde," but I wasn't too sure how Maggie and the Templars (sounds like a '50s rock 'n' roll band) would take it. Actually, I fully expected her to toddle off once her mission was complete.

As if reading my mind, she said, "I will leave once I see that I'm not delivering you into the hands of the Sicarii." She glanced at Maggie. "No offense, but I have to see these 'remnants' you're talking about to be sure. I will not leave owing Cain. The slate must be wiped clean."

Maggie's answer emerged calm, betraying not an ounce of anger. "None taken."

Time for some more answers. "Why do you owe him? He save your life?" I asked.

Minerva bit her lower lip, the first time she displayed any sort of hesitation. Up until then she'd been the perfect action hero. "I … am hesitant …."

"You can talk to me. I *am* a priest, after all. Listening is what I do."

To that, Maggie added, "And I was his apprentice for eighteen months. Hardly anything you can say would surprise me."

A faint smile touched perfect lips. "You'd like to think so, Apprentice." For a moment it looked as if she'd shut up about the whole thing, but she continued, "When we fell, after the war in Heaven, we who lost our wings were bitter, hiding in the dark places of the world, licking our wounds.

"When we grew tired of pouting and stewing in the wine of our self-pity, we showed our faces to the world once more. This was shortly after the time you people called 'The Flood,' when an early human civilization flourishing on the edge of the Mediterranean Basin was destroyed for its wickedness.

"We spread across the world quickly, thousands of the Fallen, each still with a measure of power granted us upon our creation. Every Fallen Angel had a Quality that set them apart from the next and from the humans we encountered. Many chose to live anonymously among the teeming hordes of humanity, breeding with them and begetting Nephilim, those half-breeds with the soul of a human and the power of an Angel."

Minerva paused and chose her next words carefully. "I was one of the Fallen who chose not to breed with humans. Not because I did not want to, but because I still felt unclean about my part in the Rebellion. So when the Fallen took upon themselves the mantles of Divinity, becoming the gods of legend, I chose to become Athena, the virgin goddess of Wisdom and Valor." She paused. "And when the first sacrifices and burnt offerings were made to us, the pain of our exile from Heaven lessened considerably. That was our folly—assuming a godhood we did not deserve and enjoying it."

Hesitant to break the tension, I had to ask, "And Cain?"

"Cain came to Greece a thousand years after we established Olympus, which was shortly after the fall of Troy. It was Cain who convinced me that what we were doing, using mortals for sport and worship, was wrong. It was

Cain who sowed discord among the various pantheons of the world, exposing how vulnerable we Fallen really were. It was Cain who proved to the humans that even a 'god' can die."

"What did he do?"

"He killed Hephestiel, who was known as Hephaestus, God of the Forge."

"Wait-a-minute," I replied, rubbing my eyes. "If I remember my Greek mythology, Hephaestus was injured by Zeus, who threw him from Olympus when the lesser god challenged him. He didn't die."

Before I finished my sentence, Minerva was shaking her head. "No, it was Cain. In front of humans, he slew Hephestiel and scared off Ares, showing him to be a coward. Zeus created the legend of throwing Hephaestus off of Olympus and asked Nurenial, of the lesser Fallen, to assume his place. Because Cain is stronger than most Fallen, and fearing God's Curse should he kill him by stealth, Zeus cooked up a story about him as a Titan who displeased the gods so greatly that he was chained to a rock in Tartarus, where a giant eagle ate his liver every day."

"Prometheus," I whispered. The Titan who gave man fire, or in this case, knowledge. Deadly, dangerous knowledge.

Minerva nodded. "That's all Zeus could do, make up stories. Even the gods are afraid of Cain. Prometheus. Loki. Kokopelli and Manannan Mac Lir. Cain never seeks to be a god, only to teach mankind either through trickery or object lessons. But wherever he goes, godhood is thrust upon him."

"Holy mackerel." What could I say?

Maggie turned to me, her dimples visible. "Well, that's about enough of that happy horseshit, Mike. Let's get down to brass tacks." Maybe she realized the lighthearted tone wasn't sitting too well with me and a frown replaced her smile. She nodded abruptly. "C'mon." Tossing me a black motorcycle helmet that was sitting on the coffee table, she added, "You have to meet the rest of the gang."

I gathered the *Codex* box and papers, along with the manila envelope Cain had given me, and loaded them into the Harley's saddlebags. There was no way I could leave them behind. A quick motorcycle ride through Calais brought us to the port along Pont Vetillard, where Maggie steered the motorcycle into a mostly deserted parking lot. The sky above was darkening to midnight blue as the sun slipped past the horizon, but she kept the headlight off, parking the bike near a brace of white Volvo semis parked side by side.

Seven people boiled from the semi trailers, three women from the right and four men from the left. The women looked a heck of a lot tougher than the men except for Renaud, who looked like he could handle the Cornhusker defensive line all by himself. As for Minerva, she parked the tiny blue Renault rental nearby, sat on the hood, and stared, face stony.

Before I knew it, the seven Knights, their eyes shining in the lights of halogen lamps that dotted the lot, surrounded me. A woman of about thirty, who had shoulders broad enough to suit any pro linebacker, reached out and took my right hand. Reverently, she brought it to her lips and kissed my knuckles softly, tenderly. When she lowered my hand, her eyes were moist.

"Thank you, Father," she said hoarsely, and moved aside for the next person, a fortyish man with a round face and thinning hair. He, too, took hold of my hand and brought it to his lips. I was too flabbergasted to resist, merely staring as one after the other the remnants of the Knights Templar kissed my hand.

Maggie was the last to bestow that honor.

"What …?"

"We know who you are, sir," said a thin man with a thick German accent. He had sallow, acne-scarred cheeks. "Maggie has told us your story."

"My story?"

All nodded. "Yes, Father Mike, the story of how you helped defeat Julian Deschamps, of your exorcism of the Bephemaloch Cazzizz, how you were able to perceive the Holy Grail and your destruction of the Silver. You have been touched by the hand of God Almighty and are the vessel of His will."

We were one mile from our target.

"Okay, gang," I began once Maggie checked my slim backpack, Kevlar body armor, and utility belt, giving me a thumbs up. "GPS off. Anything that emits a signal that can be intercepted … off." Without argument, they did so. "Radio silence unless there's an emergency. We all know where the cabin is. What I want is an even, steady pace through the woods as quickly and as quietly as possible. We will rendezvous just outside the clearing at zero three-hundred." I checked my watch. "It is now zero two-twenty on my mark." Long pause. "Mark." As one, the group nodded as they synchronized their watches.

Butterflies fluttered in my stomach, but I quashed the feeling ruthlessly. Fear is fine. Fear gets the juices going, lets a body know it's alive and keeps it that way unless the fear becomes dominant. Once that happens, it's all over and it's time to get measured for a casket.

"Okay, by twos now, like we discussed. Renaud, you're odd man out, so you're on your own, but keep an eye on Simon and Richard. You ready?"

The big man nodded solemnly.

"Remember, don't hesitate because they surely won't."

One of the women, a dirty blonde named Amy who had a cute, elfin face took a step forward. "Will you bless me, Father?" she asked, eyes wide and wet.

"Yes, please."

"Please, Father Michael."

"Yes."

A chorus of please and affirmations assailed me, and of course I could bestow a blessing because it's what I do, what I am. A Catholic priest, a man of peace in an insane circumstance, but still a priest, a man of God. I searched my mind for a prayer, a blessing, something that would comfort my new congregation, something that would give them peace, and ultimately, hope.

It came to me as if kissed into my mouth and it flowed out to caress the ears of the Knights:

"The Father of Mercies has given us an example of unselfish love in the sufferings of His only Son. Through your service of God and neighbor, may you receive his countless blessings."

All responded. "Amen."

"You believe that by His dying, Christ destroyed death forever. May he give you everlasting life."

"Amen."

"He humbled Himself for our sakes. May you follow his example and share with His resurrection."

"Amen."

May Almighty God bless you, the Father, and the Son, and the Holy Spirit."

"Amen."

The Liturgical Blessing on the Fest of the Passion of the Lord. Not sure it was the correct prayer and blessing, but it felt *right* and I had to go with my gut on this one. One after the other, I touched each of them on the forehead and that felt right and proper. Each one, Maggie included, crossed themselves, their eyes brimming with unshed tears.

"Thank you," said Renaud in a voice like sandpaper over rough stone. "Thank you, Father."

"Thank you."

"Yes, thank you."

"Thanks, Father Engle," and variations on that theme were wafted to me.

I felt … good. It had been a while since I'd administered to the truly devout. Don't get me wrong, I love my parishioners back in Omaha, but sometimes I felt they were just going through the religious motions. Going to church simply because it was expected of them, a social convention rather than in response to a deep and abiding connection to the Lord. Looking into the shimmering eyes of those who *truly* believed in their hearts and souls gave me a measure of satisfaction I had never felt before.

"And thank you very much," I replied with all due gravity.

Twenty-Nine Hours Earlier

"You're making me sound like a rock star." My voice remained steady despite my unease. The way those Knights looked at me made me want to find a convenient rock to hide under. "I'm no rock star."

"Of course not, sir," the thin man with the acne-scarred cheeks replied. "You're a hero."

Good Lord, save me from people with an acute case of hero worship. Before I could respond, he continued, "All of the Knights know your story and the results of your actions."

All the Knights? I looked at the dim stars shining through the veil of light that shielded Calais from Heaven, gathering my thoughts. "There's more of you?"

Maggie nodded. "Ten more. A couple of pilots, computer technicians, and even a doctor. The rest are financial experts who manage the money that keeps us stocked with munitions and pays the mortgages on our safe houses."

"I thought the Vatican supported you? The Church is pretty darn rich."

"His Holiness can only do so much, considering that the Vatican is awash in Sicarii spies. Unfortunately, all he can offer is spiritual support, but we take what we can get."

That brought me up short. I'd forgotten that Morgan had told me of his Family's infestation of the Church. It bothered me some then and now it really set my blood to boiling … hot enough, in fact, that I had to visibly restrain my temper.

The look on my face must have been frightening, because a couple of those battle-hardened veterans actually took a step back, alarm writ large across their features.

Easy there, Mike, I cautioned myself. *You've been through the wringer, but that doesn't mean you can lose your cool whenever you want. These people look up to you.* That's when the realization hit, a bit of an epiphany, actually. All of them, that tough Valkyrie Maggie included, gazed at me with a sort of reverence seen only on those who stare into the eyes of an idol. Or a major celebrity.

Or a leader.

Maggie saw it first, that dawning awareness that lighted my eyes like lamps. Her soft chuckle startled everyone. Those dimples were pronounced on her beautiful face as the chuckle became laughter, then a full-throated roar of hilarity.

"Me?" I needed answers. Or a different answer than what had dropped into my mind. "Me?"

A moment later, under the eyes of the bemused Knights, she calmed down enough to grace me with a hiccoughing answer. "Of course, Mike. It had to be you. It's why Cain has been training you." *Hic … hic.* "Not just to keep you alive, but to assume the mantle of leadership you were born to." Her teeth shone very white in the light of the halogens. "Sir."

Oh, no! Not *that.*

"You have got to be kidding me," I blurted out. "Me, the *leader* of this bunch?"

"Yup."

"I was a sergeant; I *worked* for a living. I'm no officer." *Deep breaths, Mike. Deep breaths.*

"Well," Minerva drawled in amusement. "I believe my work here is done."

"Please don't." I cringed at the whine in my voice.

Her eyes with that unknown color speared me. "You have to buck up, Mike. Life as you know it has changed forever. It changed the moment you decided to assist Olivier Deschamps, and you can never, ever go back."

I didn't want to admit it, but she was right. My old life belonged to the past, and my new one beckoned, offering more than a handful of peril and fear. I wanted to scream my denial at the top of my lungs.

"It's up to you to lead us, Mike," Maggie soothed. The Templars were looking at me with such pity and longing that I wanted to pull a disappearing act. Their need clawed at me, choked me, bound me with chains of duty and responsibility. But I had other responsibilities, too … to my parish, to my parishioners, to … to ….

To God.

And here He was handing me the biggest responsibility of my life. It scared me spitless. There seemed to be only one thing for a man in my position to do. "One moment, please," I rasped, throat tight, and walked away.

From behind, I heard Maggie shush the group as my feet took me to the other side of the semis, the side facing the English Channel. God's magnificent creation before and above me, perilous and beautiful at the same time. Behind me stood humanity's concrete and steel structures—sterile and ephemeral, a child's sand castles by comparison. I let the glory of the sea and sky wash over me as my hands came together in prayer. "Dear Lord, you have watched over me, protected me against the forces of the Sicarii. Given me strength to endure torture at the hands of Boris." I licked my lips. "Is it my destiny to lead the Templars? Or have they placed their faith in a man who will march them all into failure and death? Please, Lord, give me a sign."

Nothing. I kept staring at the dimly winking stars and still felt the tremendous uncertainty in my soul. I was a man of God, a priest, and a handful of people wanted me to lead them into conflict with the most dangerous family on the planet.

Over twenty years. That's how long it had been since I'd set foot on a battlefield, ready to kill the enemy until my commanding officers told me to stop. Back then anger filled me, a directionless passion harnessed by the Army into a jagged blade ready to let loose a torrent of blood.

And I would have, too.

Still no answer. No sign … no nothing. I sighed. Not in frustration, but in resignation.

"He doesn't answer like you humans think He does." Minvera's voice floated on the still, salt-laden air like eiderdown. "As a matter of fact, God isn't a He or She or even an It. If humans had the vocabulary to describe God, I could tell you what He is, but your minds are so limited, you wouldn't understand the concepts needed to understand the concepts needed to understand." A long pause while I stared at the sky, unable or unwilling to turn around and face the Fallen Angel. "But I will give you my two cents worth, Michael Engle, and you can take or leave it. Doesn't really matter much to me."

I cleared my throat. "Go ahead."

"All this time, you've been reacting to circumstances, holding on for dear life while events washed you one way then another. You have to make a decision, and while prayer is always good, don't rely on it. Rely on yourself. Stop reacting and make a decision to do *something*."

"Skip to my Lou, my darlin'," I sang softly. The anger I felt in Paris while being chased by the Dagger Men began to assert itself again, fizzing along my nerves, and the thought *enough is enough* once more bounced around inside my skull. I continued to sing the partner stealing song.

Minerva laughed and it almost sounded like … bells. Her voice joined mine in a chorus.

> Lost my partner, what'll I do?
> Lost my partner, what'll I do?
> Lost my partner, what'll I do?
> Skip to my Lou, my darlin'.

Part Three

Fight

Chapter Twenty-Nine

"For he is God's servant for your good. But if you do wrong, be afraid, for he does not bear the sword in vain. For he is the servant of God, an avenger who carries out God's wrath on the wrongdoer."
—Romans 13:4

WE WERE A HALF MILE FROM target.

For the record, trying to sneak through a dense forest of conifers is darn near impossible. Pine needles so dry they'd flare into a raging fire at the smallest spark *crunched* under my boots as I made my way steadily closer and closer to where the target lay. From behind came a soft *popping* as Maggie stepped on a pinecone.

"Damn," she whispered. "Wish I had Vision, or nightvision goggles."

"*Shhhhh!*" The trick was not being silent, but to make only those sounds that are expected in the surroundings. The whisper of the breeze through boughs and animal noises.

We trekked through pine giants, avoiding their bristling shoulders. I checked my watch. On time, not too fast, not too slow. The fizz of adrenaline began in my blood. Not too long now.

What would we find? Sicarii, of course, but what else? A cabin in the woods where answers lay.

A pine cone *popped* quietly under my boot, just loud enough for me to hear, but not so loud to be heard ten feet away. I hoped.

"Why no Elementals?" I whispered to Maggie after stopping to listen, the words barely disturbing the cool night air. No unusual noises; the other Templars were apparently successful in their endeavors in stealth. Good, what a relief. An insect crawled along the back of my neck, but I ignored it.

"Don't know," she replied. "Fire is the easiest to coax, but it's too hungry and unpredictable, so they wouldn't use it. Air is unstable, flighty, and getting Sprites and Gales to stick around takes some effort. Water and Earth would be perfect for a setting like this with a lake nearby, but the Sprites I used for recon said there were none active in the area."

"That's unusual, considering the value of our target, isn't it?"

Her deep blue eyes, colorless in the dark, regarded me solemnly as we rounded a giant of a fir. "Yes, and that's what bothers me. What's there in that cabin that even Elementals want to steer clear of?"

Twenty-Seven Hours Earlier

THE SEMIS TURNED OUT TO BE mobile offices complete with computers, satellite communications equipment, and comfortable leather office chairs bolted to the floor. In fact, everything was secured to either the walls or floor.

"Impressive," I remarked. "Always mobile. How?"

"We own the trucking company." She smiled. "Several, in fact. All legitimate. It allows us to travel to any location needed to fight the Sicarii. The Deschamps are wonderful when it comes to brute force, but they wouldn't know subtle if it fell out of the sky onto their faces and began to wiggle. They're financial wizards, but haven't really caught on to the fact that the real power in this digital age is the internet. We Knights, because we're used to less funding, know how to make do with subtle, and no one beats our programmers." Maggie ran a hand over one of the computers, a large laptop with a glowing blue screen. "Ergo, we developed these mobile command centers."

"Mobile to keep the Sicarii from finding them, right?"

All of us, including Minerva, filled one of the semis. For some reason, no one objected to the Fallen's presence. Perhaps that was one of her little tricks, the ability to be accepted into any social gathering. Either way, I was glad she'd chosen to stay for a little while and kept close to her side as a buffer against the hero worship emanating from the Knights like an almost palpable stench.

Maggie frowned. "One of the things that's been plaguing the Knights has been the Sicarii's uncanny ability to find their enemies, no matter how well hidden. Back in the '60s, some genius figured out that boats and trucks were perfect offices because the Sicarii never knew exactly where they would be."

Minerva snorted.

"What?" I asked.

Her face became studiously blank. "Nothing. Sorry."

No. Not nothing. "Tell me."

"No." Flat. Final.

Enough was enough. Time to be the complete, dominant ass I used to be back in Iraq when things were bloody, dirty, and mean. "No? Now's not the time for no. I need intel and you have it, so spill."

She gave me the *you're not the boss of me* look every child perfects before the age of eight and said nothing. The temperature in the trailer dropped noticeably, enough that I saw my breath steam in the close air of the trailer. The anger in her face made everyone take a quick step back. The trailer creaked and groaned on its axles.

Righteous anger wasn't working; it would only spur Minerva to greater heights of anger and greater lows of temperature. I needed time to figure out how to enlist her help. "Why not?" I asked. "Answer me that, at least."

Those uncanny eyes flicked about the trailer, and suddenly the Knights found other things to occupy them. Not a man jack of them looked our way, or even appeared to be listening. We were as alone as if we stood on the surface of the moon.

SEVERAL HUNDRED YARDS FROM OUR TARGET, we heard hard, flat reports muffled by thousands of pine boughs. Not ours; most of our weapons were outfitted with suppressors, the notable exception being mine. If I closed my eyes, I could pretend those shots sounded like popcorn.

"On my six," I ordered as more barking reached us.

Faster through the woods we moved, the darkness now hot and heavy, my mind expanding, working at triple speed as excitement and dread supercharged my body. Faster and faster around the trees. My heart thudded but my mind remained clear, functioning perfectly, rationally. The barking came from ahead and to the left.

Suddenly, more barking, this time from the right, harsh, louder than before. Closer. Two weapons, one with sharp reports spaced close together— an SMG, perhaps. The other the hard *boom* of a shotgun.

"What now?" panted Maggie from behind. More booming.

"You use what Words you need to use and watch my back." I slowed, approaching the booming of the shotgun, although a stampede of elephants wouldn't have been heard over all that racket. Still, better safe than suddenly and definitively dead.

Close now. Strobing flashes of the firefight burst against my eyes and I could hear the steady *chuff-chuff-chuff* of Renaud's Mac-10 and its enormous suppressor. I moved, a shadow slipping between trees, and from behind came a Word that slid into my ear and right back out without touching the gray matter in between. My eyes drooped to half-mast because I didn't want to lose my night vision to the bright flame emerging from the auto shotgun held in the hands of a big man in black who popped around a tree every few seconds at odd intervals to fire away. A knife appeared in my hand, a K-bar, razor sharp, gleaming in the faint light. My feet pounded against the forest floor, sending needles flying. Suddenly the knife no longer gleamed as a hot rush of liquid coated my hand in metallic-smelling fluid, and I went past, hidden behind a tree out of sight from the clearing that was right *there*.

Renaud hit the deck behind one of the conifers, half burying himself in needles and loam.

"Where's the other gunman?" I asked while keeping an ear on the staccato gunfire far away to the right.

"Dead, *monsieur*. Simon killed him."

"Where's he, then?"

Simon's gut was more pony keg than six-pack, a thing of legend. Short and wide with a genial, pug-nosed face, he looked strong enough to rip trees out by the roots.

Renaud shook his head sadly.

Damn.

"Richard?"

"Here, sir," said a voice from behind. Richard, a tall, thin man with a pinched face and ginger beard, lay half under a conifer, a hand pressed to his side.

"You okay?"

He nodded. "Flesh wound. Hurts, but not too debilitating," he rasped in his thick English accent. A former SAS officer, he was as good as they come and as tough.

"All right. Stay here and watch our six. Bug out if things go pear-shaped."

"But—"

"That's an order, Soldier."

He nodded again. "Yessir."

I looked for and found Maggie. Her eyes shone in the soft light from the cabin filtering through the branches. They were wide enough that I could see the whites all around. "What?" I asked.

"Never seen a priest kill before."

The blood was swiftly drying on my knife, almost gluing my fingers to the handle. Me, a priest … a killer. For the first time I looked at the corpse of the man I'd killed. A gaping mouth below a strong chin, the edges crusted with quickly drying blood. Neatly sliced cartilage, thick and rubbery, and the gleam of bone from a cut so deep it had almost decapitated the man. I had no real memory of the strike, only the momentary tug of resistance and the sudden *give* as the K-bar entered flesh.

I shuddered, but forced myself to look. I did this—it was my handiwork— and I had to acknowledge that fact, own it down to the bone. To look away would label me a coward. That was a weakness I could not afford. Not to mention being a lie, and I couldn't live with such a canard on my soul.

"Renaud."

"Yes, *monsieur?*"

"Check the clearing. Be careful." The firefight still raged several dozen yards away, but we sat in a sea of calm at the edge of the clearing. "Then help the others."

"*Oui.*" Dark skin, dark clothes, he was a flitting shadow barely seen as he made his way through the trees, surveying the clearing and the cabin resting comfortably therein. His skill lasted long enough for him to make it halfway to the other firefight before his head exploded in a ghastly mist of blood and brains.

Twenty-Seven Hours Earlier

PERHAPS IT WASN'T THE BEST IDEA to push her, but Minerva obviously possessed information I needed, *we* needed, and just letting it lie wasn't in my DNA.

I went for polite. "Please?"

"No." The word landed hard, with a tone of finality. She abruptly turned away and opened the rear of the trailer, jumping out and landing lightly in the parking lot. That motion carried a subtle grace and elegance I could never match and didn't bother to try. Instead, my sneakers slapped down hard, my legs flexing to absorb the stinging impact I could feel all the way to my crotch.

"Wait, Minerva!" I called softly to her retreating back. One of the Knights closed the trailer door to hide the hard lighting from inside.

The Fallen Angel turned, her expression harsh in the illumination of the parking lot halogens. "What?"

"I meant no disrespect."

"Noted." An acknowledgment, not forgiveness.

"If it is my role to be the leader of this bunch," I waved at the trailer, "then I need all the help I can get."

"Understood." Butter wouldn't melt in her mouth.

"So," I pleaded, "will you help me?"

"No."

The single-word answers were beginning to try my patience. "Why?"

She shook her head, eye hot and shining with some unnamable emotion. "I am gone." Off she went to the Renault, not bothering to spare a goodbye.

" 'The only thing necessary for the triumph of evil is for good men to do nothing,' " I quoted, spitting out the first thing I could think of.

"Don't you quote Edmund Burke to me," Minerva replied without looking back. She jumped into the car and it revved to life.

When I want to, I can move pretty fast, and I made it to the car before it could speed off. I stood in the light of the headlamps and crossed my arms. Anger I had held back for far too long made my flesh tingle. Once again my world was all topsy-turvy, and deep down in the pit of my stomach, I knew I wouldn't be laying eyes on St. Stephen's again, that it was now and forever in the *lost* category, along with my youth and my innocence. Too much had happened in such a short time. Minerva had essentially told me to put my big boy pants on, then turned and walked away when the Knights—when *I*—needed her most.

Really beginning to piss me off.

"No," I shouted without thought. The word forced its way out past my lips and I could almost see the rippling pressure waves hit the Renault. Once again, "No." A curious heat throbbed behind my eyes. I felt like I was ten feet tall staring down on a vehicle that seemed to be constructed of gossamer strands. From behind, I heard the trailer doors open and several boots hit the ground. Whatever spell she held over them looked to be long gone, and they stood at a respectful distance, watching.

"Get out of the car." A command not to be refused. My voice sounded deeper, almost booming, yet emerged no louder than a whisper.

She complied, eyes now silver pools that rippled like mercury. Her skin carried a hint of a gold sheen and her long hair haloed around her head like seaweed caught in a strong current.

"Come here."

Each step was a battle fought with the will of an Angel, but there flowed through my veins a stronger spirit that could not be denied. I watched her approach as if detached from the scene, unable to do anything but play the part assigned to me.

My hand rose of its own accord, palm out. I motioned for Minerva to kneel, and her knees gave way as if her strings had been cut. She landed hard enough on the concrete that the knees of her pants tore.

The question emerged low and urgent. "How do the Sicarii always know how to find the Templar's secret bases?"

Minerva's jaw worked and a vein throbbed on her temple. For several seconds she resisted, but the power flowing through me could not be denied. "The Oracle," she said, grinding out each syllable with miserly reluctance.

Good. Now we were getting somewhere. "Where is this Oracle?"

"He … he is in Switzerland, near Lake Brienzersee."

"Where, specifically?"

What followed was a series of numbers that at first didn't make sense, but after a moment I realized they were coordinates—longitude, latitude, minutes, and degrees. To my left, Maggie nodded, letting me know she had them memorized. I grinned, heady and full of power.

"Angel Atheniel," the Templars started and stared, "you have been away from the vaults of Heaven for a long time. Why have you not asked for His forgiveness?"

The silver lamps of her eyes shone brighter, and the ringing of small bells grew louder. "I rebelled against the Throne, Father Engle," she answered, golden tears dripping down her cheeks. "For that there is no forgiveness."

An anger vast and terrible gripped me, the fury of a father sorely betrayed by a troublesome child. "You took the mantle of a false god, commanding mortals you should have been shepherding. Another sin you must answer for. You turned your back on humanity to sulk in the darkness of your own self-pity, yet another sin. You told me not to quote Edmund Burke, yet you have done nothing to battle the evil that plagues this world. Remaining passive while possessing the ability to ease suffering and promoting good is also a sin, my child."

Far in the back of my mind, I sat and watched, astounded, as the former Angel of the Heavenly Host prostrated herself before me in abject misery, sobbing. The desire to berate ebbed against the force of my compassion.

My knees hit concrete next to her and I gathered the weeping Angel unprotesting into my arms. "Atheniel, Angel of Wisdom, why have you, in all your time of exile, never asked for your Father's forgiveness?"

"I'm not worthy!" A cry of despair. "He will never forgive *me*."

I chucked her under the chin, tilting her head up. Silvery pools radiating sorrow and loss met my eyes and turned away, unable to meet the power that was bleeding through my irises. "All of us can earn forgiveness, Atheniel, even Lucifer himself. There is but one thing you must do to begin," I whispered. "Just *ask*."

"How can I?"

"Ask."

"But—"

"*Shhhh*," I commanded, then softer, in barely a whisper without a hint of command, added, "Ask."

"Forgive me?"

"Do you repent your actions, my daughter?"

"Oh, *yes*!" A sad and lonely wail.

"Will you faithfully and forever follow only God and obey His will, to be a force for Good against the Darkness?"

"Yes."

"Then I forgive you."

Stillness, absolute and perfect. No breath issuing from the mouths of the

Templars, no motion from the tears on Atheniel's face. The night became charged with an electric anticipation that seemed to suck the light out of the halogens and prickle our skin as the sounds of water, insects, and our heartbeats failed to reach ears rendered numb. Even the stars themselves ceased their winking.

It started as a faint exhalation that whispered against my skin, cold and soft. With it came a sound, which became words that caressed my ears.

"Thank you."

And she was gone. Just like that.

Once again, the night became the night with its usual accompaniment of sounds and motion. The world had returned from its momentary stasis, but the wonder I felt still lay about my shoulders like a warm cloak.

"What did you do?" asked Maggie in a voice filled with awe. "What did you *do*?"

The feeling of might and wrath and command fled my body just as all traces of Atheniel had fled the world, and I was human once again. It felt good. "I did my job," I replied. "You have those coordinates, then?"

"Yes."

Renaud strode forward, a tablet in hand. "It looks to be a cabin in the woods near a road, *monsieur*. Very close to the mountains. We can be there in a dozen hours if we do not hurry."

I shook my head. "No. Switzerland belongs to the Deschamps. Driving isn't a good idea."

Maggie stepped closer, but not too close. Her eyes were shining with unshed tears. "What then, Father? We have to stop this Oracle."

Father. Is that what I was relegated to? No longer Mike, but Father. "I have quite a lot of money in bearer bonds and you said you have pilots, didn't you?" I smiled. "What do you think we should do?"

Chapter Thirty

<hr>

"But God shows his love for us in that while we were still sinners, Christ died for us."
—Romans 5:8

As the fine rain of aerosolized tissue drifted to the forest floor, I snapped at Maggie, "Sniper!"

"On it," she replied. "But I'm smelling some things here."

Smelling some—oh yeah … a magus. Words were being used and she caught a whiff of magic. "You get that sniper. I'll cover the magus."

That went over like a lead balloon, but she merely nodded and blasted out a Word that shook the pine needles all around.

My vision blurred, or maybe she did, but whatever happened, all I saw was a flickering Maggie-shaped shadow that didn't want to register on my visual cortex. The blurry, there-not-there silhouette vanished from sight, followed by the sound of rapid footsteps over dry needles.

Cain had told me that there were twenty-five Words of magic passed down to Adam and Eve through the forbidden fruit from the Tree of Knowledge. Those outside of Cain's personal circle of apprentices thought that there were only twelve, and the existence of another thirteen would be an awful shock to the Deschamps, should they find out.

While Maggie did her stealth routine, making a beeline toward the cabin, I ran toward the other firefight. Words are great and all, but a bullet travels faster. I passed Renaud's corpse, a softball-sized hole in the side of his skull. A .50 cal, had to be, and I hadn't heard a thing. One heck of a suppressor on that thing. At least Renaud's death was quick and relatively painless. A prayer slipped past my lips for my fallen comrade. I hadn't known him long, but he was a believer and deserved better. There would be time enough afterward for last rights.

Assuming I lived through this.

A sharp cry of pain. Sounded like a woman, high-pitched and anguished, and it spurred my feet. *There.* Bursts of muzzle flare away from the cabin and return flares toward … three weapons in all and they were chattering away. No time for fear because I was high on the rush of battle lust, my people being fired at by servants of an evil being. I wasn't about to let them die, no siree. I had the Galil out—no time for the K-bar because the Sicarius had a bead on one of my people and was about to unload, had them dead to rights. There were already bodies on the loam, one writhing and three not, and I stepped on something that gave a loud *crunch.* The Dagger Man turned my way, alerted by the treacherous forest, and a Word burst from his throat, harsh and loud. It never registered, but I knew it would be bad so I dove, Galil forgotten, and rolled as an invisible *something* disturbed the air over my skull, missing me by centimeters. Suddenly I was there, next to the Sicarius, at his feet, and everything slowed, time becoming thick as his mouth stretched wide to hurl another Word at me. The K-bar was in my hand, burying itself into the forest floor, pinning a boot-clad foot.

That face, so ready to scream death at me, contorted in agony, but before I could pull the K-bar free and stick it someplace soft and squishy, his foot lifted, taking the knife with it. Another Word hammered into me.

Stinging wasps mortified my flesh, my bones splintered, and my nerves caught fire as gasoline ignited against my skin. Organs burst and muscles cramped hard enough that I thought they would tear themselves to shreds at any moment. The pain was so immediate, so intense, that I almost blacked out. Though my vision actually started to fade around the edges, I held it together with a scream that tore at my vocal cords with rusty hooks.

There is no adequate description for the Word of Pain. Imagine the worst hurt ever suffered and multiply that by a factor of one hundred. My whole world became the destruction of my senses as agony racked my body, but I could still see and I saw that Dagger Man raise his weapon, an SMG of some kind I was unfamiliar with. A trill of alarm, barely registering, ran through my mind as I stared down that barrel and caught the telltale glimpse of a finger tightening on the trigger. Strange thing, though … I was perfectly at peace, ready for my death, ready for the bullet that would slam between my eyes and exit the back of my skull. It was okay. Through the haze of pain, the terrible magic that flensed my flesh, there was a sense of wonder and relief that soon it would all be over and I could face the Lord's judgment with a clear conscience.

But the bullet never came. Instead the Dagger Man grunted and folded in on himself, falling to the ground.

The pain left. Suddenly, blissfully. I almost passed out from relief. Yeah, if I could just have grabbed a nap for a dozen years, everything would've been aces, but I had work to do. No rest for the pious.

"Are you well, Father?" That was Donald, the only other American among the Templars, a former SEAL with shaggy blond hair and muscles on his muscles. A large paw lifted me to my feet.

It took a second or two to catch my breath. "Thanks."

Was that a hint of light streaking across the sky? It seemed too soon for false dawn. "What's the bill?"

"Zachary and Antonio are down, Maude is wounded but she'll be okay." His voice was crisp, all business.

Two more to join Simon and Renaud in the afterlife. The Templar remnants were being whittled down to a nubbin. How did you recruit into a secret organization that everyone assumed had been wiped out centuries ago? Maggie told me there were others, men and women handpicked to fill the ranks. Looked like we needed them.

Maggie.

Numbskull, I thought savagely. Forgot all about her and the sniper. "Follow me and don't stop," I growled and staggered off toward the cabin, my body not fully recovered from Pain.

Off we went through the clearing toward the cabin, a cozy-looking affair with a porch surrounded by a rough wood railing. Small room above the main floor, the window dark and the front door wide open. Not a single light burning, and that had me worried because Maggie was in there without Vision to help her.

Two flashes from the second-story window. Muzzle flares and I picked up speed, panic giving my feet wings.

Up the small steps onto the porch and through the wide-open front door I ran, heart thudding madly, exultant that my head hadn't been turned into a canoe by a .50 cal. Into the greater darkness of the cabin was a darkness that eclipsed the night outside. My shin barked on something hard and wooden. The pain shot up past my knee into my hip but I barely registered it. From ahead, light blossomed, illuminating a staircase. No hesitation, only steely resolve as I took the stairs two at a time, my weapon leading the way.

A door at the top, open, inviting. Dangerous. I tumbled in, ready for bullets to shred my body. A silent prayer passed my lips, but no sudden pain, no punching rounds to pummel me into the afterlife. Instead I caught brief glimpses that pasted themselves into a whole picture in my mind:

Blond-wood floor with crimson puddle spreading from a shattered skull. A man in black with a shocked look on his face.

An overturned lamp still lit, but without the shade to soothe the brightness.

Russian .50 cal on the floor, brutal, black and efficient. The scope's glass eye broken.

Maggie standing, staring at me over the barrel of my Galil.

My finger felt cramped, tight, but I managed to not pull the trigger. As I swung the weapon away, I watched Maggie unclench, face pinched with fear. I let out a breath I didn't know I had been holding.

"Damn," she whispered.

"You okay?"

She nodded.

I stood and looked at the man on the floor, a bearded, stocky fellow who stared sightlessly at the ceiling, brains oozing along with blood from the back his head.

"That was a trifle scary," said a voice in heavily accented English.

I nearly jumped out of my socks at the voice that came from behind. Swinging around, I saw a man sitting on a small twin bed. He was swarthy and dressed like a lumberjack. "Who are you?"

He smiled, a radiant expression that showed very white, even teeth. "I am the Oracle."

Chapter Thirty-One

"And everyone who calls on the name of the Lord will be saved."
—Acts 2:21

"Y OU ARE SURPRISED, YES?"

I nodded. "More than a little. You look like an Egyptian lumberjack."

The Oracle spread his arms, smile never faltering. "What can I say? I love red plaid."

"Your accent ... Danish?"

"Norwegian."

"You're Norwegian?"

"Thrown off by the dark skin, right?"

I shrugged. "It doesn't fit the norm."

The Oracle shrugged right back at me. "All the men in my family have olive skin. The power of genetics, you know. You've heard of Black Swedes? We're Black Norwegians. Semitic blood."

"You're not what I expected."

"Most of us aren't."

This was getting me nowhere. I raised the Galil, ready to blow the swarthy lumberjack in half, but my finger wouldn't grasp the trigger. Something held me back. Was it the soulful brown eyes? The way his whole demeanor radiated peace? Whatever stopped my finger still coursed through my body, halting every muscle and tranquilizing every nerve.

"Pull the trigger," urged the Oracle placidly.

Sweat beaded my upper lip. *Kill the Oracle,* screamed the little, pragmatic voice in my head. *Kill him!*

The weapon fell to the floor. "Can't," I said, heart hammering. "In self-defense, yes, but this would be cold-blooded murder." A deep breath. "What is going on here?"

Patting the bed next to him, the Oracle scooted over a bit, indicating I should sit. I did so, having no more strength left in my tired legs. I left the Galil where it lay next to the dead Dagger Man, a brutal reminder of the long journey from being a simple priest. Without a word, Maggie left the room, leaving me alone with the Oracle.

"What is going on is that you have lost four people on this raid you have just led," began the man in plaid. "Which is surprising, considering that the Sicarii killed were all multiple-Word magi with the latest in advanced weaponry. All the Templars had was you." His smile never faltered. "One good man."

Didn't feel so good at the moment. Hard to believe that I had been ready to kill this … this … *peaceful* man. Pull the trigger and steal the rest of his days.

Those chocolate-brown eyes twinkled, and I figured he knew exactly what I was thinking, but he merely shrugged. "The Sicarii are blunt instruments of an unimaginative being," the Oracle said quietly. "They know only overwhelming force and sudden, ruthless violence. Like attack dogs, they lack the creative spark that could make them truly exceptional, because Lucifer fears that spark. He knows it represents the Divine in all humans and so encourages the Family to crush it utterly from their children." He sighed, as if profoundly saddened by what his words evoked, and I started, realizing that he was sad, profoundly sad and very, very tired. I finally saw the fine lines at the corners of his eyes and the deeper labial lines bracketing his mouth.

"Those kids don't have a chance once that spark is snuffed out," he continued. "And they become still more drones in the Deschamps army. The true enemy of the Sicarii is free will. Choice."

"Thou mayest," I said. *Timshel,* in Hebrew. What God told Cain after the murder of Abel.

"Thou mayest choose between Good and Evil." Not *will,* thou mayest. With those small, seemingly insignificant words, God granted free will to all mankind, something Satan rejected as unwise. The first among the Fallen wanted to force worship from man, not for it to be given willingly. That, more than anything, explained the true difference between Good and Evil.

The Oracle laughed. "Ah, you've read Steinbeck."

I smiled. "Loaned the book to a friend."

"Olivier Deschamps."

"Morgan Heart."

A shake of a shaggy head. "Olivier Deschamps made two major choices. One changed the fabric of the future, the other changed his soul."

I thought for a moment, then said, "When he chose to run away from his Family."

"That was the first," said the Oracle. "The one that changed the fabric of the future." He took a deep breath, his gentle smile never wavering. "You see, he *was* destined to be the Redeemer, the one who would bring about the End of Days. The whole 'second Angel blew his trumpet, and a great mountain of fire was thrown into the sea. One-third of the water in the sea became blood' bit. The whole Book of Revelation in all its terribly majesty, and Olivier would have been at the heart of it all. He was the greatest magus since Cain, the greatest Sicarius who ever lived. The perfect vessel for Lucifer."

"The Anti-Christ."

He made a face. "I hate that term. It lacks imagination, just like Lucifer. No, Redeemer is a better name for that one, even though it comes from a dark prophecy. That second choice negated the events foretold in the Book of Revelation."

"How is that possible? It is the Word of God as given to John of Patmos."

"When God sent the Angel to give John the vision, what was shown was the most probable future. Call it a ninety-nine percent certainty of it coming to pass, but that's the funny thing about the ability to choose: it can upset the apple cart at the most interesting times. The consequences of Olivier's choice are still affecting the future, causing ripples that will take centuries to subside, barring other more drastic choices."

"What was his second choice, then?"

The Oracle rubbed his bearded chin. "When Olivier fell down that elevator shaft, he did so while drinking Primal Water. When he hit the top of the elevator, his body landed on that of one of the Sicarii you killed, thus cushioning his fall so that his life did not end immediately. During that last moment, Primal Water offered him a choice of destinies: he could die right then and there, cease all pain and regret, or he could be healed and avenge your death and the deaths of your companions. Two choices, yet he chose a third option. He chose to become part of Primal Water, for a short time, to save his friends. To save *you*. He chose self-sacrifice over selfishness. He chose friendship over loneliness, love over vengeance. Good over Evil."

We sat there for a few minutes in a comfortable silence as I chewed on that bit of information. It made perfect sense. When he was a young man, Morgan/Jude/Olivier could have hunted down his brother Burke (although at the time he thought the man his cousin) and killed him, securing his place in the Family hierarchy, but he chose not to. Instead, he turned his back on vast wealth and power to live in Omaha, of all places. Who would look for the scion of the world's wealthiest family in Nebraska? My thoughts were interrupted as the Oracle continued, perhaps sensing that Maggie wouldn't wait much longer and would come to check on me.

"Don't worry about the Templars, Michael. Maggie has been a very busy woman. There are over a dozen young men and women training as we speak to become full members of the Knights Templar, and there will be more on the way from other sources. The days of the 'remnants' of the Templars are drawing to a close and a new chapter will be written. The contents of that chapter are up to you."

The fragile peace in the room shattered like cheap glass. "Me? I'm an ex-sergeant and a priest."

"And a leader. You always have been. Soon you will be confronted with a decision and that will determine the course of the world for good or ill."

Relief blossomed in my chest. Good thing I had an Oracle to help me out. "What decision?"

Twinkling brown eyes met mine. "That is for you to make, not for me to tell you. Free will, you know. It can be a bitch sometimes."

Sigh. "Tell me about it."

Something nagged at me, a little itch at the back of my brain. Usually, when I had such feelings, they would vanish in an instant upon scrutiny like water on a hot griddle. This time, however, the thought sprang full into my sights and I gave it a voice. "If you can see so much of me, how come you didn't tell the Sicarii about Olivier, dammit? Morgan, seventeen years ago? Surely Julian must have demanded to know where his wayward son was hiding."

"Ahhh," said the Oracle, his grin stretching across his face. "There's the question! I was wondering when you would ask … and *no*, I don't see everything. Even I can be surprised." He placed a companionable arm around my shoulders and gave me a gentle squeeze. "God gave me the spark that has been fanned into the flames of clairvoyance, but my prescience only extends to what He wants me to see. Because He did not want me to see you and because he hid you from my sight, Olivier Deschamps was also hidden. I think it was due to his proximity to you." A long pause. "Julian pestered my father for years, trying to find him, but God refused my father any vision of Olivier. Perhaps that is why He led the young rebel Sicarius to Omaha. To meet you."

"How did Burke find him?"

"Persistence and good detective work. The face that Olivier was able to hide from his Family for fifteen years was a miracle. Literally, I believe."

Still smiling, the Oracle stood and picked up the Galil. I wasn't worried; I knew he wouldn't use it. Not he. Of all the people I'd met, he was the most peaceful, centered. He thrust the weapon into my hands. "You have one more job to do, Michael," he said.

"What?"

A deep, cleansing breath followed by an even wider, calm smile. "Kill me."

Had I heard that right? "Now wait a damn second, Oracle!"

"My name is Joshua."

"Joshua, then. Just hold the phone."

"The first-born son in my family is always named Joshua," he said conversationally. "It's been that way for two-thousand years."

What was he babbling on about? "Be that as it may—"

"We are named after a famous ancestor. My many-times great-grandfather."

"But—"

"Think about it." I couldn't get a word in edgewise with this guy. He sighed.

What else could I do? His piercing, chocolate gaze and calm demeanor stoppered my throat and forced me to noodle over the situation. I cooled my jets and calmed down, giving his words a good hard think.

A famous ancestor named Joshua. *Hmmm.* About two thousand years ago, give or take. Who did I know—

Oh my.

Obviously he saw the realization writ large on my face. "Yes."

"But—"

"He was thirty years old when he became the Messiah. In a culture where it was common to be married by age fourteen, you think he never got busy? Never met someone who tripped his trigger?" The Oracle, Joshua, laughed. "It is the height of folly for the Church to assume that Joshua, or Yehoshuah (Yeshua for short) of Nazareth never once lay with a woman, that he did *not* take Mary Magdalene to be his wife as was written in the Gospel according to Philip. She begot a son she named Yeshua, who in turn had many more sons. My family has always carried a piece of the Divine spark that was a raging flame in the Messiah. A sort of Heavenly DNA, if you will. When the firstborn male of our line reaches thirty, the Sicarii take them to a desert where they are left for forty days and nights to fend for themselves. It is a time of pain, of suffering, of intense thirst and near-unbearable hunger, and it is through that suffering we Joshuas receive our vision from God and our gifts, such as clairvoyance. We learn the truth of our family, of the Sicarii, and what may come.

"That cycle began three hundred years ago when the Sicarii discovered our secret, who we were. It was they who created that which is called the Crucible, the sabbatical that reveals our power. It is through threats to our family that they keep us in virtual slavery. One of the benefits of my family, however, is that no Elemental will cooperate with our captivity. It is the reason Maggie found no Elemental presence in the area." He raised his arms to indicate the small cabin. "I do have to say that my time as a prisoner has been comfortable. I get plenty of lemonade.

"So, Michael, understand this: they have my wife, they have my two children—my daughter Kirsten and my son Joshua. As long as I do their bidding, no matter how reluctantly, my family will be safe. If I try to escape, if I do not honestly reveal what God allows me to see, then they will not harm my family." Here his voice became thick and husky, betraying a depth of emotion kept hidden for quite some time. "And if I do betray the Sicarii, they will inflict such suffering upon those I love that Lucifer himself would wince in pity. That I cannot allow."

Mind reeling, I said the first thing that came to mind. "Come with me." Head throbbing, heart racing, I could barely comprehend. Too many questions, too much information to be processed. It seemed that every day for the past week, I'd learned something that tore my world view to shreds.

But it made sense. Of course it did. How could it not? Two years ago Morgan proved to me that the world wasn't what I thought, that it contained more wonders than could be imagined. He showed me magic and Elementals and helped me destroy the Silver. These hands of mine held the Holy Grail, my faith banished demons and stopped bullets, so why couldn't Christ our Lord have descendants living amongst us?

The priest in me denied that argument. All my teachings told me that Jesus died childless, that Mary Magdalene was merely a boon companion, a woman he brought into the fold as a follower, the woman he cleansed of seven demons and brought into God's grace. Extra-biblical conjectures about her role in Christ's life painted her as a mother, wife, secret lover, and whore.

Why not a lover and wife?

The Vatican would screech and holler and throw a fit so big it could be seen from space should something like this become public knowledge. Sure, there's speculation galore about Mary Magdalene's role in history, but were it to be confirmed ... well, that's a whole other kettle of fish.

"Upon the shoulders of the unwilling lie the burdens most favored by God." The words were out before I could stop them.

The Oracle kept grinning, although it had faded around the edges. "Who said that?"

Who indeed? "I did. Just now. Weren't you paying attention?"

"Father Mike?" Maggie's voice arrowed into the room, filled with worry.

" 'Scuse me," I muttered.

Joshua bowed, a disconcertingly polite lumberjack. "Take your time."

At the head of the stairs, outlined in the doorway, I peered down the short staircase to see Maggie fidgeting on the bottom step. "What is it?"

She worried her lower lip with her teeth. "Just checking. I wanted to tell you the body count."

"Four of ours gone, I know."

"How—?"

"Bad news travels fast. Anything else?"

A shake of the head. Good, I had the strangest conversation in my life to get back to.

"Come with us, Joshua," I said as I turned around only to see the Oracle sitting back on the bed with one leg of his jeans pulled up from his boot, exposing a white calf-high athletic sock and an inch-wide black plastic band around his ankle.

He pointed to the band. "I'm being monitored at all times. If I walk more than fifty feet from the cabin, if I try to cut this off, if I in any way attempt to escape their clutches, my family suffers. There is only one way out. My son is ten years old; it will be another twenty years before he can attempt the Crucible. For twenty years, the Sicarii will have no Oracle, no matter how obtuse the foretellings. Twenty years without that advantage. Such a thing would be quite a boon for the Templars," he paused, "and you."

"You assume I will be around for twenty more years, fighting the good fight, leading the Templars. Men like me become old before our time." War wears many a man down to a nubbin. If I didn't catch a bullet, most likely I'd succumb to magic or some such.

"Twenty years is a drop in the bucket compared to the length of this conflict and the Lord's infinite patience." He stood, shaking his shoulders and arms as if to stimulate blood flow. "Now, you have forty-seven minutes until the nearest Sicarii arrive from Geneva. Five minutes after that, this area will be swarming with helicopters. Get this over with and be gone." He paused. "Remember, read the *Codex*. It will help you in your fight. And, someday if you can, save my wife and kids. Save my family."

With a start, I realized I still held the Galil in my hands, the barrel pointing at Joshua's chest. When had that happened?

He stood there, calm, the current Oracle, the descendant of Christ, imploring me to pull the trigger. Tears began to collect in my eyes. "I can't."

Gone was his smile, leaving a faint note of regret on his face. " 'In my Father's house there are many rooms,' " he quoted. "He has one waiting for me. Don't worry, Michael Engle. In time I will see my family again. You and I, we shall meet again, I know this. Pull the trigger."

The tears were coursing down my cheeks now. "It's … difficult."

"The necessary things often are." His tone brooked no argument, his mien resolute.

My finger found the trigger. "It's not in me."

He shook his head. "It's in everyone. Do it, Michael."

His form blurred. "Joshua—"
"Do it!"
God help me.
I pulled the trigger.

EPILOGUE

"Fail once and it can be overlooked. Fail twice and all is lost."
—*Codex Infernales*

FERGUS SAT ON THE STEPS OF the Met, eating a hot dog purchased from one of the many food carts lining Fifth Avenue. Dozens upon dozens of New Yorkers milled about, talking on cellphones, eating vendor food, and basking in the warm sunshine falling upon the museum's steps.

Hustle and bustle, the drone of cars, and conversation both person-to-person and on mobile phones. Honking horns, the occasional yell, and the soft whistle of wind through the concrete canyons of the city. It was brash and loud and just the sort of thing he loved. Fuck London with its odd combination of propriety and vulgarity and fuck Paris with its sense of moral and cultural superiority, because New York was *alive* and vibrant in a way that put most other cities to shame. Hardcore and not afraid to shove it boldly in your face along with a fistful of scarred knuckles. New Yorkers knew they lived in the fucking greatest city on the planet and fuck it if others disagreed. In this city, Fergus felt alive and connected, and he wanted to own it so bad, it was literally a taste on the back of his tongue.

Too bad it was all wasted on that cretin Blaine.

As if on cue, his cellphone rang. He checked the number. There was none, at least none on the display. His skin prickled with fear because he knew exactly who waited on the other end.

"Hello, sir," he said, keeping his voice cold and steady.

"Cain is still alive."

"Sir? I was told the drone strike was successful."

"The strike was successful," said the Patron. "It just didn't kill Cain. He has been cursed and damned by the Lying God. If his soul left his body, it would come to *me*. As it is, I have the souls of those he dispatched."

"I apologize, sir."

"Not your fault, Fergus. If anything, the fault lies with me."

"Sir?"

"Blaine failed. He should have sent a full team instead of observers. He should have found a different way to destroy Cain, but he fucked it up and I am the one who put him in charge. His business acumen is unmatched, but his large-scale leadership abilities and strategies leave something to be desired. The Family needs a general, not a businessman."

"How can I help, sir?"

"Do you have Blaine's exit strategy prepared?"

"Of course." Fergus couldn't keep the smile from his face. Nearby, a young woman in glasses and a Pussy Riot T-shirt saw it and shuddered.

"You are a good soldier, Fergus, and will rise even higher in the Family if you continue to demonstrate the competence you have so far."

Yes. "Thank you, sir." Pride burned in his gut, spreading warmth through his veins.

"Go get it done, implement the change of leadership and make your way to the HarrowInc offices Midtown. The new head of the Family wants to meet you. I think you will be ... pleased, to say the least."

"Will do, sir." Fergus paused briefly. "And thank you for your trust in me."

"If I didn't trust you, if you hadn't done everything I asked, we would not be having this conversation."

"Yessir."

"That is all."

"Goodbye, sir."

"Oh, and Fergus ...."

"Yes?"

"You have never failed, so don't start now." *Click.*

Smiling, Fergus punched in a new number and waited patiently for the other side to ring.

It was Blaine who answered. "Yes, Fergus?"

"We are going to spin this as a terrorist attack, you know."

"What?"

"Terrorists are terribly in vogue right now. Americans see an Osama bin Laden lurking around every corner and hordes of them in every mosque. To blame Islamic extremists will be incredibly easy."

"What the fuck are you on about, man?"

Fergus' grin nearly cracked his head in two. By the Patron, he felt *great*.

"The boss is very unhappy with you, Blaine. No warm fuzzy feelings at all, not anymore."

A note of unease crept into the young man's voice. "Fergus, what have you done?"

In the Scot's jacket pocket lay a powerful transmitter the size and shape of a credit card. He fished it out and regarded it fondly. "Your little room atop that tower is as secure as money could make it. I doubt a bunker buster could put much of a dent in it." With every word his Scottish brogue became more pronounced. "Those pet Elementals of yours, the ones you persuaded to guard your stronghold, are brilliant watchdogs, I'll give you that. You made one mistake, however."

Blaine snarled, "You're dead, you realize that, don't you? You won't make it to the airport in time. I'll send one of my 'watchdogs' to rip you apart."

"Not curious about your mistake? That's okay, I'll tell you: Elementals are absolutely essential for protection against external threats, but for internal ones, they're complete shite. One thing I am very happy for, Blaine-me-laddie, is that you'll have a grand view of the ground rushing up to meet ya."

He pressed a small button on the transmitter three times in rapid succession.

Large amounts of the explosive RDX (cyclotrimethyenetrinitramine) were packed around the main steel support columns in Deschamps Tower. RDX exploded at a rate of 8,230 meters-per-second and was perfect for shearing through steel, splitting each column in half. The pressure wave would continue outward, powdering stone and cement and blasting any human in its way to a red mist. At first there was a rumble, a deep, resonant sound heard by all the staff within the tower. After a brief hesitation, as if the world was holding its breath, the tower began to move.

Downward.

Blaine watched in horrified amazement as the clouds of powdered concrete billowed outward from the base of the building, obscuring the street and cars below. "Holy fuck," he breathed, as the tower shuddered around him, the large, seemingly impenetrable windows of his bunker groaning in protest. Slowly, almost majestically, the bunker accelerated toward the street.

Blaine's scream lasted a very short time.

Smiling, happy that the Patron had sanctioned the deaths of two Board members and three hundred office workers along with uncounted unlucky passers-by, Fergus strolled away from the Met whistling a merry tune. From far away the sound of sirens could be heard.

Many minutes later, his limo dropped him off at the offices of HarrowInc, a Deschamps corporation that on paper was involved in the development of medical devices. In reality, it was another cutout for the conglomerate that funneled vast amounts of money to Super PACs supporting political candidates who toed the line of the Deschamps agenda.

Top floor: a sumptuous office overlooking Midtown Manhattan, big enough to host several cocktail parties at once. In the center of the hardwood floor stood a walnut desk where a long, slender figure sat talking into a cellphone. As Fergus stepped off the elevator into the office, the figure hung up and walked around the desk, feet *whooshing* softly through a thick, white rug. A ten-thousand-dollar light-brown Briony suit, a pair of Tanino Crisci Lilian brown-leather shoes, and a Hofmann und Co AG 24-Karat Gold necktie completed an ensemble that spoke not only of fabulous wealth but impeccable taste graced the approaching man's lanky frame.

"Hello, Fergus," said the man in Romansh. His face was stretched into a wide smile. He had olive skin, a slightly larger than normal nose, and thick, sensuous lips. Hair as black as Satan's heart hung thick about his shoulders. "I am very glad to have you on my team."

Fergus took the hand. The grip proved to be strong and callused. "Good to see you again, sir," he answered with a smile of his own. "By your presence, I see Project Century is a success."

"Yes, it is. Soon it will work on a massive scale. The Templars won't know what hit them."

The Scotsman hid a wince. It was an old superstition, calling the Templars by name, but the man in front of him had never met a superstition he didn't hate. "Well, it's good to have you back. It's good to be on the winning team."

Burke smiled. "Bet your ass."

COMING SOON

The third and final book in the Judas Line Chronicles:

THE JUDAS REVELATION

Born in Helsinki, Finland, **Mark Everett Stone** arrived in the U.S. at a young age and promptly dove into the world of the fantastic. Starting at age seven with the *Iliad* and the *Odyssey*, he went on to consume every scrap of Norse Mythology he could get his grubby little paws on. At age thirteen he graduated to Tolkien and Heinlein, building up a book collection that soon rivaled the local public library's. In college Mark majored in Journalism and minored in English. Mark is the author of the From the Files of the BSI series and the Judas Line Chronicles.

Mark lives in California with his amazingly patient wife, Brandie, and their two sons, Aeden and Gabriel. You can find Mark on the Web at:

www.markeverettstone.wixsite.com/mysite-1

From Mark Everett Stone and Camel Press

⚮

Thank you for reading *The Judas Codex*. We are so grateful for you, our readers. If you enjoyed this book, here are some steps you can take that could help contribute to the success of the Judas Line Chronicles:

- Please think about posting a short review on Amazon, BN.com, and GoodReads.
- Check out Mark's website and join his mailing list at www.markeverettstone.wixsite.com/mysite-1.
- Spread the word on social media, especially Facebook, Twitter, and Pinterest.
- "Like" Mark's author Facebook page: www.facebook.com/MarkEverettStone and the Camel Press page: www.facebook.com/CamelPressBooks.
- Follow Camel Press (@camelpressbooks) on Twitter.
- Ask for your local library to carry this book and others in the series or request them on their online portal.

Good books and authors from small presses are often overlooked. Your comments and reviews can make an enormous difference.